D0727171

Please return or renew this item
by the last date shown. You may
return items to any East Sussex
Library. You may renew books
by telephone or the internet.

East Sussex
County Council

0345 60 80 195 for renewals
0345 60 80 196 for enquiries

Library and Information Service
eastsussex.gov.uk/libraries

Courttia Newland is the author of the critically acclaimed novels *The Scholar*, *Society Within* and *Snakeskin*. He has contributed to the anthologies *Disco 2000*, *New Writers 8*, *AfroBeat* and *Teenage Kicks*. Find out more about Courttia at www.courttianewland.com

'Convincing . . . Newland shows every promise of being able to reflect Britain from a distinctive and unsentimental perspective'
The Times

'An entertaining and pertinent read'
Pride

'An exciting, sustained and truthful novel, fine writing and firing dialogue. Courttia Newland knows his people very well'
Diran Adebayo, author of *Some Kind of Black*

'Newland has conjured up a world apart from the one which most Londoners know — a world in which differences are settled with bullets, where flick-knives flash and where people casually threaten "I'm gonna carve you up"'
Evening Standard

'The rising star of Brit-lit and chronicler of inner city life . . . Newland has acquired a buzz . . . his novels cover a section of British society that was not only unrepresented but oddly invisible. The comparison with [Irvine] Welsh is apt for two reasons. First there is a clear parallel in creating new literary language and second, with luck, Newland will open up the world of fiction to a whole new audience'
Guardian

'Britain's brightest black writer'
Evening Standard

'If you thought novels about life on desolate council estates have had their day, you obviously haven't heard of Courttia Newland. One of the most in-demand young writers around, his colourful tales about the seedier side of urban Britain have earned him plaudits everywhere. So much so that he's already toured with the likes of Irvine Welsh'
Touch

'As a literary culture, we are chronically short of this sort of fiction. Voices like Newland's provide a vital counterpoint to the likes of Bridget Jones'
Financial Times

Also by Courttia Newland

Society Within
Snakeskin

The
Scholar

A West Side Story

COURTTIA NEWLAND

ABACUS

First published in Great Britain by Abacus in 1997
This edition published by Abacus in 1998
Reprinted 2001, 2003, 2006, 2008

A CIP catalogue record for this book
is available from the British Library.

Extract from *Small Acts* by Paul Gilroy reproduced by kind
permission of Serpent's Tail.
Extract from *South of Haunted Dreams: A Ride Through
Slavery's Old Back Yard* by Eddie L. Harris (Viking 1993)
copyright © Eddie L. Harris 1993, reprinted by kind
permission of Penguin Books.

ISBN 978-0-349-10876-6

Typeset in Ehrhardt by M Rules
Printed in Great Britain by Clays Ltd, St Ives plc

Abacus
An imprint of
Little, Brown Book Group
100 Victoria Embankment
London EC4Y 0DY

An Hachette Livre UK Company
www.hachettelivre.co.uk

www.littlebrown.co.uk

Just for you London . . .
and also for my brother Jerome
and Regina (I didn't forget).

Acknowledgements

Thanks to all the people that had to listen to me go on about Cory and Sean – Mum, Barney Platts-Mills, Ghanim Shubber, Sledge, Jules, Bernard and Ang . . . and to Kate, my very first critic!

On the research tip, many thanks to the Royal College of Psychiatrists and St Charles' Mental Health ward . . . Big up D., respec' for the 'yit' business (you know the ku!) Thanks to Sam Lindo for reading the last draft!

Respec' goes out to Insane Wayne (for obvious reasons!) And a very special thanks to Ruscha Fields and Stephanie Cabot at William Morris, for believing in *The Scholar* . . . And everyone at Massive Video – Carly (who made me wonder why Cory was so angry), as well as Saloum, Tchekedi, Drew, and Jenny (who were all at the first 'readings'), and all the others too numerous to mention. I'll try and thank you in person!

Lastly, cheers to my good friend and cousin Lee Newall, for all your encouragement when I was broke and feeling like doing stupidness . . . And to my old English teacher Ms Youlton from Burlington Danes for teaching me everything I know!

Contents

Prologue

August 1986

It was a hot summer's day; the kind people never took for granted in London, where winters were long and summers often non-existent. Parks, normally lifeless apart from dog owners and children, were transformed into a sea of immobile bodies, all lying in wait for that elusive natural tan. People actually smiled at strangers as if they were old friends. Adventure playgrounds all across the city were stampeded by kids, itching to swing over wide spaces twenty feet across the ground.

Cory Bradley was one of those children, but the eight-year-old felt he'd had his quota of rope swinging for the day. He left the park at a run and hid behind a gleaming Ford Cortina, a small smile on his handsome brown face, eyes steady on the park gates. He didn't have to wait long before another darker boy, roughly the same age, came out onto the pavement, looked around twice and headed up the street. Giggling, Cory crept up behind the ambling boy and jumped on his back screaming: 'Sneak attack!! Sneak attack!' as he clambered over his body. The two scuffled until a sort of non-verbal truce was reached and then panting and laughing, made their way down the road.

'Fix up Sean!' Cory cried, strutting as he walked.

'I could've killed you dead boy!'

His cousin kissed his teeth.

'Don't talk crap man!' the boy called Sean replied. 'I heard you breathin' guy.'

'Bollocks!' Cory shouted, making passing adults shake their

heads in disbelief and Sean laugh wildly. 'You never heard nuttin', I'm too slick for you cuz!'

The two children walked at an easy pace, pausing only to stare lustfully at the ice cream man's picture of a 99 with a Flake. A failed scavenge for change, however, burst their bubble and the walking resumed.

'What time d'we have to meet your dad for?' Sean asked.

'Three o'clock, at that pub he drinks in. Dad's jus' waitin' for the footie season to start, so he can drink more.'

'Who'd you want to win the Milk Cup?'

'Liverpool of course! Who else . . .?'

'No chance, Man U are the best in the world!' Sean interrupted.

'Listen,' Cory started, as if going through a tried and tested argument, 'Liverpool . . .'

As they'd been talking, they rounded the last corner before reaching the Green Man where Cory's father drank. Sean, who turned the corner second, was about to ask his cousin why he'd suddenly stopped arguing. Before he could, he saw the reason all too soon.

Cory's father, Ronald Bradley, was a huge man standing six feet three inches in his socks, and weighing fifteen stone. Sean had never seen his uncle angry before and would never forget the awe he felt watching Ron fighting with three burly looking white men, who'd clearly bitten off more than they could chew.

There were a few spectators, including Sean's mother Bernice – Ron's sister – tearfully calling at both parties to stop; Sean's eleven-year-old sister Shannon, and Cory's mother Helen, who was also crying. The other watching patrons tutted, but weren't getting involved. Indeed Ron (who'd put the ring pulls from cans lying around the pub on his fingers, to tear his opponents' faces) was just about finished, when four police vans skidded to the kerb with a squeal of tyres and brakes.

The police were clearly opting for the 'questions later' approach and about ten men waded into Ron, closely followed by others, as truncheons rose and fell oblivious to the cries of the women.

'*DAAAD!*' Cory cried, his voice cracking. Before Sean could stop him, he'd sprinted across the road to face his father's attackers, only to be pushed roughly to the ground by one of the policemen. The others lifted Ron, still struggling and threw him forcefully into the back of the van.

'Oi! . . . Oi you lot!' A short balding man with bright blue eyes, wearing an apron around his waist, shouted from the pub doorway.

'You got the wrong man yer bastards! Them blokes was taunting 'im an' I called you fuck-ups to help 'im.'

One policeman turned to the man with a bored, patronising, look on his face. 'We're arresting them *all* Harry, now just cut your crap and go inside all right?' which only wound Harry up more.

'I saw what you cunts did!' he screamed. 'I'm gonna make a formal complaint to your Super and—'

'You do that and by the end of the month your pub'll get a visit from the Vice boys,' the policeman countered. 'I wonder what they'd find, eh Harry?'

To this, Harry said nothing.

The policeman turned to Helen and Bernice.

'You know where the local nick is ladies, don't you?' he asked, casually. Helen was silent and shivered despite the heat, sniffing back tears, while Bernice spat at the man's feet and put her arms around Helen and Shannon and led them away. She seemed not to notice when Cory and a moment later Sean joined them, but all three women seemed to take comfort from their presence.

The journey to the station went by in a blur for both boys, each of them deeply shocked by what they'd witnessed. Sean unconsciously felt himself gripping his sister's hand, something he hadn't done since he was a toddler and sensed her reach for Cory's also, which, considering their usual relationship, was frankly a miracle.

At the station Bernice warned them the wait would be long and left to tell the Desk Sergeant they had arrived. She returned two minutes later, looking even more worried.

'The Desk Sergeant hasn't even heard of Ron!' she exclaimed to her family, even more puzzled by her sister-in-law's lack of response. Helen was unaware of Bernice's staring and continued to rock back and forth, staring and saying nothing.

After three quarters of an hour and two more visits to the sergeant, the front swing doors slammed open. A skinny man with a suit and a small leather bag strode through. He spoke briefly to the sergeant then made his way through the side entrance to the cells. Bernice, who recognised the leather bag, made her way to the desk again.

'Was that a doctor?' she asked quietly.

'Now Ms Bradley, if you'd like to take a seat someone–'

'*Was that a doctor?*' Bernice screamed, something in her seeming to snap all at once. '*Was it? Answer me will you!*'

'Mum come and sit down,' Shannon said gently, her brown eyes full of concern.

'Any more outbursts an' you can all wait outside, got it?' the sergeant warned Shannon, pointing a podgy finger at the Bradleys, then the door. He was all but ignored by the girl, who gave only a stony look as her reply. She led her mother back to the row of plastic seats, with Cory and Sean gaping, and Helen hugging herself. Minutes later, the click of footsteps made them both look up.

'Mrs Bradley?'

It was the man Bernice had seen with the leather bag, peering intently at her. Closer, she could see the lines weariness had etched beneath his eyes, but there was kindness there too.

'Sorry, I'm not Mrs Bradley, she is.' She pointed at her sister-in-law. 'I'm *Ms* Bradley, Ron's sister.'

'All right well . . .'

The man coughed once and began again, 'My name is Dr Phillips.' He paused again seeming to notice the children for the first time.

'Can we talk alone?' he asked quietly.

'Of course,' Bernice replied, taking Helen's arm so she could join them. They retreated to a corner and started whispering, the sergeant watching with avid attention from his desk.

Sean turned to look at Cory, to see if his cousin was as puzzled as he was. The boy was amazed to see a thick trail of tears openly running down his face.

'They've killed him,' he was sobbing into his SpiderMan

T-shirt. 'They've kicked his head in,' he bawled, before he covered his face in his hands.

'Don't be silly,' Shannon taunted, in her, I'm-eleven-so-I've-got-more-brains tone of voice.

'What makes *you* so sure anyway?'

'Don't you watch *Quincy*, dummy?' Cory spat at his cousin. 'When they take the family to one side it means—'

'*Nooooo!*' Bernice wailed, falling so quickly, the doctor almost didn't catch her. Sean never forgot the sound of his mother's grief; or the look of loss on his cousin's and sister's faces: but the main thing he'd always remembered about his uncle's death at the hands of the police was the sight of his Aunt Helen, her arms wrapped around herself, staring into space just rocking and rocking and rocking . . .

In the days immediately after Ron's death, Helen took a definite turn for the worse. Bernice, Sean and Shannon came to stay in the two-bedroomed flat she'd shared with her husband, helping out in the run-up to the funeral. Helen cried constantly for two days, then one morning she abruptly stopped. The evening before the funeral she went into a fury, and virtually destroyed the living room, smashing everything she could see in front of the frightened children, calling her husband's name pitifully.

When she'd finished, she sat down in the middle of the mess, showing no emotion once more. Bernice hugged and consoled her gently, but Helen slipped into a brooding silence before locking herself in her bedroom, refusing to eat or even drink water.

That night, Cory woke up to find his mother standing over his bed. Behind her, he could see Sean fast asleep on his stomach. He was frightened for a moment, until she shushed him and kneeled down beside his bed.

'Hi baby, how are you feelin'?' she asked, putting a cold hand to his head.

'I want you to do somethin' for Mum, yeah?' she whispered, still stroking him. 'Sit up a minute.'

He sat up in his bed slowly, still groggy from sleep, his eyes half closed. The cold, clammy feeling in her hand . . . That was something Cory relived, time and again after that night. He wiped his eyes, yawned, then looked up at his mum. She was watching him with a thoughtful, yet detached expression.

'Now Cory,' she'd begun, 'I know you bin hurtin' these last few days; and I know I haven't looked after you as well as I should've. Mum's sorry. But honey, I've thought of a way for us to get over all that. A way for us to get away from all this madness, d'you understand?'

He didn't, but he nodded sullenly, his mind only on how normal she suddenly seemed again.

'So Mummy's gonna give you these . . .'

She reached into her pocket and pulled out a handful of large pink pills. Cory looked at them, scared, but willing to do anything to please his mother.

'. . . An' I want you to take them all OK? Pretty soon, the pain an' the hurt'll be gone an' we'll all be together again. Me, you and your father. Hurry up, get them down, you'll feel better in a while.'

Cory grasped the pills as his mother produced a mug of water containing three ice cubes floating lazily and knocking lightly against the mug's side. He swallowed them one by one, his mother urging him on quietly beside him, occasionally giving him sips from the mug to ease them down. Cory swallowed six before his bedroom door swung open, exposing a shadowy figure that paused in shock at the scene before her.

'Helen?'

His mother turned to the door, a classic expression of fright on her face, emphasised by the beam of light flooding in from the living room. Bernice took a couple of steps closer, her eyes widening as she saw the remaining three pills in his outstretched hand.

'What the hell d'you think you're—'

With a cry which was more like a wailing moan, his mother threw herself past Bernice and out of the room. His aunt immediately picked him up from his bed, ordered Shannon to look after Sean, then ran for the bathroom, cradling him in her arms. Once there, she forcefully pushed his head over the toilet bowl and told him to open his mouth and stick his finger down his throat.

'What for?' Cory said, his eyes closing.

Bernice hadn't wasted time. She simply opened his mouth

herself, sticking her own finger inside. Cory retched a few times before his stomach clenched painfully, everything coming up all over Bernice's hand. Many years later, Cory realised his aunt had saved him from certain death; and she became something of a heroine for him. As he'd knelt weakly on the bathroom floor, he heard a crash, some shouting, then, after a pause, more retching. Bernice had broken into his mother's room (where she'd locked herself in with the rest of the pills) and also forced her to throw them up.

Ron's funeral was held in Kensal Green Cemetery in West London. The plot was adjacent to two older graves which held Teresa and Marcus Bradley, Ron and Bernice's mother and father. Teresa and Marcus had wanted to be buried in Dominica, their homeland, but they'd never been able to afford to return home; Ron's life assurance just about covered the cost of this third burial.

The grave was surrounded by friends and family − at least forty people Sean guessed, all sweltering in the mid-August sun. Although the boy had never seen a funeral before, he felt his uncle had received a beautiful send-off into the next world. The priest talked of the 'gentle giant' who'd befriended so many before his death; but neatly skirted around the blood clot found in Dr Phillip's autopsy. He also avoided mentioning three broken ribs, which police claimed were from Ron's earlier fight, although witnesses said his original assailants hadn't managed to land any blows: they were all too drunk.

It almost seemed as though they'd get through the final nightmare without incident when Helen Bradley let out a low moan of anguish, then swayed and fell face down on the grass. Horror-stricken family members rushed to help her.

She was taken to nearby Hammersmith Hospital, and then, after a few weeks she was moved to an institution five miles outside London, the doctors stressing that the claustrophobia of the city was hindering her progress. After being treated for severe depression for almost a year, Helen was released into hostel accommodation, where the security was in fact a lot less 'secure'. Within six months she had made another suicide attempt. This time she was successful.

In the late autumn of 1986, Cory Bradley came to live with his cousin Sean and his family in the Greenside Estate, West London.

PART ONE

Boys Will Be Boys

The Black experience in England is increasingly
revealed to possess a certain uniqueness – a
particularity and peculiarity that distinguish it
from the history of Black populations
elsewhere . . .

Paul Gilroy, *Small Acts*

Chapter One

May 1996

The sound of Hip Hop swirled and flowed like an unseen mist through flat 36, Denver House, Greenside Estate. From the front room carried by silver Jamo speakers, it twisted its way past Shannon's room, where it certainly wasn't wanted, whispered by Sean and Cory's room, where it wasn't needed, then made its way upstairs to the kitchen, where it was the choice of one but only just about accepted by the other.

'Ruff innit?' Cory Bradley, now seventeen, asked his Aunt Bernice, his mouth stuffed full of bread and ham. He was a tall, cinnamon-coloured boy, dressed casually in baggy corduroy trousers and a plain cotton shirt, tucked in neatly at the waist.

Bernice gave him a look usually reserved for misbehaving tots at the day nursery she'd worked at for the past five years. She was a small, handsome woman, modestly dressed and ever ready with a smile or a word of encouragement if you were feeling down. She'd always been Cory's favourite aunt and it was obvious to everybody he loved her deeply.

'Not as "ruff" as looking at mash up ham sandwich,' she replied, laughing as the doorbell rang.

'I got it!' Cory yelled and was out of the front door before Bernice could turn.

Shaking her head, she thought about all the child had been through, in fact the whole family had been through; especially after the inquest which had blamed the three drunks – rather than the police – for Ron's death. At least, thought Bernice, none of the kids seemed to have a racial hatred for whites, although all three had an unhealthy disrespect for the law-enforcers. Bernice thought she couldn't really grumble with the way the children had turned out, especially since she'd raised all three completely alone, with no help from Sean and Shannon's father.

When her children had reached nine and six respectively (three years before Ron's premature death), Bernice had sat them both down in the living room, a serious look on her face. Choosing her words carefully, she'd explained that they'd have to be strong as their father had gone away and wouldn't be back, ever. The memory was a sepia-toned photograph in her mind, with Sean, in little boy shorts that showed scuffed knees and Shannon in a blue shirt and grey school skirt, her thin legs dangling from the large sofa.

Oh well, she mused to herself, at least the boys were in college after doing well in their GCSEs, Sean passing them all with no grade lower than C. Shannon was a door-to-door hair stylist in a business set up with some college friends . . . so all-in-all I ain't done bad, she thought.

Upstairs, Cory opened the door to be greeted by a rare treat. His cousin's friends and hair-styling partners, Adrienne, Susan and Pamela, had all chosen to visit on the same night; they looked like angels, to his lustful stare.

Adrienne was the darkest of the three, with wide black eyes which shone like twin moons in her ebony face. Susan was half-caste, a term that bothered Cory, who preferred mixed-race, although both just meant black to him. Pamela had smooth brown skin, wore her hair in a bob and at five feet three inches was the shortest of the group of friends. Cory smiled to himself and felt it must be his lucky night.

'Yes girls!' he said looking them up and down. 'Boy I 'affa say it, you're lookin' *t'ick* tonight y'get me! Furthermore, when we goin' ravin' star?!'

Adrienne looked at him coldly and with a terse, 'Move from the door nuh boy', she pushed past him into the flat. Susan and Pamela laughed and followed their friend, while Cory stumbled, cursing at the 'boy' remark. He would've even gone inside to start an argument if he'd not seen Sean's girl Sonia and some boys from the other side of Greenside coming down the featureless grey landing towards him.

'Stop harassin' innocent women,' Sonia teased, looking pretty yet tough in brown CAT boots, jeans and a brown leather jacket. She was a sweet-looking girl, with full lips and sensuous brown eyes, as well as a razor-sharp tongue that could tell you about yourself in seconds. She'd been seeing Sean for two years now and Cory guessed they were quite serious about each other. His friends sniggered and muttered amongst themselves.

'Stop harassin' me an' look after your man. My guy's all pinin' f'you now star,' Cory replied, a little stung by the way things were going.

Sonia made a face and disappeared inside with a quick 'bye' to the boys. As soon as she left, their sniggering stopped and it was down to the night's business.

'Yes blood.'

Arthur Lyne, better known as 'Art' on the estate, greeted Cory with a touch of the fists and stood back to let the others, Johnny and Raymond, give their own greetings. They were a hard-looking selection of crackheads, far enough down the road to be stealing for the habit, but far enough up it to still have their wits about them. All of them betrayed an intelligence that at best made Cory think they were wasting their lives. But what could he possibly tell them?

When they were done, Cory looked at them eagerly.

'Wha' you man sayin' tonight star? What's the mission?' he asked, smiling broadly.

Raymond, the quiet young man of the crew, answered Cory's smile with his own. As if by a sign, all three produced screwdrivers from their pockets.

'Pullouts,' they replied, speaking as one person and holding the tools out so he could see.

Cory needed no more tempting; without another word, he closed the door and made his way down the corridor and onto the night streets, which immediately embraced him as their adopted son.

Sonia spent five minutes gossiping with Sean's mum about college and her part-time job in Boots. She spent another five in Shannon's room, socialising with her friends and coughing from the Red Seal they were passing around. After more scandalous talk, she made her way to Sean's room, thinking what a good couple they made together. He was different from the other estate boys in so many ways it was uncountable. Sonia was glad he wasn't anything like his cousin, whom she liked, but secretly thought would amount to nothing.

Other boys smoked weed, ash and worst of all crack; Sean didn't even touch Benson & Hedges. Other boys spent nights robbing and chatting up girls; Sean was always studying or relaxing with a lager when he had no work. Other boys were materialistic, wanting cars, mobile phones and jewellery now; Sean was working towards his long-term future – *their* long-term future – so they could leave Greenside behind forever.

They'd first met at the secondary school they both attended, Greenside High, but were there for over three years before they actually got it together. As they were in different form classes they'd been merely nodding acquaintances until their third year. They were asked by their teachers to choose five option subjects which decided the GCSE exams they would take. They had both chosen business studies and slowly, as the year went by, they had found themselves getting closer and closer.

Sonia counted herself lucky to have him – and of course he was equally lucky, she thought dryly. She rapped twice on his door, waited for his usual yell to enter, then eased her shapely frame through.

'Hey Sonnie,' Sean said from a desk by the window. 'I almost thought you wasn't comin'.

'Tamika was sick, so I had to go chemists,' she replied, squeezing between the two beds.

The room was lit by one lamp, which showed up old wallpaper and various bits of junk Cory had collected. If the two cousins hadn't been close, the small room could've been a battleground, but each had his own space: the mountain bike with one wheel (that Bernice had wanted moved since last Christmas) marked Cory's half. The poster of Halle Berry and Eddie Murphy in the film *Boomerang* marked Sean's. The broad pine desk and most of its contents was shared between them both.

'So what, is she gonna be able to go away if she's sick?' Sean asked, his dark face shining from the lamp's glow.

Tamika was Sonia's younger sister. In two days' time she was due to fly out to Jamaica with her mother for a luxurious eight-week holiday. Sonia had meant to go as well, but her forthcoming end-of-term exams had put paid to that idea and, reluctantly, she decided to stay at home.

'It's jus' a runny nose an' a cough, nuthin' major,' Sonnie told him as she approached the desk. 'I got some kiddie's Benylin for her an' Mum's put her to bed an' tol' her to stay dere, so hopefully she'll be all right. Dem tickets ain't even refundable though, so I suppose she'll have to be on death's door before Mum thinks of cancellin'.'

Sonia walked over to the window, then lifted the net curtain and looked out at the bright lights of other blocks and kids running like shadow creatures. Then she turned, smiling teasingly at her boyfriend, who was hurriedly finishing off a last sentence.

'So what, did yuh miss me?' she asked, letting the curtain fall gently.

'I missed you,' Sean said sincerely, putting down his pen and turning to her.

Standing, he was slightly shorter than Cory, but his build was stockier and his skin colour a little darker. His eyes were deep brown and he wore a gold hooped earring in his left ear that shone pleasantly against his skin. Sonnie could hear low Jungle busily playing as she came closer, and wondered how he could concentrate without the rapid beats distracting him. She sat on his lap and kissed him before motioning to the books.

'Givin' up so early? It's not often I can tempt you this easily.'

Sean rolled his eyes and groaned. 'I bin at it since six,' he said, feigning his tiredness. 'You must 'llow me some rest an' recoup innit?'

'F'real though,' Sonia replied, stroking the side of his face absently. 'I don't want my scholar to collapse from exhaustion, do I?'

'Mmmm,' Sean muttered, already falling asleep at his girl's touch. Sonia, who'd planned a whole night with him, tried to keep him awake with talk.

'Your cousin should watch himself with dem brers he's movin' with, y'know,' she told him, her lips pouting slightly.

'Why?' He looked up at her.

'Well I don't know about the others, but Art's a blatant cat. His granny lives in Fleming House and he drummed her yard an' never felt no way, so he can't care for Cory. Certain times I see my guy all prang an' I cross the road boy.' She laughed nervously.

'Cory ain't no cat,' Sean said simply. 'He hates crack man, says it's poison from white people to make us kill ourselves an' fuck up our families. He hates it star.'

'People change y'know,' Sonia muttered quietly.

'Cory ain't no cat man,' he emphasised slowly, giving the statement time to sink in. 'An' hear dis Sonnie right? Don't cross the road when you see Art, jus' walk star, my man won't look on you, believe me. Yeh?'

'OK.' She snuggled up closer to him. 'You jus' watch that cousin o' yours too.'

'Yeah, yeah.' He put an arm around her. 'Cory's too smart to get involved in anythin' too stupid. Trust me.'

'I do,' she murmured; and she did. But even so, they both felt a shiver of doubt in their minds – planted there by themselves, but best left alone, just in case it bore fruit.

Chapter Two

'I don't *fuckin'* believe it!'

Cory took in the sight before him, with strong regret. He'd left his warm comfy house for this? He shook his head angrily and glared at the others.

They'd hopped on the first Underground train to North Acton and walked into an area that looked like suburbia, yet wasn't five miles from central London. Cory checked the car windows as they passed, looking for the expensive pullouts. Johnny laughed and eased him past the dormant vehicles.

'Cory's after a stereo,' he chuckled. The others laughed as well. By the time they reached their destination, a modest look-ing semi-detached house, Cory was already fuming.

They crept around to the back, hidden by a pathway dark-ened by large hedges which rustled spookily. They jumped the gate into the garden, careful not to shake it too hard, with Cory scowling all the way. He stayed quiet until he saw the large win-dow looking into the living room. That was when he finally understood what his friends had planned.

'You man are barmy if you're on what I think you're on,' he whispered in disbelief.

Johnny and Raymond took no notice, merely producing their screwdrivers and starting to unscrew the window from the frame with intense concentration. Only Art turned to him.

'If you ain't helpin', at least look out for us blood,' he grinned, in a voice which suggested he was being reasonable.

'It won't work. The putty'll hol' it in place,' was all the shocked Cory could manage.

Art didn't look worried in the slightest.

'We'll jus' 'ave to dig it out innit?' he answered, gesturing with his screwdriver. 'Look out will yuh?' With that, he turned to the job at hand.

Five minutes later by Cory's watch (five minutes that seemed like hours to him) he saw Johnny's head poke over the gate.

'Come nuh,' he whispered, before disappearing again.

Cory shook the cramp from his leg and followed, to see the window lying on the concrete and the living room curtains twitching restlessly. At that instant, he took back everything he'd said or thought earlier and beamed for the first time since leaving Greenside.

'Shit,' he said, following the rest inside and looking over the wide-screen TV, a Phillips CD-I and a heavy-looking black Kenwood stack system. 'Dis is dett boy! How long you bin on dis?'

'Couple o' weeks,' Art replied, glad his friend could see the reality of the move at last.

'An' you're jus' bringin' me in?'

Art laughed and clapped Cory on the back.

'Tell you what, everythin' you can take from upstairs is yours blood.'

'*Yeah*?!'

Cory could see the other two didn't like that, but they were too busy unplugging the stack system to argue.

'Yeah man. One; we do about four of these a week, an' two; I want you to stop walkin' wid the card you use to slide man. Police are wise to dat now, so it's time to switch tactics.' Cory nodded and made his way to the stairs.

The house was as dark as a tower block's basement. At first he had to grope along the walls and grip the bannister by turns to get up the staircase. He stumbled twice, swearing under his breath both times. He did have a pocket Maglight, which he carried nearly everywhere, but he was afraid the beam would be seen from outside and decided to wait until his night vision kicked in. By the time he reached the first bedroom door, he could make out posters and reckoned he was outside a child's room. With a mental shrug, he turned the door knob slowly and eased the door open, mindful of squeaky hinges.

The room was both a relief and a disappointment. Relief because it was unoccupied, the one small bed neatly made up and an assortment of Power Rangers figures in a carefully put together action scene; and disappointment at the lack of toys actually worth stealing. He settled for a handful of Sega MegaDrive games, stacked on a sturdy-looking cabinet, which he stuffed in his pockets hastily before looking for the parents' bedroom.

Cory hit jackpot on his fourth attempt, after finding the spare room and the toilet second and third time around. It was a plain room, painted a light colour Cory couldn't make out in the dark. The king-sized bed and a wardrobe with mirrored doors took up most of the space on the right side. On the left was a bar-bell and a couple of dumb-bells and a dresser.

Cory headed straight for the dresser, opening drawers and jewellery boxes until he found an assortment of rings and chains. Feeling confident, he had a rummage in the wardrobe and even tried the drawers underneath the bed. All that they contained were some musty-smelling clothes.

In a few more minutes, Cory had collected what he wanted. He was heading to join the others, when he heard a car slow down to a stop outside. He went to the bedroom window and cautiously looked into the street. He could see a Vauxhall Nova parked there, but the owner, who showed no signs of getting out, was just sitting in the dark waiting. It didn't look like a police car. Maybe someone had alerted the houseowners and they'd returned from wherever they'd been for the night. He watched the car for a second more, then checked his switchblade was in his back pocket.

'Mek him come star,' he muttered to himself. He crept downstairs slowly to alert the crew, only to find them sitting in the armchairs, drinking champagne from a large black bottle. Ray passed it over as he entered the room.

'Hear what now,' Cory said, between swigs. 'There's a guy in a car outside jus' park up an' I don't like it boy.'

Johnny got up.

'What, in a Nova?' he asked.

'Yeah yeah.'

'*Raa*, that's my cousin star, he's a cabby. I showed him to come down earlier on today man, you know say he's legal, innit Art?'

Art nodded once, his expression saying he didn't really care, he just wanted to leave.

'Come we go back to Greenside man, go check Levi, an' hold a bone, y'get me?'

Johnny laughed as Art made his proposal and collected his goods while the others did the same. They left the window on the concrete of the back yard, and as quickly and quietly as they could shoved themselves in the car with their haul on their laps.

'Nice one cuz,' Johnny said to the young man driving, who was called Simon. He had a shaved head apart from a short lock at the back, and a large jaw. He nodded easily at the crew when introduced and only asked to be 'brought in neatly' when they exchanged their stolen goods for money, or drugs.

Twenty minutes later, they were parked outside Beechwood House, home of Levi, a Rasta who lived on the third floor. He dabbled in anything that made money, from cocaine to stolen crates of Coca-Cola, which he'd successfully sold for twenty pence a can the year before, making a tidy sum.

Cory called him a fake Dredd because he sold crack at night to the same youths he preached to in the day. Still, Cory was prepared to forgive him sufficiently to sell the jewellery he'd found in the house. He'd long believed he was a diplomat at heart and his dealings with the older man had proved it frequently.

Beechwood House stood like a dark multi-eyed creature as the residents slept, unaware of the boys as they packed their haul into the lift with Ray, and took off up the stairs. They met up with him on the third floor where everything was lifted into Levi's flat quietly, apart from some mumbled curses and grunts as they strained with the two TVs.

Levi's flat, Cory had learned a few months after meeting him, wasn't exactly his. It once housed an old man and his even more decrepit dog. When the old man died, his dog was put down and the flat boarded up. It stayed empty for a while, until a group of friendly squatters moved in. Soon the place looked habitable, if not homely. Then Levi appeared like David Copperfield, with a get-rich-quick scheme that had a high profit margin. The operation had been running successfully for months to many of the neighbours' fury. Everyone on the Greenside Estate knew the goings-on at 42 Beechwood House, but the police never seemed to go near it.

The Dredd's eyes were wide, yet clear, as he led them past the front door, reinforced with three short pieces of scaffolding, placed across the top, middle and bottom. He took them along the corridor, closing doors as they passed through them and into a back room that was empty, apart from a brown carpet, three wooden chairs and black cloth curtains over the windows. The haul was piled up in a dusty corner of the room like an untidy array of prizes in a TV game show. Levi looked around, then indicated they should sit down.

'So what you sayin' for dis little lot blood?' Art began, rubbing his hands together.

The others groaned silently: Art was a man who'd come out the worse if he haggled with Mother Teresa herself.

'Weell . . .' Levi inhaled deeply on the zook, then exhaled, bathing the room in crack smoke. 'I feel say I c'n give you . . . One an' a half, two, fe dem t'ings dere.'

Johnny, tantalised by the intoxicating smell of the slowly twirling smoke, spat fine droplets as he shouted '*What*!?' The others quickly added their indignation.

'You mus' be jokin'!'

'Man's 'avin a laugh, serious boy!'

'Dat TV's a Nicam y'know. Fuck, dat's a monkey at least!'

This last was from Cory who grinned as he said it, knowing Levi would just as soon give away rocks as give them five hundred pounds for the TV.

Levi accepted their complaints in silence, then held up his hands in a gesture of surrender.

'All right den. Four an' a half fe de whole lot, tek it or leave it.'

The young men looked at each other and conferred silently. Art, who'd elected himself spokesman, nodded at the Dredd.

'Yeah, yeah, dat can run,' he said, feeling good.

Art looked around at his friends, as Levi produced a bulging wallet and counted off fifties, assessing their reaction as he always did when Levi showed off his money. Johnny and Ray sat smiling, trying to be nonchalant as the notes formed four neat piles on the table before them. Cory was sneering and slowly shaking his head, which annoyed Art. Sometimes his friend showed his feelings a little too easily for his liking. But Levi hadn't noticed Cory's hard stare.

'See it deh,' Levi said, sitting back in his chair.

Cory picked up the pile of notes nearest to him, while the others argued about the remaining fifty, eventually deciding to give it to Johnny's cousin. Cory gave his share willingly and got up to leave. Art looked at him in surprise even though it was the same every time they did a move.

'Raa where you goin' spee?' he said, smiling. 'Bones are runnin' tonight star!'

'F'real!'

'Y' get me!'

Johnny and Ray were looking up as well. Levi spoke, his voice rumbling from his chest.

'Cory refuses to journey to the Garden of Eden. For *now*,' he said, looking the youth square in the face. Cory looked into his eyes, tempted to make a comment about snakes in the grass. He decided against it and shrugged instead.

'Hear what now, you lot see the gullies at my yard innit? I wanna speech the light-skinned one a way man!'

Art snorted and waved his hand in dismissal. Johnny laughed.

'She's the only one that ain't cuss you yet!' he spluttered.

'Yeah, yeah, see you lot after college man,' Cory replied, taking no notice.

'Later.'

'Yes blood.'

'Walk careful man.'

Cory made his way to the front door, passing rooms that vibrated music, muffled but audible through closed doors. He passed a man by one, against the wall, his arm wrapped around a woman, noisily kissing her neck while his pale hand moved underneath her T-shirt. The woman was moaning softly, her eyes wide open. Cory eased behind her partner so quietly, he never even noticed his presence, and he was forced to look the woman in the eyes. She surprised him, by suddenly smiling at him and rolling her eyes upwards, all without missing a moan. He smiled back and left the flat, grinning widely.

The outside air was cold but a relief after the smoky room he'd left behind him. He trotted down the stairs and was crossing the road when a shout pulled him up.

'Oh my God, watch Cory *blatantly* walk past my house guy!'

He turned to see Rosie Joseph and Tara Wilson, two Beechwood girls, standing and watching him as he strode along the pavement. Rosie lived on the ground floor where they were standing and Tara on the fourth. They were both of a milk chocolate complexion, very pretty, and neither of them was your average loafer. They worked as well as studied and Cory felt an attraction between himself and Rosie, even though she knew he wasn't exactly a regular working Joe.

Of course, to help matters along, Tara, who was Rosie's best friend, still hated Cory after he had tried to chat her up at a party three years ago. Rosie had moved into Greenside the winter after that. Cory strolled over, still feeling lucky.

'Out late ain't we?' he questioned amiably. Tara just looked at him.

'Maddy won't let us bun inside, so me an' Tara sit out 'ere.'

'Maddy?' He looked at her, puzzled.

'Madeleine, my aunt innit.'

Rosie gave him a dazzling smile.

'Still goin' out with that escapee from Holloway?' she asked, trying to disguise her prying with humour. Cory and Tara laughed despite themselves.

'You're a dark girl,' he said jokingly, 'and yes I am and her name's Tanya, all right.'

'You could do better.'

'So could you.'

'*Me*!'

She looked around as if addressing an audience.

'Than who?'

'Jason Taylor an' don't tell me *nothin*' star, I see you—' He was forced to break off as both girls were laughing and repeating the name, while leaning on each other for support. Cory relented. 'All right, all right, so it ain't JT.'

'In his fuckin' dreams.'

'At least you know I care.'

'You don't care for me, like I care for you,' Rosie sang, her voice surprisingly clear in the crisp air. She looked at Cory and then looked away, the words replaying in her mind and making her shy, despite her former worldly attitude. Tara looked a little disgusted.

'You never know, one day I might prove you wrong,' Cory replied, backing away. 'I gotta run man. See yuh Rosie, Tara.'

''Bye darlin'.'

'Yeah, see yuh.'

Cory walked slowly, patting his pockets to check he still had the jewellery he'd kept back from the haul. Satisfied they were safe, he hummed an Ice Cube song and smiled, thinking of the last few hours.

You know what, he thought to himself, today *was* a good day. With that, his smile widened and he headed home, warm despite the chill of the breeze.

Chapter Three

'So for your homework tonight, I want you to write an essay with the title: Explain the role of the Nuclear Family in the Nineteenth Century and give your reasons for its decline in the Twentieth. OK?'

The lecturer, Sam Boyd, looked around to see his pupils shocked at such a complicated subject for an essay. One even said as much, asking if it wasn't just a cruel joke. Sam rested his lanky frame on a table and decided honesty was the best policy.

'To tell the truth, I left the real essay title for today at home and just made that one up.'

The class roared with laughter as the lunchtime bell let out its urgent call to hungry students all over the building. Sean Bradley, sitting at the back shook his head and smiled. He'd always had a healthy respect for his lecturer, mainly because Sam was the only West Indian teaching at his college. And as the months had passed he'd found him to be both wise and down to earth.

Sam was the only lecturer to eat his lunch at tables crammed with students, and talk to them without appearing to patronise. Even Cory, ever resentful of authority, had taken to Sam. Together with Amanda, another student in the class, they'd organised a charity football match – pupils against lecturers – to be held in a few weeks. The proceeds would go to sickle cell research.

While Sean was lost in thought, the class had gathered their bags and were leaving.

'Make the most of my error!' Sam was shouting as they left. 'Next week's title is definitely a five-line affair! Oh, and can I see Sean quickly please.'

Sean made his way to the front of the class and sat on the desk. Sam grinned and rubbed his hands together.

'Now Sean, I wanted to see you to get a message to Cory yeah?'

'Yeah man, safe.'

'Tell him that he's in charge of the promotional posters for the match, so he's to get designin' sharpish. And Tyrone wants him to be captain of the students' A team, so it's gonna be his fault when we whip his arse boy!'

Sean noticed Sam had relaxed into a stronger Bajan accent now the lesson was over.

'I'll let him know blatant. Dis is gonna be quite a tournament star,' he said to himself.

Sam nodded.

'You know what – that's really all. Oh yeah, if you need to store anything let me know, 'cause the caretaker has lent us a storage room for awhile.'

'OK,' Sean replied. 'If anythin' I'll let you know.'

'All right Sean. Enjoy your lunch, yeah?' Sam muttered, already busy with some files sitting in front of him.

Sean walked into the corridor and heard a door swing open behind him. A familiar female voice floated welcomingly into his ears.

'Fancy seein' you here!' it said before he'd even moved.

He turned to find Sonia pushing through some doors with 'FIRE EXIT' printed boldly underneath the windows. He gave her a warm hug.

'We in or out for lunch?' he asked when he'd let her go.

'Out definitely. I saw Tanya and she reckons everyone's in the park playing footie. It's cris' outside man.'

'Come den. I got a message for Cory.'

They walked outside arm-in-arm, Sean squinting as the bright sunlight hit his eyes. All around them, students of all shapes, sizes and nationalities milled about the building, many of them like themselves, free for the rest of the afternoon. Cars played SwingBeat, Hip Hop and Jungle; their owners trying to impress the opposite sex by drawing a gathering. Sean and Sonia waved and hello'ed their way to the shops, where they bought a bagful of munchies, then strolled to the park contentedly.

Their friends were sitting in a group of around twenty, while others played football with goals marked by two piles of jackets. The smell of weed was heavy in the air and a tinny portable tape deck played soothing Raregrooves, while a group of girls were singing along in a heartfelt kind of way. Sean and Sonia flopped to the ground near the most familiar faces and opened their bag of snacks.

'Bloodfire!' Douglas James, a large black youth with skin so dark it shone with good health, reached over to touch fists with Sean and his girl.

'Wha' you sayin' man?' he beamed up at them.

'Cool star, I'm safe.'

'Nuh man, I mean wha' you sayin' on a Twix yuh bastard. My man's bag's ram up boy.'

The crowd laughed and a few looked over. Sean flipped Dougie a Twix and fielded off an avalanche of requests from the others.

'I ain't a fuckin' corner shop,' he complained, a bit put out that everyone made him feel like a Scrooge. Douglas looked around his chocolate in sympathy.

'Build a zook nuh,' he offered generously.

'I don't smoke man,' Sean replied. He was used to this, as well as having people pass him spliffs at parties and raves. He usually passed them to Cory if he was about.

'Shit, I always forget dat blood. You drink innit?'

'Yeah yeah.'

'Tanya! *Tanyaaa*! Bring dem Holstens come man.'

Sean raised his eyebrows thinking, Cory would go mad if he heard Dougie talking to his girl like that, no matter his size.

Tanya, a light-skinned girl from Hackney, with wide Chinese eyes, a stud in her nose and shapely honey-toned legs, came over with the drinks. She was as rough as the boys and had even fought and beaten one up in the Christmas term, gashing his head with a PeachCanei bottle after he kept touching her bottom in her English class. At seventeen, she had her own flat and her own car. Cory once confessed to Sean that they'd even robbed a house together one night. Nevertheless, Sean found her funny and likeable and so did most other people – apart from the boy she'd beaten up.

'Hey Sean. Y'all right Sonnie. Oi Dig Dug my name ain't Benson y'know, you're takin' liberties guy.'

Tanya cut her eyes at Dougie, but kept a small smile on her face to show she was joking.

'Course your name ain't Benson, you're too light, too stupid an' you're a fuckin' gully,' Dougie shot back. There was more laughter from the boys, while the girls cussed colourfully. Tanya swung the tins in his direction, aiming to miss.

'Mind dem cans don't get shake up y'know,' Dougie rumbled, ducking the swinging bag easily.

'You're lucky I'm in a good mood,' she replied, laying her jacket on the grass and sitting down on the colourful lining. While they bantered, Sean took out a can, watching the exchange closely. He popped it slowly, easing the air out before taking deep swallows. The lager flowed down his throat like an icy river and he realised how thirsty he'd been. He gulped down some more, then put the can down, burping loudly and wiping his mouth with his free hand.

'Needed that boy, I was parched,' he said gratefully.

'You popped dat like a professional star,' Dougie answered, happy his gift was received well.

They sat and watched the match in front of them, cheering on their friends noisily when a goal was attempted or a tackle executed. Cory, who was playing the right wing, noticed his cousin and jogged over to sit by Tanya, ignoring his team-mates' complaints.

'Yes cuz. How are you cuz-in-law?' he panted at Sean and Sonia, as Dougie passed him a zook.

'Safe man,' Sean muttered, the weight of the heat bearing down on his shoulders, making him feel lazy. He suddenly remembered Sam's message for Cory.

'Oh yeah, Sam says you bin nominated captain of the A team an' you have to get that poster done quicktime, not blacktime. He ain't rampin' either, he reckons he's gonna kick you up in the football tournament.'

Cory stretched out and laid his head on Tanya's thigh.

'I dealt wi' dat poster from las' week, I jus' gotta get some copies done now star. Hey an' skin 'n' bone Sam bes' mind I don't roast a ball in his face, about kick me up. He don't know about my skills yet, but he'll fin' out soon enough believe me.'

There was quiet for a bit while everyone watched the match as a brief goal-mouth scuffle went on. A defender punted the ball harmlessly away for a corner.

'Come *on*!' Cory shouted. 'Cover the right post someone will yuh!'

'Get on the pitch and cover your own post!' An unseen comedian yelled back. Everyone cracked up, Cory included. Sonia said something underneath the noise, but it was all but lost to the teen. When the laughter died down he asked her to repeat her sentence.

'I said, "what's the score?"'

Cory frowned. 'Six–five to dem man. Dem African yout's are rough footballers y'know, but y'ave to watch their tackles still. Brok up a man if he ain't careful y'get me?'

While Cory had been talking a group of five black kids had wandered over to where the match was being played, talking amongst themselves and surveying the crowd curiously. They were a rag tag group, some with their heads wrapped loosely with bandanas, others with elaborate patterns and short locks. They stood watching for a bit longer, like shimmering mirages in the heat and then started talking to the goalie, who shrugged and pointed at everyone else. The corner was taken, plucked out of the air by the goalie and kicked away quickly, then the boys resumed their talk, seeming to bargain with the Africans. Cory got up and threw away a smouldering roach absently.

'Looks like they wanna game,' he commented. 'You playin' Sean? Dere's five o' dem, so we'll need an' extra man.'

'Ummm . . . Yeah, I soon come all right?'

'Dougie wha' you sayin' blood? Come we kick a ball nuh,' Cory teased gently, knowing the answer. Despite his size, Dougie made a rule of never exerting himself, especially on a day like this. He screwed up his face as if in pain.

'You got your extra man, 'llow me nuh, what'm to you? Can't you see I'm restin'.'

'Yeah yeah, same old story man. Soon come Tanya.'

'OK babes.'

They watched as Cory returned to the pitch and got into a discussion with the boys, who looked about the same age as them. Sean recognised a couple from a small estate not far from Greenside, but decided he actually knew none. He got up and joined his cousin, curious.

'All right.' The boy with the shaved head, sullen look and the early wisps of a beard was talking. 'Three on one side, two on the other, right?'

'Right,' Cory answered. 'We better take the two, 'cause my cousin's playin' for us, y'get me?'

'Fair enough blood. I'm Roger, dis is Christian, Max, Jeff and Robert.'

'I'm Cory, respec'.'

Everyone touched fists, Sean included.

'Sean, nice one man.'

The teen nodded in greeting at the sullen-faced boy.

'Let's get started den.'

They trotted over to the others and kicked off, the cheers from their friends stirring them up faster than any shrill whistle could. Sean (who was playing in defence) quickly found out Cory had been right: the mainly African side they were playing were very skilful indeed, working their way into their half with a series of accurate passes, before crossing the ball into the box. He managed to volley the Mitre powerfully back into their half, before looking around at his fellow defenders.

'Find a man and stick to him tight star,' he said quickly.

For the next few minutes play swung back and forth on the grass, everyone sweating as the heat and exercise hit them. Cory skilfully tackled one of the newcomers, then led a steaming attack up the right wing, looked for his man and crossed. It was a beautiful ball, that seemed to hang in the air, spinning slowly like a mock planet, before falling to be headed by Paul, an Irish boy from Sean's A' level English class. The goalie dived sharply to the right, but couldn't stretch his fingers. The ball whipped past.

'Six all!' Cory shouted, waving at their audience as they cheered loudly. The goalie kicked the ball back to the centre.

Five minutes later Cory blasted the ball past the goalie. In another two minutes, the African saved a cross, only to fumble and drop the ball. Paul was waiting for just such an opening and tapped it casually past the keeper, smiling happily. Eight–Six.

The main striker for the Africans called for a half-time break and was surprised by the cries of agreement that greeted his suggestion. Everyone was thirsty and a mass exodus to the watching crowd was in progress, way before the goalie could get the ball back to the centre. He looked around, seeming a bit lost, then left the makeshift pitch to join his friends too.

Sean sniffed the air, aware of a new smell besides that of weed. He relaxed, trying to see if the wind would bring it over, but then the slight breeze dropped. Paul pointed at the five boys who'd joined the game late. They were sitting in a group apart from everyone else, a cloud of smoke over their heads, laughing and joking. The breeze rose, pushing the thin tendrils of smoke towards Sean again. He sniffed once more, satisfying his curiosity. It was Paul who put a name to what his nose picked up.

'Crack,' he said gravely, the word making heads rise from whatever they were doing. Tanya's rose with a slight smile nobody noticed.

Sean pointed the boys out to Cory, who shrugged.

'Each to their own innit,' he muttered. 'As long as they don't trouble *me*, I don't give a fuck.'

There was a burst of laughter from the five boys as Roger and Max play fought on the grass and the other three gave the occasional dig when the chance arose. The Africans were looking at the boys with disgust on their faces, but a couple of the girls who'd been singing earlier went over, smiling daintily. Max passed a small pipe to the prettiest, while Roger invited the other one to sit next to him. Sonia kissed her teeth disdainfully, but remained silent.

Some of the boys started drifting back onto the pitch and passing the ball around. Sean decided to get some practice in. One by one, the other players wandered back as well, until everyone was in their positions and eager to start again. Cory sat holding his zook, seeming in no hurry to resume the game.

'Gimme a light Dougie,' he muttered watching the darting, running players with half an eye.

'Don' 'ave it y'know . . .' Dougie was lying with one thick arm covering his head, looking immovable.

'Gimme a light babes . . .'

Cory sat up, poking Tanya in her thigh playfully. After a lot of giggling and poking back, she shook her head.

'Sorry darlin', I ain' got one either; stay dere an' I'll get one though.'

She got up in a second and, before Cory could say a word, made her way over to the crew of singing girls. He watched them very carefully. After seeing the multitude of heads shake from side to side sadly, Tanya sauntered over to Roger's crew. There was a great deal of talk. Cory saw Roger hold out something, then pull it back close to his chest, smiling at the girl. Tanya looked over at Cory quickly, then crossed her arms and looked at the sky. The boys all began to shout; loud enough for Cory to hear random words, but not quite loud enough for him to guess what they were saying. Sonia kissed her teeth again.

After letting this go on for a bit longer, Tanya came back. 'They wouldn't give me one,' she told them.

'Why the fuck not?' Cory blazed.

'I dunno do I? The guy's a joker man, make him stay dere. Anyway, shop's only round the corner innit?'

Dougie looked at Tanya quizzically.

'So what was dem man sayin' all dat time?'

She scowled and looked a little embarrassed. 'Nuttin' man, they was jus' goin' on stoopid about his lighter, dat's all. Come we go shops man . . .' she walked a couple of paces then looked back at Cory. He hadn't moved.

'Wha' d'he say?' he growled threateningly, taking Dougie's cue.

'Nuttin' Cory man, I tol' you . . . Come we go—'

'Tanya, stop fuckin' around wid me man!' Cory snapped. 'Far as I can see, the brer's got a light, so what am I walkin' shops for? Furthermore, if you don't tell me I'm gonna go an' ask my man myself star.'

Tanya sighed deeply, then came back over looking a bit distressed. 'It's nuttin' man,' she said slowly. 'I asked dat guy for a light an' he started goin' on about givin' him a . . . a shiners an' all dat shit . . . *Cory, it was jus' a joke, where you goin' man*—'

Cory had got up, hard-eyed and marched over to where Roger and his friends were sitting. The youth shaded his eyes and looked up at Cory with a faint smile. Roger's friends watched sternly.

'What, you chuckin' it wid my girl spee, or what?' Cory blasted.

Tanya soon followed.

'Cory 'llow it man, what'm—?'

'Shut up,' he ordered gruffly, before turning back to Roger. 'So what, ain' you got nuttin' t'say?'

'Not to you bredrin,' Roger replied. He got to his feet and pointed at Tanya. 'But I wouldn't min' a couple more words wid *her*.'

Cory, growing more livid by the second, stepped even closer to Roger while the others watched. The footballers limbering up finally took notice.

'So what, is dat how you're goin' on? Disrespcc' mc an' you don't even know me star. You bes' min' out, dat's all I'm sayin'.'

'You bes' min' *me*,' Roger snapped back, his smile fading. 'Dis time now, yuh girl looked up for lettin' off spee – she probably would if you wasn't about y' get me?'

Roger's friends laughed at that. Tanya looked hot and flushed with shame, while on the football pitch, Sean had started making his way over to them.

'Hear what now, don't make me hafta bore you up y'know. After we was getting on an' dat,' Cory spat, his fist clenching tightly.

'Suck yuh mudda star,' Roger answered with venom.

'What?! *What*!?'

'I said "suck yuh mudda", pussy.'

Cory punched Roger in the face with a stinging blow. At once, the two boys started grappling. In an instant they were surrounded by the other players, some trying to stop the fight, others just cheering. As Sean watched, Roger's friends were reaching in their back pockets. He looked around in a panic and, seeing Dougie appear beside him, tugged his arm and pointed at them.

'Come now gentlemen, let's not spill any blood on such a fine day, hmm?'

Sean was pleased to see Paul had joined them, his Irish accent wafting as smooth as Guinness punch across to their adversaries. He was even more pleased to see a battered yet sharp ratchet in

Paul's hand and a hard look on his face. They were steadily joined by other kids from the college and even some of the African players, until the four were outnumbered by many. The boys put away their blades, sheepishly.

Cory and Roger, still shouting and swearing had been pulled apart. Roger's eye was already swelling and his right lip was bleeding, while Cory had a lump just above his own right eye and his T-shirt was ripped and torn. Sonia was holding him back, along with some others, while Tanya let loose a verbal onslaught full of profanity on Roger's mother. Roger tried to get at her but the crowd held him back, until he lashed out, freeing himself violently. Tanya stood by Cory, thinking Roger would try to come for her, but he stayed where he was and pointed at the teen.

'I know your face, pussy,' he said, looking like a madman in his rage. 'You're from the manor. I'm bound to buck you up again star and when I do, I'm gonna carve you up, blatant.'

Cory looked unshaken by this statement. 'We'll jus' have to see about dat star,' he replied, looking coldly back at Roger. They stood that way for about twenty seconds, no one moving, until Roger spat the word 'pussy', and walked off, collecting his bemused friends as he went, their faces amazed at the turn of events.

Sean ran over to Cory concerned. 'Are you OK? How about you Sonnie? Did he stab you? Dem man had their boras y'know,' he said in a rush. Sonia held his hand as he reached them.

'Yeah man, I'm safe, come we go home star,' Cory said, sounding more fed up than anything else.

'We should go look for dem man an' fuck 'em up,' Sean said, his voice betraying his outrage and a need to hurt someone. He tried not to make it obvious he was looking over Cory's face.

'Nah man, fuck 'em star, I jus' wanna go to my drum man. Come we go nuh,' Cory repeated adamantly. His cousin decided not to argue.

'Cool man, let's doss then,' he replied.

The Underground journey home was made in silence. Cory stared back stonily at the businessmen looking at his cut eye, until they were forced to look away. Tanya sat next to him protectively until they reached Greenside Station. She walked close and linked arms with him as they passed the ticket collector, then they crossed the road, past Mackenzie House, into the estate.

As they walked, Sean caught up with Cory and Tanya and made a gesture to the girl, indicating she should drop back. She left to talk to Sonia, leaving Cory looking around in mock surprise as if he hadn't noticed Sean's approach.

'What'm cuz? Where'd Tanya go?'

'I told her to chat wid Sonnic,' Sean replied, smiling at Cory's raised eyebrows. 'Listen Cory man, we gotta look for dem brers, quicktime star. We can't let dem come lookin' for us.'

His voice sounded worried. But Cory just shrugged. 'Yeah, I'll look for dem man, but in my own time an' in my own way. Don't worry about me cuz, I'm safe man, you should done know dat.'

'Dat's the thing, I am worried,' Sean countered, his gaze sombre. 'Remember what happened to Lawrence?' he finally said, the words sticking like hastily chewed food in his throat.

Cory turned to Sean in shock at the mention of the name. He eventually had to look away, as the concern in Sean's eyes was too much for him. After all Lawrence Ganton was someone most boys on the estate tried to forget . . .

Two summers ago, after a gruelling football game, Cory, his best friend Garvey and Lawrence Ganton, a large fair-skinned boy, were walking home from the pitch in the middle of the estate. They had stopped outside the shops discussing their next move, eventually electing to go back to Cory's to play on his Sega Megadrive. All, except Lawrence, who claimed he was too tired and wanted to go home to Oakhill House. Carrying his Mitre football, he waved goodbye to his friends. He made his way past Caldervale House and up towards Beechwood, according to police reports. But he never reached Beechwood.

At the corner of Caldervale Lawrence spied a man, considerably older than him, viciously slapping a girl about the face. Lawrence (who'd witnessed his father beating his mother many times) flipped, then ran over and pulled the man away from the girl, shouting: 'Leave her the fuck alone man!'

The man fell backwards, skidding on the concrete. When he looked up he saw Lawrence had picked up a piece of wood from a skip by the kerb. The youth was advancing on him, ready to defend himself.

Meanwhile the girl had recovered, seen what was happening and ran up to the fourth floor to tell her boyfriend's crew what was going on. Six men came down to help their friend. Between them, they beat Lawrence to within an inch of his life, bundled him into a car and drove away, leaving twitching curtains in their wake.

Lawrence's body was found two days later, floating in the Grand Union Canal, with fourteen stab wounds and two shots in his head.

Cory and his friends were distraught over the killing, Garvey taking it hardest. He lived in Oakhill as well and blamed himself for not walking Lawrence home that humid evening. All the boys spent many sleepless nights, dreaming of their dear friend.

'It can happen to anyone,' Sean concluded, as the street lamps began flickering on one by one, slowly transforming the roads into an orange-lit movie set. Cory sighed.

'Cuz listen man; Lawrence was in the wrong place at the wrong time—'

'Exactly!' Sean broke in, before Cory could finish.

As they reached their home block, Cory turned and called Tanya to follow him.

'Where you goin'?' Sean asked.

'Garvey's,' he flung over his shoulder, as Tanya hurried to catch him up. 'Hopefully, you'll have stopped naggin' me by the time I get back.'

With that, he walked away, leaving Sean upset and Sonia puzzled.

'What's going on?' she quizzed, her brown eyes bright in the dusk light and her face inquisitive.

'I wish I knew,' he muttered back. He didn't want to go over the Lawrence story again.

Chapter Four

The Greenside Estate, like many others of its kind, was built after the Second World War to combat the housing problems in London caused by the Blitz. At first, so the story went, the planners wanted to build an estate of high-rise tower blocks. Money restrictions proved too much and the idea was abandoned in favour of lots of smaller five-storey blocks, which eventually made up the whole estate.

The first two tower blocks, Denver and Bartholomew, were already half built when the plan was shelved. But Hammersmith and Fulham council decided to keep building, and so they became the only high-rises in the estate, Bartholomew on the east side and Denver on the west, standing like two concrete sentinels facing each other and looking over the smaller blocks.

By the time all the buildings were finished, in the early fifties, there were twenty-six blocks, not including the two tower blocks. When West Indians started immigrating to the 'Motherland' in large numbers, the estate was more than ready. Many black families found themselves housed in Greensides all over England, tucked away with the lower-class whites, where the middle and upper classes didn't have to see them.

There was a sense of pride about Greenside though, especially amongst the old-timers, black and white, who'd seen many changes between the fifties and the nineties. Not long after the Lawrence Ganton murder, a government-funded community celebration was organised. Old residents talked about their experiences of over forty years on the estate. There was music, food and a plan was unveiled that would take Greenside into the twenty-first century. The estate was to be extended by an extra fifteen blocks, and a shopping centre which would cater for the thousands of people was on the council's drawing boards.

For years now, Greenside residents had walked to Shepherd's Bush market to shop, so most trips were left until the weekend, working commitments all but eliminating weekday visits. Bernice Bradley followed this almost religious weekly trek, filling up her battered Fiat with her bags of groceries as well as those of Janet, a Cockney lady, from two floors down who had a large family and no car. She was Bernice's dedicated shopping partner.

This Saturday, Bernice was running all over the flat trying to leave as early as she could. If she left after nine-thirty she considered herself 'late'. Cory lay on the threadbare sofa in the living room, watching TV and chewing toasted hard dough bread.

The living room was his favourite area of the flat bar his bedroom. The teen found the beige wallpaper relaxing. Artist's impressions of Dominica took pride of place over the whole of one wall. They surrounded a central picture of a Dreddlocked Daniel in the Lion's Den purchased by Shannon at Notting Hill Carnival a few years ago.

Cory was feeling lazy, yet restless at the same time. He kept thinking back to the confrontation in the park, full of bright ideas about what he should've done. The bruises from his fight with Roger had faded into dark marks on his face. A week had passed since the scuffle, but the outrage he felt had only grown.

A few days after the fight, unable to take Sean's concern any more, Cory had persuaded Tanya to drive him, his cousin, Garvey and Dougie to look for the boys on their estate. They had cruised around slowly for an hour in a light rain, finally giving up as the rain turned into a downpour. None of the boys had been sighted, even though Garvey swore he'd seen Roger and Christian in Greenside several times before.

'Cory,' Bernice was saying, as she rushed past into the kitchen. 'I'm off darlin', all right? Tell them two lazy bones I'll see them later on, yeah? An' try an' keep out of mischief till I get back will you?'

'Yes Auntie. 'Bye Auntie,' Cory threw over his shoulder, as she rushed out of the front door, its slam echoing around the flat. Moments later Shannon wandered into the living room, awakened by her mother's noisy departure, with tousled hair and bleary eyes.

'Hiya trouble,' she croaked, managing to smile prettily down at her cousin as he chomped on his toast. 'Wha' you doin' up so early?'

Cory offered Shannon his plate, with one last piece of hard dough sitting on it.

'Jus' watchin' TV,' he answered, happy when she declined his offer of a minor breakfast. 'You ravin' tonight cuz?'

Shannon drew her blue terrycloth dressing gown around her and flopped on the sofa.

'I dunno. I wen' out las' night and right about now my head is splittin' man, so it all depends on how I feel. There's a Jungle thing happenin' in North London though.'

Cory nodded. 'Yeah man, I'm goin' one down dem sides as well, with Garvey an' dem man. It could all be the same rave.'

Shannon smiled her agreement at Cory. Bernice had found it amazing that, in the aftermath of Cory's father's death, Shannon had changed her views about her cousin drastically. Instead of being his chief agitator, she became his chief protector. Bernice confided to Yvette, a friend from work, that she was proud of the way Shannon had grown up, even if she wasn't altogether pleased with the circumstances that forced her to.

Sean came downstairs in his boxer shorts. He'd woken up at the sound of their voices, and was now squinting at them with half sleepy eyes. Shannon abruptly got up and ran for the empty bathroom, pushing past her bewildered brother. Cory patted the seat Shannon left.

'Si' down man,' he said, moving some magazines Shannon had inadvertently sat on. Sean sank into the battered sofa.

'So wha' you sayin' Sean, you comin' ravin' wiv us tonight den?' Cory asked.

'Boy y'know,' Sean replied, then fell silent. Cory watched him, and when he spoke again, it was with the effort of a man pushing a car up a long, steep hill.

'See the t'ing is, me and Sonnie were gonna have a little meal together y'get me? True her mum an' her sister's gone Yard for awhile, we got her place to ourselves, so . . .'

Cory groaned, remembering. 'Damn, you two like you're joined at the hip. Soon you won't even wanna be seen on road with me, innit!'

Sean laughed and shook his head vigorously. 'Nah man, don't say dem t'ings. I'm just tryin' to spen' some time with her *and* study, y'get me?'

'Yeah, yeah. You don't have explain to me man, jus' do what you're doin'. I'm only jokin', you done know I'm proud of you anyway.'

Sean grinned at Cory and they touched fists, their knuckles knocking together like castanets.

'As we're here talkin' like dis, I jus' wanted to apologise for goin' on at you about Roger an' dem man,' Sean said.

Cory shrugged and started to speak, but Sean held up his hand before he could open his mouth. 'Hold on a second cuz. I jus' wanted to explain . . . Raa . . . I mean the only reason I kept buggin' you is 'cause I was worried for you, y'unnerstan'.'

Cory sat back in his seat, his eyes back on the television set.

'Yeah but cuz; I done know dat man,' he replied, looking directly at his cousin.

They grinned at each other again and then hugged. Shannon came back into the room in time to catch the embrace and started teasing at once.

'Cor, don't let Mum see you two, she'll start to wonder man,' she said, picking up another of her hair magazines and flicking through it. Sean threw a cushion at his sister, while Cory just cried, 'Later!' and turned to the TV once more. His cousin didn't even flinch as the cushion bounced to the floor.

'Don't get me wrong, it's good to be a part of such a lovin' family, blatant,' she continued, trying not to laugh.

'Piss off Shannon,' Sean replied, good-naturedly.

'I will in a minute, but I jus' wanted to know if you two young lovers wanted breakfast this mornin'. Or are you savin' your appetites for each other?'

Sean picked up another cushion, darted across the room and pummelled his sister's head till she shrieked. She ran out of the room laughing, with her brother in pursuit, the chase echoing noisily around the flat. Cory shook his head disbelievingly.

'Man, dis is a crazy place to live!' he said to the empty room and settled down to watch *Batman*.

The rest of what was definitely a very gloomy Saturday morning passed very slowly for Cory. He sat in front of the TV until midday, then stared out of the window, looking out over the estate as the people below walked about trying to keep out of the rain that'd been falling for the past three days. His thoughts turned to his father, the dull scene outside merely adding to his gloom.

Coming to terms with his father's death had not been easy. In the years at primary school that followed, Cory took out his frustrations and anger on the other children, often getting into fights over the tiniest name-calling incidents and taunts. He usually came out on top, not because he was stronger but because of his deep aggression. When he wasn't rowing, he was an intelligent and well-mannered child. He scored high in his eleven-plus exams, easily attaining a grade one, the highest grade out of three.

In secondary school the playground scuffles escalated and became almost a daily routine, as Cory's temper and sensitivity proved to be a volatile mix. Most pupils learned to stay on his good side, knowing he wasn't to be baited in any way and woe betide anybody who started cussing over dads and mums. Midway into his fourth year, one new boy, despite being warned by classmates, spent a whole lesson cussing Cory's parents. ('Your mum's a freak man, she walks around with one tit in the middle her forehead. Everyone calls her Titclops . . .')

Cory said nothing, his face taut with anger, ignoring sympathetic words from his friends.

That lunchtime he went home and returned with a bicycle chain coiled neatly in his jacket like a sleeping snake. The outcome was inevitable. The ambushed boy had so many cuts to his face and head that he needed a total of twenty-two stitches. He never returned to the school.

These days, Cory felt he'd grown up a bit and that he wasn't so hot under the collar where his father's memory was concerned. The ache he felt now was like a fading throb, compared to the crippling pain that had burned in his stomach not so many years before. Christmas and Father's day, could sometimes be hell, accentuating his loneliness. Of course he had his new family, but it wasn't the same.

His mother, he tried to forget about completely; the last memories he had of her in her so-called secure accommodation were not happy ones. He would not admit it, but he felt deeply ashamed of her. The drooling, raving, childlike woman she had become in her final days was a far cry from the tender, beautiful person she'd once been. Thoughts of how she had stroked his head soothingly until he went to sleep when he was younger, were still too much to bear.

Cory brooded darkly most of the day, watching TV. By evening, bored out of his mind, he walked over to Garvey's house, his hooded jacket protecting him from most of the shower. Dogs cowered for shelter by rubbish bins and the streets looked like a scene from a film set in a ghost town, with the sodium lighting already casting its strange glow about the estate. He stepped up his pace, eager to get to the warmth and comfort of his bredrin's abode.

Garvey's mother Sheila was English; his father Jake, a Jamaican Rastafarian, was a social worker, working mainly with teenage children. Cory looked up to his friend's dad and could sit for hours with him, discussing anything and everything from the environment to repatriation, from nuclear warfare to joyriding. Always, Cory learned something new.

'Oh hello love, come in,' Sheila trilled, opening the door wide to Cory and stepping back to let him past. 'It's really terrible out there,' she said stepping out onto the balcony.

'I only came from my house an' I'm soaked,' Cory replied.

Sheila took his damp jacket, saying she'd put it in the airing cupboard.

Cory followed Sheila's footsteps down the corridor and found father and son bent over a small coffee table, intent on the few marble chess pieces left on a blue and white board. In the split second before they noticed him, Cory felt a sharp pain of loss and envy in his heart and he clenched his fists unconsciously.

Garvey looked up, noticed his friend standing by the door and jumped, scattering chess pieces all over the carpet.

'Yes blood,' he said, bending over to retrieve his marble soldiers. 'Wha' you doin' by the door man?'

'I was jus' gonna take off my wet trainers,' Cory said slipping his Fila's off. He padded into the room and touched fists with the chess players. 'What's bin happenin' people?' he said, still feeling weird. Garvey looked pleased with himself.

'It's a good day,' he remarked, as Jake watched him sourly. 'I got Dad checked man, maybe even checkmated!'

'Checkmate my raas!' Jake replied as he pulled his beard and lit up a large zook sitting in the ashtray.

'Jus' lemme relax fe a second and I'll get outta dat, believe me yout's.'

They waited quietly for a few seconds, looking like Bisto kids as smoke from Jake's zook wafted past their noses. The older man looked up from the board, caught their expressions and smiled knowingly at them.

'Buil' up nuh,' he puffed, tossing the bag over to Cory.

'Can Cory take it in my room?' Garvey asked his dad, trying to see how much of his spliff was left.

'Yeah man, lemme concentrate on dis star,' Jake replied, his attention back on the chess pieces.

'Come nuh.'

Garvey waved at Cory to follow him into his room, which wasn't much bigger than the one he shared with Sean. A stack system and large speakers took up most of the space, while the bed was squeezed up against the window, fighting for space with the TV, video and Nintendo, as well as a tiny dressing table. Cory always wondered how Garvey fitted everything in.

'Still ready to Rave, blood?' Garvey whispered, digging underneath his bed and pulling out a bicycle pump, some old school exercise books and a couple of porno magazines.

'How you mean star? Tonight's JungleFest man, I ain't stayin' in for no one, trust me . . . Wha' you on star?'

Cory watched as his friend pulled the bed out until it hit the dresser. He then climbed over to the exposed corner of floor and pulled out a plastic bag.

'Here y'are,' he muttered, passing him the bag, as well as a cigarette and a pack of king-size blue Rizla, all sitting on an old Elevation flyer.

Cory looked in the bag and was amazed to see it full of red and black plastic capsules, like the kind people took for pain relief. Except these didn't relieve pain . . . at least not in the traditional sense.

'Are they live?' Cory asked in a hushed voice. Garvey cackled evilly.

'Nah man . . . But *these* are.' He held up another smaller bag, which contained several white pills that looked like aspirin. 'Me and Claire was up all las' night on these . . . an' I mean *all* night,' he said proudly, which cracked them both up.

Cory asked Garvey how much he paid for the dud pills. The boy shrugged.

'Laid on star. A white guy at my work dealt with me an' gimme the live ones too. There's a couple for you an' Tanya as well if you want 'em.'

Garvey was a trainee painter and decorator with the local YTS, which meant that he got forty pounds a week and his travel expenses paid. He was only vaguely interested in the job, but he'd long ago realised the necessity of having a trade, as well as hustling for money.

Cory looked up respectfully at Garvey's last words.

'Raa . . . Safe blood, I can give you the wong when I go home tonight man,' he told him.

Garvey looked at his friend like he was mad. 'Fuck dat man, ain't we blood? I known you nearly ten years an' Sean all my life, y'get me an' I'm only fuckin' seventeen. I'll look after both o' you 'cause you've always looked out for me an' my family. Furthermore, you can help me sell couple duds tonight if it makes you feel better, yeah?'

'Course man, you know you're safe,' Cory assured him. 'Respec'.'

Garvey started firing up his Nintendo while Cory busied himself building his zook. When it was alight and tasting right, he looked at his reflection on the dressing table mirror.

'What, you can gimme a trim f'tonight Garv?' he asked, running his hand over his hair.

His friend took a second to come back from the world of computers. 'Yeah man, get the chair an' all dat out while I finish dis game. I'll be two secs.'

'What, at the same time? Cory joked. Garvey groaned, gave him a funny look and continued his game.

It was a happy Cory Bradley who walked back to Denver House, the sun shining a muted white glow behind the grey clouds covering the whole sky, making it look like a featureless ten pence coin. Cory played football with some of the young kids in the car park outside his block, until he felt the weed communicating with his stomach. He went up in the lift and into the flat, feeling a lot better than when he'd left.

'Where've you been?' Bernice called at him as soon as he hit the door. He smiled as he took off his trainers.

'Jus' over at Garv's' he answered, as he came into the kitchen and planted a kiss on her cheek. Bernice looked mildly shocked, then distressed.

'What's happened?' she said, eyeing her nephew carefully.

'Nuttin' man. I jus' got a little pee'd off earlier on, thinkin' about Mum an' Dad an' I forgot what I got here an' now. I mean . . .' He faltered, trying to find the right words. 'I mean . . . The time I spent wi' dem before what happened, I took for granted, y'know an' when they went, it was too late. I'd missed my chance to say . . . almost everythin'. I jus' want you to know that I'll never do it with you guys. Never,' he said again, forcefully.

Bernice's face softened as Cory spoke and on impulse, she hugged him tight, rubbing his back, thinking he would cry. When she let go, his eyes were dry and his face hard, as if he'd made up his mind decisively. He moved towards the door to leave, saying: 'I gotta get ready to go out man, I'm expectin' some calls.' Then he was gone.

The phone started ringing at around half-past eight, and then on and off until the Bradley family left for their separate rendezvous. Shannon decided she wanted to hear Ragga tonight, so she and her friends were heading south of the river to a Sound Clash in Clapham. Most of the calls were for her and she had to be prised away from the handset on many occasions, the others deaf to her pleas.

Even Bernice was going out raving, heading to a housewarming in Seven Sisters with some workmates, escorted by her man-friend Greg, whom the kids teased her about, but secretly liked. She dressed carefully in a velvet blue suit, cut low (but not too low) and with matching shoes, while Shannon took care of her hair, pinning it up around her face in loose curls. When she was ready all the kids agreed she looked beautiful.

Tanya called Cory at nine and they decided to meet inside the club. They talked the kind of talk anyone not in a relationship hates, then rang off, with Cory wishing she was right beside him instead of on the other end of a phone in East London. He had a scalding hot bath, then shaved what little hair on his chin he had. He ironed his clothes while Sean did the same, only Cory was much quicker. When Sean came out of the bathroom, he found Cory just finishing the cuffs on his navy blue Duck and Cover shirt, while his trousers were hanging up on the handle of their wardrobe, looking creaseless.

'Respec' cuz, for that ironin' lick, but how come you knew what garms I was wearin'?' Sean asked, reaching for the coco butter jar.

'You said you wanted to be smart, so I just drew for dem t'ings there.'

Cory put on a tape to get himself ready and built a zook. He never heard the door slam as Bernice left the flat. At ten o'clock, Shannon's boyfriend Mikey, a law student in his final year, poked his head around the door, puffed on Cory's zook, and said goodbye, all to a backing track of the latest Jungle tunes. A quarter of an hour later, Sean left for Sonia's, checking himself in every mirror he passed until he reached the door. Cory smiled, thinking it was funny how close those two still were; even though the relationship, only started in secondary school, was nearly two years old. As always, Sean was as stable in his social life as he was at school.

Cory was restless and more than ready to leave when Garvey knocked at his door at ten to eleven. With Garvey was his girl Claire, Nazra, a nineteen-year-old Asian boy who lived on the third floor of Oakhill House, and Trent, Garvey's cousin on his mother's side. Behind Trent stood two other girls – a pretty Asian (Nazra's older sister) and a blonde girl in a leather puffer jacket, who Cory assumed to be Trent's girl.

The others, Garvey explained, would meet them at the venue.

They walked to the shops and caught two cabs, Cory's driven by a Somalian who knew virtually all his passengers. Cory found himself sitting in the back with Nazra's sister, who introduced herself as Rabana, and talked like it was going out of fashion. Nazra sat in the front, his face saying he wished he'd travelled in Garvey's cab. Cory nodded at all the right places, trying not to look at Rabana's thighs, which were a creamy brown and impossibly smooth.

When they reached the club, the line of waiting ravers stretched out of the doors and away around the corner of the building, talking, laughing and blowing whistles into the cold air. Cursing, the group paid their respective cabs and made their way to the end of the line.

A white boy with a sock hat and a friendly grin intercepted them halfway there.

'Es, Trips, Charlie,' he chanted to Trent, yet his eyes wandered and found Rabana.

'Anyone?' Trent offered, making sure everyone heard.

No one answered.

'Whizz, Rocky, Skunk?' the boy said quickly as they walked away, his voice rising in a hopeful tone. Garvey turned and replied, 'Nah mate, we're sorted.'

The boy shrugged and rejoined his friends in the line, as if the encounter had never taken place. Some broad bouncers passed him moments later and eyed him warningly, but said nothing.

It took half an hour by Nazra's watch to get into the building and be searched for weapons, by which time Cory thought that he would freeze to death. A massive stage was set up at one end of the vast building, with a bar at the opposite end. The rest was given over to the ravers, of whom Cory could see thousands, their heads rising and falling like a giant musical ocean. Large laser lights shot thin red and green beams over their heads. Strobe lights tossed and spun, throwing hundreds of colours in as many directions as possible, so nothing looked the same twice. For a while, the group stood in one place, taking in their surroundings in awe. Then they started moving deeper inside, unbuttoning their coats and swaying to the boom of the 808s.

Claire, a mahogany-skinned girl with a killer laugh, linked arms with Cory.

'Where's Tanya hidin' herself babes? I ain't seen her in ages, believe.'

'She's supposed to be here already,' Cory replied, trying not to sneeze as her perfume tickled his nostrils. 'Come, you wanna look for her then?'

'OK, let me jus' tell Garv's yeah?' She wandered over to her man, who already had customers for his duds around him, looking eager to drop.

A minute later she was back. They wandered through the crowd, each of them suddenly aware of the hopelessness of their quest. They'd been around the building twice, when Claire pointed through the people at some figures dancing animatedly in the centre of the crowd. As they got closer, Cory discovered one of them was Tanya. He eased through the mob until he was right behind her, then cupped her buttock in one hand. He nearly didn't survive to tell the tale. Tanya turned quick as a flash, a look of cold murder on her face. She swore loudly, only seeing her boyfriend when he shined his pocket Maglight in his face, glad the bouncers had let him hold on to it. Her expression changed instantly and she hugged him tightly, rubbed her body seductively against his and apologised for thinking he was someone else. Then she hugged Claire, but not until they'd finished screaming with delight at the sight of each other.

When Cory felt he could walk back over to Garvey and his other friends without embarrassing himself, he grabbed his girl's hand, and told her to bring her friends over. There were three of them, two black girls and a white girl, all dressed to kill and jigging to the bass heavy music. After some talk with Tanya, they headed back with Cory and Claire.

Garvey was standing with his back to the wall, talking to a stocky black boy when Cory returned, the girls close behind him. Garvey made the sale quickly, passing the boy the pill as they shook hands, just in case anybody was watching.

'Who's dem girls blood?' he breathed. Cory laughed and put an arm around Garvey.

'Dat's Tanya's friends star. I know they're cris', but is it worth riskin' Claire cuttin' your balls off?'

Cory knew that when it came to women, Garvey had no remorse.

'That brownings is smilin' at me already man!' his friend said, sounding as if his mind was made up already. He looked at Cory and decided to put his friend's mind at ease.

'Don't worry blood I won't distress Claire tonight, star,' he smiled. Cory gave him a wry grin and clapped him on the back.

'I'm glad man, I hafta say it. I don't wanna see Claire all upset an' cryin' cause you can't control your dick in the face of temptation.'

They both laughed uncontrollably.

Rabana, who was dancing with Trent's girl and the others, looked over and flashed a sexy smile at Cory. Garvey raised the can of Holsten Pils he was drinking in salute to his friend and winked at him.

'Looks like I'm not the only one who has to tread careful tonight,' he muttered in Cory's ear, then left to talk to Claire and Tanya, floating smoothly over and worming his way into their conversation.

Cory looked at the Asian girl as she danced, and sent a prayer to God asking for guidance and strength, before making his way over to join his friend. It was at that stage, that their night really began.

Chapter Five

By contrast, Sean's evening was quiet, crowdless and devoid of any thoughts about anyone but himself and his girl. He left his mother's flat with a bottle of Martell brandy and a small Tupperware container of cooked, diced pieces of chicken he'd seasoned himself. A chill had worked its way into the air, but he was wrapped up well enough, his scarf and New York Jets cap keeping him warm, while others walked briskly around him, eager to outrun the cold.

As he strolled his way along the pavement, his breath billowing like a secret, silent language from his mouth, he watched an old man shuffling along in the middle of the road, picking up assorted bits of rubbish blown there by the wind. At first the man took no notice of Sean passing, merely keeping his eyes on the mammoth task before him scraping his feet across the hardened tar. His tightly laced trainers looked like miniature canoes, the image enhanced even further by the way they curled at the toes. Suddenly aware of Sean, he craned his head around and opened his mouth to speak, exposing a mass of rotting teeth. Instead of talking, he coughed as if his lungs were ready to emerge, shrunken and steaming, from his gaping mouth. Sean watched, his distaste turning to concern, then he edged his way over, mindful of the spittle projecting from the man in almost visible arcs. When he was two steps away, the old man controlled his fit and turned large red-rimmed eyes on Sean. His beard covered nearly all his features and along with the grime, helped disguise his race from anyone but the most curious.

'Spare any change?' the man said stretching a hand, palm upwards towards the youth hopefully. 'I need a cup of tea to ease me throat.'

The man spoke with a straightforward English accent, tinged with Cockney, but not East End born and bred. Sean shook his head disbelievingly.

'A cup of tea, at goin' on eleven at night? I don't think so mate.'

He turned to go, not wanting to waste time. Sean walked until the man was just a lone figure in the middle of the road, his desperate rantings lightweight against the heavy sound of passing cars and kids screaming as they ran around their blocks. The encounter stuck in his mind and he felt a little guilty as he entered Bartholomew House and took the lift to the ninth floor.

Sonia answered his ring straightaway. She was dressed in an old T-shirt and tracksuit bottoms, her hair tied back tightly. She led him by the hand into the kitchen, where a multitude of pots were bubbling busily on a gas cooker. Rice, peas, plantain and a joint of beef were among the items on the menu. Sonnie asked if he approved, and when he told her he did, she tugged him into a living room the exact size and shape as his own and showed him the videos she had on pirate. These included two horrors he'd never heard of before and a feature film entitled *Strapped*.

Many months after this evening, Sean and Sonia would remember it as one of their happiest moments. They ate in silence for the most part, savouring the food they had starved themselves all day to eat. They only spoke when one of them wanted the fried dumpling dish, or the plastic gravy jug. Their body language was another matter though, the way their eyes linked as they smiled at each other and the way they touched occasionally, as if reassuring themselves the other was still there. Sean found himself thinking at that moment that she was the most beautiful girl he'd ever seen and one he could easily spend the rest of his life with. And Sonia; her thoughts were almost the same as they toasted each other. She imagined that the clink of her mother's wine glasses sealed her and Sean together stronger than any marriage vows could ever do. This was their vow to each other; completely personal, unspoken and undeniable.

Sonia cried a little at the end of *Strapped* and put it down to the wine making her emotional. Sean could see she was touched and held her tightly, thinking he too had seen friends, situations and jokes on the screen that echoed his own life on the estate, save the fact it was a bit more extreme out there.

Why not? he mused as he opened the Martell bottle and poured a little into each of their glasses. We're all the same people, randomly separated by fate and slavery, until families generations apart forget each other and relatives go unseen for years at a time. That could be my cousin and I wouldn't even know, he thought, the realisation sobering him slightly and making him hold his girl even tighter.

They settled to watch the horror movie Sonia had borrowed, but found they couldn't make the transition from grim reality to morbid fantasy. Halfway through they lost interest in the film and turned their attentions to each other, eventually making love on the sofa to a background noise of decapitating heads and exploding bodies, to which they were completely oblivious. They lay entwined, Sean stroking Sonia's hair and body until she fell asleep, her deep brown skin reflecting the light of the television.

He drifted off, feeling at peace with himself for at least this one night. The film came to its conclusion, with its hero the victor; but nobody was watching. Sean and Sonia slept blissfully on until morning, their arms wrapped around each other, without a care for anything or anyone else in the world.

At JungleFest, Cory and his friends had been having the time of their lives – dancing from end to end of the crammed warehouse. The heat from the bodies and their exertions made them sweat buckets and drink water like fishes. At one in the morning, they all dropped their Es together and by two they were well away, smoking zooks and rubbing ice-cold Evian bottles on their faces in between each tune. Garvey spent most of his time knocking out his duds, while occasionally cussing the MCs, swearing he could do better.

Trent and his girl had bought a bottle of Moët at the bar and Garvey, not to be outdone, bought another. Both were emptied loudly and speedily and soon enough, everyone was not only rushing and stoned, but blind drunk as well.

Later on in the morning, some more Greenside residents turned up, including Tara Wilson with a crew of fifteen girls and eight boys. Among them, was Jason Taylor whom Cory had teased Rosie about. He ignored Tara for a while, mindful of Tanya's watchful eye. But he couldn't hold back for long and he asked the girl where Rosie was. Tara eyed him sullenly.

'She's at home catchin' up on some course work,' she said, looking as if she didn't want to say that much.

Cory nodded and went about his business, thinking he knew he couldn't be universally loved, but Tara was going a bit too far with her ice maiden act. Seconds later, the music whipped away his thoughts and he was dancing through the crowd again, searching for Tanya.

It was close to five when Garvey weaved his way through the masses towards Cory and his girl. His eyes were like saucers that had fixed themselves onto his head and he looked worried. Cory put an arm out to steady him and spoke directly into his ear.

'Raa, wha' gwaan Garv, you look well worried spee,' Cory shouted hastily. Garvey's look deepened.

'It's Claire man,' he said, his voice firm despite his expression. 'Dat E's makin' her vemit a way man. Rabana reckons she puked twice in the bogs already star, so I'm lookin' to take her home now, y'get me?'

Cory looked at Garvey, shocked.

'I feel all right an' no one else's complained,' he replied, perplexed. Garvey nodded.

'Yeah man, I feel safe, y'get me, but dis time now, it probably didn't agree with Claire, so I don't wan' her gettin' all upset and freakin' out y'know? *Plus* dem people I sold the duds to must've clocked by now, so the quicker I get out of 'ere the better innit?'

'Where y'gonna go?' Cory asked. At that, Garvey grimaced.

'I can't take her home man, my dad'll fuck me up bigtime star . . . boy y'know that's a good question . . . I dunno man.'

'Come we go back to mine's man, true Bernice ain't dere y'get me? She won't be back for ages and at least we can say Claire jus' smoked too much green, innit?' Cory proposed firmly.

'I thought you was stayin' at Tanya's tonight, spee.'

'Fuck dat man, dis is serious star. Anyway blood's t'icker than pussy, y'get me?'

'Not Tanya's man,' Garvey said, cracking up.

'Wha' you tryin' t'say star?' Cory replied, laughing too.

'Anyway, go an' get your girl an' I'll tell Tanya what's gwaanin', yeah?'

'Safe blood, I love you man,' Garvey said gratefully and was off in a flash. Cory went over to tell Tanya, who'd been watching them, what was happening. She wasn't pleased, but agreed it was the best thing to do, although the kiss she gave him made him unsure if it was. Nazra decided to join them and leave his sister with Trent and Lorna and so the four of them left the rave and walked out into the cold morning air.

There were plenty of cabs waiting outside the warehouse when the quartet emerged. They snatched a handful of flyers thrust at them from all angles, then hopped into a Toyota driven by a large Asian man with an abundance of nasal hair. Cory took the front seat and the others got in the back, Claire with her head down next to the door. He could still feel the pill in his body, making his fingers tingle and his brain feel wide awake, aching for music and intricate beats. The cabbie offered around a pack of Orbit, but the gum was declined by everyone. They rode in silence, save the one-sided chatter from the cabbie's radio.

The cab reached a set of red traffic lights just past Kings Cross Station when Claire began to retch again, as the lights turned green. Garvey, who was sitting in the middle, acted quickly as usual. He opened Claire's door just in time for her to throw up onto the road, leaning across her to hold the door with his left hand, using his right to hold his girl steady with Nazra's help.

The cabbie cursed them until Claire was safely back inside, then, seeing everything was all right, cursed again.

'Bloody maniacs!' he ranted. 'She could've been killed! I could lose my licence as well, what if the police had seen that . . .'

They got as far as Euston Station before Garvey flipped and told the cabbie to shut the fuck up and drive, before he stabbed him and drove the car home himself. The cabbie looked nervous and didn't utter another word.

Five minutes from Greenside, Garvey started talking about Linford Christie, saying what a brilliant athlete he was and how he thought he would break the world record in his next race, definitely. It was admittedly a subtle message but it was not lost on Nazra or Cory and, as they approached Greenside station, Cory ordered the cabbie to pull over. He could see Garvey making Claire sit up gently, whispering their plan of action in her ear, while Nazra shook himself awake, his face looking serene in the warmth of the car. They pulled up to the kerb slowly, all three boys keeping their eyes open for cruising police cars. But lady luck was smiling on the quartet as they carried out their plan. The three in the back got out, while Cory made as if he was searching for his wallet, then eased himself out of the car, pretending to pat himself down. Before the driver could realise what was going on, all four had broken into a run towards Greenside, with Claire struggling to keep up and the cabbie screaming obscenities at them.

They sprinted past Mackenzie, took a right at Brownswood, then a left at Goldsmith, until they reached the park and stopped to build a spliff. They laughed and joked, puffing with the exertion and crowing about their success.

'Damn, dat was simple!' Garvey said, sitting on a bench and rubbing Claire's back, his hand underneath her top.

'I tol' you, fat drivers are the lick: they can't run to save their life,' Nazra added, rolling a two-paper king size for the occasion.

When the roach was thrown to the asphalt and Claire decided she felt a little better, they walked to the shops, all agreeing to chip in for some munchies to take back to Cory's. Kareem's twenty-four-hour food store, next door to the cabbie's was their destination and Cory's stomach rumbled with anticipation the closer they got.

Claire started talking again as they walked, and when they reached the shops she looked as if life was slowly seeping back into her face, even managing a weak smile. Garvey kissed her on the cheek and squeezed her hand, only letting on by his relief how worried he'd been by her state in the warehouse.

They slowly strolled around the small shop, picking up bags of crisps, biscuits and three cartons of Just Juice. Garvey, who left the store last, his arm around his girl, looked at the others and felt a rush of love for his friends envelop him. He took in everything: the way Cory was talking quietly with Nazra; the way the street lights lit up their clothes, making them look like the boys in the old Ready Brek adverts. He turned to look behind him, to see if the streets looked as bright there as they did here. But what he saw made him stop dead in his tracks, causing Claire to look up at him, puzzled. She craned her head around to follow his gaze. Garvey saw her go pale and squeeze his hand so tightly, that he thought his bones would crack.

'Oh shit,' he breathed, for once lost for words.

Coming towards them from Caldervale House in a ragged assembly were at least ten boys, laughing and shouting noisily. At the head of them was Roger, a red bandana covering his head and a blue one across his face, leaving only his crazy eyes visible. He'd seen them even before they'd seen him. As Garvey looked, he saw him nudge Max, then point at them and rub his hands together gleefully.

There was no time for discussion. All I can do is warn them and hope they react the right way, thought Garvey. In the few seconds it had taken him to turn around and back again, Garvey had decided his course of action.

'*CORY!*' he shouted, his voice cracking with strain and sending pigeons scattering for the sky, '*RUN!*'

Cory turned around, a stunned expression on his face, then saw Roger and the mob of boys. He flung the bag he'd been holding into some bushes and sprinted as fast as he could, Nazra close behind him. Garvey started running the moment the words left his mouth and he willed Claire to keep up with him. They ran together until they reached the foyer of Denver, where they took a look behind them. The mob had increased their speed significantly. Some had sticks, others were picking up stones to throw at them. Garvey's fear intensified.

'Split up,' Cory said, digging in his pockets and pulling out a set of keys. 'Garvey you take Claire up to my drum, but go in the back way y'get me? I'll keep these fuckers busy man.'

'Be careful blood,' Garvey replied, taking the keys quickly, 'An' come straight back man.'

Cory nodded as Nazra pulled his knife from the back pocket of his jeans.

'I'm wid you man,' he said.

With that, they all ran, Garvey and Claire around to the back of Denver, heading for the fire exit and Cory and Nazra towards Flaxman, hoping they could get lost in the buildings. Ten against two were not good odds. Fighting was a last resort in both the boys' minds, only to be considered if their backs were against the wall. Cory risked a glance behind him and found the boys had split up as well, presumably to chase Garvey and his girl into Cory's block. Roger was still in sight and Cory felt an eagerness to hurt him badly for the trouble he was putting him through. He tried to erase the thought from his mind, knowing this was not the time. He put his head down and pumped his legs until they ached.

Cory and Nazra managed to stay together for all of two minutes. It wasn't anybody's fault really – just one of those things that happens when two people are running and neither has a clue where they are aiming for. If anything was to blame for what happened next, it would have to be fate, for that was what surely decided the events which took place next. Cory took a right at Lexham, but Nazra kept running straight.

Cory took a left at Solomon and continued running, until he realised the boys' shouts were no longer echoing in his ears. He slowed to a walk, his breath coming and going in frightened little gasps.

He could hear nothing, and this surely meant Nazra was being chased by the others. Cory found himself fearing for his friend's life. There was nothing he could do – the fear for his own life was just as strong or on second thoughts even stronger. He took another right at the corner of Solomon and repeated the turn again, circling the block stealthily before heading back towards Denver. It was getting light now, yet the dull sky made the dawn seem like a half-hearted attempt at daylight, urging people to stay in bed on this cold Sunday.

The two blocks on either side of him towered sinisterly, making Cory shiver as he looked up at the bright landings. The wind whistled in his ears like a lamenting ghost. Although it was not raining, he could feel the moisture in the air. Cory walked eyes fixed on the pavement, wishing they'd taken the cab all the way to his house. A slight movement made him look up.

Standing at the other end of the block was Roger, staring at him coldly, a switchblade in his hand.

Cory blinked, thinking the Ecstasy he'd taken was making him hallucinate. He blinked again but Roger was still there. As Cory stared transfixed, Roger's blade appeared as if by magic, flicked out by his thumb. He took two steps towards Cory.

'I told you I'd see you again,' he said, the bandana across his face muffling his words, so Cory had to strain to hear them. He wiped a watering eye and looked about for a weapon to use, but could see none. He'd left his knife at home and at once felt tears of rage pricking his eyes: his future at this point looked bleak and not very extensive.

Roger spoke again and Cory could hear the sadistic pleasure in his voice.

'I'm gonna fuck you up!' he screamed suddenly and ran at Cory, the blade high in the air.

Cory held his ground as Roger hurtled towards him and dodged at the last moment as the other boy brought the knife down. But he wasn't quick enough. The blade tore through the right arm of his jacket. He felt a searing pain as he turned and threw a punch with his left fist, which glanced off Roger's face, and only served to push him a half-step back.

Roger's response was to slash viciously, catching Cory across his chest, tearing his shirt, forcing him to step back. Roger advanced, lunging at him. Cory retreated until his heel hit the kerb and he fell backwards, his arms waving for balance, into someone's low-fenced garden. Roger was on him in an instant.

Cory grabbed a handful of gravel and threw it as hard as he could into Roger's face. The boy yelled as the grit got into his eyes, making him instinctively cover his face. Cory got up quickly and with all the force he could muster, jumped and planted a kick square in the other boy's chest, making him fall back over the fence and crack his head painfully on the pavement. The knife flew out of his hand and slid a few feet away. Cory stepped over the fence and rushed to grab it.

But Roger, making a quick recovery hooked his legs into Cory's from his prostrate position, tripping his adversary up, while struggling to regain his feet. Unfortunately for him, Cory only had to reach his hand out and the knife was in his possession. But he was still on the floor, and Roger aimed a hard kick at his stomach, designed to make him let go of the switchblade. Cory gasped with pain, but refused to release the blade. Roger stepped forward and swung his foot again, aiming for Cory's face. But this time, Cory brought the knife down viciously, stabbing Roger in the foot, just above a crisscross of laces.

The blade punctured the boy's trainer, but glanced off the bone in his foot. Roger stepped back again, his eyes wide with pain and his mouth wider with loud curses.

Cory didn't stop there; perhaps realising the power balance had shifted and the odds were against Roger now. Cory rose, and taking a running step towards the boy, grabbed his shoulder in a rough embrace and plunged the blade repeatedly into his stomach.

The knife punctured the skin and Cory felt an initial resistance, then the ease of entry as it slid into the boy's belly. Blood and bile gushed from Roger's wounds, until Cory's hand was covered with it. The boy screamed, his voice bubbling as more blood flooded his mouth, making his earlier curses seem like whispers. He fell to the ground clutching his belly as the light sweater he was wearing became stained a much darker shade of red.

Cory raised the knife, bent over Roger's writhing body and slashed his face one last time. Then he ran, throwing the blade as far as he could, even as doors were opening behind him and residents raced out to see what all the screaming was about. One shouted at him, but Cory kept running, not looking back until he'd left the block completely. The wind blew in his face making his eyes tear, the water running unwiped down his cheeks. Why me? he wondered crazily, nearly slipping as he slid on some sand spilled from nearby roadworks. He used his blood-stained hand to push himself back up and continued running blindly, searching for answers that realistically, he could never find.

He sprinted as far as the next block, his mind racing and his fear of the police driving his tired legs on, until he looked up and realised where he was. Beechwood House seemed to stare accusingly down at the youth and he shivered, wondering what the fuck to do next. Then he remembered what Tara had said about Rosie staying home to study instead of raving.

Rosie's bedroom window was at the back of the block, facing Woodcroft House. Cory remembered her bed was underneath her window, recalling this from a time in the winter when he and Garvey had got a draw of weed for the girl. He stepped over a small brick wall and made his way hesitantly towards the window, then stopped and cocked his head listening for sounds, trying to keep as still as possible.

In the distance, but steadily getting closer, was the wail of police sirens. Cory stepped forward, this time without hesitation and rapped on the window.

'Rosie . . . *Rosie*! Wake up will yuh!' he whispered urgently. The window stared impassively back at him. He looked around, seeing only a man walking a dog a little way down the road. Cory took a quick look the other way and decided to change his tactics before time ran out. Making his hand into a fist, he thumped hard on the window, leaving blood and sand smeared in a ragged circle on the glass. His voice cracked with desperation.

'Rosie man, open the fuckin' window come on man please God make her open it . . .' he chanted, the litany making him even more frightened instead of calming him.

Rosie's curtains stayed drawn.

Eventually, he stepped back, giving the window one last blow and hopped over the brick wall, meaning to leave and make a run for it. As he turned away, the left curtain twitched into life. A tired face stared out at him, clutching the curtain tightly. He caught the movement from the corner of his eye, and spun around in a flash. Cory had never been so relieved in his life.

'Rosie, let me in man please,' he said. But she couldn't hear him through the window. She fiddled with the latch, while Cory fidgeted from foot to foot impatiently, his ears on the sirens. After what seemed like an age the latch was defeated and the window swung open towards him.

'Cory,' Rosie said pleasantly. 'What the fuck you doin' knockin'—' She stopped, noticing his bloody hand and torn clothes.

'Hey what happened to you? Are you all right?' she muttered, the sleep still evident in her voice. Cory stepped back over the wall and towards the window.

'Rosie, you gotta let me in man quicktime, I'm in trouble man please.'

'What kind of trouble?' she said suspiciously.

'Let me in an' I'll tell you everythin' Rosie, *please*,' he implored, the wound in his chest burning him. For a minute, she just stared. Then, as the sirens came to a stop in nearby Solomon, she flung open the window and reached her hands out.

'Hurry up, climb in,' she said, as he came towards her. 'And be quiet will you, my aunt'll kill me if she catches us.'

Cory nodded and, ignoring Rosie's hands, pulled himself into the room, his wounds making him gasp. He slipped on the frame as he entered and fell on the bed, the mattress cushioning his fall and the noise at the same time. As Rosie closed the window, he lay there, puffing and blowing, his head spinning faster and faster until he thought he'd throw up. He lay still till the spinning slowed to a complete halt and only then did he open his tightly closed eyes, turning his head towards Rosie, who was looking at him with concern.

'What happened?' she asked, sitting at the head of the bed.

She was clad in a long T-shirt, which reached her rounded calves. Her wide dark eyes were so round and clear, he found himself unable to look away from them. When he finally did, it was only to take in her full, fleshy lips, the kind white people paid thousands of pounds for. He admired her strong high cheek bones, which made her face look almost carved in perfection. Stop that, he thought to himself scornfully, that's the E talkin'.

He looked away from her and tried to think of the events that had led him to this room. It wasn't a good thing to do, as images flooded his brain, threatening to overload him. He sighed and with a massive effort croaked, 'We was comin' back from JungleFest, when some brers rushed us star . . . Listen Rosie, I stabbed a guy, but it was in self-defence man. Dere was about nine, ten brers wiv boras an' sticks an' I dunno what else man, so we jus' dossed out, y'get me? Garvey an' his girl went to my gates an' Nazra (you know Nazra innit?); yeah, Nazra an' me run the other way. I lost him man, he must still be out dere . . .'

Cory turned to look out of the window worriedly, then turned back to Rosie, who appeared to be taking in what he said.

'. . . As I was comin' back, I bucked up wid the brer I stabbed. I didn't even have a bora y'know, I had to fight my man for his, look.'

Cory unbuttoned his shirt and showed the girl his wounds. Her eyes narrowed in sympathy. He sat back, the enormity of his actions rising in his brain, like the wails from the sirens outside.

'Shit Rosie, it was self-defence, I swear to God—'

'You don't have to swear, I believe you,' she replied, looking him square in the face as she did so.

'Furthermore, free talkin' for now, I want you to sleep. We'll talk about it later on, when my aunt goes to church OK?'

Cory looked at her, surprised. Then he managed a woozy smile. 'So where'm I sleepin' den?' he said, winking at her roguishly. She patted the pillows up by her end of the bed.

'Come up here,' she giggled. 'I ain't sleepin' till Maddy goes, so you can have the bed to yourself for a bit. I'll make sure she don't come in, so concentrate on restin', yeah?'

Cory crawled up to the pillow and flopped down in a dead weight, his head bouncing before settling gently.

'So what, you ain't joinin' me?' he murmured, making Rosie chuckle. She stroked his head softly, sending tingles down his spine.

'Jus' you worry about sleep man, never mind nothin' else,' she replied, still looking down on him. When she looked at the digital clock beside her bed three minutes later, and then at Cory, his eyes were shut and he was snoring lightly. She looked out of the window and, despite the growing sound of sirens, she managed to smile to herself and the walls, thinking hard.

Chapter Six

'Hey.'

Darkness covered him like a cloak, woven by his dreams.

'Hey you, wake up.'

The voice was trying to penetrate his slumber. He pulled the cloak around him and refused its commands.

'Oi, wake up will yuh? Come on man.'

The voice was silent for a moment – then as it realised the words had no effect, it brought reinforcements in the form of a hand that pushed and forced him into awakening. Cory tried to push it away, but eventually the cloak was ripped from around him. He was forced to raise himself up, as light from the window bullied his eyes open painfully, then he slumped back on the bed as his body remembered its injuries.

He raised his head to take a second look at the room and the person who'd interrupted his sleep. Rosie's dimpled face peered back at him.

'Shit, I thought you was gonna sleep all day bedbug,' she commented, as she busied herself putting in a gold earring. She was sitting beside him on the bed, with the T-shirt nightie gone. In its place were navy blue trousers and a tan suede waistcoat.

'What time's your aunt come back from church?' Cory asked, yawning. Rosie winced and the teen couldn't tell if it was a response to his morning breath or the girl's own probing with her earring. He decided he didn't want to know.

'About an hour from now,' she said firmly, finally finding the hole in her ear. After some fiddling, she let her hands rest on her thighs. 'Boy you know, she's brewin' about me not goin' church dis mornin' star.'

'How'd you get out of it?'

'Took a sickie innit,' she laughed, throwing her head back. The boy found himself smiling too. 'God, she nearly come in man an' I had to leave you in here for half an hour on your own and sit by the telly with a bowl watchin' Songs of bloody Praise. *And* she nearly didn't even go at all.'

She shook her head in wonder. Cory sat up a little, then looked down as the blanket fell from his body. For the first time he realised he had no clothes on. He yelped in amazement.

'Fuckin' hell, where's my garms?' he blurted, shocked at the sight of the ragged tear, weaving a path caked with dry blood from his breast bone to about a centimetre away from his nipple.

He pulled the covers about him once more, feeling the cold bite at the wound. Rosie was giggling, her hand unsuccessfully stifling the laughter. Her other hand pointed to a chair beside her dresser.

'They're on the chair darlin', don't worry,' she laughed again, her shoulders rising and falling with every bout of giggles. 'Cor, you should've seen your face, it was a picture man.'

Cory, embarrassed by the ugly wound and bestowed with a personality that hated being laughed at got annoyed fairly quickly.

'So what, did you have to strip me, for fuck's sake? I could've undressed myself if you'da jus' asked me . . .'

Rosie smiled her innocent smile at him and interrupted gently. 'I didn't strip you, yuh fool, you still got your boxers on,' she said, abruptly leaving the room. Cory stared underneath the blanket as if he'd lost something close and dear to his heart. When he realised the girl was telling the truth, he lay back on the bed with his hands over his eyes and sighed deeply.

It was twenty minutes to twelve, according to the digital clock glowing a pale sickly green on Cory's face. Over at his home in Denver House, his family would probably be sleeping and wouldn't be expecting him back until much later in the evening as he stayed at Tanya's most weekends anyway. Cory mused about what had happened to his friends and tried to suppress the fear that stole over him, before pushing the thoughts out of his mind altogether.

He looked about the room, smiling a little, liking the smell and the girlishness of it. There was a nice little dressing table across the way from the bed. The surface in front of the mirror was crowded with toiletries. Beside a chest of drawers was a rack full of clothes on metal hangers. They all looked very sexy and revealing and Cory wouldn't have minded seeing her in any of them.

The bedroom door swung slowly open and Rosie came back into the room holding a bowl and with a towel draped over her right arm. She moved in an old man's shuffle towards the bed. She put down the bowl and produced a bottle of TCP and some cotton wool balls from her waistcoat pocket, waving them at Cory. Then she handed him the bottle so he could read the label.

'We gotta clean them cuts babes,' she murmured, sitting beside him on the bed once more. Cory nodded soberly and handed back the bottle, a look of wariness on his face.

'Ain't it too late for dat shit?' he asked the girl, as she spun the cap off the bottle and placed it on the night table. She shrugged, screwing her pretty face up tightly.

'We did leave it for a while, but it's bes' to do it now rather than not at all man. You don't know how many brers got wet wiv dat knife, or what germs they had.'

She shrugged again and her smile returned.

'Don't worry, I'll be gentle,' she teased, winking at him and dipping the cotton wool in the warm water.

Cory watched tensely as the girl daubed the water-soaked pink ball across his chest, easing the dried blood away, and ignoring the occasional sharp intake of breath from her patient. She repeated the treatment twice, until the glistening red crystals were all gone. The cut gaped at them, the raw skin underneath pink and tender. She threw the cotton wool into her bin, tutting and shaking her head. Cory glanced at her, roused from his inspection of the wound, looking worried.

'What?' he said, eyeing Rosie cautiously.

'I was jus' thinkin', you should've got dat stitched up in hospital 'stead of comin' here,' she replied, as she pressed another cotton ball against the mouth of the bottle, turning it upside down.

'Dis is gonna sting OK?'

Cory nodded and thought to himself he'd have to be sick in the head to go to Hammersmith, which was the nearest hospital in Greenside. He could just imagine sitting in casualty with knife slashes on his chest and arms, while Roger lay not twenty feet away in a cubicle, waiting for emergency surgery, maybe even surrounded by police officers. Cory thought he could do without stitches, thank you very much . . . but he remained silent, not wanting to offend Rosie.

When she was finished, she took the bowl and the TCP away and returned with a tall glass of fresh orange juice which she placed on the night table where the bottle had been. Cory took tiny sips watching her, a smile slowly creasing his face. At first she looked away self-consciously, but then she looked him in the eyes and returned his smile with a radiant one of her own.

'Wha' you starin' at? What's up?' she muttered, ducking her head slightly.

'I was jus' thinkin' about how good you was at lookin' after me an' I couldn't work out how to say thanks properly,' Cory said, sincerely. Rosie reached out and held his hand, massaging his fingers with her own.

'You don't have to thank me,' she answered easily. 'I could never've left you out in the cold, it's against my nature.'

Cory shrugged and weaved his fingers delicately around Rosie's.

'Yeah well, I ain't gonna forget it Rosie, believe me. I think you're a very special person an' as soon as I can, I'm gonna make it up to you, f'real.'

He looked up at the girl, who was looking about the room in an embarrassed kind of way.

'Cory, let me get one thing straight yeah, kind of lay my cards on the table, y'know? I like you a lot, you must know dat, but I don't want nothin' between us until you finished wi' dat mad woman you're dealin' wiv.'

'Don't call her dat,' Cory said, getting a little riled. This was not what he wanted to hear.

'I'm sorry darlin', but dat's the way I feel. Furthermore, even if you finished with 'er I dunno if we could get together, now

I've told you dat. I know it sounds stupid but it's the way I am man, I can't help it y'know?'

She glanced at him, lying forlornly on the bed and felt a tiny regret, for saying a little too much. On the whole, she was glad her feelings were out in the open, even though she knew she'd put Cory in a kind of no-win situation. She continued to play with his fingers though, as if she was trying to rub her feelings into his hands. He picked up on something, because he looked up at her, no longer sullen, nodding towards their linked hands.

'You better 'llow dat den star,' he said, his eyes bright as they held hers. 'Dis time now, I can still feel that somet'ing in me boy.'

She grinned down at him.

'Really?' she replied, running a hand all the way down his arm, then his chest, carefully avoiding the wounds she'd plastered.

Cory chuckled deep in his throat and gave the girl a sidelong look.

'You take liberties, star, messin' around wid me like so. Leggo o' my hand man an' let me get dressed, will yuh?' he said, eyeing her as if she was the mad woman now, his arm still tingling faintly. Rosie laughed and continued to rub, now looking at him with her own roguish smile.

'All right, I'll let you get dressed before my aunt comes in on us. Jus' gimme one micro-second an' I'll get you a towel an' a flannel, all right?'

'Yeah, cool man.'

Rosie returned with the towel, a small flannel and a tooth-brush. He made his way to the bathroom and washed himself quickly, now eager to get out of the house before Madeleine made an appearance. When he returned, feeling refreshed and alive again, the room was neat and tidy, as if the events that occurred hours ago had never taken place. Even the hand print on the window was gone now, thanks to Rosie and a bucket of warm water. Cory found it hard to believe it had all happened.

He slipped his torn jacket on carefully as she watched, wait-ing for any signs of pain from his arm. It didn't seem to trouble him. Bending over, he scratched his leg absently and motioned towards the girl.

'Well . . . thanks for everythin' Rosie. I appreciate it a way, y'get me?'

'Anytime darlin',' she replied, rising to follow him out as he moved into the passage, towards the front door. When they reached it, Rosie darted in front of him, pulling back the latch quietly.

'Hol' on a second while I check outside,' she said under her breath. She poked her head into the bright light of the outdoors, glancing quickly around. Satisfied the coast was clear, she pulled the door in behind her and turned to Cory with a protective look on her face.

'Take care of yourself out dere, will you?' she finished, stepping towards him and hugging him tightly. Cory returned the embrace muttering, 'Thanks a lot Rosie, I won't forget dis.' He marvelled at how good her body felt. They kissed sincerely, yet quickly, as if neither of them wanted to push the close contact. Then Cory left the flat, while Rosie waved from behind the half-closed door shouting an instruction to phone her.

He took a right and walked one block into the park, his hood up and covering his face. He'd just reached the mud-covered football pitch when he spied a lone figure sauntering slowly towards him, taking in the playing children and barking dogs as if they were some new and amazing forms of life. The figure came a few yards closer before Cory realised it was Art, the self-proclaimed King of Thieves. As he got closer still, he saw how glazed the boy's eyes were. He made like he hadn't noticed and hailed him loudly.

'Yes blood, wha' gwaan?' he said energetically, bouncing on his toes. Art touched fists with him.

'I'm safe y'know. Did you rave las' night?' he asked, weaving slightly as if he was drunk. Cory nodded his head eagerly.

'Yeh man, it was rough star, bere gullies and dat. Music was dett, I puffed my head off . . . It was a good night.' He trailed off, suddenly thinking about Roger again.

'What was you on?' he finished, in a stilted kind of way. Art giggled like a gremlin, held his fist to his mouth and sucked in air deeply, his eyes wide, miming the actions of smoking a pipe. 'Ah, I jus' got sprang on some cold shit,' he said, watching Cory's face for a reaction. 'I was fucked up las' night, trus' me.'

Cory sighed deeply. '*Damn* Art man, it's your life but . . . it ain't exactly livin' is it?'

Art nodded, as if he'd heard the sermon before, then considered it as if it was something to be endured, but not taken in. He took a couple of pigeon steps past his friend.

'Well, hear what, I'm missin' anyway,' he said, moving into a slow motion version of his saunter. Cory nodded and was just moving off, when Art turned again and laughed.

'Hey, you should 'ave seen it dis mornin' blood, nuff police was wingin' about man. I was in Levi's drum and he thought it was a fuckin' raid, till we saw some ambulances an' shit, y'get me? I didn't even clock what was happenin' out dere, but I ain't see Levi get so paro in a long time, boy.'

Art giggled his disjointed laugh again and Cory smiled back. But his grin felt painted on, stiff and ready to crack and flake away.

'Boy, I didn't hear fuck all, I was fas' asleep dis mornin', y'get me? You ain't the only one that was sprang las' night boy.'

He paused for a second and when Art said nothing, he decided to make his escape.

'Anyway Art, gimme a call or somethin' yeah? I need to go out dere soon, true I'm brok man, so let me know what's up.'

'Yeah, yeah, I'll call you dis week blood,' Art threw back at him. They both walked away to their separate destinations, each locked in his own thoughts.

Cory walked quicker, not wanting to bump into anyone else he knew. He left the park, crossing the road and buzzing his aunt's flat on the intercom. Fortunately, there was someone in the foyer who could let him in fast. He sped past, waving and saying good afternoon to the man.

Then he raced for the lift, which thankfully, was empty. He waited impatiently until he reached his floor, and stepped out and onto the landing. He still felt uneasy, although he knew Roger's friends had to be long gone. But what he saw on the floor as he passed down the chilly corridor didn't help him feel any better.

Dried blood spotted and streaked the wall nearest the windows and the floor beside the lift. Even though there wasn't a great deal, it still made his stomach churn and he thought of Nazra, who he'd last seen with at least five boys giving chase. Shaking the thoughts away, he briskly walked to his front door and pushed on the handle, praying whoever had come in last had either forgotten to lock it or left it open intentionally for him.

He silently thanked God as the door swung open and he slid quietly into the warmth of the flat, eager not to wake anyone.

Cory poked his head around Shannon's door to see if Garvey and Claire might've bedded down there. But the only male in the room was Mikey, Shannon's boyfriend. The rest of the sleepers were Adrienne, Pamela and Susan. They were sleeping so deeply Cory didn't have the heart to wake them, so he left the room and his questions until later.

He tip-toed past his aunt's room without bothering to look inside and made for his own room. The sight of so many slumbering people made him feel tired and long for his bed. He eased open the door to his room and was surprised to see Sean sitting on his bed, intently playing *FIFA International Soccer* on their MegaDrive. Sean's eyes lit up with relief when he saw Cory. Cory closed the door behind him and stepped into the room, with a tiny half-smile on his face.

'Yes cuz, wha' gwaan?' he said, raising his hand to slap his palm against Sean's. Sean returned the gesture, clasping his hand tightly around his cousin's and pausing his game with his free hand.

'Fuck wha' gwaan wid me, where you bin all dis time star? I bin worried, fuckin' Shannon's bin crazy with worry an' even Adrienne an' dem lot was scared somethin' happened to you. So you tell me 'wha' gwaan'?' he finished, finally releasing his grip on Cory's hand and giving the teen a penetrating stare.

'Listen blood, I'll tell you everythin' you wanna hear in a sec', but firs' you gotta show me what happened wid Garvey an' Claire. I bin thinkin' about dem all mornin', so I have to know star.'

'All I *know* is Shannon gave me a call at Sonnie's, sayin' some brers rushed Garvey an' his girl, yeah? By the time I come over, everyt'ing was done, y'get me?'

'So what happened man?'

'Apparently, Garvey and Claire run up here an' Shannon was already back from 'er rave, with Mikey an' some of his spars. Roger's friends come bangin' on the door, so dem man wen' out dere an' dere was a row, y'unnerstan'. Two, two's Mikey an' his spars are big man, y'get me, so Roger's crew tried it, realised they were mismatched an' dossed out. That was it, as far as I know.'

'Did anyone get hurt? I seen blood on the floor man.'

'I feel say Wesley, the brer dat drives the Astra GTE got a little wet, but it was a minor. I know Shannon was screwin' 'cause Mikey's boys was tooled up though, so they might've bored up someone, innit? Garvey wen' out dere, but he's all right an' Wesley an' dem lot lef' before I come, case the Rads decided to visit. Nuttin' serious happened.'

Cory lay back on his bed, feeling his aching muscles relax and remembering his run from Denver in vivid detail.

'What about Nazra?' he said, sitting up suddenly and making blood rush to his head.

'Nazra?'

'Yeah, y'know, dat Asian brer, lives in Oakhill. Y'know man, wi' dat supafit sister star.'

'Oh yeah, I know who you're talkin' about. Boy Cory, I never see him at all, but Garvey an' Claire left jus' after Mum did lan'. I don't know if they see him out dere or not.'

Cory flopped back on the bed, his old worry flooding back. Sean let him lie there for a while then said, 'So what's up man? You gonna tell me where you bin, or do I have to beat it out of you?'

Cory smiled at his cousin coldly, took a deep breath and began.

The next week was hectic for both boys, as both had course work to complete and both had neglected to do any. Cory's wounds were healing, though he faced an ear-bashing from Shannon one evening when Bernice was late home from work. On the whole, the incident was put to the backs of their minds, although they knew it was far from over.

Tongues were wagging all over the estate about who stabbed Roger (who was slowly recovering in hospital) but his crew weren't saying anything. The police didn't call, even though everyone expected them to, and Garvey and Claire were fine. The only dark side to the whole thing was Nazra, whom Cory and Sean went to visit in the middle of the week and found with his arm broken and bruises all over his face. In the privacy of his bedroom, he told them how Roger's boys had surrounded him and beat him savagely, then run at the sound of the sirens. Nazra was fiercely pleased Cory had stabbed Roger, and he laughed out loud when he described the way the boy had screamed.

The following week began quietly – until the day Sean and Cory walked home from college later than usual. They'd stayed back with Sam to plan the final stages of the charity football match and everything was going well. It was a mildly hot day and people were walking about in T-shirts, but still complaining about the fickle weather. Several women and girls were about, carrying babies or pushing prams piled with children and mid-week shopping.

Sean always thought the girls looked tired and disbelieving, as if they hoped they were dreaming the mundane lives they led. The women looked resigned and fully settled into the role they'd been given as mother, breadwinner and upholder of all the responsibilities that came with raising a child on Family Credit and a prayer. They took up the whole pavement and talked for hours, probably because they dreaded going home to more daytime TV and their lifeless flats. Sean wondered if his own mother had looked that way too.

On the road cars passed by, blaring music from two-hundred-watt bass tubes. Occasionally, the odd shiny vehicle beeped a greeting at the cousins, then drove away out of the estate, heading, in all likelihood, for Hyde or Holland Park where the girls were. A group of prostitutes sat on the wall outside Mackenzie, drawn out by the sun and lively atmosphere. A small silver radio was tuned to one of the better pirate radio stations. They looked ordinary, more like the women the cousins had passed a minute ago than the hookers they'd seen in American films and TV shows.

The boys were meandering along lost in their thoughts when they became aware of the low growl of a car engine as it got closer to the pavement they were walking along. A bottle green Vauxhall Frontera was pulling up beside them, thumping loud Hip Hop, with Levi grinning from the passenger seat, his eyes unreadable behind jet black Ray Bans.

The figure sitting in the driver's seat turned down the music and the Dredd opened his wide muscled arms, hanging one outside of the wound-down windows and making his various sized chaps' jangle together musically.

'Wha' you ah say Rudebwoys!' he boomed, his grin looking as if it could grow to cover his whole face. Cory took a hesitant step towards the car window and slapped hands with Levi, while trying to gauge what the man wanted.

'I ain't sayin' nothin' blood, jus' lan' from college an' dat y'know.'

Levi nodded his head, which made a thick lock fall across his face. He brushed it away unconsciously.

'Yeah, yeah, I hear you brother,' he said, in a Yardie–American accent that wound Cory up no end. 'De yout's o' today ha' fe learn, or they can never feed de yout's of tomorrow wi' de food o' knowledge! Ah lie?'

Levi laughed and Cory heard the man in the driver's seat laugh too and say, 'Ah no lie!' before falling silent and tapping the steering wheel in time with the low pitched rhythm in the car. Sean, who had kept quiet up until now, muttered, 'F'real'. But his face was as unreadable as Levi's. To Cory's dismay, the dealer's attention was drawn to his cousin, quiet as he was.

'What'm Steve?' he said, stretching out an arm towards Sean, who shrugged and took a few steps closer. Inside Cory's head a roaring sound began and he felt his temper beginning to rise. He clenched his teeth together and swallowed, trying to force the harsh words he was thinking back down his gullet.

'His name's Sean,' he replied, so tightly that Levi said 'Huh?' And Sean said a millisecond after, 'My name's Sean not Steve', which made the older man shrug, understanding what Cory had said and not giving a damn anyway.

'Still 'ittin' dem books, my yout'?' he asked. When Sean nodded, he turned to his friend in the car. 'Now dis is an intelligent yout' we 'ave 'ere y'know. How many O' level y'ave star?'

'Eight . . . GCSEs I mean,' Sean replied, looking at his feet, embarrassed. Cory sighed through his nose. What was Levi under?

'See it deh? Brainy lickle fucker dat, believe you me, you will get far, jus' stay on the right track, seen!?' the Dredd was saying, while Sean nodded as if it was Sam Boyd talking, not Levi, the neighbourhood drug cartel.

Cory wished they'd made a walk for it when the older man's back was turned, but much as he wanted to he couldn't just stroll away when his cousin was still chatting. As far back as he could remember, Levi never stopped to talk to him or Sean (especially Sean) on the streets of Greenside, always racing by in whatever new car he had at the time. He'd always assumed the man knew how much he despised him and was returning the feeling, but now . . . None of this, the here and now, made any sense whatsoever.

As if to prove his point, Cory heard Levi say to Sean, 'Come nuh, mek we go fe a drink, seen?'

Before he could say a word, the Dredd had got out and gestured for Sean to climb into the back of the vehicle. He held the door open for Cory to join them, his face as impassive as the dark glasses covering his eyes.

Feeling angry at everybody, Cory got in the car, hoping no one from their block saw them. He sat, scowling out of the window, as Levi got back into the ride. The driver floored the accelerator, took a right at the corner of Denver and left the estate, the engine roaring like a beast straining at its leash.

When, after twenty minutes or so, the driver showed no signs of slowing down, Cory's bad feeling intensified. He moved over to the middle, in between the two front seats and took careful note of the fact they weren't even in West London anymore. According to the signs he managed to glimpse, they were in N16. He'd lived in W12 for most of his life and the old-looking buildings and unfamiliar parks were strange to him.

He leaned forward and tapped Levi on the shoulder. 'Hear what, where we goin' for dis drink star, the North Pole or summick?' he said.

Levi turned, his face vicious with anger. Cory could see that the mask of geniality he'd been wearing earlier was gone. In its place was just plain untamed badmindedness.

'Jus' cool yuh raas and sit the fuck where you was,' the Dredd spat with venom, causing Sean to look up abruptly, as if hearing a gunshot at close quarters.

Cory sat still for a second, dumbfounded, then gave Sean a look that seemed to say, 'This is your fault, I hope you know that'. He sat back in the seat once more.

They drove the rest of the journey in tense silence, until a little later, the car cruised gently up a hill. A large majestic-looking building of a rich golden brown colour loomed in front of them, like a lion resting in the heat of the savannah. Scores of families and couples were wandering around, between the building and their waiting cars. Ice cream vans, novelty balloon sellers and hot dog stands gave the place a theme park look. Despite his confusion, Cory found time to study his surroundings and be impressed.

The Frontera's driver positioned them a distance away from the other cars. He and Levi turned to face the two teens in the back seat, the Dredd taking off his Ray Bans to expose his dark, unfathomable eyes. He clicked his fingers and began talking in a low, bassy voice.

'All right yout's introductions mus' come firs' y'unnerstan'. Dis man 'ere is an associate of mine call Kenny, y'get me. Kenny dis is Cory an' Sean, yeah?'

The man in the driver's seat nodded at them and the teens both grunted by way of reply. Levi ignored their disinterest and merely toked hard on the zook, before passing it to Kenny.

'Hear I now,' he began, warming up for a speech. 'Supposin', jus' supposin' mind, dere was a man dat 'ave a plan. And dis plan was a long, long, *long* time in preparation an' co-operation an' all dem t'ings dere, seen. Two, two's you toil an you sweat so the t'ings yuh waan fe do can gwaan and . . . *BAMM*!' he shouted out loud, clapping his hands together, then spoke again in a normal voice.

'Someone come along and fuck up yuh runnin's . . . An' all dem t'ings yuh did work for, all de t'ings yuh bin plannin', go outta de window, jus' like dat, seen. Now, if yuh was a man who was under sumt'in' like dat . . . if yuh 'ad a programme . . . an' someone fuck wid yuh programme . . . what would yuh do, hmm? What would yuh do?'

The question hung in the air like a dust particle, riding the thermals and dancing around the confines of the car. Levi stared at Cory, and the youth returned his gaze confidently. When

Sean muttered 'I dunno man', hesitantly, Levi held up his hand, bidding silence.

'Is Cory question dat,' he rumbled, without breaking eye contact with the teen. Cory shrugged and scratched his nose before answering.

'If someone fucked wid my programme, I'd fuck wid dem proper, y'get me?' he said, gazing levelly back at the older man. The two in the front laughed loudly at that, then touched fists and turned back towards the boys.

'I tell yuh de yout's militant, star,' he growled at Kenny.

'Where yuh parent dem from, Mista Milly?'

'Dominica.'

'Blood seed, yuh come like a Jamaican yout' dere star, f'real man!' Levi chuckled, then got back to the point.

'See yuh right, but it a trick question y'unnerstan, ca' dere ain't one answer. I mean yeah, yuh can fuck man up 'till de cow come home, but sometime dat cyaan run, y'unnerstan'? Sometimes yuh affe use yuh head and wisdom as a righteous 'uman bein', seen. Violence only begat violence, yuh ever 'ear dat dere?'

'No,' Sean said colourlessly. 'Look, where are we an' what's dis gotta do wid us?' He looked as if he desperately wished he was elsewhere. Levi favoured him a blank look.

'Dis . . . is Alexandra Palace,' he answered easily, stretching his arm out to show where he was talking about. 'An' *Dis* . . . has nothin' whatsoever to do wid yuh an' eveyt'ing to do wid Cory, seen. Yuh see, a couple night back, yuh cousin stab a nex' yout' in his stomach. Yuh know dat?'

'Yeah yeah.'

'Good. Anyhow, dis yout' suppose ah tek part in ah arm robbery of some post office, two week from now, y'unnerstan'? Also, him juggle rocks fe me, over in dat fuck-up estate down the road from Greenside. Nex' t'ing me know, him deh ah intensive care – an' de doctor tell 'im mudda him confine to 'im bed fe at least t'ree mont's star, if dat. T'ree mont's!!' Levi repeated, working himself up into an angry mood. 'Dis time now, I got a worl' a yout's don't waan' work, talkin' 'bout revenge y'unnerstan'?'

He frowned, making the word revenge seem dirty.

'An' I 'ave me bes' worker in hospital, cyaan do fuck all for t'ree pussyclaat mont'! Yuh, an' only yuh, fucked up my programme.' He focused on Cory again. 'So wha' yuh gaan do 'bout it, ca' star, I don't waan afa fuck yuh up, man,' he finished, playing with the gearstick idly.

Cory looked at Levi, mightily pissed off. He had more than a good idea about what the dealer was getting at by now.

'Wha' d'you want me to do abou' it?' he replied, feigning ignorance, self-pity and anger coming over him once more. Levi looked at the vehicle's roof, exasperated, then brought his large hand slamming down on the back of the seat savagely.

'I waan yuh fe do the arm star,' he replied, his eyes deadly serious, his mouth whispering the words in the teen's face, like a horror book storyteller.

Cory sat further back in the spacious seat and scowled even more: 'Later,' he replied rapidly, his voice as cold as a frosty February morning. 'I ain't doin' no fucker's dirty work star, you can forget it completely. I've heard enough of dis shit, I'm missin'. C'mon cuz.'

He threw this last sentence over at Sean and tugged the latch to open the door without another word to the Dredd. After his initial push, nothing happened; he tried again with no success before realising there had to be some kind of childlock on the door – after all, Levi had got out the vehicle to let Sean *in*. There was a hurried fumbling from the front seat, then a clink of metal on metal that, funnily enough, seemed vaguely familiar. He heard Sean say, 'Cory, wait', in a small voice, and when he looked around, he realised Kenny had a pistol pointed at him, deadly and unwavering in his large steady hand.

Cory paused for one tiny second as the barrel of the weapon glinted hypnotically at his forehead then pressed his lips tightly together. Levi smiled distantly and gestured towards Kenny.

'See how easy it is to talk to de people dem, when y'ave yuh bucky,' he said, a grin on his face.

'Dat one dere a Beretta ninety-two, y'unnerstan'? It semi-automatic an' it fire nine-millimetre rounds, seen. So lemme tell you suttin' now star, don't feel fe one second dat me a play, or ramp wid you y'know. Roger is my baby mudda's cousin, so direc'ly I shoulda 'ave Kenny pistol whip yuh raas right here, seen. But I t'ink to meself wait an' see wha' gwaan . . . see if Cory can rectify de situation 'im put himself in.' He paused, then seemed to lighten up. 'Furthermore, me tell yuh wha' . . . t'ink about it fe a while. When we get back to Greenside, tell me how yuh feel 'bout it, all right?'

Sean nodded his head, his mind feeling detached from his body and miles away. Cory cleared his throat and looked out of the window, unable to deny the knot of fear inside him. That gun was silenced man, he thought heavily, trying to recall the way the black metal tube, screwed tightly onto the barrel, had looked at him, the small hole reminding him of a dark and evil eye. Kenny looked pointedly at him and rolled down his window. He checked to see if anyone was looking and pushed the gun into the glove compartment, before starting up the Vauxhall and tearing away back down the hill.

Soon enough they reentered the orbit of familiar streets and faces. Police TSG vans and pandas cruised around slowly, their occupants looking hot and bored. Kenny parked up, with Denver House looming over the vehicle. Levi turned around in his seat to face Cory, then spoke only one word.

'Well?' he said, easing the question softly between his lips. Cory thought of telling him to go to hell, but resisted the urge and did what his self-preservation thought best.

'Yeah man, I'll do it, star,' he murmured, feeling as if he was making the worst mistake of his life. He could see Sean staring at him in shock, but he ignored him and focused all his energy on the Dredd. Levi smiled, exposing perfectly white teeth and got out to open Cory's door for him. He emerged hurriedly, closely followed by Sean. When the two boys climbed out onto the pavement, Levi leaned on the open door in a relaxed manner.

'Come check me Sat'day, we can discuss de plans an' dem t'ings dere, yeah blood?'

'What time Saturday, I got a football match man,' Cory replied.

The older man shrugged. 'Mek it about eight, nine seen. An' Cory – don' fuck me about star, dis is between me an' you, y'get me? Dere's too much money at stake here for any fuck-ups an' me *know* yuh like money. Later.'

He waved cheerily at them, then climbed back inside the car. Kenny gunned the engine and the car was away again, heading for Beechwood. Sean was staring at Cory, a trace of anger showing in his face, while shoppers and a white kid on rollerblades dodged them neatly.

'Dat was clever,' he said, in disgust. Cory shook his head disbelievingly.

'You're callin' me clever? Didn't Bernice ever tell you not to get into strange men's cars eh? Lettin' my man feed you all that shit about fuckin' O' levels.' Cory said this last scornfully. Sean sighed in a mournful way that made his cousin instantly regret his anger.

'I'm sorry Cory, I wasn't thinkin' straight, man. But neither are you if you gonna knock off a post office with him. He's a crazy brer.'

Now they were both making their way inside Denver, past the foyer and to the lifts, where the digital display above the door showed a red arrow pointing upwards, informing them they'd just missed one. They sat on a wooden bench opposite the lift and waited.

'I'll tell you summick now Sean, I ain't doin' no robbery man, no way,' Cory said, forcefully.

'Yeah, but you just told Levi you would man. Dat ain't too smart cuz.'

'I know, but what am I supposed to do? I wouldn't put it past a cunt like that to shoot me one night for fun an' I bet he's the only thing stoppin' Roger's mates from lookin' a skirmish wid us, you get me? Levi's got me where he wants me, f'real.'

Sean nodded, while Cory watched the lift doors dejectedly, his head filled with worries, small and large.

'So how you gonna get out of it?' Sean wondered aloud.

'I dunno man, I'm stuck on dat one.'

The bell for the lift chimed pleasantly and the two boys stepped in and pressed their floor, both trapped inside their own thoughts. When the steel booth was moving, Cory said, 'Don't tell no one about dis y'know.'

Sean thought for a second before answering.

'Yeah yeah, all right.'

'Not even Sonnie, star.'

Sean now turned to look at Cory, as the lift jerked to a stop, then settled slowly.

'All right, I said yeah d'int I?'

His cousin turned and strode purposefully away down the corridor, Cory trailing behind him. The blood on the walls was still there, but it had faded into a dry brown, that had flaked in places. Damn, he thought, what's happenin' to my life, man?

He looked out into the streets angrily, trying to read his future in the busy people and screaming children. Try as he might, the only omens he could envision were all very, very bad.

At around the same time Cory and Sean were getting out of Levi's car, Rosie and Tara were sitting outside Rosie's flat, smoking weed and chatting. Both had just returned from work and were complaining about their hard day, each trying to outdo the other in a friendly way. As they talked, Sonia walked past. She spied them and waved, before walking on, heading towards Denver. The two girls waved back, watching Sonia as she disappeared, hidden by the bulk of their block.

'She's so pretty,' Tara said, lighting her spliff carefully. Rosie grinned.

'Yeah, it makes you sick, innit? I bet she don't have to worry about spots, or her weight or anythin' like dat. Me, I eat a big plate of rice an' gunga peas an' I'm runnin' for the scales every two minutes.'

They laughed, both of them recalling their own weight worries in their minds. Tara spoke again.

'D'you know her?'

'Not really. I used to see her in school, but I've never really spoken to her before, y'get me?'

'She's all right y'know, goes out with dat loser you fancy's cousin . . . lucky cow . . . Now *he's* the lick man, it's a pity he's taken,' Tara said dreamily.

Rosie looked at her friend, wondering if now was the right time to tell her about Cory hiding in her aunt's flat. She'd been trying to pluck up the courage for a few days, knowing what Tara's reaction would be. Should it be now, or should she wait until her nerves weren't jangling so much? Despite her brave attitude in front of Cory, she needed her friend's approval desperately.

She hesitated a moment, then she took a deep breath and decided the timing was perfect.

'Hey Tara, you know dat guy who got jook over Solomon las' week?'

'Yeah yeah, dat was dread boy, I heard nuff Rads was on the scene. D'you know what happened to him, was he a bonehead?'

'Yeah well . . . See . . .'

Tara passed Rosie the zook and gave her a strange look.

'What girl, spit it out will yuh?'

'Well . . .' Try as she might the words wouldn't come. She gave a massive effort and everything seemed to rush out at once. 'It was Cory that done it y'know an' he knocked on my window afterwards, all injured an' dat, so I let him in an' hid him till he was safe an'—'

'*What*!' Tara almost screamed, making Rosie jump, even though she knew her friend would be like this. 'What the fuck d'you do dat for? D'you wanna be like his nutter of a girl? Are you in competition with her or sumthin' now, eh?'

'Don't be silly Tee,' Rosie said, feeling a bit silly herself now it was out in the open. She fought the feelings down, semi-successfully. 'I couldn't leave him out dere man.'

'You bloody well could've girl.'

'All right I could've, but I didn't want to all right? I care for him too much to see anythin' happen to him. Anyway, it was self-defence, dat brer rushed him, y'get me?'

'So he says,' Tara replied, unconvinced. 'For all you know, he could've bin smokin' shit, got sprang an' decided to go out lookin' for my man. I wouldn't put it past 'im.'

'At goin' on six in the mornin'?' Rosie muttered sarcastically. 'Yeah *right*.'

Tara shrugged. 'You don't know what happened Rosie, it was jus' dem two out dere at the end o' the day. Don't take Cory Bradley's word for gospel girl, he's a known gower.'

'Is dat so?' Rosie sounded angry now. 'Lemme tell you summick Tee,' she said tightly, not looking at Tara. 'You tol' me you seen Cory at JungleFest dat sed night yeah? You're tryin' to tell me, he come all the way from North London back to West, buzzin' of a E, to look for some brer he had a footballin' disagreement wiv almost two weeks ago? I'm sorry Tara, but dat don't run for me, not at all star. I know the guy ain't no angel, but the way you're goin' on anyone'd think he was a ravin' fuckin' psychopath man.'

'I ain't sayin' dat at all,' Tara countered, very much wanting Rosie to grasp her point. 'I'm jus' askin' you not to get involved wid the brer blindly, dat's all. Don't forget, I known him for years man an' I see how he runs t'ings, especially wid girls. At the end of the day, the way I check it, he's only out for himself an' I don't reckon t'ings are gonna run any different wid you. Shit, you're my bredrin, bona fide, y'get me? I'm jus' lookin' out for you man, OK?'

Rosie was still pouting at the ground. Tara forced herself into her line of vision.

'OK?' she said once more.

Rosie looked up, feeling silly again. 'OK Tee, you're right. Sorry for goin' off like dat man, it was stupid.'

'That's OK. You like him anyway, dat's fuckin' obvious girl.'

They laughed a little, slightly breaking the moody spell cast by their arguing.

'Yeah, I know man.'

She looked at Tara, noticing how quiet she was and how easily she seemed to give up the argument. Rosie puffed the last toke on the zook and flicked it into the gutter with an expert's aim.

'I'll tell you sumthin' else Tara,' she muttered, wanting the last word and heading back inside the flat now. 'There's worse people than Cory Bradley on street, y'get me? A man like Levi, makes Cory look like the Pope star.'

She pointed a finger at the Dredd's Vauxhall, which was still ticking as the engine cooled down. Tara followed Rosie inside with a cynical half smile on her face, wondering how her best friend could be so naive.

'I jus' don't wanna see you get hurt over Cory,' Tara implored. 'So I fuckin' hope you're right,' she ended wryly.

PART TWO

The Big Match

Over the mountains, and under the moon
you ride, into the valley of shadows.
Along the way, you acquire some
things, you lose some things.
Someone very dear to you has died.
Someone you used to be is no more

Eddie L. Harris, *South of Haunted Dreams*

Chapter Seven

The midday sun was a hazy ball, and the air was heavy with its heat. The sky was marked only by the odd planc that passed its never ending vastness, leaving trails of vapour that twisted and turned like a toddler's first attempt at writing. The day had turned out contrary to the weather reports and many Londoners' expectations. It was the day the organisers had chosen for the charity football match and the temperature had risen to twenty-eight degrees centigrade by one o'clock. Rianna Scipio, Sean's favourite weatherwoman, had promised an overcast day, with a chance of light showers later. For once, everybody was glad she'd been wrong.

The park, where Cory and Roger had met not three weeks before, was filled with people of all ages. Most were playing on video games loaned to the college by the local arcade, throwing hoops in order to win prizes, or devouring one of the many dishes from various stalls selling hot food.

Sean had adopted a chilled-out approach to the whole event, even though his job was anything and everything, just as Sam's was. Dressed in khaki trousers, a thin silk shirt and shoes, he strolled about, calming people down.

They'd been up and running since eleven and the most dangerous and exciting thing he'd dealt with so far was changing a fuse. He made his way to where his family were seated, smiling as he saw the success the fundraiser had made so early in the day.

He walked away and over the grass, his eyes scanning all the faces he passed. Soon he reached the flagged-off area, which was packed with different teams limbering up for the match. Jerseys and shorts of every colour were on show, and boys either sat on the grass, adjusting shin pads and talking, or ran about the pitch, taking shots at whoever was in goal. Sean spied the African team they'd played weeks before, exercising near the goal furthest from him and calling to each other whenever a friend touched the ball. They looked awesomely fit.

He waded through the crowd, his progress slow yet steady. When he broke through into a small clearing, he saw Garvey, Claire and Garvey's parents, as well as Shannon, Cory and Bernice, seated on a large picnic mat. Garvey and Cory were both dressed in full kit and the mat was crammed full of food, drink and cakes. Sean, who hadn't eaten since the morning, felt his stomach roll lazily.

'Yes, people!' he cried, giving his mum a kiss, then flopping on the mat. Cory grinned at him.

'So what's happ'nin', executive?' he asked.

Sean shrugged casually. 'A worl' o' t'ings man, it's bin all go, all day, y'get me? Every stall seems to be going well . . .; well, apart from the coconut shy stall, I knew dat pile of shit wouldn't work . . .' Bernice eyed him pointedly and he rapidly switched subjects, remembering his mother's deep hate of profanity.

'Yeah, but apart from dat, everyt'ings runnin' dett. I gotta take the money from Amanda an' Kym's stall in awhile an' their till's fat man. We're gonna make nuff wong today.'

He stopped, while his sister and the others made fun of his excitement, teasing him about climbing the corporate ladder and becoming a high flyer. Jake, who was eating a bowl of rice, peas and vegetables, looked wisely at the youngsters as they laughed.

'It would be a good t'ing to see some black yout's on the corporate ladder, never min' climbin' it,' he commented.

Sean glanced around. He could see Cory paying careful attention as the Rastafarian spoke. Garvey looked bored, as if he'd heard his father's comments many, many times already. Jake spooned some more rice into his mouth and continued.

'We such a talented people, with so many ideas and t'oughts.

OK, we excel at music and sports, but what about business, eh? What about buyin' an' sellin' commodities, ee?'

He paused and looked at his small audience, penetratingly. 'Like it or not, de crack an' weed dealers of today, coulda be businessmen an' women of de future, if they put money back into the community, instead of into material t'ings, like cars an' gold, that only put lickle pittance in de oppressor's pockets. As far as I concern, dealers know de in an' out o' mekin' a successful business, far better than a student studyin' . . . Why? Beca' 'im 'ave de buyin' an' sellin' experience already, y'unnerstan'? It would be good too, if more yout's follow yuh daughter footstep Bernice, an' at least try start a lickle business somt'ing fe demselves.'

Sean could see Jake's words were making an impression on everyone. Garvey was looking at the footballers practising, as if the whole speech was too much for him. Sheila nudged Jake affectionately.

'All right Jake, spare lecturin' the kids on a relaxed day like this,' she said, rolling her sky blue eyes at her son. He nodded in understanding and scooped up another heaped spoonful of rice wordlessly, while Bernice poured out cherryade into plastic cups. Cory downed his drink in three deep swallows and gestured to his friend.

'We better get goin' Garv, I can see dem man waitin' for us star,' he said, rising and sounding eager to start.

Garvey swallowed his drink in the same manner as Cory, kissed Claire and ran onto the field with his friend. The others watched as the two boys met up with their teammates and started kicking an orange ball about, showing off to the crowd that was growing around the pitch, like an ink blot on white paper. Sean saw Sam Boyd by the sidelines, ticking off names on a clipboard, a reminder that he couldn't sit around for very long. He ducked down, so he was less likely to be seen.

'Who you hidin' from?' Shannon said slyly, never one to miss anything. Sean shot her a mean look.

'Sam Boyd, my lecturer,' he replied dryly. 'If he sees me loafin' I'm in for it, believe.'

He lay, half on the brightly coloured mat, half on the grass, his head low. Claire laughed.

'At least you're trainin' to take executive lunches for real!' she said, making everybody crack up.

The Bajan wasn't even looking his way, as his attention was fixed firmly on a tall, heavy-set light-skinned boy, who dwarfed Sam and most of his teammates. His head was full of locks which moved in the slight breeze and his face was stern with a frown which wrinkled his forehead. Even Sam backed away a little as he took his name and Sean could see his teammates treated him with avid respect.

The boy had begun laughing as Sean watched, bending over while holding his stomach as if in pain and the teen caught the glint of gold from his mouth as the sun flashed. The tall footballer looked familiar although Sean couldn't quite place him. Five minutes later, his suspicions were justified when he saw Max and Christian, two of Roger's crew, walk up to the tall boy and touch fists with him forcefully.

They talked for a while, then pointed to the field where Cory and Garvey were casually passing the ball around. The tall boy laughed again, this time with the other two joining in. Sean sighed inwardly, trying to look calm, but feeling the turmoil he was coming to know so well rise in him. Claire caught his eye, then looked silently to where Sam was, showing she too had noticed them. It made the whole thing seem terribly real to Sean and he shook himself alert, brushing grass from his trousers.

I gotta tell Cory, he thought, feeling his heart begin to pound in his chest. He rose, then swayed, nearly toppling over the food in his haste to get up and away. He couldn't even look at Claire, but directed his words to his mother and sister, feeling much safer doing that.

'I'm gonna get back to work, OK?' he said, flatly.

'All right then, have fun,' his mother replied, her attention on Shannon as they made bitchy remarks about the clothes passing girls were wearing. Claire gave him a faint smile of encouragement, then, after touching fists with Jake and saying goodbye to Sheila, he walked along the side of the flagged-off area, hoping his cousin would see him before Max or Christian did.

He walked until he was in line with Cory, then waved a hand at him from the edge of the pitch, not wanting to draw too much attention to them. He waited, then saw a lanky white boy pass him, dressed in a goalie's kit, heading towards the other footballers. He tugged at his sleeve, halting him in mid-stride.

'D'you know Cory?' he asked. The boy nodded, his brown hair falling into his eyes.

'Yeah, man, he's dat guy in the green shorts, innit?'

'Yeah yeah. Do me a favour will yuh? Tell 'im 'is cousin wants to chat to him for a sec', yeah?'

The boy nodded again and trotted over to Cory, who was talking with Paul, the Irish boy who'd backed them up three weeks previously. Sean looked back over to Sam and saw the three boys were gone now, lost in a sea of people that threatened to engulf everything in sight. Cory bounded over, looking full of energy and Sean felt proud of his cousin, just for being who he was. He slowed to a stop, panting and grinning at the same time, sweat beading his face.

'What's up blood?' he asked, between breaths. The breeze rose for a second then fell, making the flags surrounding the pitch flap loudly.

'Listen Cory, don't look about when I tell you dis yeah?'

His cousin nodded, his head held perfectly still. Sean suddenly felt he was being a bit too melodramatic. He continued anyway stubbornly. 'Dis time now, jus' after you come up here, I see Max an' Christian, y'know, Roger's boys, talkin' wid some big brer who looks like he's playin' today too. I dunno what they're on 'cause I couldn't hear, but it can't be good, y'get me, so I jus' thought I'd tell you to watch your back, yeah? My man looks like a nutter star an' they was pointin' at you y'get me, so . . . you jus' min' yourself y'hear me?'

Cory who'd looked serious all the way through laughed derisively when Sean finished. He put a hand on Sean's shoulder.

'Ah, fuck dem man, they're full o' shit, cuz,' he sneered, now stretching and touching his toes as he spoke. He said something else as he bent which his cousin missed and Sean asked him to repeat.

'I said dem man can't come on the pitch, so what can they do to me? Besides, they can't try nothin' if Levi wants me for that move nex' week, innit? I'm protected, man.'

Sean rolled his eyes, not believing what he was hearing.

'What about after the match?' he hissed.

Cory shrugged.

'What about it? Star, there's eleven man in a football team y'know. Look Garvey, Paul, Tyrone, Billy, Jameson . . . Nuff man star!'

Cory had turned and was pointing at each man as he spoke their name, before he turned back to his cousin.

'See what I'm sayin', I'm safe man,' he boasted. Sean let out a sharp breath.

'What about dat tense off footballer. He's gonna be on the pitch too you know; dat's the general point of football las' I heard it.'

Cory ignored his cousin's sarcastic tone, knowing it was borne out of worry.

'Listen Sean, unless dat brer's got his bora in his sock behind his shinpad, I don't see how he can do me anyt'ing, y'unner-stan'? You should know I don't fear no man, least of all when it comes to a man on the pitch, innit? You do know full well I can handle myself, so jus' stop worryin' man, yeah?'

Sean said nothing and just cut his eye at his cousin, while bit-ing his lip nervously. Cory tried to reassure him.

'Look, would it help if I said I think I know the fucker.'

'No.'

Cory ignored this.

'Tall red-skinned guy, gold teet', locks.'

Sean said nothing again.

'C'mon Sean is dat him, or not?' Cory said, starting to get frustrated.

'Yeah, I suppose so man,' Sean replied, scratching his chin, thinking that could be anyone. Cory smiled scornfully.

'Yeah man, I know him star. They call him Insane Shane, he plays for the QPR youth team. All right, I admit he's a milly brer, but I don't fear 'im man, he's jus' human, y'get me?'

'I ain't askin' you to fear 'im star, I'm jus' sayin' min' yourself.'

He stopped as he realised Cory was looking over his shoul-der, not even listening to his words. Sean also turned and saw Amanda Brooks, one of the organisers of the fundraiser, com-ing towards them through the crowd. He held out a palm, indicating he'd be over in a second, then turned back to Cory, who had his roguish smile back in place.

'Oi, oi, what's goin' on 'ere den? Sonnie won't be too pleased if she sees that . . . hey, where is she anyway?'

Cory switched between the two subjects as deftly as a magician switching cards, unseen in front of an audience of hundreds.

'She had to shop, so she might pass by later. What about Tanya, where's she at den?'

Cory frowned hard.

'God knows, she was about earlier. If you see her tell her to come see me will yuh?'

'Yeah man, definitely. Listen, I gotta go man, but Cory . . . remember what I said star. Dem man are on sum'ting, I c'n see it for sure.'

'Yeah yeah, an' you don't get carried away by Amanda, y'get me? She's lookin' fit today star,' Cory replied, laughing easily, before turning and making his way back to his teammates. Sean watched him for a second more, then he walked over to where Amanda was standing. She wiped a sweating brow and stared.

'Giving Cory a little pep talk?' she said brightly.

Sean almost didn't answer, as his mind was locked back at the pitch. Her words crept into his mind seconds after she'd uttered them.

'Somethin' like dat,' he muttered.

Their eyes caught for a second then glanced away.

'What's happ'nin', d'you need me to carry dat wong?' Sean asked.

'I beg your pardon?'

'The money, d'you want me to take it to the storeroom?' he repeated. Amanda smiled in an embarrassed way.

'Yes please, that till's getting too full to take much more, and the bag's way too heavy for me,' she rushed, gratefully. Sean nodded solemnly.

'All right, let's go deal with it den,' he replied, turning and walking away into the crowd, with Amanda following behind him.

Sean took big strides, weaving in and out of people with his head held high and straight, thinking hard and not feeling the bumps and jostles from the crowd.

They better not do nothin', he thought, his fists clenching as he did so, his blood rising, making him see and hear things around him with stunning clarity. His face was set and so was his mind, but only in his desire to get back to the pitch before anything serious could happen to anything or anyone close to him.

The rules of the football tournament were quite simple; eight teams, made up of four lecturers' teams and four pupils' teams, played against each other in a total of six thirty-minute games, with the winner of each match going through at every stage, until there were only two teams left.

Over to the left of the pitch, a crowd was gathered, taking close note of an illustrated playoff tree, drawn on an OHP whiteboard. Cory checked the tree and saw his team was scheduled to play first, against the science department. He smiled and made his way back to the pitch to begin his game, as the referee – a bored parent with a rule book – began calling for the captains.

From the kick off, Cory knew the game would be fairly easy. The science department compromised mainly thirty-something men, who hadn't exercised since the days of Mad Lizzie. They puffed and blew their way around the pitch, their faces red after the first five minutes. The only goals scored were by the pupils – Tyrone scored a rocket of a shot in the first two minutes of the second half and Cory got a goalmouth fumble, where neither team realised a goal had been scored for at least five seconds.

At the sound of the final whistle, Cory and Garvey headed for the drinks table at a trot, closely followed by their teammates. Sam Boyd was there, as well as two students Cory recognised from around the college. He grasped his cup of orange squash gratefully and drank the cool liquid in one go, feeling it ease the fire in his chest. Then he winked mischievously at Sam.

'You ready to take a beatin' at the hands of me an' my spar . . . *if* you get to the final?' he mocked, his face saying the chance would be a fine thing.

Sam gave him a look. 'You call that football? All dem flashy tricks an' shit dummies that wouldn't fool an infant? You English boys don't know about football man. Listen, back home we used to play football with coconuts.'

Garvey and Cory cracked up.

'You t'ink it's joke too . . . Why you t'ink me feet so hard eh? It took a brave man to go in goal, believe you me . . .'

Garvey laughed again, shook his head and walked away saying he was going to look for his family. Cory nodded and turned back to Sam.

'Sam 'llow me dem old wives tales an' face the truth. You're about to meet a superior player an' dat's dat. Don't big yourself up, 'cause you'll only feel shitty when I cane you an' your team, seen.'

Sam stopped pouring orange and gave Cory a look of mock horror.

'Cane what?' he said, his eyes wide with the injustice of it all.

'I tell you, you're gonna get a shock when you see Sam come flying down the wing, causin' mayhem in your defence, shimmyin' lef' an' right, dummyin' (real dummies mind), shootin' . . .' Sam kept talking while Cory smiled, scanning the crowd and only half listening. His smile froze in place, as his eyes caught the tall footballer Sean had been warning him about. He realised the boy was staring directly at him and had been for some time. Cory glared back, his face stern, his eyes unblinking, seeing nobody but the boy.

Insane Shane was an imposing figure standing heads above most of the milling people, a rock in a sea of humanity, refusing to bow to their force. Cory stubbornly refused to look away either and it was only when he heard a female voice behind him say, 'Oh, so dis is where you bin hidin' is it?' that he broke the deadlock and spun around.

He was surprised to see Rosie standing in front of him, wearing beige shorts, trainers and a short navy blue top that ended just below her breasts, exposing a tiny belly button. Cory smiled to himself as he noticed she was an insy. She smiled shyly back at him.

'Cor, I thought you'd disappeared off the face of the earth,' she continued, raising a hand to her face to shade her eyes. Cory finally managed to speak, a little taken aback by her sudden appearance.

'I bin proper busy wi' dis t'ing here star, ain't had a chance to think of much else y'know?' There was a pause, then Cory said without thinking, 'Shit man, you're lookin' cris' today, f'real!' which made Rosie smile again, although her smile was slow, careful, cautious even.

'Thank you,' she said, nothing else.

Cory decided he had to do something about this situation and fast, before Tanya came strolling past and made a scene. He gestured towards the drinks table.

'Wanna cold drink?'

'Yeah, thanks.'

'I'll get one for both of us an' we'll 'ave a chat, yeah?'

'Yeah man,' Rosie said, avoiding his eyes.

He made his way to the table and tried to ignore Sam's leering in Rosie's direction. He darted a quick glance over his shoulder and saw Shane was gone, probably to sign in for his match. He won't be gone for long, Cory thought, then put the boy to the back of his mind, to be taken out and dealt with at a more leisurely time.

'Anymore like that at home?' Sam said, handing the plastic cups over. Cory laughed.

'Nah, there ain't thank fuck,' he replied, as the West Indian threw a soaking wet towel at him.

He dodged deftly, kicked it lightly back, then walked over to where Rosie was standing, catching admiring looks from passing people.

'You don't mind sittin' on the grass d'you?' he asked, as he handed the girl her cup.

'Nah man, whatever,' she replied. They walked a little way until they found a clear space by the side of the pitch where they had a clear view of both goals and the strikers taking easy practice shots at their goalies.

Rosie sat watching the players limbering up, then said, 'You're quite good at football. Dat's somethin' I didn't know.'

She took a sip of orange and Cory shrugged.

'Thanks man, but you know what they say, practice makes perfect innit? I bin at it since I was tiny, in the school team and the college team an' all dat shit. I should be all right by now, innit? I mean I wanna play for a big club one day – maybe even at Wembley.'

Rosie stretched her legs out and smiled.

'Dat's what I like . . . a modest man . . . uh, I mean person.'

Cory looked at her through slitted eyes.

'Wha' d'you mean a modest person . . . what ain't I a man now, or somethin'?' he teased, making Rosie laugh.

'Nah, nah, I didn't mean it like dat, it didn't sound right, y'get me . . . I mean . . . you're still seventeen, an' I looked at you—'

'What, so I don't *look* like a man eh?' the teen was saying, sending Rosie off into another fit.

'Nah, you got me all wrong star,' she giggled, as they both cracked up.

They managed to pull themselves together, as the second match, between the African boys and Sam's team got ready for their kick off. Cory leaned over to Rosie and spoke seriously to her, his eyes never leaving hers.

'So what's up Rosie, you just come to see me play or sumthin'?' he smiled, watching her reaction. She kissed her teeth and finished her drink before talking.

'I take back what I said about you being modest,' she told him her smile fading until her face was sober.

Here it comes, thought Cory, Roger's her cousin or sumthin' man. Or her boyfriend even. Or her boyfriend's boyfriend. He stopped himself there and forced himself to pay attention, as Rosie's voice was calm, yet couldn't be more full of feeling if she'd shouted her words at him.

'I come to support the sickle cell cause first off, y'know . . . see my Mum, she died of sickle cell, not long after I was born an' I'm a carrier myself, y'get me, so . . .' She shrugged and gave a little sniff.

Cory stared at her, shocked by her frankness, talking about a subject which he'd thought nobody could tackle so openly. He called people who could talk about death that way insensitive, as he'd never met any who had lost someone themselves, apart from his Aunt Bernice. Sean and Shannon found it hard to talk about Ron and Helen too, yet here was someone who'd lost, just as they all had lost and seemed to have come to terms with it. He suddenly needed to know more.

'So where's your paps? If you don't mind me askin',' he said, gently.

'He said he needed a holiday to get over "his loss", so he dumped me on me mum's sister, went to America an' wrote back two years later, sayin' he'd married some fuckin' American Indian girl. We ain't heard from him since den.'

She spoke slowly, yet forcefully, her voice colder than Cory had ever heard it. He was silent for a moment, digesting this information carefully. 'Dat's cold man,' he said slowly, and quickly changed the subject, before he began to bawl out loud. 'Hey, so what's second off?'

Rosie looked back, perplexed. 'Second off . . . I ain't got a clue.'

Cory smiled. 'Well, you said first off, you're supportin' the cause we got. Fair enough. So what's second off den?'

Rosie laughed, exposing a thin gold chain with a ring attached to it that glinted occasionally in the light. She leaned over and held his hand tightly.

'Second off, is I wanted to apologise for what I said the other day. Y'know, about you finishin' with Tanya an' all dat shit. I dunno what come over me, but I was out of order an' I'm sorry man. Lemme tell you now though, it don't mean I'm gonna jump into bed wid you or anythin'. Let's jus' say we'll take things as they come, yeah?'

Cory gave the girl a look of admiration.

'Yeah man dat's cool, but you don't have to apologise to me, Rosie. I kinda respected you for all dat, to tell the truth,' he replied, feeling maybe, just maybe, his luck was taking a turn for the better. Rosie snorted and chewed on her cup.

'Yeah, yeah, you respected me. So how come you never phoned my yard?'

Cory sighed. 'I tol' you man, I bin hard at work . . .'

At that moment, a huge football boot appeared from nowhere. Before they could move, it kicked the half-filled cup Cory was holding, sending liquid all over the grass. He looked up, to see Insane Shane's tall lumbering figure walking away, his shirt around his waist and his broad back rippling with muscles. He turned and waved to Cory, then winked at Rosie.

'Sorry star,' he yelled back, not sounding at all sorry to Cory. He half rose to run after the boy, meaning to have it out with him right there and then. Rosie, who he'd forgotten about in his anger, grabbed his arm, her grip stronger than he would've imagined.

'Hey, hey, he said sorry Cory, leave it nuh,' she implored him, her pleading eyes making him think again.

He froze, then sat back down and watched the boy join his friends who were watching and laughing at his antics like primary school kids. He tried to ignore them and get back to the good humour he'd been feeling, but his mind was back on his misfortunes. Rosie was looking at him and talking on the edge of his hearing.

'Cor, you got a temper man,' she breathed. He shrugged his bad mood off for her and got up again, reaching out a hand to help her up.

'Hey, you tried the Mexican/African food stall,' he replied, as he pulled her to her feet.

She shook her head.

'Come then, let's go get sumthin', their food's dett man,' Cory urged. Rosie looked at him, a bit unsure.

'What if we see Tanya. What's she gonna say?' she asked, not really wanting to fight over any man, but knowing Tanya would have no such qualms. Cory smiled wryly as he steered her through the crowd.

'Believe me Rosie, Tanya's the least of my worries,' he said as cheerfully as he could.

And at that time, he was probably more right than he knew.

While Cory's football match started, Sean made his way to the food stall with Amanda and counted the money again to make sure they came to the same total. When he was satisfied, he told Amanda and Kym he'd be back and, after putting the money in two carrier bags for safety, he walked across to the college building, trying not to look as if he was carrying nearly two hundred pounds on his person.

He headed through the swing doors and towards the storeroom, the change in the bag jangling with every step. Then he unlocked the heavy wooden door and, after following a combination written on his hand, he dumped the weighty load in a safe, his hands tingling as the blood ran into them. He walked out, locked up easily, then realised the keys he held in his hand were also the keys for the college office. He thought for a second, then decided he'd ring Sonia to see where she'd got to. He'd expected her to put in an appearance way before now and he needed her around to talk to, mainly about Cory and Insane Shane.

Sean bounded up the stairs without another thought and in no time found himself in the familiar corridor leading to the college office. Once in he walked over to the phone, pressed line one to call out and smiled when he heard the dialing tone. He tapped his girl's number out effortlessly. It rang a good few times, before he heard a loud click, the sound of fumbling and a cautious voice saying,

'Hello . . .'

He grinned to himself. 'Hey you, where you bin?' he asked. Sonia chuckled and Sean could hear the sound of a hoover, roaring in the background.

'I knew it was you. I jus' got in from Safeways an' I was hooverin' the place—'

'I know, I can hear.'

'Hold on a sec',' the girl said and disappeared for a minute. Sean heard the hoover switch off with a dying whine, then a click as Sonia returned to the phone.

'All right I'm back,' she said happily. 'How's it goin' out dere? It's bakin' today innit?'

Sean nodded, then remembered Sonia couldn't see him.

'Yeah man, it's roastin' out here.'

'What about the football tournament,' she wanted to know.

Sean sighed.

'Boy, dat's jus' started man and it looks like it'll be OK . . .' he waited a second, then told Sonia about Shane and how worried he was for Cory. Sonia was vaguely sympathetic, but she stressed Cory was a big boy and that he could look after himself.

'For the past two years I seen you worry about a guy dat don't seem to worry any about himself,' she was saying in Sean's ear. 'It's not good for you Sean, you gotta let go sometimes, y'get me?'

'I know Sonnie, but every time you say dat, I do an' somethin' happens. Look at when we was in school man. Remember every incident. Ain't it true, Cory got in more trouble when I left him to himself?'

'I suppose so man.'

Sonia paused.

'You want me to come up dere, don't you?'

Sean smiled to himself. It was hard to hide anything from his girl, she knew him too well.

'I suppose I do man. I'm kinda missin' you.'

'You saw me yestiday.'

'So? Do I have to take into consideration when I see you an' when I don't.'

Sonia laughed. 'Of course not, I'm just tryin' to explain I've got a worl' of things to do an' I might not be able to get down dere at all.'

'Yeah?'

''Fraid so. I tell you what, why don't you come over here when dat's all done?'

'Yeah man, sounds safe Sonnie. I'll be dere straight after we pack up.'

'All right babes.'

'See you later.'

''Bye Sean.'

He got up and left the room, pausing at the door to see if everything looked as it had when he entered. It was much the same. He locked the door before turning towards the stairs leading outside. He'd only taken two steps, when he heard the low murmur of voices again, floating just short of his hearing from the far end of the corridor. He stopped to listen again. The murmurs continued, ghostly and mysterious in the otherwise empty building. Sean's curiosity was aroused. He stepped slowly forward, trying not to make his heels click, then he stopped dead, listening hard.

The voices had stopped.

Sean turned to head back outside, feeling like a prize fool. At that moment, a low laugh wafted towards him, echoing between the walls. He marched up to the far end of the corridor, peering into every classroom he passed. He reached the last room and looked through the glass.

Oh man, he thought, what's going on today star . . .

It was not a good sight.

Sitting on a table, facing his direction, was the tall unmistakable form of Dougie James, the boy that'd been Sean's back-up when Max, Christian and the others had attempted to rush Cory. Sitting on his lap and kissing him hard on the lips was a girl who, sadly, was unmistakable too. She had long jet black hair, her skin was the colour of cocoa butter and her smooth supple legs were twitching in pleasure even as he watched. Anger rose in him like mercury in a thermometer on a hot day. The girl on Dougie's lap, was Tanya.

Sean grasped the battered handle of the door and pushed it open forcefully, smelling the overpowering odour of crack, and making the couple jump and look up quickly. The air from the open door rushed in as Tanya tried in vain to pull down her skirt, her face red with the shock of being caught in such a compromising position.

'Hey Sean . . . uh . . . y' all right?' she muttered, breathing heavily, nervousness making her tongue stupid. Sean's rage forced him deeper into the hot oven of a room, as he dismissed Tanya and focused his eyes on Dougie.

'Listen man, I know dis don't look right, but—'

Sean interrupted him in a second. 'You're tellin' *me* it don't look right!' he exploded, his temper taking both of them by surprise. 'Or do you make a habit of fuckin' your bredrin's girl, huh?'

Tanya stood up, her face still flushed.

'Hey Sean, don't be like dat will yuh?' she said, pleadingly.

Sean turned on her. 'You jus' shut the fuck up for now, yuh slag,' he told her, menacingly, his displeasure growing every second he remained in the room.

Dougie made a face like he'd had enough.

'Hey Sean, you're fuckin' out of order y'know,' he said, beginning to lose his cool as well. Sean sneered at him.

'You think so? You think *I'm* out of order, do you? Hear what, you know what I think? I think dat's a fuckin' crack up star, dat is, if crack ain't too close to the *bone* for you two right about now.'

He walked to the table and picked up a small plastic self-sealing bag, that held a glittering white crystal and some shiny dust. He scowled at the pair.

'You better pu' dat down,' Dougie cautioned, his face as hard as rock. Tanya silently watched the scene unfolding. Sean waved the bag at them.

'What dis?' he teased, opening the bag up slowly, his eyes never leaving Dougie's face. 'It seems to me, my closest cousin's friendship don't mean half as much to you two as a bag of shit an' a shag. Am I right or am I right?'

'Sean, I love Cory, you should know dat.'

Sean snorted, shaking his head, while at the same time Dougie said, 'I'm warning you, pu' down dem t'ings, star', his own rage rising.

Sean gave a laugh as if he'd heard neither of them. He proceeded to empty the bag's contents on the floor, until there was nothing left inside. Then he crushed the small rock with his foot until it was a chalky nothing on the floor, laughing in Dougie and Tanya's faces.

'Whoops,' he said simply, smiling.

'*You fuckin' cunt!*' Dougie yelled, launching all his considerable thirteen stones in a murderous attack. Chairs and tables flew everywhere as the room erupted in noise.

Sean knew he had literally seconds before the enraged teenager reached him. Strangely enough, for the first time today he felt calm. Everything seemed to move in slow motion, allowing him to find something to defend himself with in the blink of an eye.

Behind the half-closed door was a red metal bin. Sean picked it up, hoping Tanya could keep a hold on Dougie. The youth had struggled his way closer. Sean lifted the bin and brought it down on his head with a metallic clang.

Dougie stepped back, his hands clutching his head, while Tanya screamed and moved quickly out of the way. Sean brought the bin down again, across Dougie's face, splitting his lip and making him look like a dazed boxer. Then he hit him once more, striking the side of his head with a blow that made Tanya yelp from across the room. Dougie fell to the floor, his arms and legs waving madly and the side of his face cut and bloody.

Tanya rushed past Sean and crouched beside Dougie's prone body, examining him fretfully.

'Happy now?' she spat viciously at Sean.

Sean dropped the bin with a faint clang.

'Hey Tanya, fuck you, y'hear me? Fuck you star, cause I didn't cause any of dis. It was all down to you an' Mr Loverman over dere. Jus' don't you dare blame dis fuckin' shit on me all right?'

'Are you gonna tell Cory?'

Sean decided enough was enough as he walked backwards slowly, his eyes never leaving Tanya. He wouldn't put it past her to attack him when he least expected it.

'Wha' d'you reckon?' he replied, thinking the answer had to be obvious.

Tanya was silent, then she turned back to Dougie. Sean closed the door and headed off, his mind set on finding Cory and telling him the bad news as soon as possible.

He steamed through the park's tall gates and roamed aimlessly for at least five minutes, asking everyone he knew if they'd seen his cousin. An avalanche of contradictory answers threatened to bury him. Some people said he was by the football pitch, others said they'd seen him by the jungle sound system with some of the other footballers. Sean decided to see if his own mother had any idea of her nephew's whereabouts and he headed back in the direction of the pitch.

Shannon, who was lying on the mat, holding her belly and smoking a zook lazily, informed him Bernice was out looking for a bargain in the second-hand book stall. He asked his sister if she'd seen Cory and she nodded.

'Yeah, I did as it goes,' she waved smoke from her eyes. 'He said he was going for a walkabout before his second match which should be in about . . .' She glanced at her gold Seiko, a twentieth birthday present from Mikey. '. . . Five minutes. He was wid some girl from Greenside man, a really nice lookin' one.'

Sean rubbed his head, trying to erase the ache growing there. He frowned at Shannon.

'You're the second person to tell me dat,' he complained, squatting down on his haunches. 'Who is she? He never said nothin' to me about her.'

'Why should he? You're only cousins for fuck's sake. I thought she was very nice anyway, seeing as she's got more manners than dat red-skinned sumt'in' he's bin seein'.'

'So who the fuck is she den?'

Shannon pulled a face. 'Fuck knows Sean. All I know is that she's from somewhere in Greenside, cause I've seen her about wid her mum, and that she impressed *our* mum a way, so she must be pretty decent. All right now Sherlock?'

Sean gave his sister a sarcastic smile and got up.

'All right Shannon, if you see him show him I'm lookin' for 'im, will yuh?'

Sean headed off and pushed through the crowd again, his head swivelling left and right, as alert as a radar on a battleship for any sign of his cousin and his mystery companion. He walked straight into Sam Boyd.

'Where de backside you been?' Sam asked, his face showing the strain of the day's toils. Sean held his eyes firmly before replying.

'I was lockin' the money from the Mexican stall in the safe,' he told his lecturer, knowing a half truth was better than a whole lie. Sam accepted this with a quick nod and waved his hand at the mass of people.

'I need you to do the same with all the other stalls Sean, while I deal wi' dis football t'ing yeah? Grab one of the college security guys an' make him escort you every time, you got it?'

Sean groaned noisily.

'Dat's gonna make me an even more obvious target,' he argued. Sam was having none of it.

'I don't care, you're not doin' it alone Sean, no way. Put all the money in the safe, labelled mind, so I know which stall it's from. When it's been done, come and see me. I've got lots more jobs for you to do and for Cory if you see him OK?'

'Yeah yeah. Did you win your match?' Sean inquired. Sam gave a big belly laugh.

'Sean my brother, we got our arses kicked man. Five one, at full time.'

Sean cracked up and Sam smiled back.

'You're doing a great job Sean, you've impressed everyone, includin' me. Keep it up son. I'll catch you up later, yeah?'

'Yeah, later Sam.'

Sean walked away slowly, wondering which stall to start at. His search for his cousin would have to wait indefinitely now.

He reflected on Sonnie's words, telling him to let go and let Cory make his own mistakes. I'll see him after the match, he convinced himself. He headed for the security tent, with his cousin put to the back of his mind, at least for the next brief, busy moments.

Chapter Eight

Meanwhile, Cory was unaware such a fuss was being made over him. He and Rosie strolled on the other side of the park, where it was peaceful and quiet. The bass from the sound's heavy speakers was just a whisper carried to them by the wind and the crowd, a multi-coloured mass that ebbed and flowed endlessly.

They sat on a bench, their food still warm in cardboard containers, and tucked into some spicy beef chimichanga. Afterwards, they relaxed and continued to chat while Cory built a spliff. Then they walked back at a leisurely pace towards the crowd in an easy silence which Cory eventually broke when he passed her the zook.

'So where's your man at, if he ain't Jason Taylor?' he suddenly asked, thinking a straight question could only lead to a straight answer. Rosie smiled to herself, then bit her lip to hide it and gave the teen a sideways glance.

'Uhh . . . actually he's in Feltham,' she said, her eyes watching him carefully.

Damn, Cory thought, I didn't think she'd be that honest.

Feltham Young Offenders Institute was a notorious prison in South London. Most youths who were criminally minded and unlucky enough to be convicted in court were sent there.

'So wha' d'he do then?' he continued, his voice casual. Rosie shrugged.

'GBH, attempted robbery, possession—'

'Of what?'

'A firearm.'

'Damn,' Cory said, 'we'd probably've got on man. When's he out?'

'Nex' summer, if he's lucky. He'll be twenny den, so he ain't missed out on too much of his life, but I don't think I'll be seein' him after all dis. He's too off key for my likin' man, y'know? Don't give a damn about nuttin' star. I wanna go places man, do things like travel anywhere I want to go, whenever I feel like it, y'get me? I could hang around, waitin' for him to lan' an' pretty soon it'll be the same old story: five point five children by the time I'm twenty one an' I'll be stuck wid a job I'm financially unable to leave. I want more than dat Cory man, I want a hell of a lot more.'

She turned to look at him, her face determined and the tendons in her arms as taut as a bowstring. A moment later she relaxed and looked away towards the approaching army of stalls and people.

'Is dat a selfish thing?' she asked Cory, in a low voice, her eyes still looking piercingly at the seething crowd. He nudged her with his shoulder, wishing they were alone again so he could hug her. Then he remembered she'd asked him a question.

'Dat ain't selfish, dat's human star,' he told her and was caught off guard by the return of her dazzling smile.

They pushed and shoved their way to the football pitch, where Garvey was standing with Claire, sucking a cherry brandy ice lolly. He spotted them in an instant.

'Hey Cory, where you bin star, man's bin searchin' everywhere . . .' He finally saw Rosie and did a double take, before composing himself.

'Hey Rosie, wha' gwaan?' he barked, spitting out ice sucked free of juice, making it look old and white.

'Nuttin', I'm all right man. When's you lot's match?' she asked, staring at the players flooding the pitch, her hands on her hips. Garvey gave Cory a meaningful look, which wasn't lost on him.

'Any minute now star,' he replied, while hurling the lolly stick as if it was a boomerang.

Cory turned to Rosie.

'You gonna hang around?' he asked, hoping she would, despite Tanya. He found himself not caring. He felt reckless, able to deal with any situation that came his way. He was pleased when she smiled and said yes.

'Have a chat wid Shannon or Claire if you want. I think my cousin likes you an' you two can have a smoke,' he told her, before turning and jogging onto the field with Garvey, who quickly began filling him in on what he'd missed.

Sam's team had failed to get through the first round and faced a humiliating defeat at the hands of the African team. The final score was five–one. Insane Shane's team, led by a goofy white boy from Hammersmith, succeeded in outclassing their lecturer opponents too, with a convincing three–one victory, including a hat trick from Shane himself. The remaining game, between the grungy biker students and the PE department, finished initially in a nil–nil draw, then the PE team scored a goal in extra time to win.

There were four teams in the semis: the PE department (who were the only lecturers to get through), the Africans, Insane Shane's team and Cory's side, who were to play the Africans again. Cory was determined to win this time.

To speed things up a little, the PE department commandeered more flags from their storeroom and a second pitch was set up for the match between them and Shane's team. As they were doing that, Tyrone scored another goal for the pupils over on the first pitch, which turned out to be the only one of the match, even though the Africans fought back bravely. When the final whistle blew, everyone agreed it'd been a skilful game. Both sides settled down with some anticipation to watch the last semi-final.

Shane's team got through to the final in an easy win. Cory sat on the grass watching the celebrations, his manner outwardly relaxed and calm but his mind racing furiously. Garvey looked at him with concern, then patted his shoulder and muttered, 'Everyt'ings gonna be safe star, dem man can't fuck wid us.'

He wandered away, saying he was going to see his girl before the match started. Cory stayed, his eyes on the team he had to face, wishing he'd never laid eyes on Roger. There was a feeling deep inside him that there was going to be all kinds of fireworks when he and Insane Shane took to the pitch for the seventh and final match of the day.

Eyes closed, Sean breathed deeply, taking in large amounts of air. Two girls passed him, laughing quietly as he puffed and blowed. He opened his eyes, smiled back at them and continued oblivious to anyone else who passed him by.

He stayed there for six maybe seven long minutes. From the other side of the park came the shrill of whistles, followed by cheering and long blasts from foghorns which sounded like a call to battle to his tired ears. He sat upright, looking towards the commotion with one hand shielding his eyes. He could see nothing past the mass of writhing bodies. He looked at his watch and knew exactly what time it was.

He got up, stretching and yawning, and made his way slowly towards the crowd. It could only be the final, this late in the day. Pushing and elbowing, he entered the crush and found it took a lot longer to get through than it had previously. The whistles, yells and people screaming directly in his ears made him want to shout.

He finally got through the crowd to a point where he could see the players. Cory's team had made it to the final, as he'd known they would. It took him a second to realise who their opponents were. Then he spotted Shane, powering through the opposition's defence. He held his hand to his head in despair – events had gone ahead without him.

Cory was tired. He couldn't see, but he could sense the crowd, as his mind pushed his body into finding space, dodging his marker . . . then running with Tyrone and Paul, and calling, his hand raised in a silent signal. Paul, who was on the ball at the time, found himself taken down in a crunching slide tackle. The ball rolled out of bounds and came to a stop near some young girls, who all said, 'oooh' sympathetically when Paul hit the ground. As he ran to pick up the ball, Cory twisted his body slightly, so his shoulder smashed against the offending boy as he passed him, jarring his body and making him stumble. Cory looked back, smiled and yelled 'Sorry'. The boy glared back at him.

The referee wagged his finger at him. Cory mouthed his apology again, before picking up the ball. He held it in the air, looked around, then threw it down the line in a high, spinning arc, that was powerful despite his aching muscles.

Tyrone took control of the Mitre as soon as it bounced in front of him, trapping it with his left foot, then pushing it away in front of him until there was enough space for him to switch it to the right. The manoeuvre looked as natural as breathing, and the crowd cheered. He tried for a cross, but it was intercepted by the defence and volleyed back into his own half. Cory ran back in a half-hearted manner and watched Insane Shane receive the ball, then sprint away from his markers with long accelerating strides. He dummied the keeper flawlessly into diving, then shot the ball over his body.

Cory walked back to the centre spot, his chest rising and falling rapidly. Shane eyeballed him as they passed each other. Cory looked casually back, refusing to be psyched out. He even managed to wink confidently at Shane, which made the boy blink, then look away, angrily. When he turned, Cory held up three fingers at Tyrone, who nodded, understanding completely.

Cory rolled the ball under his foot, waiting. When the whistle blew he passed it to Tyrone; his friend gave it back quickly. Cory sent it across to Garvey on the left wing, just before Shane reached him. As the tall boy stopped to change directions with a snarl of frustration, Cory forced his muscles into a headlong run.

Cory knew almost exactly when to break off and look for his position in the box. He found the area in an instant: the right corner of the penalty area stood empty, as every other player watched Garvey's movements, their backs away from the danger lurking in their midst. To Cory, it was just perfect.

With one hand in the air, he watched Garvey dodging defenders, willing him not to lose possession. Two seconds later, his friend pumped his legs a little more and took a few steps past his markers, before chipping the ball high over their heads.

Cory saw the ball coming and knew it was going to fall

exactly where he wanted it. He glanced at the goalie and saw he was completely absorbed by the ball's flight pattern.

All Cory had to do was get to it first. He stepped to the left, hearing the crowd going crazy around him and prepared himself for the cracking equalising goal. He was so mesmerised by the leather sphere he didn't hear the heavy footsteps and panting breath behind him, or the sharp yet quiet whisper of grass being torn from the earth by sliding metal studs.

Sean saw the whole thing from the touchline, his eyes transfixed by the speed of it all, his mouth screaming his cousin's name as he saw Shane running Cory's way at breakneck speed.

He saw his cousin tensed ready to shoot, as the ball flew towards him, curving gently.

He saw Insane Shane reach Cory and plough into his legs a split second before the ball reached him, sending them to the ground in a jumble of arms and legs.

He heard Cory scream in pain while the referee frantically blew his whistle. Then he watched as Shane pushed himself up to a crouch, using Cory's twisted leg as leverage, while the crowd booed and swore at him.

Garvey, incensed at seeing his friend in so much pain, ran up to Shane as he was levering himself up and put all his weight behind an uppercut to the taller boy's chin. The boy fell backwards, biting his tongue as his jaw slammed shut. He very nearly tumbled into the referee, who was blowing his whistle and pointing at Garvey, his face red with disbelief at what he'd seen. A player from the opposing team ran over and threw a wild punch at Garvey, who ducked easily. He turned back towards Shane, ignoring his attacker completely.

In seconds, the other players ran over and joined in.

The referee was lost among the crowd, as players started punching and kicking at each other, while others rolled around in the grass, butting and tearing at heads and shirts, until confusion was the order of the day. People from the crowd who were friends or family of players on the pitch, started running onto the grass as well. Sean joined the rush, thinking only of Cory lying on the grass, completely defenceless in the stampede.

Tyrone, Paul and a shaken-looking midfield player were all

standing around Cory acting like human shields. Their faces were hard, as the crowd came towards them then eased away. Tyrone spotted Sean and looked relieved.

'I think it's broken star,' he nodded towards where Cory lay. Sean smiled his thanks at the trio and squatted near his cousin.

'Hey Cory. Cory wha' you sayin' blood?' he babbled, above the roar. The boy's head turned to him.

'Fuckin' . . . bastards,' Cory spat, his voice cracking with pain. Sean swallowed back aching tears and grabbed Cory's hand squeezing it tightly.

'Where's that cunt?' he growled.

'Who d'you mean?'

'Who the fuck d'you think?' Sean spat, releasing his cousin's hand and standing up again, scanning the pitch for Shane. He kissed his teeth in frustration, looked again this time for his mother and sister, but couldn't see them.

There was still no sign of Shane, but Sean was surprised to see how quickly the crowd had dispersed from the pitch, though some were still fighting. The reason for this rapidly became apparent as police riot vans flooded the area. Sean watched people being bundled, shouting and swearing, into the backs of the vehicles.

A dodgy-looking white man wearing stonewashed jeans and a Def Jam T-shirt walked confidently up to Sean and took in the scene behind him with suspicious eyes.

'What the fuck's up with him?' he barked pointing at Cory.

'I think his leg's broken, Cid,' he replied.

The man had the good grace to blush mildly at being spotted, then he flashed his badge at Sean, as if that could regain his pride.

'Detective Sainsbury, Harrow Road CID,' he said, all traces of embarrassment gone now. 'Is this the first boy that got injured?'

'Yes.'

'And who might you be?'

'His cousin . . . uh, Sean Bradley. His name's Cory Bradley.'

'OK Sean. Now I don't suppose you were involved in all that fighting were you?'

Sean gave him a dirty look.

'I bin here wid Cory. I don't suppose you could call for an ambulance, could you?' he replied, sarcastically.

The man eyed him curiously.

'There's one on its way. If you could just calm down.'

'I'm calm, I'm calm, don't worry about me man,' Sean assured him. He saw Bernice coming over, her face a mask of worry, with Shannon close behind her. They both introduced themselves to the policeman, then went over to where Cory lay on the grass, offering words of comfort. Sean joined his mother and sister where they were crouching.

'Where's Jake and Sheila?' he asked Shannon. Shannon motioned at him to follow her, and they walked a little way from Cory's prone body.

'Garvey got shif', chasin' after Shane while all the madness was going on, so his mum an' dad's gone down the station,' she explained. 'I think the police caught Shane as well.'

Sean shrugged.

'Big deal, no one's gonna press charges, are they?' he said to his sister scornfully. She ignored him and pointed a finger across the grass to where a white Bedford van was heading towards them, the blue lights on the roof flashing fitfully, commanding people to get out of the way.

'Here comes the ambulance,' she muttered, putting her hands in her pockets.

They watched the ambulance race across the grass and come to a stop parallel to Cory. Everyone in the vicinity, including the detective, Cory's trio of guards and the slightly bruised referee, made their way over to see what was going on. The paramedics, dressed in green jump suits, leapt out and looked over the teen.

The white of bone could be seen through broken brown skin covering the lower half of Cory's leg. Averting his gaze from the injury, Sean knelt down again and took Cory's hand. His cousin opened his eyes, saw him and muttered something incoherently. Sean shushed him, telling him to relax and cool. His eyes closed again and his cousin forced himself to look at the young, clean-cut man feeling around the limb.

'Hey.'

'Hi there,' the man smiled at him.

'Don't worry, it looks worse than it is,' he assured the worried looking boy.

'How bad is it?' Bernice asked. Sean got up and put an arm around her shoulder comfortingly and the young man rose, looking satisfied.

'I think it's a clean break,' he told them, 'the tibia's the bone that's gone west, but we'll need X-rays to make sure there aren't any other little bits floating around in there. I'm fairly sure he'll be as right as rain in six weeks' time.'

Bernice wiped her sweating brow.

'Thank God for that. I don't know what I'd do if anything happened to that boy, really I don't. Do you think we can ride with him in the ambulance?'

'Sure you can. We're only going St Charles' anyway.'

The second man busied himself setting up a folding chair to carry Cory into the waiting vehicle. They splinted his leg, then gently lifted the boy into the chair and into the ambulance. Bernice and Shannon decided they'd go to the hospital with Cory, while Sean opted to catch them up after he'd found Sam, of whom he'd seen no sign. Looking around at the aftermath of the mayhem in the park, it was easy to see why.

There were tables and chairs overturned everywhere. The whole place looked like a bomb site. Litter and black bin bags were strewn everywhere, while stewards tried to chase the rubbish and put it into more black bags.

He turned back when he heard the ambulance's motor turn over, then start revving. It moved away slowly, its backlights large and ugly to his eyes. Detective Sainsbury strolled across and stood in front of Sean, as if the youth was planning to make a run for it. He waved at the stalls absently.

'Who's in charge?' he asked.

Sean looked at him strangely, as if he'd just noticed the man was standing there.

'Come with me man, I gotta find him too,' he mumbled, his voice a monotone.

Two hours later, Sean was striding through the corridors of St Charles' Hospital in Ladbroke Grove, with a green plastic bag swinging in one hand and an assortment of magazines tucked under his other arm.

Men and women were shuffling like robots on zimmer

frames. Doctors rushed from place to place, as if it was against their code of practice to stay in one area too long. Cute-looking nurses smiled at everyone. Looking at a large map on the wall, Sean saw that Cory's ward, C6, was on the fourth floor. He bounded up the stairs, not trusting the ancient lift that stood beside the concrete stairwell.

After they'd tidied the mess in the park as best they could and collected the money, he, Sam and the other organisers had all been gathered in a small classroom to be interviewed by the detective. He'd asked them what they'd seen in the lead up to the final, whether they'd noticed any antagonism between the players or the crowd, and if anyone had been acting strangely before the final game.

Amanda turned to Sean, a knowing look on her face, which didn't go unnoticed by Sainsbury. Sean wasn't surprised when, after the others left, the policeman placed a large bony hand on his shoulder and said, 'A quick word please Mr Bradley.'

Sean sat on the desk at the head of the room trying to maintain the candour of an innocent man. Sainsbury picked his teeth with a match and looked around the room.

'So Sean, what did you see go on today?' he asked easily. Sean shrugged and made a face.

'I dunno . . . I mean I saw the same as everyone else an' I told you all dat already. Dat guy with the locks pulled a wrong move on my cousin, innit? I didn't get to see if anyone was arguin' beforehand 'cos I was so busy, but I do know dat brer's well known as a dirty player.'

Sainsbury was nodding, his head down, scribbling in his pad.

'So you think I should talk to Cory?' he suggested, looking up and fixing Sean with piercing grey eyes.

'I suppose so, if you think dat'll help, but I know dem two ain't never met before.'

'How d'you know that?'

Sean made another face and smiled.

'I jus' woulda known. It's one o' dem t'ings,' he told the man, his expression saying Sainsbury couldn't possibly understand 'them things'. Sainsbury smiled and put his notepad in the inside pocket of his faded denim jacket.

'OK son, fair enough. It should be all right for me to pass by the hospital sometime, shouldn't it?'

'I think so. Cory should be dere for a few days.'

Sean rose, slightly surprised at the sudden end to the questioning, and together they left the building, blinking like owls in the brightness outside. It was Sean who spoke first.

'I'll chat to my mum about when you can see Cory,' he proposed, taking the concrete stairs in one leap. The older man called him back, then held out a small white rectangle of card which the teen took and put in his pocket.

'Get her to call me at the station,' Sainsbury answered firmly. 'Oh and thanks for your help, Sean.'

He crossed the road, got into a blue Astra filled with uniformed police and took off, leaving Sean standing on the hot steps, feeling a little better now the interview was over. There were no other cars parked by the pavement. Sean looked over to where the Astra had been sitting and chuckled to himself. Fuckin' bastard didn't even offer him a lift. He made his way to the bus stop, still smiling.

Cory's ward was filled with old white men, who stared at Sean distrustfully as he walked by. Drips and bottles of plasma hung from iron stands, and televisions blazed silently, the men using headphones to tune in to the Saturday evening entertainment on the box. Nurses delivered pills and water to patients, while relatives sat close and concerned beside their loved ones.

Bernice and Shannon were just picking themselves up to leave as he entered. They were talking quietly and carefully and piling yet more fruit and magazines on top of Cory's bedside cabinet. Shannon poked Sean in the ribs with her elbow, as he grinned down at his cousin, happy to see him looking better already.

'Took your time,' she sneered at her brother. 'I thought you'd bin nicked as well.'

Sean laughed, making an old man on the other side of the ward spill his tea and then curse at them in a whining tone of voice. Cory laughed as well, his eyes focused on a mini computer screen.

'You don't know how close I was to dat, f'real star,' Sean told his sister seriously. He told everyone about the group interview with the plain-clothes detective and their solo meeting. Bernice fumed to herself quietly as she fussed around Cory.

'He should've seen me, I would've had loads to say,' she steamed, as she put on her coat.

Sean decided not to mention the card he'd been given, as he wanted to show it to Cory before letting his mother loose on Sainsbury. Shannon poked him again.

'Tanya was here earlier,' she said, eyeing him as she spoke. A voice from the bed interrupted them.

'Did yuh tell her to come back?' Cory mumbled from the bed. Shannon sighed.

'Yeah, yeah, I told you I did. But she was askin' for you as well Sean.'

Sean looked at Cory who was playing the GameGear intently, his eyes locked on the screen.

'Yeah I saw her earlier, but I was too busy to chat an' I said I'd *talk to her later*.'

He said these last four words slowly and deliberately. Shannon gave him a measured look and picked up her bag.

'All right then, as long as you know,' she said, kissing Cory tenderly on the cheek. Bernice kissed both boys and fussed around Cory for a few minutes. When they'd gone, Sean sat down by the bed and beamed at his cousin, who immediately switched off the GameGear.

'So . . . here I am cuz,' Cory said, with a disgusted look on his face. Sean handed him some magazines and put the fruit on the cabinet with all the others.

'Sam said to tell you he's comin' up to see you on Monday an' Amanda tol' me to send you her love. Dat park's fucked up big time man! I can't believe you caused a fuckin' riot today!' Sean paused for breath, scrutinising his cousin's face. 'By the way, how's your leg, star?' he asked apprehensively. Cory waved one hand in a see-saw motion.

'S' all right. All they done here is put a piece of metal down my leg to stop it from bendin', y'get me. They killed me puttin' the bone back in place, but tomorrow I get a big off cast an' the painkillers'll help me ride it until den. It was fuckin' agony earlier though spee, I'm tellin' you, I thought I was gonna pass out at one stage.'

Sean winced in sympathy. Cory's right leg was a strange-looking lump underneath the blanket, staying completely still no matter which way the teen turned his body. Cory meanwhile, had looked through Sean's offering of magazines. He found a copy of *Skank* and was soon chuckling with pleasure as the pages rustled together.

'Hey Cory, how will dis affec' your footballin' man?' Sean wondered, half to himself. Cory's gaze was flat and accepting.

'Boy cuz, I spoke to the doctor, an' he said I can't even think of playin' professional football 'cos o' dis. Ever.'

He bit down on the last word menacingly, making Sean rub his arms as if there was a chill in the air.

'Shit Cory man. You sure you're all right?' he questioned, feeling hopelessness at the harsh and unexpected end to Cory's lifelong dream of a career in soccer.

He'd spent hours curled up in front of the television, watching videos of his newest favourites, Manchester Utd (Sean finally converted him), and studying every move executed by Ryan Giggs and Eric Cantona, about whom Cory would hear no wrong from anyone. He'd then go out to the park with Garvey and practise overheads, fake passes and diving headers, sometimes until one or two in the morning, which caused serious eruptions in the Bradley household from time to time (usually when Garvey and Cory came in singing, 'ooh aah, Cantona', at the tops of their voices).

Now the dream was fading but Cory shrugged off Sean's last question, eyeing his cousin gravely.

'Hear what now cuz. Yeah, it is kinda bad what happened to me today, but fuckin' hell man, look around you. Go on, have a look will you?'

Sean let his gaze travel across the large ward then come back across to his cousin.

'Yeah what?'

'Yeah what? Listen Sean, all around dis room are people that are in more pain than me an' you've experienced in both our lives, fuckin' put together, y'get me?'

'So what's the point man?'

'What's the point? You bin smokin' bone today or what? I'm tryin' to say dere's worse things than a poxy broken leg in dis life y'know. Like fuckin' Parkinson's disease or AIDS or fuckin' sickle cell, for Christ's sake. All right, I can't play football professionally. So what? I got my good health still, innit? I got my life man.'

'F'real cuz.'

Sean stared at Cory, as if seeing him in a new light, nodding his head in agreement.

'Looks like you're turnin' into a scholar now,' he joked, referring to the name Bernice and Sonia had given him upon passing all his exams. Cory raised an eyebrow and lifted the GameGear up with a smile.

'Yeah man, I can drop science as well y'know star. Hear what, I bet I can brush you at Chase HQ too. I got up to the Porsche earlier, so I'm ready for you.'

Sean laughed, and for the next half hour the two cousins attempted to outrace each other, their eyes glued to the tiny colour computer screen in concentration, as it beeped and whistled in their hands nosily.

Sean found himself suddenly recalling what had happened with Tanya, the scene worming its way into his mind as they played. The clang of the rubbish bin against Dougie's head reverberated in his skull every time he heard something bang against metal in the busy ward. He wanted to tell Cory, but so much had already happened in this one tense day. He decided to wait, at least until the next day, when, he hoped, there would be less on their minds.

While the nurses brought Cory's dinner, Sean found Detective Sainsbury's card at the bottom of his pocket, covered in dusty lint from a crumbling tissue. He showed it to Cory, who sneered and glanced at it through slitted eyes.

'Throw it away man, I don't wan' dat. For people to think I'm a grass.'

Sean did as he was instructed, throwing the card in the wastepaper basket without a second thought. He made a gesture at Cory's untouched plate on which was a boring looking meal of meat and two veg swimming in a paper thin gravy, with chocolate mousse for afters.

'Don't you want dat?' he said hopefully.

'Nah man, you can kill it, I ain't too hungry. Leave the mousse though, I'll 'ave dat later.'

'Bastard.'

They laughed and Sean tucked in, ignoring the bland taste of the food, only aware of his stomach's relief at being filled. He ate with his head down and only looked up as he was scraping the last bits from the plate. Sean saw Levi enter the ward, bags in both hands. He looked around till he spotted them.

Cory whispered, 'Damn, I forgot about my man,' a second before Levi's tall frame towered above the bed. He eyed a passing nurse then borrowed a chair from the bed opposite. He sat down, handing Cory one of the bags.

'What'm my yout's?' he growled, taking off his dark glasses. Cory shrugged a little flippantly and looked inside the bag. Chocolates and more fruit. He put them to one side.

'You see me here, innit? You must done know what happen, a lie?'

The Rasta nodded his head.

'Yea' man, I heard,' he muttered. 'Now it seem to me, we got some sortin' out to do, concernin' dis t'ing nex' week.'

'How yuh mean? I'm in fuckin' hospital man, I can't do nothin' for six weeks man, simple.'

Levi laughed a little, like a parent about to tell their child the truth about Santa Claus.

'Nah star, it ain't dat simple believe. I tol' you the other day dere's money at stake here, y'unnerstan' an' I ain't losin' the chance of gettin' my hands on it, jus' because you decide to bore up one of my runners an' den brok up your leg. To tell you the trut', dis whole t'ing is startin' to piss me off Cory, an' you know the fuckin' reason why? It's 'cos *you*, seem to feel you're exempt an' untouchable from anyt'ing dat goes on in the real worl', y'unnerstan'. I'm tellin' you now star, it ain't fuckin' so.'

'So what the fuck can *I* do?' Cory shouted at Levi, losing his cool at once. Heads turned to look, then looked away rapidly when three pairs of hard eyes challenged them. A nurse started to come over, her face angry and her finger to her lips. Levi told her that Cory was upset about his injury. After some prompting, he made the boy apologise. When the nurse was gone Levi turned to Sean.

'See what I mean?' he growled, arms outstretched. Sean gave the Dredd a disbelieving look and spoke in low tones.

'Levi, can't you see he can't even fuckin' walk let alone do an' armed? How the fuck d'you expect him to take part like dis man?' Levi looked bored.

'Someone has to do it, if Cory can't. It's all down to him man, y'get me?'

He turned to Cory. 'Ain't you got no frien' to go t'rough for yuh star? What about dat half-breed yout' yuh move wid?'

Levi's attention was back on the bed-ridden boy again speculatively. Cory cut his eye at him, then made a farting noise with his mouth.

'Garvey? Later on star. I wouldn't make him do dat, dat's sick. You must think I'm a dark cunt, to come off wi' dem talks dere.'

Now it was Levi's turn to get mad, but his rage was quiet, cold and laced with the threat of pent-up violence. Cory sat back, hoping the Dredd's voice wouldn't carry to the other beds.

'Let me tell you sumt'ing star. You got till five pm dis T'ursday to get me a replacement Cory. If, for any reason concernin' you or Roger, dat move doesn't go on, you can consider yuhself a hunted man when you come outta here, seen. A hunted fuckin' man.'

Levi pulled back his jacket slightly, to reveal a bulge above the front of his waist, possibly made by Kenny's gun. The youths stared hatefully at the Rasta, while Sean visibly paled at his words. Levi let his jacket fall again.

'Yuh bettah start pullin' in some favours quick my yout', cause I'm not nice Rasta, I ain't fuckin' nice. It ain't good to affe walk lookin over yuh shoulder, believe me, so jus' do de sensible t'ing Cory . . . sort yuh shit out will you? Do dat an' everyt'ing can done dere, y'get me? We can forget de whole t'ing.'

Sean fiddled with some loose skin flapping on his thumb and tried to block out the angry voices that were going on and on, in aggravating circles around him. Every time he looked around, things seemed to be getting steadily worse. Cory seemed to be getting deeper into a situation spinning way, way out of his control.

He broke off the thought as he noticed Levi getting up to leave out of the corner of his eye. He gave a tiny, inaudible sigh of relief.

'Get it sorted an' I'll be off your back, trus' me,' Levi was saying, his expression forgiving now. Sean noticed how small his cousin looked against the large hospital pillows, how tired his eyes were and he felt a pang of hurt deep in his chest. He watched as he lifted his head and tried to smile, but eventually gave up, as his aching facial muscles couldn't hold the expression up for long.

'Maybe I'd be able to think a little clearer if you weren't t'reatenin' me every two minutes innit?' he told the Dredd. Levi walked over to the bed and knocked him lightly on his shoulder with his fist, in a 'we're buddies now' kind of way, making light of his words.

'Me nah t'reatnin' yuh rudey, me jus' advise yuh, seen? Tek time an' head my advise, will yuh? It'll serve you well. You got me moby number, so gimme a bell dis week, yeah?'

'Yeah yeah.'

Levi touched fists with both boys and nicked an apple before strolling out of the wide hospital doors. Cory and Sean said nothing until he'd been gone from their view for at least half a minute. When Sean looked back to his cousin, he could see he was seething silently, trying not to let on how upset he was. As their eyes met, the words forced themselves past Cory's lips, gaining speed and power like an avalanche.

'*Bastard*. I'll kill the fucker man, I'll cut his t'roat star . . . 'ey listen, when I get out I'm hol'in' my t'ings star. I'm gettin' my bucky blatant an' man's gonna go on different, f'real.'

'Sssh!' Sean hissed, his fingers on his lips. Cory shushed, but still mumbled curses under his breath. Sean looked him over.

'You all right man?'

'Yeah man, 'course star. He jus' burns me up.'

'Yeah man I know, jus' don't let him scare you, we'll think of somethin', dere must be a way to get you out of dis.'

Cory snorted bullishly at his cousin.

'Scare me? Levi? Raa cuz, you're on some joke business believe me. I ain't frightened of Levi star, no fuckin' way, y'unnerstan', it'll take a bigger man than my man for dat, f'real. Hear what, pass me dat pen will yuh? Behind dem fruits man. Yeah yeah, lovely.'

Sean looked on the cabinet for a second, then found the Bic. He passed it to Cory, wondering what was going on in the boy's mind.

'Got any paper?'

Cory scribbled in the air, illustrating his problem. Sean searched his pockets and came up with lots of nothing. Then he remembered the detective's card again and bent over to fish it out of the bin. Cory made his disapproval plain.

'Fuckin' hell Sean, dat's a bin man.'

'Fuck it, dat card's the only thing in it,' he stated, in a matter-of-fact tone of voice. Cory kissed his teeth.

'Dustbin raidin' ain't from Bernice's side of the family, must be from your paps man, innit Sean?'

'Fuck you star,' Sean grumbled, offhandedly.

He handed the card to Cory, who looked at the print for a second, then kissed his teeth and turned it over to the blank side. He began to write in a small, neat script. Despite his earlier claims that he wasn't scared of Levi, Sean could see his hand was shaking slightly as he wrote. He waited trying to work out what Cory was up to before asking him straight out. A ghost of a smile pulled at the corners of Cory's mouth, then was gone, making his face look solemn and a great deal older than its seventeen years.

'I want you to do me a favour,' he said to Sean.

'When you go home, I want you to look in my bag with all my clothes in, y'know, the one I use to carry my football kit.'

Sean was nodding intently.

'Look in the back pocket of my jeans and you'll find my address book. I want you to look for these names for me, find their addresses an' go an' see 'em to let 'em know what kinda situation I'm in. They might, just might, be able to help me out man.'

Cory handed Sean the card. The boy could see three names scribbled close together, as if fighting for space on the card.

1/ Danny Campbell
2/ Ricky ???
3/ Razor

Sean read the card, then looked up. 'Razor? You mean Ray Clark dat used to go our school an' got expelled for dat t'ing wi' the CS gas?'

Cory smiled. 'Yeah man, I know he's off key, but all dem man owe me favours an' I was thinkin' on what Levi said. If you can get one of 'em to come in for me, everyt'in' should bc copa, y'get me.'

Sean looked dubious. 'Shit man, d'you think they'll go t'rough with an armed robbery out of the blue like dis? I mean they'd have to owe you a big favour man, an' we ain't even seen Ray or anyone from his firm in ages.'

'Boy Sean, I know it's a long shot, but direc'ly they're the only man I can think of dat'd do sumt'in' like dis for me. Danny's sellin' bone up in his manor as far as I know an' dat brer Ricky's on some kinda move nearly every time I go out dere myself, so I know they're capable of helpin' me, y'unnerstan'?' He looked at Sean mischievously.

'So what, you reckon you could deal wi' dat ku for me?' Cory asked, knowing what he'd say. Sean laughed.

'Course I will,' he said, pocketing the card once more. 'I'll deal wid it firs' thing Monday mornin'.'

Cory lay back in his bed and closed his eyes, his hands behind his head, relaxing for the first time since Sean had seen him. He looked at his watch and decided it was time to go and see Sonia before she went loopy.

'All right Cory I'll come an' check you tomorrow man,' he promised his cousin, brushing himself off and getting himself together at the same time. Cory opened his eyes and managed the smile that had been eluding him for so long.

'All right cuz, later on man. Thanks for helpin' me out, I appreciate it properly star. An' I'll tell you one thing; in future I'm gonna listen to you when somethin's worryin' you, dat's a promise.'

Sean laughed. 'You fuckin' better man.'

They touched fists, and Sean headed back towards the swing

doors leading to the stairs. He only looked back at the ward once. By then, his cousin's bed was swallowed up by the many others in sight.

Chapter Nine

On Sunday, Sean and Sonia went to see Cory in the hospital, bringing him rice and peas, curry chicken and fried dumplings in a plastic Tupperware container. When they arrived, they found Tanya sitting next to the bed looking upset and mildly annoyed. It was clearly obvious that they'd walked in on a heated argument.

Cory looked vexed when he saw them but winked at Sean when the boy hugged him, and showed off his gleaming plaster, pulling back the blankets and wriggling his toes through a hole in the bottom.

The couple hung around for five minutes, but eventually left, deciding to let Cory and Tanya sort out their problems in private. Neither Sonia or Sean spoke a single word to the girl – but once outside they agreed, at least, that she'd been courageous to come and confess the whole thing to Cory. Both of them felt a little sorry for her, but they kept it to themselves for the time being, not wanting their sympathy to be seen as forgiveness.

Sean woke up at ten o'clock on Monday morning, instantly knowing what he had to do. When he had finished showering, dressing and eating, he pulled Sainsbury's card out of his pocket, then searched through his cousin's Nike sports bag. He found the address book in a pair of black jeans and flicked through it carefully, easily finding the names he needed. Then he wrote them down on a separate piece of paper for future reference.

There was a phone number with Danny's name (the address next to the name was a music studio in Ladbroke Grove), and Razor's name had a mobile number scratched beside it. He took them down, but only as a last resort as the things he intended to talk about couldn't really be discussed on an open phone. That done, he found his exact destination in a battered A to Z, then made his way to the front door.

'Later on, Shannon,' he yelled at his sister's door. He heard a muffled shout in reply. The second name on the card, Ricky, lived in a block of flats in Hammersmith. Sean had heard Cory mention the boy before, but he couldn't recall the face for the life of him. Shrugging mentally, he decided to try for Ricky first. He walked to the bus stop, his keys jangling in his pockets.

The bus was warm, cosy and comfortable. Sean dozed gently as they headed around Shepherd's Bush Green and up a long straight road to Hammersmith. He got off at a stop just parallel to the Hammersmith Apollo which was advertising Keith Sweat Live, in big red letters at the front of the building. He darted across the street through slow-moving traffic towards a small council estate, hidden behind a bulk of shops and pubs.

He found himself a map of the estate by the entrance and saw that the block he was looking for, Felix House, was over on the far side of the manor. The only person he passed on the walk, was a black girl pushing a pram, her head straight and her eyes as unseeing as a soldier on parade. Apart from her, the whole estate looked like a ghost town and the battered swings in a small park moved slightly in the wind, with no children to propel them further.

The building had a fairly decent lift. As there were only four floors in the block, Sean decided to risk it and take the ride to the top floor to number 40 Felix House where Ricky's flat was.

The door of number 40 was a dark maroon colour and the old paint was flaking away. Sean looked up at the ceiling which was also flaking, then knocked on the letter box three times.

There was no answer for a while, but Sean heard a baby crying and the sound of movement, so he didn't knock again. He heard the sound of locks being turned. The door swung open, revealing a large half-caste girl, with a baby in one hand and a cricket bat in the other. Her bulk seemed to fill up the doorway, and her eyes were dark and clear, yet they were expressionless and didn't move from his face.

Sean could see flies buzzing around the flat behind her. One flew out of the doorway, escaping into the sun, even as he watched. He took a measured step backwards.

'Yeah?' she said. The baby stared at Sean, with a slimy trail of snot running into its mouth.

'Uh . . . I'm lookin' for Ricky . . . is he about at all?' he asked.

The girl raised the bat threateningly.

'Whatoo wan' 'im for?'

'I . . . I'm jus' a friend of his, come to chat some business with 'im,' he stuttered.

She shook the bat at him and heaved the child back up to her shoulder.

'Well he ain't 'ere an' I dunno when he'll be back. If you see 'im on your travels tell 'im not to bother cumin' back ever. Fuckin' cunt stole my rent money.'

The door slammed shut, before he'd time to even think of a reply. He looked at its impassive face for a second more and considered knocking again, then thought the better of it. Shaking his head, he walked back down the landing and down the stairs, only starting to laugh when he hit the ground floor. Taking the paper out of his pocket, he looked at the first name, Danny Campbell, and decided he'd be his next stop. He made his way to Hammersmith tube station, looking back at the block occasionally, but wanting to get as far away from Felix House as he could.

Half an hour later, Sean found himself outside the Metronome Music Studios in Ladbroke Grove. He pressed a silver buzzer on an intercom and a woman's voice pleasantly greeted him.

'Hello, Metronome!' the voice sang brightly.

Sean asked for Danny Campbell and was rewarded with a buzz and a click. He responded by pushing the door open. He found stairs ahead of him, leading down into semi-darkness. He took them and followed a passage into the reception, glad to be off the street.

He saw a door slightly ajar at the end of the passage. He

opened it to find a room painted a lively electric blue, with a large black desk at the far end and an array of plants by the one window which was on the street level. Posters advertising various groups were on the right-hand side of the wall. Sean noticed an Eternal picture smiling down on him and he wondered if Danny had ever met any of the singers.

He stepped slowly inside, peeking around the door like a jungle explorer. The receptionist, a pretty white woman wearing a black silk blouse waved him in.

'C'mon in, you're all right luv!' she trilled, as she busied herself looking over some papers. He walked over to the desk and stood, somewhat awkwardly, to one side.

'Y' all right dere. Uhhh . . . I'm lookin' for Danny, Danny Campbell? Uhh . . . I rang the buzzer.'

The woman smiled at him as the light from the window shot a broad beam across her desk. A phone rang and she held up a finger and picked it up, looking at once brisk and businesslike.

Sean looked around the room, thinking about Danny as the woman chattered. He could remember him from school as a lively boy, with a reputation for being a trouble-maker, yet very clever with it. For six months, Cory and Sean had moved with him around the fields and playgrounds of their secondary school chasing girls and giving the teachers hell. Soon, they found other people to hang around with, and Sean had lost touch with him. It would be interesting to see how he'd turned out, Sean mused.

'Sorry about that,' the woman was saying as she replaced the receiver. 'Danny's in a session at the moment, but if you gimme your name, I'll see if he can give you five minutes of his time.'

'Thanks a lot,' Sean said gratefully. 'Tell him it's Sean Bradley, from school.'

'OK.' She paused as she tapped into the phone once more. Sean heard the rings from where he was standing and also the muffled garble of a voice from the receiver.

'Yeah Danny . . . I've got a Sean Bradley to see you in reception . . . yeah? . . . OK . . . No problem.'

She placed the handset in its cradle and flashed another smile at Sean.

'Obviously he doesn't want to keep such a handsome young

man waiting; he said to show you right in,' she told him, getting up to show him through. She was wearing a tight mini-skirt that moulded the shape of her curved body. Sean kept his gaze averted, merely smiling politely at her flattering comment.

They walked to the opposite side of the passage to a small door covered in carpet. She grasped the tiny handle and pulled it towards them.

The first thing that hit him, as he followed the woman through, was the solid wall of noise. He stepped inside the room, fearing the heavy bass would blow his head away. There were three men inside, seated in black leather chairs, surrounding a mixing desk. LED's bounced up and down, in time to the music pumping from massive black speakers.

A rack of unrecognisable machines, topped by an Apple Macintosh and a small monitor were by the desk. Sean could see another man through a glass window in the far wall, singing lustily into a microphone, his eyes closed tight, lost in the tune. One of the men, dressed in a baseball cap, T-shirt and tracksuit bottoms, turned to face him. Sean was shocked to see it was Danny. The boy hailed him loudly.

'Fuckin' 'ell, wha' you sayin' blood?' he said, grasping his hand tightly in two of his own. He'd grown a beard since Sean last saw him and his eyes looked deep and adult now, yet they still had some of his old sparkle. The receptionist smiled and left them to it, presumably to deal with more paperwork. Danny pulled a fader on the desk, introduced him to the two black men as, 'my childhood spar' and told him to build a spliff, pointing at a king size pack of Swans.

Sean declined and Danny slapped his head, remembering, then went for the blue packet himself.

'Between you and Cory, my head used to be baffled at school man. I never see two people so close, so different.'

He ripped the packet and pointed at a chair.

'Si' down star, what'm to you? Wha' you bin on since we left school?'

Sean sat, feeling the soft lines of the chair draw him in warmly.

'I bin studyin' star, like a madman,' he replied. 'It's like, I thought it'd be hard an' dat, but you jus' afta do your homework an' you're copa. Sonnie complains, but I know say she can handle it, really.'

Danny glanced up at that.

'What, you still wid Sonia?'

'Yep.'

'Gwaan.' He smiled as he crumbled the weed into the sheets.

Behind him, Sean could see the man in the voice room, still singing into the mike, his arms waving about energetically, though he could hardly be heard. Danny rolled up carefully.

'So what, 'ow's Cory, the fuckin' nutter,' he shot at the teen, still grinning. Sean kept his face serious as he replied.

'Well direc'ly, dat's who I come to chat about star.'

'Is it?'

'Yeah yeah.'

Danny sparked the zook and let out a plume of smoke, that spiralled upwards towards massive revolving fans. The two said nothing for a moment, then Danny turned and signalled to the man in the other room, before addressing the two sitting with them.

'You don' mind us takin' five do you?'

The men shook their heads and reached for their coats, looking glad to have a break. After giving them a long list of food to bring back from the West Indian shop across the road, Danny swivelled his chair around and faced Sean.

'You hungry?'

'I had breakfast man,' Sean rubbed his stomach.

'I'm gettin' some for you anyway, so eat what you want, leave what you want, innit?'

'Big up, respec', star.'

Danny sat back in his chair, his face contented.

'I'm tellin' you Sean, dis is the fuckin' life man. I can smoke when I want, have lunch when I want an' I'm doin' somethin' I love and makin' wong at the same time. I can't screw, y'get me? I got a couple of tunes comin' out dis mont' as well.'

Danny rolled his chair over to a tiny compact refrigerator and pulled out two cans of Ting grapefruit flavoured drink. He tossed one to Sean and popped his, with a click and a fizz.

'So what's happened to Cory den?' he asked, morphing from cheeriness to seriousness.

Sean took a breath, then explained the situation with his cousin from the beginning. The phone rang a few times, but the young engineer ignored the calls. For the most part, the story went uninterrupted, save Sean's sharp pauses for breath.

Danny's face was unresponsive as Sean spoke and he merely built spliffs, while he took in the whole story soberly. The men came back with the bags of hot food as Sean got to the part where he'd knocked at Ricky's flat and met the mad-looking girl. Danny nodded as he unpacked his meal eagerly and, when the men left again, he started to talk in a flat, casual way.

'Yeah man, Ricky's kinda fucked up dese days star, f'real. I think he's in Wandsworth, for rapin' some girl in Ealin' wid a couple of other brers.'

'*What*!'

'Yeah man; when we left school I used to bop about wid 'im. It was one of dem times dere, Cory saved us man, so direc'ly your cousin's right, we do owe him a favour.'

'What happened?'

'Wid the rape or the other t'ing?'

'The other t'ing man. I don't wanna hear 'bout no rape.'

Danny looked up at the ceiling, his face reflective.

'We was in Kentucky in Hammersmith, y'know the one?'

Sean nodded.

'Yeah man, anyway, it was jus' me an' Ricky sittin' dere an' we was runnin' a kinda partnership theory, 50/50 capital, 50/50 profit, y'get me? Anyway, we was sittin' dere eatin' and chattin', when dis one brer called Clifford comes in wid 'is girl. Now, dis guy's one of Ricky's customers, but we both know him, so I call him over, jus' to chat an' dat, and Ricky . . . fuck star, Ricky went inta one. Turns out dis guy's got a tick list as long as my fuckin' arm, an' he owes Rick a hell of a lot of money, so Rick's brewin', making up a whole heap of noise in the place.'

While he'd been talking, Danny had been shovelling hot food into his mouth mechanically, speaking in between swallows. He took a large spoonful of rice and meat before resuming his narrative.

'Where was I?' he started, chewing on a bone.

'Kentucky, Ricky cussin',' Sean said helpfully.

'Oh yeah, Rick's brewin', shoutin', "where's my money,

where's my fuckin' money", but Clifford he's *paro*, true he's wid
'is girl an' dat, an' he feels a way cause Ricky's shoutin' an'
swearin' at him bareface, in front of nuff man. I could see he
was holdin' it down, an' two two's he jus' dossed, didn't even
hol' no fuckin' food y'unnerstan'? From dat, I knew dere was
gonna be trouble, I jus' knew man.

'About a week later, me an' Ricky was in Greenside 'cause I
was seein' some girl from dem sides, an' who do we see?
Clifford innit, wid nuff man boy, all lookin' a fight. They ruffed
up Ricky star, an' true we were smokin' bone, prang Ricky
tried to bore one of dem man up. Star, I thought I was gonna
see a man get 'is t'roat cut live-o in my face, he was dat prang,
but they got the knife off him an' started to slap him about, not
even takin' notice of me. Den I hear Ricky say, "What about my
man, he's my partner, he should get licks too."'

Sean gave Danny an unbelieving glance, as sauce dripped
from his fingers.

'No word of a lie, Cory heard the whole t'ing,' the bearded
boy said sombrely, wiping his bit of gravy from his cheek.

'Anyway, Clifford an' 'is mates rush me a little, gimme some
kicks an' dat, den I see 'em flyin' all over the place an' no one's
on me no more. When I look around I see Cory, Garvey an
some other brers, kickin' shit out of dem yout's star, properly.
Fuckin' Ricky was missin', probably as soon as I got rushed. I
was gonna go home an get my uncle's gun for 'im, but your
cousin got me thinkin' rational an' I jus' 'llowed it star.'

He shrugged his shoulders and pushed some rice around with
his fork.

'An' dat's it man, dat's how Cory saved me from getting my
head kicked in. Ricky made me think seriously about what kind
of business I was in too. I mean, sellin' crack gives you a worl'
o' money, but more an' more man ain't livin' to spen' it an' I
wanna live, y'get me? I thought about you y'know Sean, passin'
all your GCSE's first time . . . I thought: I can do what I want,
if I really want it. Two two's, I took the money I had saved,
went to college to study Studio Engineerin' an' now, here I am,
number two engineer. Not bad eh?'

Sean smiled his agreement.

'Dat's fuckin' wicked man. So what, you give up rocks too?'

'Yeah, yeah, dat was after I'd bin at college a couple of months an' I realised I weighed eight stone man. Eight fuckin' stone! Ricky was supposed to be after me as well, sayin' I set him up dat night, so I ate and did weights till I was pretty much back to normal. When I did see him, he was too fucked to do jack shit an' nex' thing I knew, he was locked up star. We won't see him again till '99, if we're lucky.'

The two boys laughed coldly, more at the madness going on around them than out of genuine amusement. Sean sipped his drink and played with the zip on his hooded top.

'So what Dee, can you help Cory out or what?' he said, in a straightforward, no nonsense tone of voice. Danny sighed, looked around the room as if afraid to meet Sean's gaze, then coughed self-consciously.

'Dat's what I'm tryin' to say,' he told him, his own tone sorrowful. 'A year ago when we left school, I would've bin bang on it, especially after what your cousin done for me dat night. Now I'm jus' like you, I'm straight up legal, y'get me. Dere's so much perfectly legitimate scams you can pull in business, I'd be a mug not to get involved an' I'd be a bigger mug to fuck it up. Basically, what I'm sayin' is an' armed is jus' what I don't want to do now Sean. Sorry man, I can't do it.'

Sean rose, his face drawn as he stood and shrugged casually.

'You got your life together man, dat's good. I can't expect you to fuck it all up on Cory's behalf.'

Danny said nothing, his hands covering his face for a second. Then he looked up at Sean.

'What, you goin' straightaway?'

'Got to star, dere's a worl' o' t'ings for me to do.'

Danny looked like a man who'd been promised a glass of wine to drink and had been given petrol as a joke. He got up with Sean, his eyes begging forgiveness.

'Star, I feel like a cunt,' he told his school friend truthfully, reaching in his pocket for something. When he'd found what he was looking for, he passed it to Sean, who looked at it, sighed and put it in his pocket. It was another business card, with Danny's name splashed over it.

'I'm truly sorry Sean,' he muttered gravely. 'Jus' make sure you phone me if dere's anythin' I c'n help wid, yeah?'

'Yeah yeah. If you could try an' see Cory in St Charles, dat would be nice. Ward C6, he's in.'

'I will man, I promise.'

'All right blood, later.'

'Later on Sean.'

Sean headed for the stairs and went up, pushing through the doors and the gate until he reached the bustling street, where he sighed and stretched, feeling hurt inside despite his forgiving words to Danny.

One more left, he thought and made his way to the bus stop again. Even as he walked a back-up plan was forming in his brain, growing and gaining more life the faster his legs pumped on the hard concrete pavement.

The address for the last name on the list was a large recently built estate in North Acton. Huge industrial diggers stood unmanned on empty plots of land. Elsewhere were foundations with pipes woven intricately into the ground and windowless half-built yellow brick structures that looked cold and uninviting.

Razor lived on the edge of the estate in a ground-floor flat. Sean knocked twice before the door was opened by a pretty black girl who readily invited him in. Razor, a short black youth with a gold tooth and a cheeky grin, was lying on the sofa in the living room. He looked surprised to see him and immediately motioned him to sit down. He asked the girl, Melisha, to bring a bottle of Rum Punch from the fridge and in no time the three of them were knocking back the ruddy liquid, while Sean and Razor talked fondly about their old school days.

'Dis flat's the lick,' Sean told the couple, looking around, impressed by what he saw. A Nicam TV, and an expensive stack set-up were just some of the expensive possessions in the flat. Razor shrugged modestly.

'Spee, I affa look after myself an' my girl y'get me? Dis time now, I know nuff man prangin' dat jus' let demselves go, but I ain't 'avin' it, seen. Jus' 'cause I was raised in the gutter, don't mean I affa stay dere, y'unnerstan'? Innit Mel?'

Melisha nodded, sipping her drink.

'Better believe it. I keep goin' on at Ray to move out, but he says the money's too good here.'

Razor turned to Sean and rolled his eyes at her remark.

'Listen spee, I'm killin' it here star. My phone rings as soon as I switch it on and true every man's on somethin' to make wong around here, dere's the most raises you can make, if you know the right people. I'm gonna save at least ten gee before I go anywhere, star.'

Melisha smiled distantly and smoothed down her skirt, saying nothing.

'Wha' you jugglin'?' Sean asked the boy.

'Bone, powder, greens, y'get me? I had some brown customers, but they kept wantin' to jack up in here, so I tol' 'em to piss off an' find a park or summick. The nex' time they come, I wen' out to the shops after they'd left an' found some New Age fucker sittin' on the pavement, wid a fuckin' needle stuck in his arm. I would've beat him up, but I was too scared to star – I don't want AIDS. From dat, I said fuck heroin.'

Razor sparked a zook sitting in an ashtray made from half a coconut and waved the smoke in Sean's direction. The odour of crack wafted towards him.

'So wha' you sayin' star, what brings you here anyhow?' he asked the teen, looking like a dragon as smoke spiralled from his nose in twin jets. 'Still studyin'?' he puffed.

'Yeah man, I'm still at it, but y'know what Razor? I come to ask a favour on behalf of my cousin man.'

'Cory?'

Razor sat up, his relaxed posture instantly gone now.

'What happened to my man den?'

'Boy y'know,' Sean said hesitantly. 'It's kinda a private matter, no offence Melisha.'

Melisha shrugged and got up to leave, but Razor held her arm and pulled her back down.

'It might not look like it, but me an' Mel don't 'ave secrets. If she goes now I'll probably tell her later anyway an' get it wrong so . . .' He held his arms out, not even bothering to finish the sentence.

Sean decided he knew enough about Razor's own dealings to cover himself, and that he had nothing to lose.

Melisha was enthralled by the tale, her mouth hanging open, while Razor looked plain indifferent, smoking and gazing around the room as if he wasn't listening. Sean thought bitterly, It's jus' dat to them. A tale, something divorced from reality, set around a situation that contained more problems than their life already had.

Unless you're *in* it, you can't feel anything *about* it, he decided mentally – you can say how sorry you are and how much you understand, but how can you understand if you don't know? No one's got a clue what my cousin's goin' through, maybe not even me, he mused. The plan that had been blooming in his mind since he left Ladbroke Grove, grew another off-shoot and dug its roots in deeper into his brain. He took another swallow of Rum Punch and got his mind back to the present.

'So after dat, Levi left the ward. Cory gave me your number and said you owed him a favour. I come here to see if you're up for it.'

Razor said nothing for a long time, swirling his drink around and gazing into its cloudiness. Then he smiled and looked up.

'Lemme get dis straight,' he muttered. 'Cory was supposed to do a job an' he brok his leg, so he can't. Now, cause of dis tiny favour I'm supposed to owe from nearly a year ago, you want me to do it?'

Sean eyed him, guessing the boy's answer from his tone of voice. 'Yeah dat's right. If you consider yourself a mate, as well as knowin' you owe him a favour, it'd help him out man. His fuckin' life's been threatened star.'

'Bollocks,' Razor spat, picking a piece of tobacco from his lip. 'Dis ain't South Central y'know. I bet you dat bucky Levi had was a replica anyhow. Man was tryin' to shit you up an' it fuckin' worked.'

Melisha looked from her boyfriend to Sean, like a woman watching a strenuous game of tennis, her head turning left and right as they talked. Sean realised straightaway that any further arguments he made would be futile. He shrugged and knocked back the last of his drink.

'Well Ray, I can't make you believe if you don't wanna,' he said, zipping up his jacket while still seated.

Razor rubbed his chin, contemplating.

'Boy, a man would've had to've saved my life or summick for

me to do a armed for him, jus' like dat. You see how t'ings are runnin' Sean, I can't bait myself up man. I got myself a nice drum, you was sayin' so yourself y'get me? I can't risk all dat for a minor favour star.'

Razor's tone had changed as he spoke, from derisive to apologetic, just from the sight of Sean zipping up his jacket. Sean rose, embarrassment making him feel claustrophobic in the flat. He focused his energies on leaving and tried to ignore the way his head was pounding.

'What was the favour anyway?' he asked Razor, not really caring, his mind and his mouth still operating on autopilot. The boy looked a little stumped for a second, then looked at Melisha and said, 'You better off askin' Cory dat, he'll tell you better.'

She eyed him suspiciously.

'Why can't you tell us now?' she complained, her eyes narrow.

'Because it's a t'ing between Cory and me an' I don't wanna bring him out.'

'Don't gow,' the girl responded, 'I know you were doin' somethin' you shouldn't, so you might as well tell me now, innit?'

'What's wrong wid you woman? I tol' you it's more Cory's secret than mine an' you're still on my case man, wha' gwaan?'

'I know you're lyin' man, dat's why. You're out of order Ray, you think I don't know what you get up to, but I ain't stupid y'know.'

'Ah, shut up star, you're givin' me a fuckin' headache.'

Razor lay back on the sofa, his hand covering his eyes.

'Don't fuckin' tell me to shut up!'

Sean, who'd been standing motionless through this exchange, decided he'd heard enough.

'All right people, I'm wingin' out anyway, star,' he told the irate couple. Razor got up to see him to the door, with another apologetic grin.

'Yeah man, sorry I can't help you out y'get me, but I ain't doin' dem t'ings dere yet. I'll be eighteen in July and I wanna be outside for dat, not birded off in a cell with some Rad playin' my stereo an' smokin' my t'ings, y'get me?'

'Yeah man, I get you,' Sean replied, his voice sounding morose.

'I'll see you aroun' man.'

'Yeah later Sean, good luck an' dat.'

'Yeah yeah.'

Dejectedly, Sean walked along the tarmac path leading from Razor's front door to the street, not even hearing the sound of the door snicking shut behind him. He stopped, standing as still as a statue when he reached the corner. Then he walked in the direction of home. It was a long, long journey back to Greenside.

He got back to Denver at around half past two and let himself in to find that the flat was empty. There was one message from Sonia on the answer machine, asking where the hell he was and saying Sam Boyd had been looking for him. Sean listened to her voice, then wiped it off the tape, not wanting his mother to hear what she had to say. He then sat in his room sullenly for a while, watching the brainless programmes that made up afternoon television.

He lay there for almost an hour, lost in his thoughts, before getting up, going to the kitchen and snatching a pack of crisps.

He left the flat and headed for the street, his walk determined. A group of kids was standing by the fence that surrounded Greenside Primary School, chewing Hubba Bubba and waiting for their parents to pick them up from the play centre. They yelled at Sean, and he waved as he passed them.

He reached Levi's front door and rang the doorbell forcefully. Within seconds a skinny white man in a faded T-shirt and jeans answered.

'Yeah?'

The man peered at Sean.

'Is Levi dere at all?' he asked. The man shook his head.

"'E's gone to dat pub, the Moon on the Green, or sumthin' like dat.'

He coughed and stepped past Sean to the balcony, to spit on the landing below. Sean turned to face him.

'What, dat one on Bush Green?'

'Yeah, dat's the one, on the corner. He said he'll be dere all dis afternoon, so he should still be about.'

The man winked at Sean.

'Wanna score?' he said, in a stage whisper.

'Sumthin' like dat.'

'I got some lovely shit inside man, you can smoke a spliff an' try it if you don't wanna walk to the Green.'

The man looked around as if there were spies everywhere.

'I gotta chat to my man anyway, so I bes' take a walk,' Sean responded, smiling a little.

The man stretched and yawned, looking indifferent about losing a potential sale. Sean took that as his cue to leave.

'If you see 'im tell him Sean come to check 'im.'

'No problem geezer.'

Sean walked back down the landing, looking over the balcony to the sprawling rows of buildings, standing like some concrete army that had just invaded the area and was awaiting further orders.

Levi's swannin' about in some pub, while my cousin's layin' fucked up in some hospital bed, he thought. It's time to do somethin' about it.

He trotted down the dank, urine-stained steps and out into the street, his face a battle between determination, fear and a minuscule slice of anticipation.

For Levi, the day had been going fairly well since he got out of his girl's bed at one. He'd rolled around on the large futon with his baby mother, Shawna, for another half an hour and showered and dressed by two. (Levi believed he was the quickest dresser in the world.) He left Shawna in her Hammersmith flat with the baby crawling all over her.

He phoned the Beechwood flat as he drove past the pub on the corner of Shepherd's Bush Green, only deciding to park up when he saw the long queue in the dole office, which was right next door to the pub. Giros would be cashed today. Levi intended to be there to collect what was owed to him, and what was coming to him by way of new sales.

He was pleased to see Everton and Mark, a white guy and a black guy who dealt mostly in brown, talking and joking with a few men from next door, their pints spilling over as they moved about restlessly. Levi felt glad he'd decided to give Greenside a rest for today. He was a man who believed in following his instincts and he loved it when they were proven right.

Levi waved a greeting as he swung the Vauxhall around the corner and parked. He hailed the men in his booming tones, getting several offers of a pint from them in return. He refused all and showed them his bulging wallet, promising the next round was on him. There were loud cheers from the men.

The breeze was icy, chilling them to the bone, yet each man stayed outside, knowing that in an hour, they could make an easy two to three hundred pounds. When a sale came, they would walk around the block and exchange a note for the drugs, for the most part, in full view of the surrounding houses and young mothers bringing their children home from school. Levi's days of being scared to juggle in the street were long gone. Everton and Mark paid police to leave them alone, so they too showed no fear.

Business was steady, and Levi enjoyed profiling, even though he knew he didn't need the money this kind of dealing brought him. He simply got a buzz out of people seeing him and knowing what he was. There wasn't any other deeper motive.

'Boy I shoulda put me longjohns on today, it's cuttin' out here!' the Dredd chattered to the circle, holding his sides to keep in the warmth.

The other men laughed.

'Think I'm stickin' in dis country much longer. Soon as I can I'm flyin' out man. I'm duckin' England dis winter too, believe me,' Everton complained, his long blond hair waving in the wind like seaweed on an ocean floor. Mark nodded and raised his drink in salute to his friend's statement.

For the most part, the other men sipped their drinks in silence. Ninety per cent of them earned in two months what Levi, Everton and Mark earned in a day. The big three could afford to take frequent holidays anywhere in the world, but they were too greedy and proprietorial about their patches.

As a result they never left England and merely spoke of travelling year after year, winding each other up constantly with talk of hot climates like the West Indies or the south of France. Everton had been to Majorca with his girlfriend and children two years ago, but came back saying it was like England without the rain. He claimed that because of that, Spain didn't really count as a holiday destination. Levi and Mark tended to agree with him.

The blond man took another sip of his drink, then looked up and saw a tall black youth walking towards Levi with a resolute look on his face. Sean came square up to Levi and looked him dead in the face, ignoring the cluster of men surrounding him loosely.

'I need to talk to you,' he told the older man sternly.

Levi rolled his head around, easing the cricks in his neck. 'So talk nuh.'

'Not in front of these lot. Can't we go inside?'

Sean nodded at the lively interior of the pub. Everton was struck by the lifelessness in his voice and the blank way he seemed to ignore the presence of the six men, all staring at him curiously. Levi looked around at the group of men and nodded to them.

'I'll be two minutes.'

'Yeah yeah.'

Everton craned his neck to watch them walk through the pub's entrance, then turned and rolled his eyes at the others.

The Dredd and the teen stumbled through the crowd, all packed like sardines in the modest-sized bar. They slowly made their way to a semi-quiet table, where they could ignore a greater part of the hundreds of conversations going on around them. Levi offered Sean a drink. Sean asked for a Holsten Pils, then sat back and viewed the clientele as Levi disappeared into the seething mass.

It was a yuppified crowd, with many of the men and women dressed in suits. Sean guessed most of them worked in the BBC building, not two minutes from his estate. The locals were there too and some were talking and drinking with the classy-looking business people. Others were huddled in corners much like the one he occupied now, giving the well-clad crew a wide berth.

Sean asked himself who could've planned putting a multi-million-pound government-funded industry bang next door to a funding-starved council estate. Madmen maybe? It was crazy, but that was the way London was built and it had been that way for centuries. And they wonder why there's so much crime, the teen thought, shaking his head.

Levi returned with two pints and placed them on cardboard mats, sliding Sean's drink over to him.

'They only 'ave Budweiser,' he rumbled.

'Yeah, dat's safe.'

Levi took a gulp of Guinness.

'So talk nuh,' he said again, unhelpfully. Sean talked.

'Listen, I've bin all over the place lookin' for someone to help Cory out, but no one can do it. He's lyin' messed up in hospital man, it's not his fault he can't do the job.'

'*Keep yuh voice down man*!' Levi hissed, not too quiet himself. A large man in a beige raincoat glanced over, but looked away quickly when Levi stared back coldly. The Dredd leaned towards Sean and spoke again in a lower tone.

'Hear what now, me nuh care what position Cory in. If him never stab Roger I wouldn't be in dis shit now, y'get me? I didn't put Cory in hospital either y'know.'

The Dredd squeezed his words out between clenched jaws, causing tendons to jump and strain in his neck. Sean was so incensed, he was past noticing – he probably didn't care much anyway.

'Yeah, but you know the brers dat done it. Shit, dat was Roger's fuckin' mates man, you got to know dem!'

Sean sat back in his seat, looking angrily all about him, taking deep breaths of air through his nose. He hadn't realised when he walked up here just how upset he really was. You got to calm down, he told himself, soothingly. Levi was talking almost as soon as he'd stopped.

'Ain't my problem. What I say still stan' – if Cory don't do the move, I can't be held responsible for my actions. Money at stake star.'

Sean looked away from Levi as he heard this, unable to take his unrepenting gaze any longer. His drink sat ignored on the table. 'I bin slappin' about all day, tryin' to find a replacement for you man,' he eventually managed.

Levi chose not to reply to the teen, instead turning to wave and smile at a smartly dressed black woman, calling his name above the din. He then turned back to Sean.

'Wha' yuh waan me fe do?' he muttered, sounding as if he was lost and he needed Sean's help to get back to what he knew.

Sean closed his eyes and felt his headache return. The words he wanted to say, the words that would tell Levi to take his guns, his money and his rocks, and stick them as far up his own backside as he could get them, just wouldn't come and probably never would. Levi was just so immovable, so set in getting his own way, he was a man obsessed. Sean cursed himself for believing, even for a second, that Levi could be dissuaded. In the end, as it had been so often in his relationship with Cory, Sean HAD to sort things out.

'Let me do the robbery man, I'll take Cory's place,' he blurted, the words splashing like a glass of lager in the older man's face, with much the same effect. Levi started, then couldn't help the sneering tone that came into his voice.

'*You*?! Boy y'know, you sure you can handle it? We're gonna be armed to the teeth, coarsin' up people . . . You sure you can handle it?'

Sean frowned at the man.

'I shot guns in Cadets so I'm all right man. Besides, we won't need to kill anyone will we? The guns are jus' there to frighten people, innit?'

'I suppose so.'

Sean sat forward again.

'C'mon man, you might as well let me do it. I won't let you, or my cousin down. When you check it, I'm the only option, unless you want Cory to do the move on crutches.'

Levi's poker face broke and they both chuckled at the thought of a man trying to pull off a robbery with a broken leg. The Dredd then looked about thoughtfully, seeming to be weighing up Sean's request carefully.

'Supposin' we say yes. How I know you won't gee me up to de Rads dem?'

Levi took another swallow of Guinness after his words, trying not to laugh at Sean's contrite expression.

'Wid my cousin in hospital? Dat'd be stupid. Anyway jus' 'cause I study an' dat, don't mean I'm a grass y'know.'

Sean sounded offended.

Levi held his hands up, in a pose Cory would have recognised easily.

'No offence, you know how it go – can't trust no fucker nowadays.'

'Yeah, I know dat, but I ain't doin' it for money or nuthin' man, I'm doin' it to help my cousin,' Sean pointed out.

'So yuh naḥ waan Roger's cut den?' Levi ribbed, good-naturedly. Sean snorted in disbelief.

'I din't say dat, did I?'

Levi smiled broadly, thinking, you never know, this kid might have some more surprises up his sleeve. He was shocked that the boy even thought about getting involved. For years he'd thought Sean was as square as a pub's plastic ashtray. However he also considered him the best of a bad bunch, when talking about the Bradley family. The other members always seemed stuck up and full of themselves. Sean's show of balls, plus the stylish way he carried himself, oozed difference to the older man and he liked smart black kids. They reminded the Dredd of a half-brother he'd grown up with back home in Jamaica, who was now an assistant manager of a bank owned by a large company.

'Yeah yeah, yuh know wha' Steve – I t'ink I'll gi' yuh a go man.'

Sean beamed brightly, then remembered what he had talked himself into. His smile vanished in a flash.

'My name's Sean not Steve,' he reminded the man absently, his brow furrowed.

Levi wafted his words away like cigarette smoke.

'Yeah, whatever yuh say. Tell yuh wha', yuh know what number I'm at in Beechwood House, innit?'

'Yeah yeah.'

'Come check me Wednesday about one an' we'll go over the plans. But Sean . . . I tell yuh like I tol' Cory. Don't fuck me about. Dis is the big boys you're in wid now, star.'

Sean nodded gravely, taking in every word.

'I won't mess you about star,' he promised sincerely.

Sean took a look at his watch and gasped with shock. He got up, knocking his chair into the one behind him, making the man in it start violently. He apologised and turned back to Levi, who was eyeing him with amusement.

'Shit man, I gotta get to the hospital and tell Cory, star. Visitin' hours jus' started.'

Levi lit a cigarette and exhaled thin blue smoke. He squinted at Sean through the haze.

'Later den,' the Dredd rumbled. 'Come check me Wednesday, about one. Cory's lucky to have a man like you in de family. Mek sure yuh tell him dat.'

Chapter Ten

'Aw, Sean man, you didn't, tell me you're lyin' star.'

Cory lay on his hospital bed with his hands over his eyes, hiding his despair from the prying eyes of the other patients, but not from his cousin. The ward was quiet, as some of the old men had been allowed home at last. The atmosphere was relaxed and the nurses able to spend more time with the remaining patients, smiling and cracking jokes, sometimes even sitting on the edges of their beds to talk good-naturedly about whatever was ailing them.

'Well what was I supposed to do man? Levi jus' wasn't listenin' to reason an' your firs' plan failed miserably, so I didn't have much of a choice at the end of the day. Can you think of any other options?'

Cory put his hands on his thighs and faced Sean seriously.

'Yeah man, I can think of one. You could 'ave left me to deal with my own shit man, simple. You don't know nuffin' about pullin' off an' armed man, you're a bona fide student star. You should be bashin' the books, not fuckin' post office clerks. I don't believe dis man.'

'I suppose you know all about it den?'

Sean sounded more than a little annoyed with the teen.

'Nah, I ain't sayin' dat, but I got more of a clue than you mate. Cadets ain't nothin' like firin' a real bucky you know, in a real shoot-out. If anythin' goes wrong, there's gonna be security guards, armed police an' ARVs on your case in minutes, all lookin' to pop your arse. If you think Levi's gonna be lookin' out for your well bein', you'll be sadly mistaken star. My man only cares about himself.'

'What's an ARV?' Sean wanted to know.

Cory raised his eyebrows and let out a pent-up breath, his frustration clearly visible. 'Armed response vehicle man. Jus' more Rads with guns. An I'm tellin' you Sean, they don't shoot to miss either. Are you really sure you wanna go t'rough star, cause I'm lettin' you know now, you don't have to, y'get me? I appreciate what you're tryin' to do an' all dat, but I'd fuckin' go crazy if you got into trouble over my shit, y'unnerstan'?'

Sean was silent for a moment, thinking hard and weighing up Cory's question seriously. He'd known his cousin wouldn't be pleased, but now he was easily pointing out scenarios Sean hadn't even considered in the heat of the moment. Cory was right: ARVs and police snipers were forces Sean hadn't had the slightest thought about. He was starting to believe the decision he'd made in the noisy pub had been a teeny bit rash, to say the least.

He couldn't let Cory down though, or let him see he'd rattled him. Sean decided on a show of optimism, the more his cousin's worried eyes rested on him. He took a tangerine from Cory's collection of fruits, then peeled it and answered his question.

'Yeah man, I'm up for it an' don't fret either. Levi must have a plan an' if it seems a tiny bit dodgy, I'll jus' 'llow it innit? Listen man, I don't see you got much choice in the matter anyway, how long you in here?'

Cory gave a little grimace.

'They wanna keep me till nex' week at least star.' He seemed none too pleased at the prospect.

'Dere you go. Levi's sayin' it's goin' down dis week, so dere's no way you'll be around for dat. I ain't plannin' to stan' around while your life's being threatened, so it's a foregone conclusion, really. You think I wanna alms up people? Later, I jus' wanna get you out of dis mess. Look, I promise you I'll be careful man, how about dat, is dat all right?'

Cory shook his head from side to side, as if trying to cancel his cousin's words.

'If your mum finds out, I'm history man,' he told Sean, fretfully.

'She won't man, I mean, how hard can it be?'

Cory glared at him, his expression saying, *hard* extremely *hard*. But he said nothing and for Sean, that was enough.

Sean took a deep breath and when he spoke again, it took supreme self-control not to scream the words at his cousin.

'You can't stop me Cory, I'm gonna do it whether you want me to or not, y'get me? Now will you shut the fuck up an' let me look after dis t'ing for yuh eh? Do you think you can do dat for me, huh?'

For a short time they remained completely silent with only the sound of Sean's ragged breathing between them. Stony faced, Cory tore open his box of Roses and emptied the chocolates onto the bed beside him. Taking a handful, he proceeded to unwrap every sweet he had and shovelled them into his mouth, pointing at the pile with his left hand.

'Want one?' he said as he chewed, the words hidden behind a mash of chocolate, but the intention plain to Sean. Sean picked up a few of the colourfully wrapped sweets, glancing at the box to check the fillings before popping them in his mouth, one by one. They were both quiet as they chewed, then Cory laughed a little and gestured at the blue box.

'Nick me a box of these when you're out dere, will yuh?' he grinned at his cousin with a forced geniality he clearly didn't feel.

'No Sean.'

Sonia's voice was cold and lifeless, the voice of a disembodied spirit that floated about the room. She shook her head and wrapped her arms around herself, not looking at Sean.

'No fuckin' way man, you ain't doin' it,' she told him once more. Sean reached for her, but she moved back, forbidding his touch.

'Sonnie, I ain't got a choice 'ave I? I wouldn't even dream of it if Cory wasn't in hospital, would I, huh?'

Sonia's head snapped forward, with the speed of a king cobra on the attack, and her voice was full of venom.

'Cory, Cory, Cory, is he all you think about Sean? What about *me* huh, what'll I do if you get caught?'

Her tone then changed, from accusing him to pleading.

'You could get hurt, or somethin' Sean. Please don't do it. Please, we'll think of somethin' else, jus' wait for a bit.'

Sean took a deep breath. 'I can't wait for nuffin' Sonnie. You say I could get hurt, well Cory *will* get hurt if Levi has his way. I dunno, I never clocked it before, but dem two don't get on at all star. I don't wanna risk callin' Levi's bluff, y'unnerstan'?'

Sonia kissed her teeth loudly and, all at once, got up from the bed, picking up her coat at the same time. She struggled to slip into it quickly, while Sean leapt over the bed and held her arms.

'Hey, hey!' he said, half laughing. 'Where you goin' man?'

Sonia glared up at him, her eyes damp, yet as hard and as sharp as flintstone.

'Dis ain't a fuckin' joke Sean. If you mus' know, I'm goin' to the hospital to talk some sense into your stupid cousin, so let go of my arms!'

Sean's smile faded into nothing.

'Sonia don't be silly. Talkin' to Cory ain't gonna change my mind is it? You gotta understand, I had dis same argument wid him, so it ain't 'is fault. I've made up my mind Sonnie an' I'm sorry, but dere's fuck all anyone can do about it. I jus' thought I should tell you, dat's all.'

'Dat's all? *Dat's all*? Let go of my arms Sean!'

Sonia wrenched herself away from Sean's grasp and looked him stubbornly in the face. Then she ran to the bedroom door, tugging it open forcefully in her haste to leave the flat. Sean ran after her, not wanting to touch her again and implored her, in a hushed voice, to stop what she was doing.

'Hey Sonnie, will yuh stop so we can talk . . .'

Sonia ran past the closed living room door, stumbled up the stairs and flew past the kitchen, where Shannon was about to place a large jug of cold drink on a tray with a ragtag assortment of glasses and mugs. She glanced up, frowning as Sonia steamed past. Sonnie threw the front door open brutally, much like the words she tossed to Sean over her shoulder.

'*Fuck off Sean, I ain't got nothin' to say to you*!' she raged at him. In a flash she was gone, leaving the letterbox shuddering in her wake. Shannon poked a head around the kitchen door, as Sean stood feeling terrible at the top of the steps. She rolled her eyes at her younger brother.

'Oh God, what's up with you guys now?' she asked, ever the nosy one. Sean shrugged.

'Ah she's just brewin' with me 'cos I wasn't at college today, it's a minor.'

'Are you sure it wasn't 'cos of you gettin' seen, chattin' with Levi?' Shannon replied, her eyes sparkling.

'Seen by who?' he blurted, before his brain could tell him to watch his words and actions, as it was Shannon, the neighbourhood bloodhound he was talking to. Shannon wiggled her eyebrows.

'Jus' me. But it looked like an interestin' talk from where I was.'

'Is it?'

Sean was thinking fast. 'An' where was you?'

Shannon walked back over to her tray. 'Drivin' past, comin' home from college in Mikey's car. Why was you up to sumthin' you shouldn't 'ave bin?'

'Yeah, I was holdin' a bone,' Sean joked to give himself more time to think, laughing a little. Shannon didn't join in and his weak laughter tapered off.

'Nah, I'm only jestin'. We was talkin' about Cory, an' Levi was sayin' if I need a hand with dat Shane, to come check him, dat's all. No big t'ing.'

'You looked so serious,' his sister told him.

'It's a serious matter innit? Hey BabyShan, you didn't tell Sonia about dat did you?'

Shannon shook her head as she wound her way around the door, balancing the tray carefully. She gave Sean a light kick in the shin for his use of the name the family had given her, then she went, one step at a time, down the stairs, her brother in tow.

Sean breathed a sigh of relief. He thought of the robbery at the end of the week and told himself, this is only the beginning. There's plenty more lies an' a lot more deceit to come.

It didn't do his cheer any good at all.

In the days preceding his move with Levi, Sean found himself unable to keep his mind on much else. At home, he wandered around aimlessly, thinking only of the day and what it would bring. For the most part, he stayed in his bedroom, playing Sega and listening to music, even though Garvey and a few others from the manor had told him to come and check them any time.

There were some days when he almost did just that, but the thought of sitting around laughing and joking was too much to take. He'd stay in his room often in a total silence, hearing only the sound of his heartbeat in his ears. Even college work, his usual pleasure, just became something to get him through the day. His concentration was becoming worse the closer the robbery got. He felt as though a giant clock was in his head, counting down the days, hours and minutes.

He wouldn't forgive himself if somebody got hurt on the day, he thought. In a way, he was more scared of what he could do with a pistol in his hand than of what harm could be done to him. Violence had been close to him all his life. He'd usually neatly sidestepped it. But whenever it had headed unswervingly towards him, he'd always dealt with it with a ferocity that surprised everyone.

He managed to come to no sane conclusion to the whole affair and, up until the day he went to see Levi, he thought his head was going to burst with the strain of it all.

He sat in a small, featureless room, with Levi and three boys he'd never met before. One of them, a baldheaded boy who was obviously team 'leader', made Sean's stomach muscles clench, he looked so much like Roger. He almost made to leave the flat, as rage threatened to engulf him.

Sean quickly realised his mistake, and relaxed a bit, even though there was a sombre atmosphere in the room. The other two boys were a Chinese-looking teenager, dressed in baggy jeans, and a dark black youth, wearing an Armani sweater and large chaps, who sneered at everyone and chewed gum non-stop.

He looked over the crew as Levi talked, and could see them sizing him up, and each other too. He came to the conclusion none of them knew who the others were and decided wherever these boys were from, it wasn't Greenside.

Levi's 'plan' turned out to be sketchy, but on the whole fairly straightforward. Their tactics would be to drive in two cars, each one carrying two masked boys up to a post office on the outskirts of London (Levi wouldn't say where). They would rush in and demand all the money in the tills and safes. Levi told them there was an Asian postmaster working in the building who was in on the plan. He instructed them not to talk to him, so he wouldn't be interrogated more than anyone else.

They would collect as much cash as they could and leave within sixty seconds of arriving, without firing a single shot. After that, they would get back into the two cars (driven by Levi and Kenny) and head back to Greenside, hopefully triumphant and a great deal richer than they'd been before. Sean thought there wasn't much that could go wrong and he was satisfied he seemed to be in no unnecessary danger.

'So when d'we get our cut?' Clarence, the bald youth wanted to know.

Sean thought it was a good question and one he would've asked himself. Levi looked up from his A4 sheet of paper seriously.

'As soon as we get back we'll split the wong, nuh worry 'bout dat star,' he told them. Everyone barring Sean smiled.

That was all they'd need to know for now, Levi concluded. The boys got up to go back to their respective homes, each feeling nervousness tugging at their bellies, but each playing hard and bouncing nonchalantly across the room.

'One at a time star, what'm t'you yout's? Sean, yuh go first, seen, seein' as yuh live closest. Mek sure yuh 'ere one o'clock Friday, yeah?'

'Yeah yeah,' Sean said glumly, hating the way the older man was dictating to him, but unable to find the words to tell the Dredd to stop. He left the flat, to be greeted by a cloudy grey sky, that matched his mood perfectly. There was nobody on the streets and the estate was unusually quiet, bar the solid wall of noise from the primary school. He ignored the kids and kept his head down and his hands buried deep in his pockets. Walking slowly, he thought of going back to college to catch his afternoon lesson, but decided he couldn't face any more lecturers today. Instead, he turned back and headed towards Oakhill House to see if Garvey was in.

When all this is over, things'll get back to normal, he thought miserably, I'll get all my college work done an' I'll get Sonnie back, jus' let me get through dis thing on Friday . . .

He supposed he was praying to God, but as he didn't go to

church and he didn't usually pray, he wasn't sure if his pleas would be heard. He looked up at the sky, but all he could see were dull grey clouds that seemed to stretch into infinity.

On Friday morning at around three o'clock, Cory lay in his hospital bed, unable to sleep. I've bin restin' for days, he told himself, turning slowly in the bed, so as not to wake the old men in the beds surrounding him. I want some action man, dis is pissin' me off big time.

The nearest thing he'd got to excitement, was a visit from the detective who'd interviewed Sean; the last thing he needed. The man apologised for turning up out of the blue, but stressed that Cory's aunt had been meant to phone him and up to now he was still waiting for her call. Cory, in turn, apologised for Bernice (saying she was far too busy at work, even to visit him), then told the man a vague kind of truth concerning the happenings on Saturday. He was careful to leave out anything that would connect him to Roger. Sainsbury seemed to swallow it.

Yeah man, Cory thought, happy for a second. Maybe I should take up actin' now, I'm still young enough to change careers.

He tried to turn over onto his side and felt a burst of pain shoot up his broken leg, which made him swear. Inevitably, he found his thoughts turning to his cousin, the worry reappearing to plague him again. Sean had been up to see him during the day and he had explained Levi's plan to the letter, omitting nothing. When he'd finished, even Cory had to admit it sounded like a fairly simple thing to pull off. He asked how much was expected to be taken, in an off-hand, I-don't-give-a-damn way.

'Levi reckons four, five grand maybe,' Sean answered, as if the Dredd had told him four or five Jamaican dollars. Cory whistled long and low and when he'd collected himself, he said, 'Fuckin' hell Sean min' yourself spee, I'm tellin' you. I swear to God if anythin' happens . . .' He trailed off, unable to express himself fully and unable to imagine what he'd be capable of, if something happened to his cousin. Sean laughed and touched his shoulder gently.

'Hey, don't jinx me star,' he joked. They laughed, somewhat uneasily. Sean left not long afterwards, saying he was going to get an early night. Cory had watched him go, hating himself for the position he'd put his cousin in.

The only really good thing dat's happened to me lately, he told himself, is fit Rosie, comin' to check me.

It was true that without the girl's positive presence, he could've easily turned to depression. It was also true that the more he saw her, the more he found himself becoming intrigued by the girl. He began to look forward to her visits. He liked to make her laugh, just to see the dimples appear when she smiled. Not that he'd tell anyone besides Sean or Garvey that.

Since the first day she'd come to the hospital, with a much mellowed Tara, she'd been back every day, mostly alone. She'd comforted him over his break up with Tanya, so all thoughts of his unfaithful girl were banished from his mind. He couldn't wait to get his cast off, so he could take Rosie out raving.

'I tol' you you could do better,' she said, quite a few times, until he'd turned and replied, 'I'm tryin' to ain't I?' as he held her hand, making sure she got his full meaning. Rosie smiled and sat on the bed looking at him with her wide brown eyes.

'Man, you're in love star!' Garvey laughed when Cory told him about it later, but Claire elbowed him in the side and told him to leave Cory alone.

Smiling a little, Cory stared at the ceiling, wondering if things could ever go back to how they'd been before. It seemed as though his life, and the lives of those around him, had been turned upside-down in a matter of weeks. The man responsible for that, as usual, was Levi.

I hate dat fucker man, Cory thought. Instead of turning his anger inwards, towards himself, he focused on Levi.

In five minutes, he was asleep and snoring deeply.

Chapter Eleven

The two cars sped along a quiet back road at an easy cruising speed, their occupants looking for all the world as if they were on a countryside jaunt, or a visit to some distant relative. Heads turned as they rolled by, amazed at seeing so many black people at one time. The curious stares made them feel tense and nervous, as if they were under surveillance.

Sean sat in the back seat of Levi's car, with the stern-looking Chinese boy. He stared out of the window, hypnotised by the view of large fields full of farm animals and tall electricity pylons that seemed to march on past the horizon. The Chinese boy, who'd introduced himself as Gary, lit up a Benson & Hedges. Sean had been silent for most of the journey, deeply afraid, but not wanting to open his mouth in case the fear leapt out and betrayed him.

They'd not been driving long, he thought, looking at his watch. They'd only been on the road for a couple of hours, but in that time Sean saw the street lights, red buses and black cabs disappear — a new and foreign world reared its head in sharp contrast to the West London estate he'd been raised on. He vowed to himself he would travel a great deal more, if he got himself and Cory out of this mess. It shocked him to realise the world he thought he knew, could be this much different elsewhere.

I wonder if black people live out here? he pondered, staring in wonder at a green and yellow double decker bus that roared past them, on a road with no pavement. He hadn't seen any yet, though he was sure there had to be some, maybe more towards the centre of the small town. We're everywhere man, he grinned to himself, as they pulled up at a T junction.

Earlier that day at Levi's, the Dredd had ushered them into a room which had hitherto been locked, to wait for Kenny who ran on BPT – black people's time. Levi had left the four boys briefly to go and attend to a crack sale. They'd stood in an awkward silence for a while, none of them knowing what to say. Clarence had grinned at Sean and pointed to a large plastic crate in the corner of the room.

'You know what dat is spee, innit?' he asked the teen, going over to the crate and crouching down in front of it, a move that made the other boys draw near like moths around a flame. Sean shook his head, but Gary and the gum-chewing black boy (who was called Darren), slapped palms as they prised open the folding lid and capered around the room at the sight of what was inside.

'It's the buckys star, bere worries a gwaan now, believe!' Darren was saying. He reached inside and hefted a bulky-looking pistol in a badman's pose, with one hand on his chin. The other three boys cracked up. In no time at all, the trio had each picked the guns they respectively liked the look of. By the time Levi came back into the room, they were chatting animatedly amongst themselves, all previous inhibitions forgotten. Sean cradled his gun against his chest and smiled, despite the depression he'd been under earlier in the morning. Levi grinned back.

'So you fin' de t'ings dem?' he said, looking like he'd led them to this room for a reason greater than just waiting for Kenny. Gary was in heaven and told the Dredd so.

'But, but, is where yuh get these kinna arms star?' the boy stuttered, startling Sean with his strong Jamaican accent. Levi touched his nose and shrugged.

'Let's jus' say someone very "grim" gave 'em to me,' he answered, mysteriously.

Levi then changed the subject by telling the boys about each pistol they held. He was a mine of information, seeming to know every minute detail about the weapons. When he'd finished, Darren, Gary and Clarence built weed spliffs. Levi produced a gleaming crack rock from his pocket, making the trio yell and touch fists happily, all of them asking to build cocktails.

Luckily for Sean, Kenny arrived at half-past one, just as the trio had wrapped their zooks. Without further ado, they each picked up the black balaclavas they'd be wearing in under an hour's time, and made their way downstairs to where the two stolen cars were parked. As Levi started the car, he told Sean and Gary that hidden in the boot of each vehicle were two sawn-off shotguns, one for each of them.

'I t'ought we did jus' choose our buckys,' Gary complained. Levi grinned into the rearview mirror.

'Nah man, you can't expect people to give up wong, wid dem small suttin's dere, y'get me? See de t'ing is, yuh point a hand-gun at someone in a armed an' you know some hero's gonna try an' get it away from you: they figure they got less to lose dat way, seen. But if yuh hol' a sawn-off on a brer now . . .' Levi kissed his teeth.

'Listen, from time yuh do dat, yuh coulda walk out, go round de corner fe a piss an' come back an' de fucker woulda still 'ave 'im hands on 'is head, y'get me? A sawn-off don't ask for respec' it deman' it star, y'unnerstan'?'

The two boys laughed, Sean starting to feel a little better, despite himself. Soon enough, he started to talk to Gary, about their lives, their schooling and their families.

Now, just a couple of hours later, Levi was swinging the car onto what looked like a fairly busy main street. He caught their eyes in the rearview mirror.

'All right yout's, keep lookin' lef' an' you'll see the place. It's the row of shops jus' afta de zebra crossin'.'

'Where's Kenny?' Sean asked, about to turn around.

'Sit still!' Levi snapped at him, catching the teen in mid-turn. He gazed somewhat apologetically at Sean in the rear mirror and spoke again, the strain in his voice very evident.

'Don't worry about dem man, all right? Until you go inna dat post office, dat car don't exist, y'unnerstan'? An' don't worry, it's still dere, Kenny can flex fe himself.'

Sean sat back in his seat as the post office rolled slowly past his window. It was a typical village shop, modestly sized, with no long wooden railings to hold large queues like the ones that came on giro day, back in London. There didn't seem to be many people inside. Sean was intensely grateful for that, his lips moving together in a silent prayer of thanks, surprising himself. It was only the second time in as many days that he'd prayed since Ron had died. It seemed like blasphemy now, but his belief in God had died with his uncle, many years back.

Before he could get a better look inside, the shop was gone. Levi headed on, out of the town centre, only pulling up when they were surrounded by fields and lush grass again. He lit a cigarette and waited for Kenny to catch up, remaining inside the idling vehicle while he puffed away silently. Gary rolled his eyes at Sean and sighed deeply in anticipation. Sean smiled back mechanically, as he caught sight of the powerful blue Escort Kenny was driving, just crossing a junction a little way from them.

Levi looked at the youths and jerked a thumb backwards, then rolled his window down and hailed his friend. The four boys got out of the car and opened their respective boots, to retrieve the powerful sawn-offs hidden underneath an old, oily blanket.

Looking at the weapons carefully, Sean could see what Levi had meant about people respecting shotguns more than pistols. The guns were smooth, grooved masterpieces, with no scratches or signs of former use. Sean marvelled at how something so beautiful looking could be so deadly. He squinted at the name etched in by the shotgun's trigger; Benelli, made in Italy. He lifted it out of the boot slowly, grinning at Gary.

Anyone would shit themselves if they had one of these in their face, he thought. He also liked the weapon's weight – you could tell the gun meant business. He got back inside the car quickly and placed it on the back seat, laying it across horizontally, so he had to sit forward. A moment later, Gary got back in and did the same, placing his weapon across Sean's.

'Are they loaded?' Sean asked Levi, instantly thinking it was a stupid question and immediately regretting opening his mouth.

'I fuckin' hope so,' the Dredd replied off-handedly, before he leaned out of the window, facing Kenny and ignoring the teen.

'Everyt'ing cool?' he barked at the man.

Kenny nodded once.

'Yeh man. You 'ave dem gloves fe de yout's?

'Course star.'

Levi reached in the glove compartment and rooted around, until he found two see-through plastic bags and an old rag, which he tossed into the back seat on the youth's laps. Sean and Gary tore open the stapled packets, each to find sleek black leather gloves inside. They put them on and dusted the guns, wordlessly.

'Mek sure they never come off yuh hands, y'unnerstan'?' the Dredd told them, his own knuckly gloved hands tight on the steering wheel, the only outward sign of his tension. A motorbike passed the two cars. When it was just a speck in the distance, everybody donned their balaclavas. Levi turned to the boys in the back seat once again, the cut out eyes and mouth of the mask making him look like a raving lunatic.

'Ready?' he asked.

Sean and Gary nodded, Sean swallowing the lump in his throat, merely making it bob back up. Here we go, he thought unhappily. His mind flashed pictures of Cory in his hospital bed and he shook his head angrily; he wanted nothing to impair the solid concentration he'd need, not long from now.

'Ready?' Levi repeated, this time talking to the occupants of the Escort.

'Yeah yeah,' Kenny said. He pulled his mask down and executed an easy U-turn.

Levi waited until the man was facing the same direction as him, before shouting; '*Go!*' and putting his foot down on the accelerator as hard as he could. The two boys were thrown back in the car and when Sean had scrabbled himself upright again, he could see the trees that lined the country road, flashing past them at breakneck speed. Instead of braking when he got to the junction, Levi pushed the car from third gear to fourth and then into fifth, making the engine roar and Sean's pulse rate treble. Sean reached behind himself to grasp the sawn-off, as if its weight could ease the nervousness that gnawed at his stomach. Before he knew it, they'd screeched back onto the town's main road. Levi eased the vehicle to a stop, directly outside the post office.

'*Move it, move it, go on*!!' he shouted at Gary and Sean. The two boys jumped from the car as quickly as they could, guns drawn and at the ready, startling the assorted people strolling on the pavement.

Sean took a hurried glance up the road and could see shoppers with their children in tow, some screaming, some just staring at them in disbelief, while a group of pensioners covered their mouths and cowered against a packed bus stop. He looked up, to catch a glimpse of Clarence and Darren rushing past him, entering the shop. He quickly followed Gary inside, his SIG-Sauer pistol tucked in his waist, making his belly feel cramped and uncomfortable.

There were only two customers inside. One was an old Asian woman, who was at the front of the queue when they burst in, busily fishing around for change to buy her stamps. The other, was a young podgy white girl, her face plagued by acne wearing a Take That jacket.

The boys swung their guns wildly in all directions, trying to cover everybody. Sean stood by the door as instructed by Levi, his own shotgun by his side.

'All right everyone, get your fuckin' hands up an' no one'll get shot!' Clarence screamed, making the girl in the Take That jacket wail like a fire alarm. Gary leapt over the shop counter and levelled the sawn-off at the old woman, commanding her to open the till, which she did with a metallic ting.

Darren strolled over to the Asian postmaster, causing the old woman at the front of the queue to flinch and mutter in her own language. The podgy Take That fan was still screaming and Darren pointed the barrel of his weapon at her face angrily.

'Shut up man. Shut up I said, don't let me afta tell you again star!'

The fat girl vainly tried to stop her crying, then choked on her tears, abruptly shut her mouth and slid down the counter in a semi-faint, her eyes fluttering as her legs gave way beneath her.

'Dat's better,' Darren said, satisfied now.

Clarence kept his gun trained on the woman behind the post office counter and stepped forward confidently.

'What do you want, please don't shoot me, I'll give you anything, please . . .' the woman begged tearfully.

'Jus' shut up will you? What you think I want, huh . . .? *Eh?*

I want the money innit? So what I also want is for you to grab one of them sacks *there* an' fill it up with all the cash you got behind *here*, got it? You c'n start wi' dat safe over in the corner.'

The woman picked up the coarse brown Royal Mail sack and crouched by a bulky grey safe, tears running down her cheeks and her neck, onto her neat-looking blouse.

'But I don't know the combination,' she wailed at the teenagers sorrowfully. Clarence rolled his eyes as if this was all too much for him. Darren looked over and gestured at the postmaster absently.

'All right den, you do it mate. An' gimme one false move an' I'll blow you away right here. Even if the police do come, it won't make no difference you'll still be shot up, understan'? Get to it, quickly mind.'

The Asian man nodded and hurriedly spun the dial on the safe, in a blur that made Sean's eyes ache.

Outside, people were gathering about and pointing, but they stayed in a small crowd on the far side of the street, where they felt they were safe and secure. From the moment they entered the shop, Sean had been watching the thin hand on his watch and was surprised to see they'd only been inside for thirty seconds. He glanced at Levi seated in the car outside, who was making hurry up signals, then at the postmaster, who'd moved to the tills and was emptying them rapidly.

If I didn't know better I'd swear he was an innocent victim, Sean thought, chuckling slightly. Gary moved slowly over to his side, the carrier bag he was holding jangling with change from the shop's till. The Chinese boy's eyes were hard behind the black mask and his mouth was like a thin, tight line, drawn by a lazy cartoonist who couldn't be bothered with detail.

'Everyt'ing nice star?' he asked the teen coarsely.

'Yeah yeah,' Sean replied, his eyes dancing around in his head, attempting to take in all the cars, motorbikes and people rubber-necking outside.

Levi was now revving the stolen car's engine to a roaring pitch and, not far behind, Kenny was doing the same in his. Sean thought of keeping his ears open for sirens, but then shook the thought away, cursing himself for his stupidity. He doubted the police would warn them of their arrival on the scene. The silence outside was far more ominous than the sound of a platoon of police cars could ever have been.

He recalled countless occasions when he'd been walking with friends in Greenside and had seen police cars speeding through the estate's streets with their lights flashing manically, but the siren silent.

'Someone's gettin' bagged,' he and his friends would say to each other morbidly, as the cars flashed by in a blur of light. Usually, if the police were coming for you, you were the last person to know.

This train of thought worried him no end. He turned back to Darren and Clarence, who were urging the postmaster on, with threats that were very real, despite the man's allegiance to Levi. The two women on their side of the counter were cowering in a corner by the still form of the Take That fan, while the woman on the postmaster's side did the same, weeping openly. Sean tried to ignore her and focused on the two boys.

'Oi, hurry the fuck up will yuh? Rads'll be here any second.'

He took another fearful glance outside. Clarence turned to Sean, nodded once and then moved fluidly to a side door, which led to the postmaster's side of the counter. He gave it a harsh kick. It flew open with a bang that made the weeping lady scream in terror. While Darren kept his weapon trained on the Asian man, Clarence put down his own gun, snatched the postbag from the man's grasp and looked deep inside.

'Yeah yeah, time to wing out,' he said in a satisfied tone of voice. The others could see his smile, despite the mask.

'Let's get out of here, star,' he finished picking up his sawn-off again and walking backwards, his gun never leaving the Asian man's chest.

Suddenly, Sean started shouting crazily.

'*OH SHIT, HERE COMES THE FUCKIN' POLICE*!' he yelled as loud as he could manage, terror lending his voice box extra decibels.

There was a micro-second of silence. It was over in a flash, as suddenly the women started screaming again. The teenagers lifted their weapons, collected the bags of money and prepared to leave the shop, somewhat apprehensively. Sean watched the events unfold outside, in a numb kind of horror.

The police Metro may have just been passing by on a routine patrol: it certainly seemed that way, as there was only one man inside the vehicle, emerging now, as Sean watched. He was a young white man and Sean found the prayers running around in his head: please God, don't make him get in our way, don't make me have to shoot him.

The young policeman was staring at Levi's masked face in fixed concentration. He moved a step towards the car slowly, as if trying to fool the Dredd into thinking he wasn't really moving. He didn't appear to notice Kenny's car, though he must've heard the idling engine. He definitely failed to see the four masked boys, who were crowding the shop door's small window, while the people behind were forgotten. The policeman stepped forward once more, causing Levi's hand to reach down carefully and return, holding a wicked and ugly-looking black pistol.

'Don't even t'ink it,' the four boy's heard him warn the pale young man, as his arm snaked out of his window and aimed straight at him. The surrounding crowd gasped and a few women screamed, while some actually ran away. From inside the shop Clarence looked at Sean, his expression scornful.

'Is dis what you were screamin' about? One countryside Rad? I thought we was in real trouble star.'

The others laughed nervously and Sean's face turned hot beneath the mask.

'Raa, so what, I was meant to look out innit, so I looked out an' see a Rad car, blatant. If you wanted me to wait till I see how many man was in there, you should 'ave fuckin' said,' Sean shot back, stung by the accusation in the boy's voice. He liked Clarence and wanted his respect. Gary spoke up.

'Yeah man, 'llow my man, he was jus' doin' what he was meant to,' he said.

Clarence raised his gun in apology, then suddenly remembered they had company. He swung the barrel around, making sure their unwilling associates weren't planning any silly moves.

The Asian man, the Take That fan and the two women hadn't moved a muscle since the boys had rushed to the door. The weeping lady had finally stopped crying and was just getting to her feet quietly, when three pairs of eyes settled on her. She rapidly sat back down on the hard floor with an audible thump. Clarence could see that everyone else in the shop took his look as fair warning of the consequences playing hero could bring. He turned back to Sean, who was still watching the antics outside with a hard eye.

'So wha' d'you reckon we should do, spee?' he asked Sean amiably.

Sean gestured outside, now feeling strangely excited.

'I feel say we should get out dere while we still can, we've bin over a minute,' he told the youths sternly, amazed at the nods of agreement that greeted his words.

On the street, the policeman was talking to Levi in a wavering voice, instructing him to put the gun down while he still had time. The Dredd screamed obscenities and told him repeatedly to back off. Sean knew the policeman was stalling for his back-up and they had to act fast. He looked at the boys and raised his sawn-off for the first time, his face resolute.

'On the count of three,' he instructed them sternly. Clarence and Gary hefted their bags while Darren kept a steady eye on their captives.

'One, two, *THREE*!' Sean shouted, giving the door an almighty kick and charging into the daylight. In the space of one second, the four boys created instant pandemonium.

They rushed out of the small door, while all around them people screamed and ran for cover. The policeman stalling Levi stood by the small Metro, his mouth hanging open in shock as they spilled onto the pavement. To Sean, he resembled a Madame Tussaud's waxwork dummy, his eyes and hands pale and perfectly still, as he sized up the threat from this new danger.

Sean made his way around the bonnet of Levi's vehicle, heading for the passenger seat, his finger wrapped tightly around the sawn-off's hair-trigger. All around him were darting, shouting faces and the noise and mayhem was driving him crazy. He raised the weapon once again.

'Don't fuckin' move!' he screamed at the lawman, his ears not even hearing the words, even though the man had scarcely moved a muscle. At the sound of his voice, the policeman started, as if just waking from a light sleep. He turned quickly and headed for cover behind his shining white car, fear lending his stumbling legs speed.

Sean, his mind racing as he stood by the passenger door, suddenly decided this man could become a threat if he allowed him to be. He aimed the shotgun unprofessionally and tightened his finger on the trigger on an impulse, guided by his nerves and his body, more than his mind.

BOOOOM!

Sean was thrown against the passenger's door, everything around him forgotten for a second, as jarring pain embedded itself in his arm. The policeman had managed to make it to the back of his mangled car. Sean caught one glimpse of the undeniable fear in his eyes, before Levi pushed open his door quickly, hitting the teen in his aching arm and making him shout at the contact. He moved out of the way and, as he threw himself into the roaring car, he saw Kenny's Escort shoot past the police vehicle and disappear. Clarence and Darren were staring out of the windows in amazement. They were on their own now.

'*Drive, drive!*' Gary and Sean screamed at the Dredd as he spun the wheel and turned the vehicle around. He slammed his foot on the accelerator and the car picked up speed. Levi tried to avoid the men and women darting everywhere. Gary looked in the rearview mirror and saw the scenes were much the same behind them. Women clutched their children, while shopkeepers shook their fists at the shimmying car, brave now that the danger had passed.

They'd barely gone fifty metres, when a little boy darted across into the car's screaming path.

Sean had heard the boy's mother on the opposite side of the street yelling at him to join her and his brother on the right-hand pavement, as he'd leapt into the passenger seat. The boy had stepped out from the hefty kerb, thought the better of it, then changed his mind again and sprinted away from the safety of the pavement, perhaps believing he could outrun the speeding car.

Sean screamed at Levi to turn, and the Dredd spun the wheel left, sending the car skidding towards the kerb, missing the frightened child by inches. The wail of brakes and the smell of smoking tyres filled the air. All three were thrown forward; Levi crashed straight into the steering wheel, emitting a grunt of pain as it turned his stomach muscles into jelly. Gary hit the front seat and cracked his skull on Levi's headrest, while Sean hit his head against the glove compartment. He rested there for a moment, breathing deeply, glad he was still alive. He looked around at the others and then shook the older man in the driver's seat.

'Levi! Levi, are you all right man?'

Levi held his stomach and clenched his teeth. Sean asked the second most important question.

'Can you drive?' he shouted, fear holding him, controlling his every action now. The Dredd shook his head, making Sean want to cry out in anger.

'Get in the back seat!' he yelled at the man. 'Hurry up man, go on!'

The Dredd raised his body up and threw himself painfully into the back seat, landing on Gary. Sean glanced in the rearview mirror as he slid over into the driver's position and felt the panic start to rip and tear at his belly again, his hands shaking uncontrollably. It was almost too late.

Behind them, the police reinforcements had arrived. Men in helmets and bulletproof vests ran about the street, taking up various positions. A tall man with a peaked hat spoke into a megaphone.

'Can all members of the public clear the area right away!' he boomed, as people ran about him.

Sean could see the mother of the little boy they'd almost hit, sitting in the middle of the road and cradling her shocked son. He knew that soon, either she would be forcibly moved, or someone would pick them off from a position where the mother and her child would be safe from harm. He reached under the steering column and pushed two limp hanging wires together, making them spark and causing the car to pitch forward, as if in a fit. Gary kissed his teeth and Levi moaned, pulling the ugly pistol from his waist again.

'Put it in neutral!' he screamed crazily.

'All right, all right!' Sean screamed back.

'Where the fuck did you get your licence!' Gary shouted over the noise outside.

Behind them, the man with the megaphone was yelling at them to stop. Sean was incensed.

'*I AIN'T GOT A FUCKIN' LICENCE, MY SISTER TAUGHT ME, OK? NOW SHUT UP AN' LET ME CONCENTRATE!*' Sean barked back at them, before putting the gearstick into neutral and touching the thin wires together again.

The car started easily and he slammed the gearstick into first, hearing metal crunch underneath him. He ignored the thought that Shannon stopped teaching him to drive awhile ago, saying he needed proper tuition to pass his test. He moved into second, his mind hoping he could get them out of there. This will be my real test, he told himself, as they lurched away, steadily picking up speed.

Behind them, the policemen were jumping into their cars and starting them up quickly, eager to give chase. Before they left the main road behind, Gary turned and could see the cars struggling to get around the crying woman, who still hadn't moved from her position on the hard tarmac, her son's head cushioned gently against her breast. Gary raised his gun in salute.

'Thanks luv,' he muttered, underneath his breath.

Levi gave him a strange look and the Chinese boy smiled inwardly, knowing the Dredd thought he was crazy. I must be, to be in dis car, he thought to himself, turning his head to Sean. Sirens sluggishly wound themselves up behind them.

Other cars beeped at him, then moved out of the way as they spied the black masks. The speedometer read sixty-five, seventy, then eighty, as he pushed the vehicle harder and harder, with Levi screaming directions at him from the back seat. A mile further down the road, they flashed by a police patrol car lurking in a side road for speeders. Before they knew it, this car was on their tail as well, swinging in and out of the many other people on the busy country road, as if it was linked to the stolen vehicle by an invisible rope.

Levi looked out at the determined faces of the policemen glaring at them and decided he'd had enough. Smashing the back window with the butt of his gun and yelling his defiance to the amazed men, he opened fire, with a hail of shots that sent spent shells falling with a tinkle onto the glass covering the back seat. Gary covered his ears painfully, his mouth wide open in shock. The result was pure destruction.

The police car skidded uncontrollably from side to side, as

bullets ripped the bonnet, the grille and eventually the windscreen. A police car behind screeched as the driver forced the gears down, but too late. It crashed into the back of the first car, pushing it across the road, into the path of the motorists driving the opposite way. Soon, the air was filled with the sound of metal crunching against metal. The resulting pile-up was inevitable, as more and more cars ploughed into the wreckage.

Levi let out a whoop of delight and fired another shot just for sport, while Sean kept his attention on the road, grinding his teeth silently.

'Fuck all y'all, country police!' the older man was crying, the pain in his stomach momentarily forgotten.

His cry roused Sean from his reverie and the teen blinked a bit, looking at Levi's wide eyes in the rearview mirror. Sean's own eyes were tired and strained.

'So what, where we goin'?' he asked, his mouth and hands shaking in delayed shock. Levi shrugged, pulled off his mask and was quiet for a long time, thinking deeply. When they'd driven another three miles down the road, he spoke again.

'Pull over here,' he said, motioning with the gun to the side of the road and ignoring Gary's splutters of disbelief. Perplexed, Sean did as he was asked. They watched as Levi tucked his gun back in his waist, got out of the steaming car and limped across the road, holding his hand in the air, his mask tucked in his back pocket.

'He's a crazy fucker man,' Gary said to Sean as they watched two cars speed past the Dredd, without even slowing.

The older man turned to the boys, then pulled the mask back out, put it on and levelled the gun at the next car to pass, a silver Ford four-door Orion. The driver screeched to a halt and Levi strode over, pulled open his door and threw the shocked man onto the floor without a single word. Sean and Gary stared at each other. The teen shook his head.

'You're not wrong,' he told Gary. 'C'mon let's get goin' star.'

They jumped out the battered car, running for all they were worth across the country road. Gary threw the money into the back seat of the Orion, while Sean headed for the driver's seat straightaway. Levi held him by the arm forcefully and wagged a long finger at him.

'I t'ink you done enough drivin' fe de day,' he told the teen firmly. When Sean shrugged, he turned back to the man, cowering at the sight of so many guns, shielding his face with his hands.

'Take it, take it, it's a company car anyway, just don't hurt me!' he yelled. Levi nodded and got in the car.

'T'anks. Jus' keep yuh mout' shut, y'unnerstan'?' he said simply, before spinning the car around and powering away up the road, very aware that all the traffic on their side of the road had stopped, due to his nicely orchestrated pile-up.

Sean and Gary sat back in their seats, and were quiet as the car cruised along, Levi driving as if he was in no hurry whatsoever to get back to Greenside. Gary nudged Sean, then picked up the bag of money he'd taken from the old woman at the post office till and shook it once, smiling.

Sean hesitantly touched fists with the Chinese youth and smiled back.

They dumped the car in an industrial estate, somewhere in Highgate. Levi then called for a cab on his mobile to take them back to West London. They waited for the car in the local McDonalds, eating Big Mac meals and trying to ignore Gary as he continually complained about having to carry the heavy plastic bag of cash.

When the cab arrived, Levi told the driver their destination was Hammersmith, ignoring the puzzled looks shot at him by the teenagers. Kenny had recommended the cab firm so Gary's bag was thrown into the boot unceremoniously and then they were off.

The car was warm and the ride was smooth. Sean lay his head against the back seat, his mind tired, but unable to rest, replaying events that ran over and over in his head. Capital Radio was on enthusiastically playing a screaming Indie record. The music might well have been a whispering dirge for all the attention he gave it as they rolled through the pre-rush hour traffic.

Sean kept seeing the looks on the people's faces, in the street, in the shop and on the country road, shouting, pointing and cursing at him.

All his life he'd known white people feared his race and that the fear spawned hate and pre-judgement. This was obvious in the way the women clutched at their handbags when he passed them, as well as the way shopkeepers would follow him around the aisles of their stores, as though they were branding him before they even knew him. All his life Sean had seen these things and he'd accepted them, knowing they were out of his hands, knowing he couldn't change the white way of thinking.

But he'd always prided himself on being different. Before today, he hadn't robbed, mugged, rioted, or taken part in any of the numerous crimes people believed were natural for boys of his colour and age. He'd spent his whole life trying to prove to himself he was different. And now, circumstances and the environment he lived in, rather than a conscious decision had forced him to become a participant in an act completely against his nature. But had the white people noticed his difference, today, or at any other time in his life?

'No,' Sean thought angrily. And did they care that they offended him every time their newspapers blamed his people for *their* moral decline?

Did they care if every black man in most TV police dramas was a criminal, insane, or a drug pusher and that this negative image was put into homes the length and breadth of the country?

So why should I bother to be different? Why should I care? Sean thought to himself, as the car wound its way smoothly.

He stared at the gun-grey sky and the bored faces of the motorists around him. Seeing them stare back at him, just the same as they always had, he couldn't think of one single reason why he should be different, anymore.

It turned out that Hammersmith was the home of one of Levi's many girlfriends, Shawna, whom Sean had never seen before today. It was also the rendezvous Levi and Kenny had decided on weeks before the move. They parked outside the house, a tall Victorian building, with two upper floors and a basement. After Levi paid the cabbie with money from Gary's carrier bag, and gave him an extra fifty and a warning to keep his mouth shut, they climbed the steps wearily. Levi let them in with his own key. Once inside they were immediately assaulted by music and the smell of hard drugs.

Levi walked into the living room where Darren and Clarence were smoking and lying back on the leather sofa with their shoes off. The blinds were drawn, giving the room a gloomy, hazy look. A massive wooden pipe stood in one corner of the room next to a large black cupboard which held the television, and a silver Bang and Olufson hi-fi set up.

Sean took his shoes off and followed Levi inside, marvelling at the soft, ticklish feel of the carpet between his toes. The older man slapped palms with the youths cheerfully.

'What'm yout's, yuh cool?' he boomed.

'Yeah star, laughin',' they replied in unison.

They caught sight of Sean and Gary behind the Dredd and went into fits of laughter, jumping about on the sofa.

'Yes blood, wha' you sayin' star, touch me nuh,' Clarence yelled almost knocking over a glass of champagne hidden by his foot. Sean touched fists with him, wondering what they were so excited about. Darren saw his confused expression and raised his bubbling glass of liquid.

'You fucked up dat Metro proper man, had dat Rad runnin' for cover y'get me? All I heard was *BOOOOOM* star, it was like a fuckin' earthquake man. Hear what, I don't care, my man's a dapper for dat move!' He said this last to Clarence, who nodded and gave Sean the Moët bottle respectfully.

'Dere you go spee, 'ave summa dat,' he told the teen, who in turn drank deeply, sending champagne frothing down his face. Levi laughed and frowned warningly at the same time.

'Mind de carpet star!' he growled at the teen.

'Yeah yeah,' Sean replied, wiping his mouth with his hand. Levi turned to the boys on the sofa.

'Where Kenny?'

Darren looked up. 'He went Chinese wid Shawna.'

'Where de wong?'

Clarence went over to the tall cupboard and tapped a bottom drawer with his wine glass. Levi went over and opened it, pulling out the coarse sack with a faint grunt, holding his stomach.

'We put it in stacks of hundreds,' Darren injected into the silence.

Levi pulled the blinds fully closed, switched on the lights and then poured the bundles onto the carpet. He made as if to start counting, then paused and looked at Sean, who was standing by the sofa, amazed that Clarence and Darren hadn't just made off with all the money after being left alone and unguarded in the flat. Obviously the Dredd was feared and respected more than he'd thought. His own respect for the man grew at the sight of all the cash lying spread out on the carpet.

As if reading his mind, Levi winked at him from his space on the floor and grinned.

'Buil' a spliff man,' he told the boy. Sean smiled.

'I don't smoke,' he replied, slightly embarrassed. The other three groaned.

'Don't tell me dat, don't tell me dat!' Clarence was yelling, making Levi glare at him warningly. He pitched his voice lower and threw a small bag at the standing teen, which hit him in the chest lightly.

'Someone who can blas' a Rad car like dat, must bun,' he said, ignorantly.

Sean took one look at the crystal and felt uneasy again, as if he was on the threshold of a door that would take him places he'd never been to, and never wanted to visit.

Levi was watching him, the money spread out in little bundles around him, forgotten for the moment.

'Yuh smoke bone before?' he asked the teen, in a gentle manner. Sean shook his head silently.

'Try it, before yuh decide yuh don' like it,' he rumbled, before turning back to the piles of money.

Darren and Clarence were watching him studiously, while Gary snatched up the Rizla, took two sheets and passed the packet to Sean who held it for a moment, then thumbed out two, his face wearing a 'what the hell' expression. The two boys squeezed onto the three-seater, all of them watching the older man as he sat in the centre of the room, muttering numbers beneath his breath and moving the piles from his right side to his left.

Sean took the sheets and crumbled a chip of cigarette he'd ponced from Gary, then shaved the crystal with the Chinese boy's penknife. He broke it in on top of the tobacco, like he'd seen crackheads do a thousand times before on the estate. Someone passed him a piece of cardboard torn from a Rizla packet, and he rolled it between his fingers like Plasticine, until it was a round tube which he carefully placed on one end of the papers. While he was doing this, Kenny, Shawna and Levi's baby returned laden with sweet-smelling bags of food. Sean inwardly groaned. He looked around the room to see if anyone could see how nervous he was, like a student sitting a final exam, who finds his mind has gone blank for no apparent reason.

Gary, who was beside him, had his attention on his own zook and was paying him no mind. Darren and Clarence were watching the television and Levi at the same time. The Dredd was still counting money on the carpet. Shawna, a slim half-caste girl with shining grey eyes, was sorting through the cartons of food with Kenny. He was holding the baby, laughing and describing their getaway to the girl in hushed tones. Sean caught the girl's eye once and she smiled, then turned back to the bags. Sean's own stomach rumbled quietly. He closed his eyes, then got back to his task, glad no one seemed to be watching him.

He took the papers between his first and second fingers, then folded them over with his thumb, while pulling his fingers away. 'Clamp it, clamp it,' Cory's voice said in his head.

His fingers slipped and the papers rustled noisily, but no one looked up. Sean continued rolling with his thumb and fingers pausing only to lick the thin line of gum at the top of the sheet, before rolling some more, until the sticky side had disappeared.

'Clipper?' he said, pleased with what he saw.

Gary took a puff on his own zook and passed him his red Clipper lighter, his look full of admiration.

'See star, yuh a natural,' he said, as Kenny handed the food and some plastic knives and forks around the room. Meanwhile, in the middle of the room, Levi finished counting the wads of money and was beaming broadly at anyone who looked his way.

'Guess 'ow much,' he teased the boys, who were as one, sitting upright, all previous concerns distant memories now. They studied the piles and barked figures at him, like crazed antique dealers in an auction.

'Ten grand!'

'Come off it star.' Levi gave them a mystified look, as if they were morons.

'Eight!' Gary spat.

'Lower.'

'Seven an' a 'alf,' Sean threw at the Dredd. Levi laughed and spooned his food lovingly.

'Nearly dere yout's, yuh nearly dere.'

'Six gee!' Clarence said coolly, blowing his smoke sideways, away from Levi's child.

The older man put the first finger of his left hand on his nose and pointed at the teenager with his right hand, like Lionel Blair in *Give us a clue*. The room erupted in a wave of laughter from the adults and shouts of glee from the boys, who were hugging each other and touching fists happily. When the noise died down, Clarence spoke up.

'Oi, dat's a gran' each innit? Look one, two, three, four . . .'

'Yeah, yeah, I c'n count star, wha' do you?' Levi shot back at him, his rough tone for once failing to deliver the impact it usually carried. Clarence simply sat back and rubbed his hands together like an oil baron, as Levi sorted the money into equal shares. Then, picking up one of the piles, leaving the rest on the carpet, he walked past Sean, looking down on him and motioning at somewhere out of the room.

'Come nuh,' he muttered, not even stopping, or looking behind to see if Sean was following. The teen picked up his Chinese and his zook and followed the Dredd into a compact red and white kitchen, looking out onto a spacious garden below. Sean sat on a broad wooden bench, wondering what Levi was up to now.

'Yuh all right?' the older man said, his spliff jerking and moving stiffly in his mouth as his lips moved together. When he said he was, Levi pulled out a large leather wallet. With a sly wink, Levi opened it up, exposing crisp notes. He steadily counted out fifties onto the table as Sean watched, astounded and excited in equal measure. The Dredd counted until he reached three hundred pounds, then he stopped, gave Sean another leery wink and continued rolling the notes off, until five hundred pounds sat on the table in front of them, large as life. He pushed the grand he'd taken from the living room to Sean,

then sat back, saying nothing, looking pleased with his handi-
work. Sean looked at the pile then into the dark eyes of the
older man. Levi puffed on his zook, relaxed.

'What's dis?' the teen challenged.

'T'ink of it as . . . a bonus,' Levi crooned easily. Sean
frowned.

'What for, I didn't do nothin' dem man couldn't do . . .'

'Yes yuh did.' The rumble came from deep inside the man's
chest.

'Yuh got us outta a sticky situation back dere, when you tek de
wheel like dat. Yuh a good driver Sean, so yuh should go fe yuh
test, now you got de wong to do it. Or buy somet'ing to help yuh
mek up wi' dat fitness y'ave, some jewellery or sumt'in'. Yuh
cyaan neglec' a gyal like dat y'know, someone'll always be waitin'
fe you to slip up, y'get me? Anyway, fuck dat, yuh can do wha'
yuh like wi' de money. It your's y'unnerstan'. I'm jus' showin'
me appreciation for yuh quick t'inkin', all right?'

'Yeh man,' Sean replied, smiling as they touched fists. 'How
did you know me an' Sonnie had an' argument?'

Levi laughed.

''Ey star, we live in Greenside y'know,' he reminded the
teen.

Sean shook his head.

'Yeah man, ain't no secrets in the Green,' he admitted.
'Thanks Levi, it'll come in proper handy.'

'F'real,' the Dredd muttered, crushing his spliff end like an
ugly bug in the kitchen's one tin ashtray.

Sean removed the pistol nestling reassuringly against his
stomach and placed the wads of hundreds along the waistband
of his boxer shorts. Then he pinrolled his jeans tightly, so that
if the money slipped, it would get caught by his ankles and
wouldn't give some lucky bastard an unexpected great start to
the weekend. That done, he checked the safety catch and placed
the small gun in his jacket pocket, where it disappeared without
a trace. Levi eyed him as he worked.

'Yuh like dat bucky innit?'

Sean smiled. 'Yeah man, it's cold, Wha' you sayin' c'n I keep
it?'

Levi waved a hand casually and made a face. 'It yours. But

mek sure yuh look af'er it an' mek sure it stay in yuh possession, y'unnerstan'?'

'Yeah man, dat's easy,' the teen replied, thinking he couldn't wait to show the man on the estate his weapon. Levi meanwhile, got down to business, now that the pleasantries were over.

'So yuh happy wid de way t'ings run,' he asked, levelly.

Sean nodded casually and said, 'It wen' all right innit. No one was hurt, except for us an' dat was a minor sumthin'. I got myself a gee an' a half, for a minute's work . . .' Sean paused for a second, his sentence replaying slowly in his mind. Levi was silent.

'Yeah I did innit? I earned a gee an' a half, in jus' over a minute,' he laughed out loud. 'Dat's dett star!'

Levi seized his opportunity as soon as he saw it, imagining a wriggling fish: he'd hooked the teen with the bait, now it was time to bring him gently in.

'So what, 'ow would you like to earn double dat in a couple o' weeks' time.'

'How you mean?' Sean looked dubious.

'Well dis time now, we got a jewellery store raid goin' on soon, t'rough a friend o' my girl's. We lookin' to clean up star. Dat's de big time money an' if we can pull it off, we'll all be rich, y'unnerstan'? Yuh seen how easy it is to pull off a move like dat, so don't worry about gettin' nicked or nuttin', we run t'ings too smooth for dat, yuh know dat innit? So wha' yuh sayin' star, yuh in?'

Sean looked up, his eyes misty with fatigue and stress. 'I dunno man, I thought we were on a one lick t'ing star, to get my cousin outta trouble. I ain't no thief.'

'Nah, but yuh a natural getaway driver man. An' yuh handle dat shotgun wicked rudey, like a cold-blooded killer bwoy.'

Sean closed his eyes when Levi said this, his mind in turmoil. The lure of the money was so great, he could already see the gold and cash in front of him, all of it sparkling enticingly. He wanted to be part of this (and was even starting to like Levi, against his will). But at the end of the day, he wasn't a criminal and could never really be one. He'd been more scared today than ever in his life and his heart rate still didn't seem completely back to normal. It just wasn't the life for him, his cousin had been right.

He opened his eyes and stared at Levi determinedly.

'I better go man, I don't wanna do no more moves star,' he said, getting up quickly and putting on his coat.

'Hey, hol' on star,' Levi said quickly. He made as if to stop him, then changed his mind, as the teen's haunting eyes found him, probing at him distantly.

'We had an agreement,' Sean reminded him quietly.

Levi nodded and held his hands up, not knowing why he was so easy with the boy. He decided he would wait until Sean got back to normal, mundane life before he wrote him off completely.

Behind the boy's polite exterior was a dark well of anger, as yet untapped. He sat back down at the table as Sean went into the living room to say goodbye. Laughing and promising to link up with the boys again, he came back into the kitchen and looked at Levi as if he wanted to apologise once more. Shrugging, he jangled his front door keys, nervously.

'All right Levi, I'm gone man.' He reached out to touch fists with the man.

'Yes my yout', walk careful, y'unnerstan'? An' if yuh change yuh min' . . .'

Sean shook his head. 'Boy, I don't think I will star.'

Levi shrugged too and studied the youth, who was standing in the shadow of the doorway, leaning against the wall as if he was holding it up, not the other way around. With a great effort, the teen pushed himself away and with a croaking, 'Later on', he left the flat, clicking the middle door quietly behind himself.

Chapter Twelve

Sean sauntered down the road, his hands firmly in his pockets and his chin pushed deeply into his neck, trying to escape the biting wind that swelled up around him, occasionally pushing at his body like a giant hand that forbade him from moving forwards. He walked along the backroads of Hammersmith, deciding he would get to Greenside much quicker if he took these streets instead of waiting for a bus or tube. He wanted the time to think about the things that had happened to him today, as well as brood over Levi's offer of involvement in the next move.

I've sold it, he thought to himself, somewhat unfairly, as the light from the street lamps sent orange pools down onto the pavement. He wondered if the others at the flat were laughing at him even now, over their Chinese dinner and glasses of Moët.

He pulled his hands out of his pockets to make sure he hadn't lost his front door keys; as he did so, he also retrieved the slightly crumpled zook he'd rolled at Levi's flat, crushed, but still looking smokeable. He recalled the Dredd's words; 'try it before you decide that you don't like it', then, in a split second decision, he looked up, spotted a tiny corner shop and walked inside, his eyes blank.

When he came out he was clutching a blue Clipper, which he flicked a couple of times to make sure it worked properly. He also had a can of Sunkist. He waited until he'd walked a little further on, before spinning the lighter's wheel and holding the orange flame to the spliff, hearing the paper shrink and crackle as the warm glow crept up it hungrily. He waited for another second, at the threshold of the unknown again, then he took a deep pull, filling his lungs with the potent smoke.

The first taste was terrible. Sean only remembered as he took the smoke into his lungs that Cory had always said, 'I never take the first blast down, it's pure paper an' cigarette star.'

He tried to blow it all out, but a wracking cough took over him, scratching at his chest like claws, painfully tearing at his lungs. He doubled over as the coughs came again with more force and he found himself glad he'd chosen to do this out in the street, instead of back at the flat, where he would've made an exhibition of himself. Sean spat violently onto the pavement and stopped to open his can of drink, hoping it would ease the wracking in his lungs. He took large swallows which only soothed his dry throat.

The zook had gone out. He placed the can of Sunkist on somebody's front wall, sparked the spliff again and took the smoke in once more. The coughs came back, but with some effort he eventually held them down and managed to walk down the street, the zook held between his first finger and his thumb. Soon, he felt good enough to take a few more puffs.

The buzz crept up on him; he could feel it slowly flowing from his feet, spreading through his torso and into his head, where it swelled and grew. He walked on, stepping over the occasional pile of dogshit while keeping his eyes open for patrolling police cars, his legs carrying him forward mechanically.

The light breeze creeping up felt refreshingly cool on his forehead, like a cold damp towel on a hot day. He felt and saw the passing people and cars more clearly now; his lethargic feelings that threatened to overcome him back at the flat were all gone. Instead, he felt excitingly alive. He walked with a confident stride, not even moving aside when he was headed on a path leading directly towards someone. The colours and lights of the busy roads seemed blindingly clear.

When he got back to Greenside and entered his small flat, he found it dark and empty. It was only half past five and he had an urge to ring Sonia, as she was usually back from college by now, waiting for *Home and Away* to come on. He cautiously made his way to the phone, but stopped before he could pick it up as the buzz in his head intensified. The room became hot and he turned away from the telephone, heading towards his bedroom hurriedly to lie down for a bit.

Once inside, he shrugged his jacket to the floor, hearing the gun thud dully on the thin carpet; then he pulled his sweater over his head and placed it on top of the jacket. Sean closed his eyes, thoughts of college and Sonia light years away now.

Soon he heard clicks and suspicious noises in the flat that had him sitting up, concentrating hard to guess their origin. With every sound he heard, he was more and more convinced the police were massing outside, guns at the ready, to take him away. He listened. There was nothing. He lay back down, reassured for a while, but when further creaks and taps occurred, he got up, reached into his jacket and produced the pistol, staring in wonder at its hard, sharp lines and smooth barrel for a moment. Then he lay down with his arm across his chest, his finger curled around the trigger, waiting for the buzz of the rock to pass, feeling like a carved statue, solid and immovable, hewed from the flesh of mountains. He stared unblinkingly at the rugged ceiling, listening.

That night nobody came for him.

Fate was an odd thing.

In the course of the week following the robbery the teen looked at his neighbourhood, his flat and his family through new and interested eyes. For the first time in his life, he took in the surroundings he was accustomed to, in terms of money.

On the estate, he *really* noticed how old and dishevelled the place was, instead of just talking about it in disgust with his friends: he noticed the way rubbish piled the streets, smelling so bad, he made sure he never ate breakfast until days after the binmen had come, sometimes not even then.

He also saw the way the battered and heavy-looking front doors to the hundreds of flats were all shades of colours; purples, pinks, blues and greens.

Most of all, he saw the estate as a tired old clock that had been overwound, its springs slowly uncoiling, until they could do so no more. Not so much the people: Greenside was a lively place and there was always something happening, or someone to go and see. But when you looked around at the buildings . . .

There had been rumours of asbestos flying around the flats for months, yet Sean, when he looked at the cracked boarded up windows and steel lifts streaked with vomit, believed asbestos was the very least of their worries.

He now had only one way to describe his mother's flat and it was a fairly simple one. It was a shithole.

Yeah, he'd lived there all his life – but maybe that was why he'd been so blind to its failings. He now knew there really was more to life than this; he'd seen it in the plush sofas and luxurious carpets at both Levi's and Razor's flats.

Sean wasn't sure how much the grand and a half had helped him in his realisations. He had suspicions it had given him at least a little prod, forcing him to open his eyes. He wondered if Cory, Shannon or his mother knew what wonderful things there were out there and how reachable they were.

He *did* know that his newfound wealth and insight had made him aware of just how much Cory's injury had affected his mother. He understood how she felt. Cory was a prized possession in the Bradley household, as he was Ron and Helen's only son. Letting anything remotely bad happen to him was just not on.

At least Sean and Shannon could let off steam (and lately there had been a few tense, petty arguments in the Bradley home). But for their mother there was no such release, and there'd been none since his uncle's death. Bernice had always been the strong one, both father and mother to them all, able to take control and ride a bad situation to its peak.

Sometimes Sean wondered if things would've been different if his father had stayed around. The unseen man he was named after didn't register in his mind often, but when he did, it was usually with a great deal of hate. Sean could see Bernice struggled with three of them to look after and no one had heard anything from his dad in all those years. When they were younger, he and Cory had argued over who had it worse: Sean, who knew his father wasn't interested in him, or Cory, who knew his father *had* been interested in him. It had been a pointless argument at the time, but sometimes Sean remembered their shouts and tears, and now asked himself the same question.

Only this time he came to the conclusion his mother had it the worst out of all of them.

He'd spent the weekend trying dismally to contact Sonia, but failing on every attempt. On Sunday, her phone rang on and on, presumably with no one to answer it. Later, the same day, it rang twice, then the receiver was picked up with a click.

'Hello?'

He'd smiled at the sound of her voice.

'Sonnie . . . ?'

Click.

When he rang back, all he got was an engaged tone, infuriatingly loud in his ears. He'd thrown the phone on the floor in anger, then picked it up again, feeling like a fool. Luckily, everyone else was still in bed.

On Monday, he counted out five hundred pounds from underneath his bed and took a ride to Hatton Garden, home of London's best gold and jewellery dealers.

He stayed there for hours, mindful of flashing his money in front of the coarse-looking men who roamed the streets. He bought Cory a rope chain of medium thickness, with a gold weed leaf attached by a thin hook. For Shannon and his mother, he purchased rings with small but sparkling diamonds in them. But he could hardly give them their gifts, seeing as he wasn't even working and he had no feasible explanation for his wealth.

The real reason for his journey was to buy Sonia a present to make up. He settled for a beautiful necklace and a pair of diamond earrings that looked like crystallised tear drops. The salesman told him he'd made an excellent choice.

Once back at the estate, he made a beeline for Sonia's block. The gloom and grey skies of the last few days were steadily passing over the city, revealing a blue so clear, it was nearly white. It wasn't hot, but it was warmer than it had been. The estate was full of people roaming around, or hanging about the corners of their blocks, smoking weed, mindful of passing police cars. There was a cluster of people standing by the entrance to the high rise, while a car parked by the kerb was thumping Jungle into the air. Sean raised a hand in greeting.

'Raa, Sean, wha' you sayin' rudey!'

Jason Taylor, the boy Cory had thought was interested in

Rosie, smiled at Sean and shook his hand firmly. Johnny and Raymond were there, their faces screwed up and mean. Stacey Collins, a young black youth of about fourteen was there too, still dressed in his school uniform. Raymond nudged Sean.

'Long time star, innit?' he said, swaying to the music as he talked.

Sean looked at the others standing in the high rise's awning and nodded his hellos to them, touching fists with the boys and kissing the girls on the cheek.

'Hear what, I'm gonna go check Sonnie,' he told the crew, who nodded and told him to say hello. He headed inside, followed by many pairs of eyes. In no time the crowd were talking about something and somebody else.

Sean got to Sonnie's landing and rang the bell once. He felt a tug of anticipation as the door swung open, but was disappointed to see Marlena, Sonia's college friend, standing at the door like a sentry.

'Yes?' she barked, sounding as if she was trying to be as unfriendly as possible. Sean ignored her tone.

'Hey Marlena, how's it goin'. Is Sonnie dere please?'

'She don' wanna see you,' she told him simply.

Sean took a deep breath, looked at the ceiling and rolled his eyes. 'Come on man, I bin tryin' to say I'm sorry for the whole fuckin' week an' she won't let me. What more c'n I do eh?'

Marlena shrugged her slim shoulders. 'I dunno, cause she won't tell me what you done, y'get me? All I know, is you're gonna have to do more than huff n' puff to bring her roun'. She's fumin'.'

Sean rested his head against the door frame, eyes closed, feeling relief that Sonia had kept his plans to herself. Marlena watched him, sympathy creeping into her face reluctantly.

'You wanna give her a message?' she asked, a little more gently now. Sean shook his head, then changed his mind and dug into his pocket for the two jewellery boxes, shoving them into the girl's hands unceremoniously.

'Jus' tell her I said I'm sorry man. I'll come back another time, yeah?'

He wandered off down the corridor, half hoping Sonia's voice would call him back to the door.

No voice came.

When he got out into the streets below, he was amazed to see the crowd scrabbling around in the dust and fighting over something on the floor. The girls watched and kept their distance. Laughing at their antics, Sean asked them what was going on.

'I dunno,' a white girl called Caroline said, as the boys punched and kicked at each other. Jason held something up in the air, out of the reach of the others. Sean couldn't see what it was and he moved closer, interested.

'We were jus' standin' 'ere, when summick come flying out the window. Someone musta chucked it innit? I think it's jewellery . . .' the girl continued, oblivious to the fact Sean had now left her side.

While she was talking, he'd managed to get a better look at the object that they were brawling over. He ran over to the fighting youths and held Jason's hand tightly.

'Oi, dat's my t'ings man,' he said, as the girls watched this new unfolding drama. Jason tried to pull away, but Sean wasn't joking and he tugged tighter.

'Don't talk shit, it jus' fell out the window,' the tall boy replied, his conviction that all was fair lending his voice power and strength. Sean twisted his arm and bent it backwards, trying to force his grip to loosen. The others backed away and voiced their opinions from afar.

'Sean, Sean, it did fall man, what'm t'you?'

''llow it man, don't fight over dem t'ings dere star.'

'Raa, man's goin' on darkheart, f'real,' they said, but made no attempt to get involved. Sean got angry rapidly.

'I jus' bought dat to give to Sonia an' I . . . want . . . it . . . *back*!'

He prised the necklace from Jason's grasp with his left hand, while clutching and bending his wrist with his right. Jason let out a shout of pain, and the necklace glinted in his palm, its tiny links wrapped around his fingers. Still holding the boy in his iron grip, Sean unwrapped the necklace from Jason's hand, while snatching quick glances at the others to make sure they didn't try anything.

Soon enough the chain was free. He looked it over to check for scratches, then craned his neck towards Sonia's window, shielding his eyes from the sun. It was closed. Angrily, Sean looked at the others.

'All right, where's the earrings?'

Everyone looked at him, blankly.

'Don't fuck around man, I bought 'em today, jus' gimme 'em for fuck's sake. I know Sonnie dashed 'em, I can see the box dere.'

Sean pointed to the concrete pavement, where the tiny earring box lay dented and open, the burgundy interior looking pitifully empty. When he turned back to face the youths, Stacey and his friends were inching away slowly, their guilt written all over their faces. Sean rested his gaze on the young schoolboy.

'I ain't rampin' y'know. Gimme my t'ings man, 'fore I have to get milly on the situation.'

'I ain't got your t'ings star,' Stacey shot back, looking Sean straight in the eyes, showing no fear.

Sean laughed disbelievingly, then reached in his waistband for the weight of the SIG-Sauer, exposing the rough-looking black handle. The youths gasped collectively, stepping back as quick as they could. Stacey's eyes opened wide in shock and the fear that had been missing before was there in full view now, making Sean almost feel sorry for him. He recalled Levi's words about people and guns again and smiled inwardly. The Dredd was more right than he knew.

'Okay, okay, okay, all right, you c'n 'ave 'em star, Jesus!'

Stacey dug into his pocket and passed over the earrings, quick as a flash. Sean inspected them carefully and gave the youth a cold stare, before walking over to the box, picking it up and taking one look at Sonia's closed window. He walked away without a word to anyone. Jason rubbed his aching wrist, watching the teen stroll along the street and avoiding the glances of his peers.

'Raa, Sean's goin' on dark spee,' he grumbled, as Stacey and his friends raved about the teen's gun, as though threats with a pistol were an everyday occurrence. Johnny, Raymond and the assortment of girls watching looked at each other, shocked at what they had seen. Collectively, they all thought those words were the biggest understatement from Jason in his entire life.

*

Depressed, Sean went back home. He let himself into his flat quietly. The smell of cooking assailed him, making his stomach rumble painfully. There was nobody in the kitchen, so he went into the living room, where he found his mother ironing a hefty looking pile of clothes. Steam puffed around her, making her look like a tired Genie, sapped of her magic.

He said a brief hello, then went to his room, after knocking unsuccessfully on his sister's door. Bernice continued ironing, the TV blaring beside her, lost in her own troubles.

In his room, Sean lay on his bed listening to the radio, trying not to think about the crack he'd smoked on Friday, and failing dismally. After all the things he'd heard, all the talk of how bad the drug was, it turned out it wasn't that bad at all. He'd been drunk plenty of times, but a crack buzz was somewhat cleaner, less controlling than the buzz of alcohol. There were minuses to go with the plusses though; chief among those were the way it made him feel hard, as if he was untouchable by his peers or the police. He knew he didn't really have the balls to shoot someone cold bloodedly, but when he'd been walking and smoking that zook, he'd wanted to draw his SIG and let off a shot, just to see how it would sound. Of course now, he thought that was crazy, but back then . . .

He switched on his Sega and was getting into some *Mortal Combat Two* when there was a loud crash from somewhere outside his room. The sound of his mother's voice, swearing in anger came to him, slightly muffled behind the door. Sean was up and he raced to the living room, only to find it empty.

The ironing board lay on the floor, along with the grey Tefal iron which his mother had had the presence of mind to unplug. One of the skirts she'd been ironing lay burnt and steaming on the floor. Bernice was nowhere in sight, so he headed for the kitchen calling her name.

'Mum? Mum, are you all right?'

He heard the sound of running water from the bathroom. Slowly, he walked over, sure she was in here. He knocked twice.

'Mum?'

He pushed at the door handle. Locked. Then he heard his mother speak up.

'I'm all right Sean, I jus' had a little accident with the iron.'

His mother's voice was quivering, not like her usual firm tone at all. Sean pushed the door handle again, then pressed his face close to the chipboard and spoke again, coaxing her.

'Mum, unlock the door will you?'

'I'm all right Sean, gimme a second.'

'Mum, I'll take the lock off if I have to.'

He waited for her reply and was rewarded with the click of the lock turning slowly. The door swung open. His mother was sitting on the side of the bath, her eyes red from crying and her hand underneath the running tap. Sean could see the heel of her hand was red too, presumably from being burnt. He went over to her and put a consoling arm around her shoulder.

'What's up Mum, why you so upset?' Sean asked, as he studied the red mark on her hand. It was a small burn, that would probably need some cream, but that was all. Sean was sure he'd seen his mother get worse burns than this doing many other things around the house.

'I was tryin' to do two things at once,' she replied, her tears clogging her throat. 'I ran to the kitchen 'cause the rice was boilin' out an' the iron must've fallen on the clothes an' burnt my good skirt. It's ruined! Then I picked it up and managed to burn myself in the process . . .'

Her eyes glinted in the light from the sixty-watt bulb above them. Sean hugged her tighter.

'Don't worry about the skirt, I'll get you a new one,' he choked, without thinking.

'With what?'

His mother gave him one of her looks. Sean stumbled a bit and gave her a smile.

'Uhh . . . I'll save up?' he said, in a tiny, questioning voice.

Bernice waved his offer away with her good hand. 'No thanks, you save what little money you got for yourself. Besides, we need more than the price of a new skirt to help us out.'

'What d'you mean?'

'Well, the phone bill's come, that's one hundred and eighty pounds; the gas bill's on its way, 'cause it always comes a couple of days after the phone bill . . . *Then* I got my poll tax . . . I'm just fed up Sean, I can't take it anymore. I was upstairs ironing earlier an' there's just so many things for me to think about, my head was nearly spinning. Cory comes out of hospital this week and he's goin' to need lookin' after . . . I can just about pay the bills, work and feed you lot, without more on my plate . . .'

She paused, looking at the ceiling, 'I suppose I've just had enough of the whole thing, that's all. No money, no escape, that's what your uncle used to say an' I used to disagree with him. Look how long we've been here an' nothin's changed. In fact, it's got worse. I just don't know what to do anymore Sean, I mean, how long am I supposed to handle this for?'

Sean was quiet, for the first time in his life thinking maybe his mother had dreams and ambitions that went further than raising three kids alone on a council estate. He never really thought about how the crime, dirt and inadequate housing – freezing in winter, baking hot in the summer – affected his mother.

The thoughts she'd just expressed, were ones he heard time and time again, all over Greenside. They begged for a change, almost any kind of change. At the end of the day, he'd forgotten his mother was a human being. Instead he'd seen her as some force that would always be there to listen to his complaints, impervious to the many things wrong on the estate.

How could he help her though?

Sean looked at his mother thoughtfully. Bernice saw him and tried to fix herself up, with a strained attempt at lightheartedness.

'Oh well, don't mind me, I'm just goin' through my mid-life crisis a little early,' she told him, wiping her eyes. Sean kissed her on the top of her head and stood up, helping her off the bath carefully.

'I jus' want you to do one thing for me,' he said, as he led her from the small room, his tone brooking no argument. 'I want you to go in your room, lie down an' not get up until I finish the dinner, yeah?'

'But Sean . . .' his mother started.

'No arguments,' he interrupted sternly, holding up one finger and wagging it like a schoolmaster. Bernice gave a laugh, making Sean feel a little better about her state of mind.

'Looks like I got no choice,' she joked, as her son steered her into her bedroom.

Looks like I ain't got no choice either, he thought, as he came to a major decision.

An hour and a half later, Sean was knocking at 42 Beechwood House a little apprehensively, feeling the night air bite at his cheeks. Levi opened the door and beamed at Sean, his zook hanging out of his mouth unlit, as though it had been there for days.

'What'm my yout', wha' gwaan?' he said touching fists with Sean from the doorway. Scan shrugged and looked at his feet.

'Nuttin' man . . . I wanted to chat t'you about dat jewellery t'ing, y'get me?' he mumbled, his chin by his neck.

Levi looked stunned at first, but he soon collected himself and motioned for Sean to enter as he walked back into the flat.

'What, c'n I blast dat ziggy?' Sean asked Levi, surprising the Dredd once more. He pointed at the unlit spliff and licked his lips, probably unaware his mouth even moved. Levi passed him the zook and his Clipper without a word, only smiling when his back was turned to the youth.

Sean, sauntering behind Levi, lit the zook, stepped into the Dredd's back room, and entered a whole new world.

The doctor attending to Cory at St Charles' hospital finally decided he could go home the Thursday after Sean's successful post office raid. Cory grabbed an apple from his dwindling supply and for the millionth time, he wondered where Sean had got to, after nearly a week of no visits. To put it mildly, the youth was annoyed.

He knew Sean had pulled the raid off successfully; he'd spoken to Shannon and Bernice and they showed no signs of any major upheavals in the Bradley home. He found himself reluctantly thinking, maybe a worse thing had happened: maybe the raid had gone *too* well. Needless to say, that thought scared him. It scared him a lot.

Even when Thursday came and he'd packed all his things into carrier bags, he looked up at the clicking sound of approaching feet, to see Shannon and his Aunt Bernice coming down the centre of the ward, but no Sean. Disappointed, he sat on the bed, fuming inside, yet trying to maintain his composure.

'Where's Sean man?' he asked Shannon, as Bernice gave back the flower pots they'd borrowed. His cousin shrugged and pulled her face into a derisive sneer.

'College, he says,' she growled in a low voice. Cory stared at her.

'Why d'you say it like dat?'

He looked around to see Bernice returning, looking strained and tired.

'I'll tell you later,' she said quickly. She punched him on the arm, making him yelp.

'I'm glad you're comin' back squirt,' she told him, which made him smile and rub his arm, not knowing whether he should be pleased or angry.

Fifteen minutes later, his aunt was swinging the car through the chunky blocks of the estate. It felt undeniably good to be back and the sight of so many familiar faces made him want to get out of the car straightaway, touching fists and slapping palms like he'd never been gone. When the car pulled up by Denver, the kids from the block rushed around him inquisitively.

'Cory, when you gonna play football with us?'

'Cory, when's your leg gonna be better?'

'Oi, you gonna brok up the guy dat did it?'

A round-faced white youth joined the kids late and squinted through the thin glass of the window at the Bradleys.

'My dad says you're in a gang. Are you?' he asked innocently.

Cory got out of the car carefully, trying to ignore the children for now. When he was free from the confines of the small car he turned to face the kids.

'Pass, pass, pass an' pass. Ask me another time man, I'm too tired to be interrogated now.'

'When you're better, I'm gonna smash you at World Cup,' the white kid screamed, before the three Bradleys entered the building, shaking their heads and grinning. Once on their floor, Cory looked out of the window and smiled at the estate spread out below him. Despite all the things he'd been through here it was good to be home.

While his aunt and his cousin headed for the living room to relax over a cup of tea, he made straight for his bedroom. He'd hidden a half ounce of weed under Sean's bed, safe in the knowledge that no one would think of looking for it there. Prior to the armed, Sean brought weed to the hospital for him to smoke in the toilets, but when he had failed to turn up in the last week, Cory had to roast until his evening visits which never happened.

Cory opened the door awkwardly, cursing at the way the crutches restricted him. He hobbled inside and pushed the door closed with the plastic end of one crutch. He studied the tiny space between Sean's bed and his own like a mountaineer at the foot of a steep and treacherous climb. He placed his crutches in a corner and, wary of hurting his leg, he put both hands on Sean's mattress and lowered himself down slowly, the muscles in his arms jumping.

He soon touched the plastic bag and heard a familiar rustling, so he grabbed at it and pulled until the bag could be seen in the light of the room. It was then, with faint surprise, he clocked it was not the same bag he'd pushed under the bed, weeks ago. He looked inside, thinking Sean had changed the bags since he'd been away. What he saw made him gasp.

The bag was crammed with an assortment of pound notes. Fifties, twenties, tens and fives were all together, in no kind of order, filling the bag to the brim. Cory looked around himself, sure he'd heard a noise outside. But when he listened closer he decided it was just his imagination.

'Well cuz, you sure bin busy!' he muttered, putting the bag back firmly where he'd got it from, then hunting around again. After pulling out some old *Star Wars* figures he hadn't seen in ten years, and an old D lock with no key, he finally heard that satisfying rustle of plastic again. He pulled his arm out once more, gripping it tightly. This time, he was happy to see his bag of weed in his fist.

He opened it, still lying on the floor. Immediately, his nose was caressed by the sweet smell of herbs. He put the bag on the bed and raised himself up as well.

I'm gonna wrap the biggest zook ever built, he told himself as he sat on the bed, his leg protruding stiffly in front of him. Hold on a sec', he thought, as he looked at the bag's contents more carefully. There didn't look like anywhere near a half ounce in the bag; he didn't even think there was a quarter, from what he could see. Before he'd gone to the hospital, the half had been compressed into a hard block, making it easy to weigh and cut. Now the block was gone and in its place were broken up buds and dust, which half-filled the bag. Cory hopped over to the desk, trying to control his fury. There was only one other smoker in the house. That was his cousin Shannon. He'd be having words with her soon.

He pulled open drawers until he found a slim black set of digital scales, as accurate as you could possibly get. Then he emptied the weed onto a piece of cardboard kept in the room solely for chopping or separating drugs, and placed the bag on the scales. When he'd weighed it, he tipped the weed back inside and weighed both, with a practised eye. His half was now an eighth. The results were as he'd expected.

He tied the bag back up, pushed it into his side of the desk, and left the room, looking for Shannon and using one crutch to lean on. When he reached the living room, where he'd left her, he found Bernice sitting in front of the television, half asleep.

'Have you seen Shannon Auntie?' he asked, not sure if he should wake her.

'She's in her room,' Bernice yawned, covering her mouth delicately. Cory peered at her.

'D'you wanna blanket?' he asked, a little concerned at the bags underneath her eyes. She nodded and lay back.

'Thank you Cory, you're an angel my dear. I should be looking after you, not the other way around anyway, it's a liberty.'

Cory kissed his teeth and headed for the airing cupboard, throwing his words over his shoulder. 'You looked after me for long enough Auntie, I can't screw. Anyway I c'n look after myself, so don't you worry about me.'

He came back slowly, with the thick blanket in one hand, which his aunt took gratefully.

'I'll just have a quick nap before I make the dinner,' she croaked. By the time Cory left the room, she was breathing deeply. He hobbled to Shannon's room, where Garage music was thumping from behind her heavy door and knocked with his knuckles.

'Come in!' she yelled, over the loud beats. Cory fumbled with the doorknob and entered. Shannon was lying on her bed, pen in hand, busily writing in her thick college folder. She looked up as her cousin came in the room and turned the music down with her remote.

'Bet you're glad to be home,' she said, with a knowing smile. Cory nodded.

'I sure am,' he agreed. 'Dat hospital food's shit star, no substance. I can't wait to get my teeth into some o' your mum's chicken boy.'

They laughed and Shannon patted beside her on the bed.

'Come an' sit down instead of standin' by the door silly, you make me feel bad. What's up anyway, you look like you're brewin'.'

Cory went over to the bed and sat down, leaning heavily on Shannon's bedside cabinet, making it quiver with the strain. When he was as comfortable as he could get, he turned to his cousin, trying to keep an accusing tone out of his voice.

'Yeah, I am brewin' slightly Shan, dere's mad t'ings gwaanin' in dis house. Dis time now, before I was in St Charles, I put a half o' green under my bed, for safe keepin', yeah? Today I come back lookin' forward to a big ziggy an' when I look, dere's about an eighth lef', I swear to God.'

'An' you think *I* took it?' Shannon said, in a monotone that spelled trouble. Cory winced and squirmed about, before answering.

'Weell, I don't think you took it, I jus' thought raa, Shannon's the only smoker, so I bes' start wid you innit.'

She watched him, then reached into the glass ashtray and passed him half a zook sitting there.

'Smoke dat,' she ordered, firmly.

'Shannon—'

'Nah, go on.'

She pushed the zook at him. He took it, motioning for the lighter, and lit it, drawing in deeply. The unmistakable flavour of Rocky hit his tastebuds, making them water as he inhaled. Nodding, he took another two quick blasts, before passing it to Shannon, who was laughing gently.

'S' all right innit?' she chuckled.

'Yeah yeah,' Cory smiled back.

'I bin smokin' ash all week Cory, I ain't even got no weed an' I certainly wouldn't sting yours.'

She blew smoke rings absently. Cory squirmed again and shrugged. 'Yeah man I know, when I thought about it, it jus' didn't make sense. But if you didn't take it, who the fuck did?'

Shannon said nothing and eyed him, one eyebrow raised, puffing away. Cory didn't understand the look at first, but it didn't take him long to see what she meant. His mouth hung open as he finally got the message.

'Sean?' he laughed, holding his belly and shaking his head in disbelief. 'Nah, you're havin' a laugh Shannon, seriously. You can't tell me Sean, of all people, smoked over a quarter. What d'you think his name is, Chong?'

Cory laughed out loud again and nudged Shannon's arm, mystified, despite his mirth. Shannon clicked her pen and looked morose.

'I ain't tellin' you nothin', I'm as baffled about your weed as you are man. But what I do know is Sean's bin acting proper weird since you wen' into hospital. You know him an' Sonnie ain't speakin' innit?'

Cory stopped laughing and frowned deeply. 'No, I didn't know dat. What happened?'

'I dunno. I asked an' Sean gave me some crap about him not goin' to college.'

'Eh?' This was getting worse by the second, Cory thought.

'Yeah man, he's bein' the livin' secretive these days, I'm tellin' you. I know he ain't bin college dis week, cause his lecturer called, askin' if he was all right. Luckily mum was at work an' I covered for him, but I don't see why I should, if he won't even tell me what I'm doin' it for. He goes out like normal, bag an' everyt'ing an' he comes in when everyone's in bed, sneakin' about like a fuckin' thief or summick. I don't even think he knows you're out an' about star, cause no one's seen him to tell him, y'get me?'

'Oh man.'

Cory was covering his eyes with his hands, suddenly feeling faint and dizzy at the same time. He closed his eyes, wishing he could close his ears as well. He just couldn't take in what he'd been hearing, without feeling like his whole world was turning upside down.

Sean not going to college?

Sean breaking up with Sonnie?

Sean *smoking*!

He could not, *would not* believe how badly things had fucked up in his short time away from Greenside. 'An' you know who's fault it is, don't you?' a little voice said in his ear.

'Nah man,' he said aloud, his eyes closed tight, causing Shannon to stare at him, finally noticing something was wrong. She opened her mouth to ask him if he was okay, when the phone rang insistently, startling them both. Shannon leaned over and picked up her extension.

'Hello . . . yeah, he's right here . . . I'm okay, not too bad . . . yeah, yeah . . . all right . . . 'bye.'

Shannon held the receiver out in Cory's direction.

'Who is it?'

'I think it's Rosie.'

Cory lifted the phone to his ear delicately.

'Hey.'

'Hiya!'

The voice on the other end of the line sounded lively and full of high spirits.

'How's it feel to be home?' she asked, her husky voice tickling his ear. Cory smiled.

'It's safe star, I'm glad to be outta St Charles' I'm tellin' you. All I wanna do is bun some greenery an' put my feet up for the rest o' the day, y'unnerstan'?'

'So what, you ain't comin' out den?'

There was a touch of pique in Rosie's voice, which made Cory laugh gently, not wishing to offend the girl.

'Hey, I'm the sick one, you should be comin' to check me!' he told her, truthfully. The girl sniffed and whispered her next sentence temptingly down the line to him.

'Yeah, but you ain't got the house to yourself, have you now?' Cory's ears perked up.

'What, you indoors on your Jack Jones?' he squeaked, not daring to think of the implications in her words. Rosie chuckled.

'Yeah, my aunt's gone my cousin's in Stratford for the evenin'. She won't be back for ages star. Why don't you come by, I'll even come over to your block an' walk you if you want.'

'Nah, dat's all right man, I'll jus' come straight over star.'

Cory tried not to sound too eager, but failed dismally. Shannon raised her eyebrow again, but this time she was grinning.

'Make sure you do,' Rosie was saying, close in his ear. 'I bin lookin' forward to spendin' some time alone wid you, you know dat innit?'

'Yeah man, same 'ere star. Hear what, I'll be over shortly, yeh?'

'OK, jus' don't be too long,' Rosie told him, before ringing off.

Cory put the phone down. Finally, the wide grin fighting to appear on his face burst out like a flower blooming in spring sunshine. Shannon nudged him and winked like a dirty old man.

'Oi, oi, you an' Rosie gettin' serious now are you?' she teased. Cory got up and reached for his crutches.

'Yeah man – listen, if you see Sean, tell him to come check me at Rosie's no matter what time it is, yeah?'

'All right, she lives on the ground floor of Beechwood, innit?'

'Yeah, yeah, the blue door. I'll see you later.'

'Have a good time,' Shannon leered. Cory shut the door on her dark smiling face, feeling a little better now, a little more alive. Hopefully, his time spent with Rosie would help him take his mind off his problems for a while.

Sean was standing on the third-floor landing outside Levi's house wondering what to do. He'd been knocking on the thick door on and off all day, desperate to talk business with the Dredd, but unable to get into the flat. Instead, he hung around with the loafers of Greenside – boys like Art, Johnny and Ray, as well as a handful of others who didn't go to college, didn't work and didn't even juggle. His head felt strange from the after effects of smoking in Art's bedroom. His mouth was dry and aching for a drink, but he couldn't shake the feeling he shouldn't move, just in case someone came. He thought back to the last few days, pulling at his top lip absently with his right hand.

From the moment he'd decided he'd do the jewellery raid, he'd been exposed to a life that previously he'd regarded with disdain, believing he knew better and that his studying was the way to make real money and a real life for Sonnie and himself. On the day Levi had passed him the cool-tasting crack spliff, he had led him into the back room, saying there was someone he wanted the teen to meet. Sean had nodded and puffed on the zook, coughing a little but managing to do it quietly.

He had entered the room behind the dealer to see a broad black man with a handsome half-caste man dressed in Armani, sitting on the wooden chairs, surrounded by large dirty-looking holdalls. They looked hard, their eyes set deep in their skulls. As one of them built a bone spliff, he noticed their knuckles were gnarled and lumpy like old tree stumps, as if they'd given and received a lot of damage over the years.

The three men proceeded to talk about guns (which, Sean assumed, were in the holdalls), drugs and women, while he listened to their tales, entranced by their supreme confidence. It was obvious they were far higher up on the crime scale than even Levi, and Sean sat in his uncomfortable seat, feeling uneasy and out of place. Yet he could not move, as the stories that they told made their powering getaway on that Friday seem like kid's stuff. The dark-skinned man held the zook straight up so Sean could see it. Apprehensively, he got up and took it, again a little scared of embarrassing himself. Levi smiled, motioning at him.

'Dis de smartest yout' inna Greenside, believe,' he'd told the men, sounding proud. 'He a cold getaway driver too, don't even 'ave 'im licence, yet 'im a handle de ride like Mansell on dat post office job.'

The men nodded and looked at Sean in a stern, but not unfriendly way. The lighter-skinned man stretched his arm out and shook Sean's hand, prompting his friend to do the same.

'Dem call me Shakes,' he said, smiling and exposing his gold front tooth.

'Trevor,' the broad one said, his designer glasses catching the light, making his eyes impossible to read. That done, the men discussed prices for the guns, bartering skilfully and in a manner befitting old comrades. They agreed to leave the weapons in the flat until they were sold, when Levi would then pay for what was gone and return the rest. The men ruminated until Trevor's phone went off, loud in the comparative silence of the room.

After a few rapid, hushed words the two were quickly off, telling Sean to look after himself and enjoy the zook. The teen raised a hand as Levi saw them out.

'Y'know dem?' the Dredd questioned, when he came back into the room, smiling toothily. Sean shook his head. 'Dat's de Bruddas Grimm star! Well, two o' dem anyway.'

'Yeah an' who're they?' Sean asked. The name had been mentioned to him before around the manor, but he couldn't remember who'd said it. Levi laughed and beckoned for the zook.

'Star, dem man wha' yuh call gangsta!' he said as he lifted the spliff to his lips.

'Me know dem since we was yout's man. They bin runnin' t'ings inna de Grove since then. They will juggle anyt'ing, kill anyone, y'unnerstan'? I heard one of their people, some brer call Jus' Juice, shot a man in front of 'im bredrins an' dem couldn't even say a word, dem 'affe jus' stan' up an' watch y'unnerstan'? Dem man don't ramp believe me.'

Sean had been a little sceptical, thinking there was no way a man would let his friend get shot barefaced and just watch. Then, recalling the men's faces and their hard hands, he supposed anything was possible.

'Dat's de difference between Yankee gangsta an' English gangsta,' Levi was saying contentedly. 'A Yankee 'ave a big car, nuff, nuff gold, bere gullies, y'unnerstan'. He run 'im shit tight, but dere's one problem. Everybody knows what my man does an' who he is, y'unnerstan'? Man wanna move to him, be they Rads or 'im enemy, dem know where fe fin' 'im. Dis time now, yuh coulda pass a English gangsta on street, tear up jeans, tatty hat, ole car an' yuh don't know what de man on, y'get me? Why yuh t'ink de police dem so afraid an' bawl fe weapon to shoot we wid? It ca' dem can't tell who's who, y'get me? Dem don't know star.'

Sean had nodded, seeing the sense in Levi's words. It had been the first of many lessons in that week.

Now, standing outside Levi's flat, Sean put his hood up with a smile as the memory faded. The evening wind was strong this high up from the ground, pushing and pulling at his hood. He looked down, wondering if he should just go home, sure Levi was gone for the whole night. A lurching figure came around the corner of the block at a steady pace. It took Sean a second to realise the lurching was due to crutches. He recognised the face a second later.

'Cory!' he yelled, waving his arms to catch his cousin's attention. Cory looked up, peering at the block, until Sean shouted.

'Hol' up a sec'!'

Sean raced down the hard steps, coming very close to breaking his own leg a few scary times. When he reached the ground floor, he sprinted over to the teen, alive with joy at the sight of him. Cory watched him come over, feeling apprehensive and a little let down, imagining he could see Sean's changes written all over his face. Sean stopped as he got closer to the boy, finally seeing his stern expression and noticing his aloof manner.

'What's up cuz?' he asked, his face concerned. Cory shrugged and pushed a piece of wood on the pavement with his crutch.

'I should be askin' you "what's up?"' Cory said seriously. 'Dis time now, I come outta hospital today an' you wasn't even dere to see me home man. Dat's cold.'

Sean looked at the floor, upset.

'Shit Cory, I'm sorry, but dere's so much goin' on man . . . I didn't even know you was comin' out star.'

'You would've known if you bothered to come an' check me. You didn't even phone to tell me if the move wen' OK or fuckin' nothin' man . . .' Cory looked around as if suddenly realising where they were. 'An' wha' the fuck you doin' comin' outta Levi's block? Don't tell me you bin movin' with my man Sean, don't star.'

Sean rolled his eyes. 'All right I won't. But Cory, I c'n understan' why you're screwin', if you jus' gimme a chance, I'll explain it t'you, y'get me?'

'So what,' Cory barked, his temper getting the better of him. 'You gotta explanation for my half ounce of weed becomin' a fuckin eighth eh? Wha' you sayin' about dat star?'

'Why don't we go home an' I'll tell you all about it,' Sean proposed, deciding the only way to bring Cory around was to bring him in. His cousin groaned and kissed his teeth.

'What, right now Sean? Listen, I was jus' goin' over to Rosie's, true I'm sure she invited me over for the wuk! Can't we talk tomorrow spee, I'm fuckin' horny star.'

Sean shrugged and made a face.

'Listen, you bury me for not comin' to check you an' not explainin' myself, then when I try to, you tell me you can't chat 'cause you wanna *fuck*? Rosie ain't goin' nowhere.'

'Neither are you star.'

'All right fuck it, forget the whole fuckin' thing!' Sean shouted, causing Cory to jerk his head up in surprise. He couldn't remember the last time Sean had lost his temper, but he was sure it was a long time ago. Tanya had told him about his cousin's ruck with Dougie, but it had been years since he actually witnessed Sean blow up and lose his cool. The shock froze him in place, as Sean started to stomp away without a backward glance. He looked longingly at Rosie's front door, torn for a second. Then he turned and hopped in pursuit of Sean, as quick as he could.

'Hey! Hey Sean, wait up!' he shouted. 'Sean, slow the fuck down man!'

Up ahead, Sean turned to face him, hands in his pockets, frowning. Cory hobbled over to his side and eyed him curiously.

'*Damn*, wha' you gettin' so steamed up for?' he asked, panting as he joined him. Sean's face didn't change.

'I jus' had enough of everyone goin' on at me man, stressin' me out. It's too much star. Oi, you ready to walk.'

'Yeah yeah.'

They strolled along the pavement slowly, the only sound the steady thump of Cory's crutches as they hit the ground. Sean spoke without looking at him.

'I got the money for dat green at home. I was jus' sellin' it, dat's all.'

'I know, I see some of it when I was lookin' under the bed,' Cory answered.

He looked back, wondering if Rosie was watching him stumble away from her block, cursing his name. He tripped, and quickly turned back to Sean, inwardly lamenting his loss.

'So who's bin stressin' you out cuz?' he asked, not wanting to think about the girl anymore.

'Ah, you know, Sonnie an' Shannon; Sonnie mostly,' Sean admitted. 'She ain't spoken to me since I showed her the ku dat day. I tried everythin' I could to make up wid her, even bought her jewellery. You know what she did?'

Sean's face was tight, his jaws working. 'She threw 'em out the fuckin' window innit? Diamond earrings an' a solid gold chain an' she threw the lot out the window. What more can I do eh?'

Cory attempted a shrug which wasn't easy on his crutches. He gave up and looked at Sean sympathetically.

'Boy, you know what Sonia's temper's like innit? I'd hate her to get vex wiv me star, dat's why I wanted to avoid it. You didn't even have to tell her man, ain't you heard ignorance is bliss?'

'I dunno man,' Sean replied. 'I jus' didn't want her to be the las' to know, if we got caught. She'd 'ave gone mad at dat.'

They crossed by the back of Eltham House, the long line of cars pausing respectfully to let Cory pass.

'Now she's the first to know an' you two ain't together because of it. I think dat's a little worse,' Cory pointed out when they reached the other side of the street. Sean nodded, seeing the truth in that and he smiled at Cory suddenly.

'It's good to have you back blood. I've missed havin' someone to talk to about all dis. I feel better jus' seein' you star.'

Cory laughed as they entered the foyer, while an old white woman held the door open for the limping teen. They waved at Ken, then made their way to the lifts.

'Save your sweet talk for Sonia,' he told Sean. 'You're gonna need it to speech 'er, now dis is all over.'

Sean said nothing and pressed the call button for the lift impatiently, ignoring Cory's words. They got out on their floor and walked along the grey, damp passage. Sean opened the front door for Cory and let him pass, watching him carefully. He then stepped into the darkness of the flat and shut the door quietly behind him, his eyes dark and contemplative.

'Is Mum up?' he asked, as they walked past the kitchen.

'Nah,' Cory threw over his shoulder, making for their room. 'I left 'er sleepin' on the sofa.'

'D'you wanna drink?'

'Yeah yeah.'

Sean went into the small kitchen and hunted for a carton of orange juice in the fridge freezer. Finding two tumblers in the cupboard, he put one inside the other, then carried the carton to the bedroom.

Cory was lying on his bed building a spliff when Sean kicked the door open. He flexed his arms as he placed the tumblers on the desk.

'Man, dem crutches can build you up y'know. My arms are achin' a way,' he said, studying his biceps.

Sean poured out the drinks and passed one over to his cousin, then at the desk facing him. Cory rolled his zook expertly, then raised his eyebrows at Sean.

'Well, wha' gwaan? You said you wan'ed to chat.'

Sean relaxed in his seat, a little nervous now the time had come to speak his mind. He spun his glass around, eyeing the contents for a bit, before he spoke.

'Cory . . . man, I've had some strange things happen to me the last few days star. You already know dat raid wen' all right. Right now, our options are bigger than they've ever bin, y'unnerstan? I jus' bin thinkin' an' thinkin' man, what can I do now? What can I do to get us out of here I mean, an' I came to the conclusion it ain't as hard as we thought, y'get me? I suppose, true we live in the middle of the estate, we see more people sucked in, than escapin' – but the way I see it, it's jus' a matter of time, backin' and luck. We certainly got the time an' we can raise the backin', true we got a head start. Now all we need is the luck, y'get me?'

Cory drew on his spliff, not understanding a word Sean was saying. He lay back, perplexed.

'How much wong you got?'

'A gran' or so,' Sean replied. Cory whistled.

'So wha' you sayin' blood?' he wondered aloud, still mystified by his cousin's words, as well as his actions.

'I'm sayin' we should get our act together, an' start runnin' t'ings in dis estate y'get me? I've seen how much money Levi makes from jus' sittin' in his drum all day man, it's fuckin' nutty. On a hot day, my man kills it spee, I'm tellin' you – all the cats come out, buyin' two, maybe three bones each, an' when their money runs too low for bone, they'll buy a draw a weed y'get me? Levi canes it out dere, believe me, I know.'

'I bet you do,' Cory muttered, under his breath. 'So what

Sean, you're movin' wiv my man now? After all the shit we went through at Ally Pally, you're linkin' dis brer now?'

Sean held his hands out and smiled, wordlessly.

'Damn, you're a nutter y'know? What about college? I thought you was gonna pass your exams an' try for Uni star. You can't pass your A' levels an' sell crack at the same time can you?'

'Nah,' Sean looked a bit ashamed now, as he remembered his college work. 'But I c'n always go back an' finish up when I feel like it, innit?'

Cory coughed out smoke in disbelief.

'Go back? How you mean star, you ain't thinkin' of leavin' college are you?'

'Kind of. Cory I got the chance to earn some proper money *now* star, not in four, five years' time. To tell you the truth, I'm goin' for it, y'get me? I'm fed up livin' like a pauper man, it's time for us to come outta dat star, time for us to make a change. It won't be easy, but it'll be easier innit?'

Cory passed Sean his zook, watching him closely. Sean took it and drew deeply, only just suppressing his coughs. Cory shook his head sadly and glared over at him.

'Dis is cos of dat fuckin' Levi innit?' he spat at the teen. Sean shook his head.

'Hear what, I got my own mind you know spee, I c'n think for myself star.'

Cory waved the boy's words away, feeling like a man watching a speeding car head for the family he loved, close enough to see, but too far to help in any way. He put his hands behind his head and feigned interest.

'So what d'you propose man? Wha' you gettin' at?'

'I dunno . . . I was jus' thinkin' dat between me an' you, we know enough people to get a little t'ing together, y'know. I met a couple o' man the other day, from some crew in Ladbroke Grove, called the Brothers Grimm, only they're a big man crew. We could run sumtin' like dem man down these sides an' clean up innit?'

'Brothers Grimm?' Cory winced. 'Dem man juggle big time star, you don't even wanna do the t'ings they do. They deal in heroin, charlie an' anythin' else dat gets you sprang, y'get me?

Fuck dat shit Sean, deal wid your education man, dat's the best thing goin' for you, believe. I don't wanna see you in jail star, so go back to studyin' your books, f'real.'

Sean covered his face in exasperation. When he removed his hand, his eyes burned with anger.

'Ain't you bin listenin' to a word I said? Fuck college y'unnerstan', dat ain't puttin' money in my hands. I'm fed up o' havin' brok pockets all the while, it's time to change the flex y'get me? Dis time now, Levi's asked me to do another armed, on a jewellery shop nex' week an' I'm in star, believe. I c'n even bring you in if you want, as a look-out or summick.'

Cory struggled up, ignoring the pain shooting up his leg in his own anger, his mind detached from his mouth for a few, tense seconds.

'You fuckin' *fool*!' he rasped, whispering his fury. 'I tol' you Levi's no good an' you're gonna go in wid him again. Maybe it takes gettin' shot to make you come to your senses. Sean it's fuckin' *dangerous* can't you see dat? Dere ain't no such thing as easy money in dis world, everything's hard, an' if you jus' stick at your exams . . .'

Sean was holding his belly and cracking up like it was all a big joke.

'Man . . .' he chortled. 'Man, I can't believe you're tellin' me dem t'ings star. Cory y'know, the man who never took time to study nothin' except gyal an' football, now tryin' to tell me sumt'in'—'

'Don't try an' switch it on *me*,' Cory retorted. 'I ain't the one dat passed all my fuckin' exams am I? I had to struggle jus' to get three passes din't I? You, you got no excuse whatsoever, you could sail t'rough dem A' levels, y'unnerstan'? It's jus' a waste man, a waste of a good fuckin' mind.'

Sean stubbed out the zook and shrugged, smiling into the ashtray.

'So wha' you sayin' blood? You wanna come in wid me an Levi an' start fuckin' t'ings up, or you gonna go on like a ol' woman?'

Cory managed to sneer and glare at his cousin at the same time. 'Fuck you man, do wha' you want star, you seem to know it all,' he told him spitefully.

Sean shrugged, then got up and scrabbled underneath the bed for a second, finally pulling out two twenty-pound notes from the Mark's and Spencer's bag and pushing them into his pocket. That done he stared at Cory, who was staring back at him coldly from the bed.

'I'm missin' star, gonna go an' try to make up with Sonnie,' he told the teen, before heading for the door. He'd taken two steps, when Cory called his name.

'Yo Sean, hol' up a second, lemme ask you summick star. You bin smokin' bone?'

Sean shot his answer at Cory like an archer, knowing exactly where to aim.

'Sure bloody,' he said and walked out, slamming the door before Cory could even think of a reply. As he walked to the front door he heard a crash from the bedroom, as if his cousin had broken something in a fit of anger. He felt a moment of reproach, but he wiped it from his mind, convinced he was right.

Cory glared angrily at the crutch he had thrown, his leg throbbing as he breathed heavily. It had merely knocked a few bottles and a tub of pencils off the desk, nothing major. He was tempted to create more destruction, but he was fearful of waking his aunt up.

Fuckin' idiot, he thought as his heart pounded, thinking of the sex he had missed just to end up seeing Sean go out and visit his own girl. He could go back over, he supposed, but his arms were still aching and he couldn't be bothered to travel to the other side of the estate again. He supposed nothing could really run for today. Besides, he wasn't really in the mood for sweet talk: Sean, the fuckin' bastard, was on his mind now. He wanted to brood a little and feel sorry for himself on his own.

I'll ring her later to explain he promised himself, as he wrapped another spliff.

Chapter Thirteen

Rosie knelt on her small bed, gazing out of her bedroom window and smoking a weed spliff. Her Akai portable cassette player was playing her favourite Raregroove tune 'Riding High' and she lost herself in the strings and horns, trying to kid herself she wasn't excited about Cory coming over. She'd been studying before she called him, but her mind had begun to wander. On an impulse she'd picked up the phone, thinking all work and no play turned Jill into a nervous wreck.

The trees outside rustled, just above her hearing, adding to the relaxed mood the music was putting her in. She blew the smoke through her net curtains, out of the open window, not wanting her aunt to come back to a flat that smelt like a she-been.

A crew of girls passed her window, all of them drinking Bacardi breezers; Rosie, recognising a few of them from WoodCroft House, called them over. Cassandra, a tall dark-skinned girl, waved and motioned the others to join her on the other side of the wall. Cassie leapt it nimbly and gave Rosie a sip of her drink.

'Yes rudegirl, wha' gwaan?' she said, as the others gathered around.

'Jus' studyin',' Rosie replied. She tipped the bottle back grate-fully. 'What's 'appenin' wid you lot?'

The crew muttered and moved around. Cassie screwed up her face.

'Nuttin' man, I'm fuckin' bored silly. The youth club's closed till summertime, so all we can do is roam the streets like vagrants, y'get me? It pisses me off man.'

'Why's the club closed? I seen it all boarded up, but I thought they were paintin' or summick.'

Another dark-skinned girl Rosie had never met before, spoke up. 'I feel say they did fin' asbestos in dere, so they gotta pull it down an' start again,' the girl told her, in a bored tone of voice. Rosie looked across at them, concerned.

'*Asbestos*? Raa, dat's a dangerous t'ing boy, dat ain't good. You know what though, you guys should min' yourselves walkin' street star, dere's bere nutters about. I know you're in a crew but boy can't you jus' cool at someone's house?'

The girls shook their heads, causing assorted braids and plaits to jiggle about.

'We ain't as lucky as you, we can't smoke in the house,' Cassie replied, jealously. Rosie laughed.

'You're jokin' innit? The only reason I'm bunnin' in here is cause my aunt's gone East for the night. If she was *here*, she'd have me out *there* with you lot star, I'm tellin' you.'

They all laughed, as Rosie handed the zook to Cassie and blew the smoke into the still night air. Cassie's dark-skinned friend stamped about on the grass and held her sides to keep in the warmth, before looking imploringly at Rosie.

'So what, c'n we come in for a bun or summick, seein' as you got a free drum,' she asked with no shame. Cassie gazed at her, shocked, yet laughing at the same time.

'Oi Leonora, 'llow it man, what'm t'you? You don't even know my girl an' you're askin' her dem t'ings, you're dread star!'

Rosie shrugged and joined in the laughter.

'Nah, dat's all right, it's a minor. I would let you guy's in, but I got a male friend comin' aroun' an' I kinna wanted the yard to myself. You're welcome to come around any other time.'

'A male friend,' Cassie was saying, eyeing the grinning girl, while her friends 'oohed' and 'aahed' collectively. 'Who's the lucky guy den?'

Rosie tapped her nose and smiled.

'I'll tell you guys if it all works out all right?'

'OK, dat's a deal.'

Inside the house the phone started ringing, making Rosie jump. Cassie gave her the thumbs up.

'Soun' like dat could be him. I'll see you about Rosie yeah?'

'All right Cassie 'bye. See you guys later man. Come check me anytime yeah?'

As the girls hopped the wall again, Rosie ran into her living room and snatched up the phone, sliding into a chair at the same time, a move she'd been practising for years.

'Hello?' she said smiling.

Her face fell. 'Oh, hello Auntie, it's you . . . Course I'm pleased to hear from you . . . no . . . I'm jus' studyin' . . . No, Tara ain't here . . . she *ain't* I promise! . . .OK . . . Are you enjoyin yourself? . . . Dat's good . . . Give 'em my love . . . All right . . . See yuh . . .'

She put the phone down and gazed around the room, with its many pictures and statues of Jesus Christ. She propped her head up with her hand, her elbow resting on the chair's wide arm. Where was Cory?

'I suppose you better come in then.'

Sean stared at Sonia, not believing it'd been this easy, this time around. He froze in place, open-mouthed, until she said, 'Hurry *up*, it's freezin' out here', and turned to go into the flat, not waiting for him. Sean stepped inside, closing the door behind him and followed Sonia into the living room, happy at achieving even this much. His good feelings collapsed as he saw a figure sitting on the couch, facing the TV.

The boy was tall and dark-skinned, with a gold hoop in his ear, the latest Air Max trainers and a short back and sides hairstyle. He was suavely dressed, wearing a colourful knitted jumper over a plain shirt and Armani trousers, even though Sean was sure they were fake. When he entered the room, the boy looked up, smiled and raised his fist to be touched. Sean tapped him lightly with his own fist, then gave Sonia a quizzical look and flopped on the sofa beside the boy, while she sat across the room watching them. She introduced them both, tentatively.

'Uhh . . . Sean, dis is Marcus, Marlena's cousin an' Marcus dis is my boyfriend Sean.'

'Nice,' Sean said, as the boy replied.

'What'm star?' in a deep voice.

Sean sat back, thinking, Marlena the bitch, tryin' to set up her fuckin' cousin with a married girl. He controlled his face not wanting to show the anger that raged beneath.

No one said anything for a long time. The tension in the air was obvious, until Marcus suddenly got up and said he had some things to do up Harlesden sides.

'Later on spee. Nice meetin' yuh,' the boy said as he left, Sonia behind him, seeing him out.

'Yeah yeah,' Sean replied, watching his broad shoulders as he left the flat. He's lucky I didn't 'ave my SIG, I would've shot him in 'is back, blatant, Sean thought, chuckling. He heard the door slam and Sonnie's steps coming back so he fixed up his face quickly before she entered.

'Wha' you smilin' at?' she asked, as she bounced back down on her chair, eyeing him.

'Ah, nothin' I was jus' thinkin' dat's all. So what, where did my man spring from all of a sudden, eh?'

Sonia stared back at him easily. She was wearing a mini-skirt and a baggy LA Raiders T-shirt. From where he was sitting, he could see the insides of her thighs, smoothly enticing in the light of the small room. Sean knew the boy, Marcus, had been sitting in much the same position. He wondered if he'd been thinking the same thing. Of course he had, he told himself, feeling the green in his eyes already.

'If you mus' know,' his girl was saying, 'he come to check on me, to see if I was all right, seein' as I'm in here on my own. He's jus' a friend dat's all, he's *concerned*.'

Sean kissed his teeth and looked away.

'Concerned my *arse*. If he's such a mate, how come I never see my man before in my life, 'til now. I know all o' your male friends an' I never see or hear of my man once star.'

'So what, I can't make new friends or somethin'?' Sonnie asked.

'Nah, I ain't sayin' dat, it jus' seems as if Marlena's puttin' the knife in a bit, y'get me? She ain't even here star, it's jus' you an' my man, so don't tell me dat he don't like you Sonnie. Dat's jus' insultin' my intelligence.'

Sonia sighed.

'All right, he likes me. So what? Dat don't mean I'm gonna run after him fallin' at his feet jus' cause he's into me, does it? The fact o' the matter is, you ain't bin around, so Marlena's gettin' me to meet new people, dat's all.'

Sean got up and started pacing around the room, while Sonia watched him, thinking he sure looked good. She smiled and hid it underneath her hand.

'Sonnie man, can't you see I'm tryin' to be forgiven, I'm practically beggin', but you won't bring me in at all star. You won't talk to me on the phone, you threw my gifts away, you won't see me—'

'I'm seein' you now in't I?' Sonia broke in.

'Yeah, I suppose so an' I'm fuckin' glad you are. Gives me a chance to stop Marlena playin' Cilla Black, innit.'

He winked at Sonnie, who giggled and smiled brightly. Feeling on safer ground now, Sean sat on the arm of her seat and took her hand.

'Shit Sonnie man, I fuckin' missed you, you don't know how much man. Cory's jus' come back today and I decided I'm gonna sort the rest of my life out, either way, today, y'unnerstan'? Even holdin' your hand like this . . . it jus' feels right, y'know, I feel better already star.'

'Ah shut the fuck up,' Sonnie spat, but she was smiling as she said it. 'You're layin' it on a bit thick ain't you? You ain't even told me what happened with the robbery yet.'

Sean laughed and rubbed her hand a bit more. 'Boy, it wen' all right star. No one was hurt thank God, and we ain't heard nothin' from the police yet, so I think we may have got away with it. That's why I bought you dem t'ings man, as a peace offerin', y'get me an' to say dat from now, we can get back to our normal way of life again.'

Sonia eased her hand out of Sean's, trying to maintain her frosty attitude. She fiddled with the rings on her finger, gazing at them.

'See Sean, you gotta understan' that I don't want none of dat jewellery at all. I'd make a fine one wouldn't I? Dissin' you for doin' the armed, yet posin' off with my earrings an' necklaces an' all dat. It wouldn't be right, in fact, it would be downright hypocritical, innit?'

Sean nodded in agreement with his girl, seeing her point. Sonia wasn't stupid. Sometimes he forgot just how clever and right thinking she was, and how much she valued her own set of rules to life, which she stuck to rigidly.

He rubbed his chin, in thought. 'You know what Sonnie? You're right man, I should've thought about it. But you gotta believe me when I say dem t'ings are done wid man, I'm outta dere, y'unnerstan'. I got my whole life ahead o' me man an' I don't wanna fuck it up star. So give me a chance at least, true we were the closest couple in the world before all dis.'

'Promise me you finished wi' the gangstuh business,' Sonia muttered sternly.

'Dat's easy,' Sean replied. 'I'm out Sonnie, blatantly. I swear to God.'

A thought popped into Sonia's head, which she brandished at Sean like one of the spiked clubs popular with the Grimm Brothers.

'I heard about you anyway, threatenin' dem lot downstairs with a gun. Where'd you get dat from?'

The question came out of nowhere, taking Sean by surprise. Still, he never faltered, and later he was proud of himself for his quick reply.

'Levi giv' it t'me, innit. Don't worry though, I didn't threaten dem lot, I jus' showed 'em the handle star. If Stacey hadn't tried to sting dem diamond earrings I got you, I wouldn't have even had to do dat.'

'Little Stacey tried to nick the earrings?'

Sonnie's mouth was open and Sean smiled, taking back her hand and holding her beautiful brown eyes with his own.

'See they didn't tell you dat, did they? I ain't some kind of maniac Sonia, I ain't changed dat much.'

'I know, I know.'

They looked at each other, half smiling, then by mutual unspoken consent, they leaned forward and began kissing passionately. Sean touched her face lightly, feeling the strong lines of her cheek bones and, in between kisses, he also touched her lips, losing himself in their softness. He edged closer to her and she took his hand, guiding it underneath her T-shirt to her breasts. She held his head with her other hand tightly, pulling him forward so their tongues could meet, making her close her eyes in pleasure. The chair slid back on its castors a little with their weight. They laughed mutely, with their lips still pressed together, then got up, looking around the room for space.

'Come,' Sonia said, taking a cushion from the chair she'd just been sitting on and placing it on the floor.

Sean took off his top, while Sonia slipped out of her skirt and T-shirt, exposing a black lace bra and knickers, her slim body gleaming in the light.

'You ain't been with anyone else have you?' she asked him, her wide brown eyes innocent and trusting, probing his face like headlights.

'Nah man,' he replied easily.

Sean smiled at his girl to reassure her and slowly slid the lace knickers past her shapely hips, her thighs and eventually her ankles, before placing the underwear on the sofa, taking in the lines and curves of her body with undisguised relish. He took off his jeans and boxer shorts, then did the same with those and slid his way along her soft torso, until they were face to face, the heat from her warming him, relaxing him. They kissed again lazily, taking their time, then, she opened her legs and arched her body to meet him, as he entered her smoothly, feeling her hands tighten on his shoulders, and hearing her low moan of pleasure.

I'm home man. I'm home, he thought to himself happily.

It was a good feeling.

Cory's first day back at college was on Monday, something he'd been looking forward to for a long time. He hobbled along the corridors, seeing smiling faces around every corner, patting his back and welcoming him with warm smiles. There was a mad rush to sign his plaster cast in his sports and leisure class (where he grudgingly sat out a five-a-side football game, instead of catching up on theory work he'd missed) and for most of the day he was treated like a king. Nearly everyone had witnessed what happened at the charity football match and they all sympathised.

He saw Tanya briefly in the dinner hall at lunchtime and he waved at her from his place in the queue, causing her to wave back tentatively. He couldn't be bothered to be vex with the girl, as he felt they'd split up in an adult way and should continue to act the same now, despite what had gone on. More to the point, she had some fit friends and some of them were smiling at him now, as he bought his usual cheese roll and a Club chocolate biscuit, which he put in his pocket for safe keeping. He went to the Coke machine and fed in his coins, pressing the button for Fanta and waiting for his choice to tumble into the bottom of the machine. Then he took his drink and headed over to the girls' table, somewhat unsteadily. Tanya looked confused at his manoeuvre. She gazed at him distrustfully as he sat down.

'What'm Tee? Wha' you sayin' Yvette, Sianna, Becky, Beth? Yuh cool?'

There was a barrage of replies from the smiling girls and Tanya's face creased with understanding.

'How're you my darlin', feelin' better?' Sianna asked him, as she spooned chocolate mousse mechanically into her mouth.

'I'm OK,' he told the girl, as he unwrapped his roll. 'I'm jus' brewin' about dis cast star, the t'ings hinderin' me a way man. Can't rave, I can't . . .' He made a face and smiled while all the girls apart from Tanya laughed. 'You know, I can't get intimate . . . it's a liberty man.'

'Why, who was you plannin' to get intimate *wid*?' Sianna asked him directly, looking him in the eyes and playing along with him. Cory waggled his eyebrows and watched, as she spooned the mousse into her mouth slowly. He wondered if she knew what it was doing to him.

'Boy y'know, I ain't sure, but I got a cravin' for some chocolate mousse all of a sudden, f'real! I wonder why?'

Sianna gave him a demure look, giggling, and he was about to continue, when a heavy hand rested on his shoulder and a body moved in beside him at the table. He looked up to see Sam Boyd's cheerful face beaming at him broadly.

'Raa, Sam, wha' gwaan spee?' Cory blurted, touching the Bajan's fist with his own. His lecturer shrugged.

'I'm cool man an' I'm glad t'see you lookin' so well too. Hi girls.'

The girls gave a chorus of hellos.

'Well y'know how it go, I can't let man keep me down, y'get me?' Cory said, seriously.

'I sure do,' Sam replied and his face abruptly changed, making him look a little more like a lecturer and less like a student. 'I really come over to have a word in private, if you don't mind. It's very important,' he said gravely. Cory wrapped his roll back up easily, wondering what was happening now.

'Yeah man, it's cool. Where we goin'?'

'We'll find an empty classroom,' the man told him.

Sam eventually found one not far from the hall. They entered the dusty class to see light streaming in from the large window, giving the room a pleasant warmth that heralded the coming of summer at last. Cory got as comfortable as he could on a chair usually reserved for lecturers. Sam sat on the table, smiling.

'You're takin' a risk eh? Chattin' up your ex-girl's friend!' he said, as if it was a major crime. Cory grinned and popped his drink with relish.

'Ain't no different to what she did to me, except she didn't wait for us to finish innit?'

Sam nodded, conceding the point.

'Anyway, that's not what I asked you here to talk about,' he said, his face stern again. 'What I'm really worried about, or *who* I'm worried about for that matter, is your cousin, Sean.'

Sean.

Cory relaxed in the seat, finally remembering what Shannon had said a few days before. Sean, she suspected, had been bunking college from the time he'd gone to link up Danny Campbell, Razor and Ricky to today. For anyone else maybe, that was a minor. Everyone took days off when they didn't feel like going in, it was like an unspoken rule held by students. If you don't feel up for it, don't bother going in. You could always catch up from somebody else, providing you never overdid your bunking.

But Sean never took days off, ever, until now. His drive for success and his determination to leave Greenside meant that even on days when he was ill with flu he'd still attend his lectures, afraid of missing even a lesson. It seemed now, his energies were focused on something a little more lucrative and a little more dangerous, despite Cory's warnings. Even this morning, Sean said he had things to do before his lessons, and that he'd catch Cory up later instead of taking the train with him, something they'd done together since they began college. Evidently, he hadn't made it.

'I'm gettin' very worried about your cousin's state of mind, to be frank,' the Bajan was saying, his voice betraying his concern. 'The few times I've seen him in my class, he's been withdrawn, moody even an' I know that's not like him at all. I was worried he was takin' your injuries to heart, blamin' himself for not being there for you, maybe even blamin' me for making him work so hard that day. I was gonna ask him what was up, but I decided to wait, to see what developed. An' you know what Cory? Since then, I ain't seen him at all, at all an' for that matter, neither has anyone else in the college. I asked Tanya and Sonia about it an' both o' them bit my head off, so I gave up an' decided to wait for you to come back. Do you have any idea what's up with him?'

Cory sipped his Fanta, feeling masochistic, as the bubbles burst painfully on his tongue.

'Nah y'know,' he said slowly, feeling his way around the lie. 'I ain't got a clue man. To tell you the truth, I ain't seen much o' Sean, true I only come out of hospital Thursday, y'get me?'

'Are you sure?'

Sam was peering at him.

'How you mean? I'm as sure as I can be star.'

Cory couldn't hide his unease with the question and he felt on the spot. What did his tutor mean, 'was he sure'? Sam shifted in his seat.

'The only reason I ask that is 'cos I heard some rumours about your "accident" with that big boy at the charity game. Someone told me he might have had a more valid reason, other than plain old sportin' aggression, to want to hurt you. You know what I mean?'

Cory laughed and looked Sam steadily in the eye.

'You don't wanna believe college gossip,' he said lightheartedly. Sam's reply, was anything but lighthearted.

'Well, in my limited experience, even though most gossip

tends to be wildly off the mark, there's usually a grain of truth hidden inside it, like a pearl in an oyster, y'know.'

Cory grinned. 'Ah you dat, with dem lyrics dere.'

Sam joined in with a chuckle.

'Seriously though,' the older man continued, 'I think you should talk to Sean, before it's too late. There's an end-of-year assessment examination coming up soon an' if Sean don't buck his ideas up, he won't pass, no matter how brainy he is. If he fails, he has to do the whole year again and I know neither of you want that. Hold on, let me show you somethin' a second.'

Sam turned to his leather briefcase and spun the combinations before clicking the pair of locks open and digging around for something inside. Cory relaxed his expression while the lecturer's back was turned, thinking if he was to tell the man even a portion of his tale, Sam would think he was lying straightaway.

People couldn't be forced to see what they didn't want to see. To some people, black or white, stabbings and shootings and junkies were all thousands of miles across the Atlantic, only to be encountered if you were unlucky enough to get mugged while on holiday. To those people, his walking around with a knife meant he was either looking for trouble or insanely paranoid, not that it was simple survival. They just couldn't, or even wouldn't, ever understand what was going on underneath their very noses.

He readjusted his face, as Sam turned back to him, a class register in his hand.

'Here's how many classes Sean's missed in the last two weeks,' Sam was saying, opening the large book and placing it on the table so they both could see. Blue or black X marks showed the days his cousin attended, red ones marked the days he didn't. Over the last two weeks there were nine red marks, not including one for today. In the previous weeks, there'd been an abundance of blue or black marks. Cory had a hollow feeling in his stomach at the sight of all those red X's. He puffed loudly.

'Damn . . . So how much work's he missed?'

Sam closed the book and sighed.

'A couple of essays I suppose. I usually ask for a shortish one every week and you're supposed to do your ground work in the preceding lessons, so he'll have to copy someone else's, providin' he comes back in time. But I can't stress enough how important it is for him to get back here, preferably as soon as possible. Talk to him Cory, I know he'll listen to you man.'

Oh yeah? Cory thought derisively, feeling targeted again. You don't know shit about Sean no more. Fuck I don't even think *I* do man, he mused.

Sam was still talking. 'When I first saw Sean, I swore he'd never make it. I know it sounds stupid, but the way he was dressed, baggy jeans, trainers . . . y'know, I judged him by his appearance, before he'd even opened his books. Two months later, he's still here, but back then he was runnin' rings around the whole class! I don't think I've been that pleasantly surprised for a long time and to tell you the truth, I'd be very upset if he dropped out now, when he's already proved me so wrong. Try an' bring him around would you Cory? My wife's fed up with me bringing my worries home at night.'

Cory looked up at Sam, knowing how sincere he was, and knowing this was more than a job to him. He nodded and touched fists with the man, more solidly than they had in the dinner hall, pressing their knuckles together, oblivious to the pain.

'I'll try,' he muttered. 'But right now, I gotta flash man. I'm gonna go and see Sonnie, true I think she saw Sean las' night.'

He downed his Fanta and rose, reaching for his crutches. Sam passed them over. Cory made it to the door, where he stopped and looked at the older man.

'Listen Sam, I'm gonna get on it tonight, believe. The ol' Sean'll be back before you know it.'

He raised his fist at Sam, before easing the door shut behind him, looking around the corridor. Two girls he recognised from Sonia's study group passed him, their heads down, deep in conversation. Cory watched their rears, his tongue nearly touching the floor, as they glided down the corridor. Then he sorted out his crutches and made a valiant effort to catch them up.

'Hello ladies!' he called, as he hopped along. 'I don't suppose you know Sonia Chamberlain, d'you?'

Sean slipped into the Bradley flat around five in the afternoon.

He called out hello, not even expecting to get a reply and he was surprised to hear his mother's voice calling back.

'I'm in my bedroom!' he heard her yell, in a strident tone of voice. He made his way to the door, knocked on it once and went in when he heard her tell him to enter.

His mother's room was a mixture of order and chaos, with a large king-sized bed in the middle and on the left hand side an old mahogany wardrobe, full of clothes and more shoes than Sean had ever seen in anyone's possession. That was the orderly side. The right side of the room was piled with papers and old bags of clothes that belonged to Cory, Shannon and himself when they were kids. Bernice lay in her bed, with her dressing gown on, while Greg, her long-term man-friend, lazed fully clothed next to her.

'Hey Mum, how's it goin' Greg? Wha' you doin' home dis early?' He touched fists with Greg as he came close to the bed.

'They sent me home early from work,' his mother told him happily. 'They said I was too tired lookin' and even the kids was askin' if I was OK – so they sent me home and said I can come back when I feel better.'

'What, they're still givin' you sick pay innit?'

'Of course!'

His mother gave him her sassy look; Sean got a glimpse of what she'd looked like at his age. Greg laughed.

'Hear what Mum, I wanted to tell you summick anyway,' he said sitting on the bed. His mother looked wary and Greg said, 'Uh-oh', quietly but audibly. Sean smiled.

'Hol' on a second,' his mother said. 'Let me ask you somet'ing first. What's all this, "hear what" an' "y'get me" business that you kids are goin' on with? Born an' raised in England you lot are an' you still talk more slang than me! I should've sent all of you to private school, innit Sean?'

Sean winced and shook his head. His mother gave him a sour look. Sean switched subjects.

'Anyway Mum, I jus' wanted to tell you I'm goin' to Sonnie's to stay for the nex' couple of days, so I won't be around for a bit, yeah?'

'Sonnie's to stay? What for?'

'I got some end-of-term exams to study for an' I need peace

and quiet for a while. I'll only be across the way if you need me an' true Sonnie's mum's gone away so no one'll disturb us. Her end of terms are coming as well an' we're gonna study together. Makes sense innit?'

His mother nodded.

'As long as you don't hold no wild parties or anythin'. Anyway, I know Sonia won't, she's far too sensible an' besides, Samantha would skin her alive an' leave her bones out to dry if she got back an' the house was wrecked. Innit Sean?'

Sean laughed and nodded. Samantha was Sonia's mother, a tall, stern-looking woman you didn't want to mess with. Everyone on the estate knew her and treated her with respect, knowing she was as militant as they came, having been born and raised to be a survivor in Kingston, Jamaica.

One night a crackhead tried to rob her, right outside Bartholomew House, seeing her rings and thinking she was an easy mark. She'd turned the tables on him, beating him with her umbrella and holding him in a bearhug, while screaming until the police came. The poor guy never stood a chance.

Sean told the story to his mother and Greg, making them crack up, before eventually leaving them and going to his room to play on Cory's Sega.

For the first time in weeks, everything was falling into place and going exactly to plan. Only time would tell if things would stay that way, but for now, Sean felt everything seemed to be flexing neatly.

Garvey and Cory were sitting in Rosie's house with her Aunt Madeleine, waiting for the girl to come home from work, feeling a little scared. Cory had called for Garvey half an hour before, saying he wanted to see the girl, but he needed moral support, as he wasn't sure what her aunt was actually like. He was glad he had.

He leaned forward and sipped some of the tea the lady had made, courteously trying to ignore the fact they'd been waiting for Rosie for twenty minutes. He smiled at Madeleine.

'Mmmm, good tea,' he remarked, trying to sound respectable. Madeleine sniffed, just like Rosie, and looked at him coarsely.

'Is where you meet me niece from?' she shot at him, not

seeming to know the art of tact, simply wading in with whatever was on her mind. Cory could hear Garvey sniggering uncontrollably beside him, thankfully hidden by his body and he cursed his friend silently, thinking he was a great help. Trying not to laugh himself, he shrugged and forced himself to look Rosie's aunt in the eye.

'Uhh, she used to go to my school, I think she was a year above me—'

That was the wrong thing to say.

'So yuh younger than her den?' the woman replied quickly, jumping at the chance to point out something negative. Cory conceded.

'Yeah, but only by a few months. See, if you're born too close to the beginnin' of September—'

A key sounded in a lock and the front door opened, bringing fresh air into the living room. Cory broke off, relieved and smiled at Garvey, winking.

'Dat sounds like Rosie,' he told her aunt.

'Yuh very perceptive,' she replied.

Garvey covered his mouth and pretended he had a harsh cough, which had sprung up from nowhere. Cory ignored the woman and waited for Rosie to appear. When the girl entered the room at last, with Tara in tow, she was shocked to see them, to say the least.

'Raa, wha' you sayin' people, wha' you lot doin' here?' she said, as she dropped her bags on the floor, cutting her eyes at Cory. He looked away guiltily.

'You all right Auntie?' she said in a lively manner, kissing the stern woman on the cheek. Her aunt patted her back in return and gestured at the boys.

'I'm fine, I was jus' entertainin' yuh man frien' dem,' she told Rosie, who laughed as she took her jacket off.

'Oh yeah? Dat sounds like fun!' she replied. The woman waved a hand in disgust.

'You can stop dem talks right dere Miss Joseph! Dis is a house o' de Lord, we'll have none o' dat in here girl. Yuh mus' respec' me wishes, even if yuh a big workin' 'ooman now. Right or wrong?'

'You're right Auntie,' Rosie said humbly, giving up without

a fight. She rolled her eyes at the others and put her coat back on, pointing at the boys, then the front door, from behind her aunt's chair. She then picked up Cory's crutches, which were behind the living room door and put them on her own arms, capering about and making Tara laugh.

'Hey Maddy I'm gonna go shop, d'you want anythin'?'

'But yuh jus' come in an' yuh 'ave visitors. Yuh can't jus' go back out.'

'They c'n come wid me. Anyway, I don't wanna get on your nerves, so we'll go an' plot somewhere else all right?'

'All right den, I suppose so . . .'

The woman was clearly not happy with the way things were going. Cory hopped over to Rosie, very aware of the dark looks she was giving him, and thinking he didn't understand why adults had to lay down the law so much. He was glad his aunt was so easy going, letting them smoke, drink and have girl-friends (or boyfriends, in Shannon's case) over, preferring that it was all under her watchful eye rather than on the street. Following Tara, who for once was smiling at him, he left the house and stood outside, waiting for Rosie to appear.

Garvey came out first, his face straining with the effort of holding his laughter in.

'Oh my days, dat was a crack up star, properly!' he was saying, his round face red with glee. Rosie came out a minute later to find Cory and Garvey comparing notes on what had happened in the flat, even making Tara laugh as they described how scared they'd been.

'Don't cuss my aunt,' she told them mockingly, walking slightly ahead, with Tara. 'She's a very nice person I'll have you know. She's put up with my shit for long enough anyway, innit Tee?'

'Truly,' Tara replied. 'But you gotta look at it from these lot's point o' view as well. Maddy don't like boys comin' around innit an' she don't mind showin' people either.'

'Believe!' Cory broke in, shaking his head. Rosie laughed and spun around, turning to face the following boys.

'Boys an' drugs an' parties are all the devil's temptation!' she boomed suddenly, sounding like an excited preacher looking down on her flock from the pulpit. 'You must resist an' give your soul to the Lord! Don't smoke the illegal weed (which God put on dis earth anyway!) an' don't have sex until you've bin wi' dat person for five fuckin' years or more, if you c'n help it. Can I get a Amen!?'

'No!' the teenagers chorused, cracking up.

'So what, are you really screwin' wid me?' Cory asked later, as they walked towards Garvey's. They'd decided to go there so they could smoke in peace. Rosie looked at him, her expression dark, yet confused.

'I dunno – I mean, on the one hand, I *know* things are kinda crazy for you at the moment an' you got a lot on your mind; but on the other hand, you could jus' be blaggin' the ku an' you could 'ave even got a call from Tanya dat night, y'get me? I don't know, do I? All I *do* know is I was waitin' for you the other night until three in the mornin', even though my aunt had bin back since eleven. I sat dere, thinkin' you was gonna tap on the window or summick an' you didn't even turn up man. I mean, what am I supposed to think, huh?'

Cory stopped and scratched his good leg for a second, while up ahead, Garvey and Tara were crossing the road that ran beside Garvey's block. Rosie smiled as she watched them.

'They're gettin' on well,' she said, as they entered the block. Cory got up and smiled too.

'Yeah man dat's good. But hear what Rosie, what would you say if I told you I had a complete explanation for not turnin' up the other night? Something dat could be checked quite easily as well?'

The girl thought for a second as they resumed walking, her eyes bright and clear. Finally she told the teen, 'I'd say, "Lemme hear it nuh!"' which made them both laugh warmly, the attraction between them still apparent, each time their eyes met.

Cory pushed the call button for the lift with his crutch, then turned to Rosie, all traces of laughter gone now, looking almost as stern as her aunt.

A problem shared is a problem halved, he thought. This time he believed he had the right person to talk to. Rosie was trust-worthy, she'd already proved that and she knew a lot of what was going on already, so that would make the telling of the story even easier. He took her hand, as the lift came to a noisy stop beside them and looked at her sincerely.

'Rosie,' he told her, the lift forgotten in his concentration. 'If I tell you dis, it can never go any further right?'

The lift stood silently open, bidding them to enter.

Chapter Fourteen

Cory was dreaming.

He dreamt he was in the Greenside Estate, walking alone and unaided by crutches. It was the thick of night and his hood was up, protecting him from the cold. The street lights were on, casting a meagre light onto the pavement. He had no idea of his destination; he couldn't even recognise the road he was taking, although by the look of the blocks, it could well have been Durham, the street that passed directly in front of Beechwood. All was silent and he couldn't hear the sound of his own breathing.

Suddenly, out of nowhere, he could hear voices echoing behind him. He strained his ears, eventually picking up some slang and the sound of laughter with it. The voices sounded like street youths, a whole crew of them if their footsteps were anything to go by. Cory tried to turn around, but his neck muscles wouldn't budge, merely tensing, as hard and immovable as solid steel. He could only hold his head straight, feeling irrationally fearful. His heart pounding like a panelbeater's hammer, he started to run.

The footsteps behind him started to run too. Cory was really scared now and he sprinted with his head down, looking at the pavement as it flashed beneath him. He couldn't tell how far he went, but soon enough, he heard a car rolling smoothly beside him and bright light washed over his body, making him stop, knowing it was useless to run any further. His head was locked into looking down at the concrete – he closed his eyes in fear as more voices came to him. These voices were adult males, speaking with a white English accent and Cory realised they sounded just like police.

He wanted to keep running but he couldn't move. There was a knocking sound on the edge of his hearing which he couldn't fathom. He felt cold panic constrict him. He was paralysed. He couldn't even fall to the ground. He was helpless. He had to open his eyes.

Had . . .

to . . .

open . . .

his . . .

eyes . . .

With a mighty effort, he forced his eyelids upwards, seeing only darkness around him now and shiny black police boots. The knocking had returned, louder, more insistent, from somewhere far away. It was then that he realised he was dreaming and he knew he had to wake up as soon as possible.

Open your eyes for real! He told himself, as the voices appeared, now in his head, teasing him, urging him to throw the blanket of sleep away. They screamed and yelled and cried and begged.

Wake up.

Wake up!

WAAAKE UUUPPPP!

His eyes snapped awake and he found himself in his bedroom, which was dark, but at least familiar. He bounced his head on the pillow twice, smiling and touching his arms and his cast to make sure he was really there.

'Damn, it was a dream,' he muttered, relieved he was back in solid reality. Outside his room, he heard the front door opening and the sound of talking, though he couldn't make out the words. He lay back on his bed, wondering what this new dream signified and whether it had anything to do with what he'd told Rosie last night.

Cory had felt better having bared his soul, glad he'd put his trust in someone at last and glad he'd chosen the girl, rather than anyone else. He respected Rosie and he knew if he told her to keep something to herself, she would, even a tale so secret he hadn't even told Garvey. He'd stalled telling the boy because he knew what his reaction would be; he would want to hurt Levi, never mind the dealer's reputation. Cory didn't want to risk his friend getting seriously injured, or Sean getting into trouble if certain things came to light.

Sitting up in his bed, Cory took a sheet of king-sized Rizla and built a spliff lazily, thinking he could do with sleeping some more. His first college lesson wasn't until the afternoon, starting at two. He sprinkled in some weed, then looked up as he heard a furtive knock on the door.

'Come in!' he yelled, thinking, hopefully, it was Shannon with some breakfast.

The door swung open. To Cory's surprise, Sonia walked into the room, looking harried and upset. Cory felt fear wrench at his stomach at the sight of the girl and he wondered what had happened to his cousin this time. Across the room, Sean's empty bed seemed to shout questions at him, none of which could be answered yet.

'Hey Sonnie, what's up?'

Cory hadn't seen Sean's girl since he'd been in hospital, so he'd missed feeling the brunt of her anger when Sean confessed about the robbery. Still, when she looked at him, Cory could see he wasn't her favourite person, and harsh words were on the tip of her tongue. She sat on Sean's bed and shrugged, smoothing the patterned quilt down with her hand.

'Nuttin',' she said, her face tired and sad. 'I was jus' wonderin' if you seen Sean at all on your travels. He was meant to come an' see me las' night an' I'm still waitin'.'

Her voice sounded low and morose, causing Cory to feel pity for her. He knew she felt for Sean, and if she was experiencing even a quarter of what he was going through, he knew she deserved sympathy. He lit his zook and frowned at her statement.

'Have *I* seen him? He was meant to be stayin' at yours las' night man.'

Sonia shook her head.

'Dat's what I'm sayin' innit, he was meant to come, but he never turned up.'

She looked at him as if he was a bit stupid. Cory gave a nervous laugh.

'Nah Sonnie, you don't understan'. Sean told Bernice he was stayin' at yours last night, innit? Well, as you can see, he ain't here now an' I know he never slept here las' night, cause *I* did, y'get me? So if he wasn't at *yours* an' he wasn't here, where could he be?'

He said this last thoughtfully, contemplating the answer as if his life depended on it.

'Wait, wait, *wait*,' Sonia said, holding up her hands, as if commanding a speeding train to stop dead in its tracks. 'You're tellin' me, Sean told his mum he was stayin' at mines too?'

'Yeah yeah. He even said he wouldn't be back for days, not jus' one night.'

'So how d'you know dat, if you ain't seen him?' Sonia shot at him, her tone instantly distrustful.

'The same person who let you in told me,' Cory replied dryly. Sonia opened her mouth in a gasp of shock, as she realised Cory was telling the truth.

'Shannon?' she muttered under her breath, not believing what was going on. Then she panicked.

'We gotta look for him, he could be hurt somewhere or lost, or anythin' man. You hear dat all the time on the news, people goin' missin' an' no one hears from dem an' anythin' could have happened to him, anythin' man . . .'

Her eyes were wide and fearful as she spoke. She got up and paced around the room, imploring Cory to get out of bed. Cory looked up, worried she was finally losing it. He shouted at her, hating the lifeless way she moved around the room.

'Sonnie! *SONNIE*! Si' down will yuh!'

The girl snapped her head around to face him. 'Don't *you* talk to me like dat!' she spat, her anger reaching him at last.

'Well jus' relax will yuh, before you wear a hole in the fuckin' carpet star. He ain't hurt an' he ain't lost man, Sean's an able brer, he c'n look after himself, y'get me? Now will you sit down for a minute, so I c'n talk widout twis'in' up my neck?'

Sonia made as if to say something else, then changed her mind and walked back over to the bed, flopping down and looking at the boy, impatiently waiting for him to speak. Cory offered the girl his spliff and in reply, she simply shot him a sour look and turned away.

'Are you tryin' to wind me up Cory, cause if you are—'

'Jus' listen will yuh?' Cory cut in, fed up with her threats. 'I shouldn't even be tellin' you dis Sonnie. It goes against all of my principles, but I see the way you're actin' an' I know you check for Sean a way—'

'I love him, I don't *check* for him,' Sonia said, irritated. Cory looked at her until he was satisfied she'd had her say, then he continued.

'Anyway, I think I know what my man's on an' why he's ducked out all of a sudden. See . . . when I come outta hospital, Sean asked me to come in on a nex' robbery of some jeweller's. Anyway, when he was tellin' me about dis t'ing he said it was nex' week . . . Dat was like, las' Thursday, so boy . . to tell you the truth, I think dat's what my man's on, he's gone to do the robbery man . . . I'm sorry Sonnie, but dat's what I reckon star.'

Sonia said nothing, looking around the room as if in a trance, seeing nothing. She turned back to Cory and pointed at him, with a shaking finger.

'Dis is your fault.'

Cory jumped and he felt a chill go through him. Was she reading his mind?

'*DIS IS YOUR FAULT*!' she yelled, leaping over to him and throwing punches at his face and chest in a blind fury. Cory shielded his face with one hand, calling at Sonia to stop and trying to hold her hands with his other at the same time.

'You bastard, dis is 'cos of you!' she growled, connecting with a hefty punch on the side of his head, that made him smash into the headrest and see stars momentarily. He shook his head and grabbed at her arms, just about resisting the urge to lash back at her, until suddenly, she broke down in tears and sat on the bed, all of her strength gone.

Cory sat up in the small bed and put his arms around her as she sobbed, stroking her hair and patting her back occasionally. The bedroom door knocked and Shannon's voice came through, sounding concerned.

'Hey, are you guys OK in there?' she yelled. Sonia bit back her sobs, wiping her eyes fiercely. Cory aimed his words at the door, not wanting Shannon to come in and see him and Sonnie like this.

'Yeah yeah, everythin's cool star,' he replied, in a fearful voice.

'OK . . . I'm goin' to college in a minute yeah? Are you sure you're all right Sonnie?'

'Positive,' Sonia gulped, not even looking at the door.

'All right den, I'll see you lot later OK?'

Her footsteps faded as she left the door.

Cory wondered how long it would take for his cousin to raise the question, if Sean was staying at Sonia's, what was Sonia doing at their place? Thankfully, either she didn't think about it or she decided to wait and ask him in private, where she could wring it out of him in minutes.

Sonia cried forcefully, but almost silently, her head against Cory's bare chest, her tears leaving damp patches on his body. Cory held her, thinking he didn't need or want this, on top of everything else going on. It would've been cool if Sean had chosen an ugly girl to go out with – he could have held her like this all day and not felt anything. But Sonia . . . she was too nice, too warm and this was wrong, completely wrong. But what could he do? He couldn't leave her on the bed to cry alone, he had to comfort her.

He wiped the tears from her deep eyes softly, then, wondering why he'd done that, he passed her some clean tissues, moving away from her to sit by his bed's headrest.

'Thanks,' the girl croaked, dabbing at her eyes. 'I don't know what come over me, but I feel better now.'

He shrugged, still a bit confused about what he'd just felt. He rubbed his head where Sonnie had hit him.

'It does you good to 'ave a cry. Gets all the stress outta your system,' he told her wisely.

'Have *you* cried lately?'

Cory sighed and averted his eyes.

'Nah . . . I think the las' time I cried was years ago man. Too long for me to remember. Maybe I should jus' bawl once and den my stress wouldn't get people into so much trouble innit?'

Sonia smiled.

'I recommend it, as of now. Oh an' Cory . . . I'm sorry about what I said earlier man, dat was shitty. I can't blame you for somethin' Sean done of his own free will, dat's not right. I apologise.'

'Fuck it,' Cory told her. 'I know what I'm to blame for an' what I'm not. I c'n live wid it.'

Liar!

The little voice in his head was back.

Cory ignored it.

'So what now?' Sonia questioned, her eyes still sparkling from her tears of moments before. Cory thought for a second, rubbing his head before he spoke. Sonia looked around the room, embarrassed.

'Uhhh, well, I feel say we should get out of here first off, true I don't want Bernice or Shannon findin' out about dis t'ing jus' yet, y'get me? I don't think Sean'll come here, 'cause he ain't meant to *be* here, so I think we should plot at yours an' wait to see what happens. Your mum's still away ain't she?'

Sonia nodded. 'Yeah yeah.'

'OK, well we should do dat. If you c'n gimme a few minutes to get washed and dressed . . .'

'Of course.'

They smiled at each other, all the ill-feeling between them gone. Sonia got up and walked over to the door, still smiling faintly.

'I'll be in the sittin' room,' she told him before leaving.

Cory nodded and sat back in his bed for a moment, his eyes closed. Then he got up and started picking his clothes out, thinking about his dream again.

Maybe, he thought, just maybe mind, it was a warnin'.

Of what, he didn't know, but he didn't feel too good after this morning. He had a sinking sensation things were rapidly going to get worse.

Sonia let them into her empty home not long afterwards. Cory swung his way inside, thinking to himself he'd done the wrong thing, yet again. The girl flicked on the TV, then went in the kitchen for a while, returning with two tall glasses and a bottle of pina colada under her arm. Cory watched as she poured, then passed him the bubbling yellow drink, sipping experimentally as she dealt with her own glass. When she was finished, she sat back and sighed.

'So how long you plannin' on stickin' around?' she asked, out of the blue.

'I'll wait until Sean gets back innit. I'm as worried about him as you are y'know,' Cory replied, the words out of his mouth before he could stop them. Sonia grinned at him.

'Relax will yuh? I ain't gonna bite your head off, I'm glad you're hangin' around. I couldn't handle this on my own, I'd go nuts believe me.'

'Yeah well, I 'ave got to link up wid Rosie sometime today,' he said quickly, mindful of his earlier thoughts. Sonia gave him a motherly look.

'*Really*? How you two gettin' on now?'

'Good y'know. I spent ages wid 'er yesterday, true I was meant to meet her the other night an' I couldn't cos . . .' he stalled, remembering why. 'My leg, my leg was hurtin' too bad y'get me? I check for her y'know, she's not stupid or nothin'. She's safe man.'

'You'll have to introduce us properly,' Sonia muttered absently, her mind on other things. Cory nodded once, then they watched the figures on the television for a while, until Sonia asked if he played dominoes.

'Yeah man, come mek me thrash you star,' Cory said, rubbing his hands together. It looked like they had a long day ahead of them and he was glad of anything to pass the time.

11 a.m.

Cory and Sonia had been playing for a few hours now, with Cory finding the game harder to read, with only two players and an abundance of 'prints' to pick from. Nevertheless, he still managed to beat Sonia four times to her two, and the steady snap of the dominoes was therapeutic for both of them. All he knew was they were laughing and talking now, instead of just sitting in a pocket of silence. Like he'd thought before, it did pass the time. Of Sean, there was no sign.

1 p.m.

As Cory built a spliff, the lunchtime news came on the television. Both teenagers looked up at once, each hoping they
wouldn't hear anything about Sean. It was only the usual rubbish; the country was in a mess and no one had a clue how to
get out of it. Late ambulance services (where people died waiting), missing children, date rape cases, where no one really
knew who was telling the truth . . . race attacks – the list went
on and on, causing Cory to shake his head in wonder. The worst
bulletin of all was one saying half a million pounds worth of
cannabis had been seized by customs officials, who'd been following a boat cruising along the river Thames for days. He held
up his spliff and blew smoke at the screen when a police
spokesman appeared on the TV to crow about the haul. Sonia
laughed and said he was crazy.

2.30 p.m.

While Sonia went to the toilet, Cory sat building another zook.
The phone rang abruptly and he hurried to pick it up, hopping
painfully on his good leg, which jarred his injured one quite a
bit. When he first picked up the receiver, he thought the deep
voice on the other end was Sean. He felt an instant rush of
relief. When the person asked for Sonia, without even questioning who he was, he realised his mistake. He tried to be nosy
without being blatantly obvious.

'Who shall I say's callin'?' he asked gruffly.

'Marcus,' the mystery speaker replied confidently.

Marcus? Cory thought, Who the fuck was he?

'Hey Sonnie, some brer's on the phone for you!' he yelled in
the direction of the toilet door.

'I'm comin'!' she yelled back and soon she was strolling into
the living room, her face blank. Cory gave her the phone,
mouthing, 'Who's Marcus?' while giving her strange looks.
Sonia smiled and took the receiver, sitting on the arm of Cory's
chair.

'Hello? Hello, how are you? . . . I'm fine, I jus' felt a little ill,
so I took the day off . . . Did you? . . . Dat's a shame, 'cause

boy, I don't think I'm comin' in today, y'get me? . . *Nooo*, dat's not a good idea either . . . *Huh*? . . . Oh dat's my cousin–in–law Cory, he's lookin' after me . . .'

She smiled at Cory. He scowled at the phone.

'Yeah, yeah . . . OK . . . I'll see you around, 'byeee.'

She put the phone down and winked at Cory.

'Cor, you and Sean are jus' the same. He gave me exactly the same look as you did when he met dat brer Marcus.'

'What, so Sean knows my man?' Cory replied. He hadn't mentioned it to him.

'Yeah, he met him the other day. Y'know my friend Marlena, dat goes to our college? Well he's her cousin. He came up to the college to see me, but of course, I wasn't dere.'

Cory decided to keep his mouth shut, even though he felt protective of Sonia, if only for his cousin's sake. It seemed strange the guy was calling her up at home and looking for her at college, but at the end of the day, it was up to her what to do with her life. He knew Sonnie was fairly honest and he didn't think she'd see other boys usually . . . but the way Sean was behaving lately, he wouldn't blame her for wanting to meet new people and broaden her horizons. He just hoped she wouldn't do a Tanya on Sean.

4 p.m.

Children's ITV had just begun. Cory and Sonia sat on the sofa together, the dominoes in a pile on the table, put down hours ago. Both of them were bored, bored to tears by now and there'd been no word from Sean, as well as nothing on the news. They talked about him, as Daffy Duck got his beak slapped off on the TV, leaving a blank space for a face as he felt around attempting to retrieve it.

'I don't know why he's doin' dis,' Sonia was saying, half an eye on the screen. 'I thought he was happy the way he was. I really thought I knew him, but in the last few days, he's bin doin' some really crazy things. The other day he came here an' he blatantly lied to me, tellin' me that he was finished wid Levi an' he was goin' straight. Now *dis*.'

Cory was silent for a moment, thinking he was the one who'd

told Sean not to confess to Sonia about the first robbery. Presumably, his cousin had decided that since she already knew about the first one, she'd no need to know of the second. It might've worked as well, as Sonia hadn't had a clue about what was happening, but who had turned around and told her what was really going on? *He* had.

Sean was going to go mad.

He shifted uncomfortably in his seat and looked across at Sonia. 'You never know, we could both be wrong an' Sean could be doin' somethin' good. Jus' 'cause he's gone missin' don't mean he's up to summick, does it?'

His words were hesitant, unsure and Sonia picked up on it easily.

'I dunno,' she said, equally hesitantly. 'Levi's car ain't parked out dere, I've looked.'

'Don't mean nothin',' Cory shot back. 'He ain't gonna do a armed wid his own ride is he?'

Sonia nodded, realising the truth in that, then she looked at him, smiling.

'You know what; in a way I'm glad we got dis chance to chat. I know we've known each other for time, but . . . it's hard to say dis, but I think I had a wrong impression of you. I've always seen you as a miniature Levi, y'know sellin' weed, robbin', all o' dat shit. I never looked into your personality, cos I assumed you didn't have one.'

Cory barked laughter.

'No it's true, you'd be amazed how many people around here don't have their own personalities. Everyone's gotta front, y'know, pretend they're someone else and try an' fit a role y'get me. It's always the same old roles. I'm hard, I'm a cat, I'm a . . . I dunno, I'm a *mugger* or something, y'get me? I thought you wasn't no different, but I was blatantly wrong, so forgive me all right? Now I can see what Rosie sees in you, properly.'

Cory laughed again. 'Seen, now it all comes out. You thought I was no good all that time man, dat's cold.'

'I never hid it. I was wrong dat's all.'

They talked some more, for the first time actually enjoying each other's company, instead of just bearing one another for Sean's sake. On Sonia's mother's mantelpiece, a brass clock ticked away the passing time slowly. To Cory, sitting facing the clock, it seemed to take forever.

6 p.m.

'*COORRRY!*'

Sonia's yell cut through the silence of the flat, easily reaching the teen, who was in the bathroom urinating when the cry came. He pulled his tracksuit bottoms up, over his bulky cast and as quick as he could, he fumbled out of the door and into the living room, knocking his leg painfully.

'Quick, quick, I think it's happened,' Sonia was saying as he came in. He almost fell onto the sofa in his haste and he turned to the TV feeling scared, more scared than ever. The dominoes of fate were falling, picking up speed, every action causing a reaction . . .

The face of Leon Hawthorne, a black reporter for the ITV news programme, *London Tonight*, filled the screen. Behind him was a jeweller's shop window, the bullet holes clearly visible, even though he was standing in the middle of the street. On the corner of the screen, a blue sign flashed the word 'Live' at them, so they could tell how recent the incident was. On the edge of the picture, a badly damaged Vauxhall Astra could be seen, as well as a couple of kids waving and saying, 'Hello Mum' and capering about. As Leon Hawthorne talked, a policeman appeared and took them away.

'Drama came to the North London suburb of Arnos Grove this afternoon,' Leon was saying, in his well spoken tones, 'in the form of a daring armed raid on this high street jewellers behind me, by four masked men. The men pulled up right where I'm standing now, then rushed inside, demanding everything they could get their hands on and brandishing sawn-off shotguns, as well as a number of automatic pistols. In the following panic, one brave man, whom the police are reluctant to name at this moment, attempted to wrestle the gun away from one of the men. The results were horrendous.'

The camera cut to an earlier interview, placed on the same street, a little nearer to the shop. Cory counted eight bullet holes in the shop's window, before turning his attention to the man talking, who claimed to have been inside the jewellers when everything went down. Sonia sat beside him frozen, her hand covering her mouth, hardly daring to breathe.

'D'you think it was—'

'Sssssh!' Cory replied, leaning forwards in his seat. The man on the screen was talking, loudly and rapidly.

'Well, they come runnin' in shoutin' an' swearin' like troopers sayin', "Get your effin' hands up, get 'em up now!"'

The man talked excitedly, clearly enjoying his moment of fame, however brief.

'Then they had us all on the floor, hands over our heads, while the girl behind the counter got 'em the money. One of 'em had, like a duffel bag an' he was emptyin' trays of rings an' dat into it, not payin' attention to what was goin' on. So dis coloured geezer there, he had a go y'know, like you do and he tried to get the gun off 'im. Uhh . . . they fought for a bit, y'know, then the guy pushed him away an' one of the others shot him. That's all,' he finished, as if that wasn't enough.

Off camera a voice said, 'Where?'

'Eh?' He held a hand over his ear.

'Where was he shot?' the voice repeated.

The man sighed. 'Uhh, in 'is stomach. Point blank I fink.'

He stared straight at the camera, looking slightly sick, before they cut back to a shot of Leon, with forensic policemen pacing around behind him, clearly looking for fallen shells.

'The police are particularly interested in this case, as some of the weapons used seemed to be the latest available on the black market and they're keen to trace where they came from. After leaving the scene of the crime, the masked men jumped into a car, which was chased, but eventually was lost somewhere in the Seven Sisters area.

'Police are looking for a blue Nova GTE, registration number D578 TYN, that's D578 TYN, with a sunroof and a body kit. Police are also urging the public that if this vehicle is seen to use extreme caution, to phone them immediately and not to approach it, under any circumstances. Meanwhile, in a North London hospital, a man is fighting for his life, a tragic victim of the rising tide of gun violence rapidly taking over our city. This is Leon Hawthorne for *London Tonight* in Arnos Grove.'

Cory stared, as the face of Fiona Foster replaced Leon's in the *London Tonight* studio, looking serious and tense as she gave the number on which to phone with information about the raid. Sonia goggled at the screen, still holding the same position Cory found her in when he'd entered the room. He glanced at her, worried by her inactivity.

'Oh my God,' she said slowly. 'He done it, he really done it man.'

Cory edged over to her, cautiously.

'Hey, are you OK? D'you wanna cup of tea or anythin'?' he muttered, as Sonia wrapped her arms around herself, even though the flat was warm and the weather outside was bright and sunny. The shocked girl nodded and he hobbled to the kitchen calling back, 'How many sugars?' as he went.

'Two,' Sonia replied, barely audible. He turned the kettle on, his head against the refrigerator, shaking it from side to side, as if he was trying to erase his thoughts, begging himself to hold things together. When he heard the click of the kettle automatically switching itself off, he stood up and called into the living room, his voice hopeful.

'It could've bin someone else y'know, nuff man's on a armed vibe these days.'

He spooned out some sugar and put in the tea bags. Sonnie's voice floated back to him, low, but assertive.

'It was him Cory. It's too much of a coincidence for it not to be.'

Silently, Cory agreed. He poured in the water and milk, stirred while cursing himself for the millionth time, then carried the cup stiltedly into the other room. Sonia was crying again, her fist against her mouth, stifling the sound of her tears.

'I'm sorry,' she sobbed, trying, but unable to hold her emotions in check, 'I jus' want my Sean back.'

Cory closed his eyes, the guilt surging through him like a strong electrical current, rooting him to the spot for an eternity.

10 p.m.

Sonia lay on the sofa, a blanket wrapped around her body like a bed-ridden pensioner, while Cory sat on the chair across the room from her, his eyes red and his head feeling like a squidgy sponge. Sean's girl had been sleeping for the past hour, leaving Cory alone with only his conscience for company. He didn't care. His conscience had been harassing him since the day Sean walked into the hospital ward, flushed with his pleasure at saving him from Levi's clutches. He should have been well used to it by now.

Levi . . .

Fuckin' fake Dredd, Cory thought.

His conscience told him not to blame other people. His conscience said it was all down to him.

Cory only half agreed. True, he'd been the principal reason Sean had been brought into this whole thing; he'd been the catalyst that had turned the spark into a burst of flame, igniting something in Sean that no one had believed existed. But that hadn't been intentional. The Dredd was the one who was using Sean for his own devices, like some drug-selling Fagin, more than likely feeding him crack too, for where else would Sean have got the taste from?

It wasn't that late, but Cory was bushed. He'd phoned Rosie earlier, ignoring her aunt's sharp tone and told her he couldn't see her tonight, because it had 'happened'. She guessed what he was talking about straightaway and offered to come over to Sonnie's to keep him company. Cory refused, not wanting her that intimately involved in things. He liked talking to her because she was completely detached from the events that had taken over his life. Ultimately, he wanted to keep it that way. Rosie had been cool about it, saying she definitely wanted to see him tomorrow as they had some 'unfinished business' to take care of. If it wasn't for Levi fucking up the programme, he could be with her now.

He laughed at himself in the dark, Sonia's snores just audible. He wished his cousin would come back. He wished he was rich, so he could just pick up his family and leave the country to go somewhere else, anywhere he could see a clear sky, instead of clouds for weeks on end. He wished that Levi would leave his cousin alone and let him get back to what he was good at – studying and being a best friend to him, the person who needed him around the most, the person who *missed* having him around.

'If wishes were horses, beggars would ride.' This was another of Bernice's sayings and one that always made the Bradley children laugh as kids, the image of horseriding tramps hilarious to them. Now he was older, it made undeniable sense to him at a time when it seemed that wishes were all he had left. Sean was off and riding his own wish, chasing and hunting for life's material things.

Chapter Fifteen

Levi's bottle green Vauxhall Frontera pulled into its usual space outside Beechwood House at around nine in the morning. All was quiet on the estate. The few people who passed the vehicle were either parents, late taking their kids to school, or older schoolchildren in a crew, late too, but not half as bothered, as well as the occasional hurrying worker. The occupants of the car talked for a while, then got out, each of the four passengers carrying hefty-looking sacks that clinked and rattled as they moved. Levi went into the boot and fished out two similar-looking bags, while the passengers – Sean, Clarence, Gary and a fair-skinned boy named Mo – waited at the foot of the stairs to Levi's block.

A small white youth played football with an empty Tango can in front of them, oblivious to their presence, looking neat and tidy in his smart black school uniform. As Levi passed him, the boy looked up from his noisy game and noticed the boys and their loads for the first time.

'Raas man, where you lot goin' wid dem big bags deh?' he said, peering up at them inquisitively. Levi ruffled the boy's head as he passed and laughed, with the teenagers joining in, amused by the white boy's attempt at chatting 'yard talk'. The boy grinned up at them.

'Jus' cool yuh lickle self an' go school man,' the Dredd replied easily, as he went up the stairs with the teenagers close behind him. He turned to face them as they climbed and whispered in a low tone.

'Dat yout's mudda love black man a way star! She's fit too

y'know, I t'ink me affe pass her drum again one night! Furdamore, we should all pass star!'

The youths all laughed dutifully, while Sean smiled, thinking about Amanda Brooks from his sociology classes. He hadn't thought of his class, or Amanda, or even Sam Boyd in a very long time. He wondered what was going on there, a world away from the things he'd seen and done in the last twenty-four hours. The hand holding his bag shook with unreleased tension and Sean's face was lined and dry looking. He didn't feel so good either.

He'd already been sick in Shawna's house, as quietly as he could so the others wouldn't hear him. He felt his gorge rise again as his sick brain replayed the moment of the sawn-off's impact, the moment when blood flew everywhere, including his own clothes. He retched silently, then lifted the bag higher on his aching shoulder, trying desperately to forget.

Levi let them into the flat where it was quiet, dark and cool. Sean headed straight for the toilet, dumping the bag in the hallway and hearing one of the squatters come out of the pipe room, congratulating them for a job well done.

He locked the door behind himself, and just made it to the toilet bowl before everything he'd eaten that morning came back up in a noisy, stinking rush, filling the bowl. He clutched the smooth porcelain sides, breathing weakly and painfully and retching some more until he was sure he was done. Then he got up and washed his face, trying not to look in the mirror. Eventually he had to and he peeked anxiously at his reflection.

His eyes looked wild and even though his hair was cut short, it was sticking up all over the place, which added to his unkempt appearance. He looked over his garms (which were old anyway) and could still see bits of the man who'd been shot, dotting his jacket and jeans, like a crazy pattern that had a meaning somewhere. After waiting until the spinning in his head had abated, he unlocked the door and picked up his bag, heading for the back room.

Levi was building a spliff. Gary and Clarence were comparing items from their bags, while Mo sat apart from them, looking lonely and a little afraid. Levi had used the youth as a replacement for Darren, whom he claimed was 'too bright'. Mo had seemed full of high spirits until the unfortunate man had lost his stomach. He'd hardly spoken to anyone since then and he rejected all efforts to cheer him up, becoming lost in his own world. Levi ignored him, telling the others he was young and it'd been his first job. Mo was twelve.

Levi emptied all the bags out and after studying the gleaming haul for a minute, he told the youths to fill up their bags with whatever they wanted. Clarence and Gary went mad, going for the biggest things they could find. Sean saw no use in taking things he wouldn't be able to carry, and he didn't want to get nicked on his way over to Sonia's.

He asked Levi if he could borrow a rucksack he'd seen lying around the day before and then made himself busy, filling it up with as many small things as he could find, including rings, necklaces and watches. There were many things to choose from, as they had over six bags worth of gold on the floor. When they were done, Levi gave them their cut of the cash, which worked out to just under a grand. Sean gave Levi a sly look.

'Dat's somethin' I was meant to ask you,' he told the man casually. 'What d'you do with all the cheques an' all dem other t'ings from the till?'

Levi laughed and tapped his nose. 'Yuh a smart yout' but yuh affe know when an' how to ask de right questions, y'get me?'

Shaking his head, Sean took a few quick blasts on his zook, before passing it to Mo. The boy took it silently, then drew on it hard, pulling the smoke into his lungs. Sean felt hurt at seeing this young boy, who had been so vibrant, reduced to this pathetic-looking person, but it really wasn't his problem. Bidding the others goodbye and promising to link up with Levi soon, he left the flat, his eyes bleary and his rucksack full of gold heavy on his back.

It was time to see his girl.

He let himself into Sonia's flat with the spare key she'd lent him. The light that came through the main window in the living room was bright and warm. The chattering of birds, loud in the room's prevailing silence, made Sean feel a little more buoyant as he walked into the flat, closing the door behind him.

He spied a comatose figure on the sofa, covered by one of Sonia's thick blankets. Instantly thinking of Marcus, he walked sternly over, meaning to have a serious talk with this brer, who always seemed to turn up when he wasn't around.

When he got closer, he saw the crutches lying on the floor next to the sofa and he realised it was Cory. Baffled but glad, he looked down on the sleeping teen, then decided he looked knackered. He left him to go into Sonia's room on tiptoe.

At the sight of his girl, snoring lightly with one hand thrown over her head, her mouth open slightly, Sean felt a stirring in his loins that made him smile. She looked like a goddess when she was sleeping, or a child princess, innocent and radiant with the unconscious beauty only sleep, or death, can bring. He sat on the bed and watched her for a few minutes, studying her lips, her hair, the lines of her cheeks and her slender neck, treasuring the moment in his mind, attempting to use it to block off the distressing thoughts that tried to take over his brain.

Remembering the rucksack on his arm, he shook it onto the floor with a shrug of his shoulder and then pushed it underneath the bed quietly. That done, he took one more look at his girl, then shook her by her shoulder, leaning over and whispering her name. She opened her eyes, then saw him and smiled, before recollection came back, freezing the smile in its place. It withered and died like an unwatered flower.

'Sean?'

She struggled to sit up, roughly wiping the sleep from her eyes and pushing Sean further down the bed in one quick motion. He grinned at her, amused by her confusion.

'Where the fuck have you bin then? I've bin waitin' for you all night.'

He looked at her in amazement, stunned by her ferocity. It just didn't gel with the innocent visions he'd been having of her seconds before. Uncomfortably, he shrugged, falling back into a defensive position.

'I 'ad some things to do man, some runnings to take care of, y'get me?'

Sonia kissed her teeth, her look of amazement matching Sean's equally.

'Sean!' she said again, her voice rising an octave this time, unhinging her anger. She launched into a furious tirade, the words spilling into the air. 'Sean, what's happenin' to you?

You've lied to jus' about everyone to do your . . . *runnings* and now you're tryin' to mask up dis thing from me again. I'm not havin' it Sean, I jus' ain't havin' it.'

'I'm not lyin' to you Sonnie—' he began.

'Sean, you robbed a fuckin' *jewellers'* shop . . . Somebody got *shot*,' she blasted. 'Can't you see what you're gettin' into, with that fuckin' Levi an' his crackhead mates? Have you turned stupid or somethin'?'

In the living room, Cory heard the muffled shouts that prised the lid away from his sleep and he yawned as he sat up, meaning to go into the room and give moral support to whoever needed it most. He pushed a leg from underneath the blanket and then heard Sonnie launch into another blast of words, making him sit back on the sofa, at once changing his mind. He wasn't stupid.

In the bedroom, her anger partly spent, Sonia stopped shouting, though her vexed gaze still held. Sean was staring at the floor, rubbing his lips together, like he always did when he was thinking deeply.

He wanted to tell Sonnie about his fear yesterday. He wanted to tell her how he'd felt as the pellets started flying – but it was impossible. All of his pride was wrapped up in those dark moments and he refused to let his girl in on his moment of weakness, however justified. Startling himself, Sean realised he was deeply ashamed of his nausea over the wounded man. He now knew he could never bring himself to tell Sonia about that.

His girl leaned forward, trying to sound less intimidating. 'Do you know how worried your sister is about you?'

Sean looked at her sharply. 'Shannon? Don't tell me she knows.'

Sonia's icy look thawed a little. 'She doesn't . . . but she suspects. None of us are idiots y'know, no matter what you an' your cronies think. D'you know Cory was up virtually all las' night, waitin' for you to come back? Of course you couldn't, you was too busy gallivantin', playin' at being a gangster, innit?'

Hurt, Sean squirmed, feeling guilty. He glared at his girl spitefully.

'Cory was here las' night?' he said thickly. 'I mean in *here*?'

She chose not to answer, her eyes not wavering from his in

the slightest. Eventually he looked away, leaned over and began pulling the rucksack out from underneath the bed, a manoeuvre that perplexed Sonia no end. When he glanced back at his girl, he held an apologetic expression on his face.

'All right, dat was out of order I'm sorry. But Sonnie, look at dis, no . . .' He held up a hand, as Sonia made as if she wanted to speak again. She relented and sat back, waiting. ' . . . don't say nothin' for a minute, lemme have my say. You know how much is in here Sonnie?'

He lifted the heavy bag onto the bed, then opened it up in her direction. Sonia could see the gleam of assorted jewellery, things she'd stared achingly at while window shopping countless times before. The rings were heavy looking, some set with sovereigns, others with large precious stones, with soothingly cool colours. Bracelets and chains lay in a tangle, so you couldn't tell beginning or end.

'Dere's about three gran' in gold in dat bag, not countin' the cash,' Sean was saying, his face full of passion. 'All together I've got more than the unemployed get in a year, an' dat's wiv two moves . . . Two moves Sonnie! I don't even 'ave to go out dere again, y'get me? Things can be back to normal, like they was before.'

He was pleading with her, while trying to sound like he wasn't.

I've heard dat once too often, Sonia thought to herself, Sean's words bringing her back to reality and breaking the sparkling lure of the bag. She looked away from it and Sean, as if she couldn't stand the sight of either, although they remained in her peripheral vision no matter which way she looked. Sean closed the bag, worried as Sonia's voice floated to him in a monotone, sounding infinitely tired.

'All right Sean, you've had your say. Now can you take the bag from my yard an' get out, right now. You don't even seem to care dat a man – a *black* man at dat – was shot by you an' your friends—'

'*I DIDN'T FUCKIN' SHOOT NO ONE SONIA!*' Sean exploded, swinging around to face his girl, desperate for her to believe him. She gave an involuntary gasp, fearing him for a moment, as his eyes were crazy for that split second.

In the living room, Cory fidgeted uncomfortably. Should he go in? He wanted to, but he could not bring his legs to move and instead he lit half a spliff that he had left in an ashtray the night before deciding, yet again, to wait.

Back in Sonia's room, Sean was swinging the bag onto his shoulder by one strap, his face as hard as stone. Sonia said nothing as he got up, then crossed the room to the door, merely averting her eyes from him, wanting to call him back, but letting her stubbornness rule. Sean stopped at the door, then turned back to face her hesitantly.

'Listen Sonia . . . If anyone comes askin' . . . police I mean . . . well, if you could jus' say I was with you yestiday.'

His girl finally looked up, her eyes full of tears, which rolled easily down her cheeks, leaving a trail that she wiped away.

I hate cryin', she growled to herself, distressed with the way it made her look. She redirected the hate at Sean, letting it colour her words in anger.

'Get out will you Sean. An' don't come back till you've fixed up will you?' she told him, with as much feeling as she could muster.

Sean sighed very audibly, then slammed out of the bedroom, feeling as though Sonia was using her tears like a knife to gouge and rip at his heart. He waded forcefully into the living room, where his cousin was sitting awake, if not fully aware, just outing a spliff. Cory looked up at Sean, not a trace of a smile on his face.

'What's up cuz, wha' you sayin' star? Can't you see boy.'

Sean nodded, glad for Cory's presence, as always.

'Safe an' dat. You know how it go.'

He shifted the bag from his left shoulder to his right, a little lost for words, as he knew Cory must have heard the argument with his girl. Cory gestured at the bag.

'So what, is dat the t'ings dere den?'

'Yeah man.'

Sean looked around, as if just realising his surroundings.

'Hear what now, come we doss out star, true Sonnie's goin' on dark.'

Cory nodded in agreement and grabbed his crutches, using them as leverage to help himself up. They left the flat, walked down the corridor and caught the elevator in silence, then emerged onto the sunny street.

'You gotta help me with my alibi man,' Sean blurted. 'Sonia won't bring me in. I'm gonna have Rads on my case if things don't go to plan an' I gotta have a story, y'get me? I thought Sonnie would sort me out, but she's goin' on like she hates me star, so dat's out of the question. Wha' you sayin' star, c'n you defen' it or what?'

Cory thought for a while, even though in the back of his mind, he knew what he'd do at once.

'What the fuck happened star?' he eventually managed, changing tack. 'Who shot dat brer?'

Sean's face screwed up in righteous anger.

'You know what cuz? Dat was that bastard Levi. He didn't even have no cause to do dat, he jus' let off on my man . . .'

The teen paused, looking at the sky as if it was a giant cinema screen, his memories projected onto the blue heavens for his eyes only.

'He was cryin' an' shit man, until he passed out, y'get me? Dere was blood an' . . . nasty stuff dat looked like digested food all over the floor . . . my man was shakin' like a leaf an' everythin' boy. One brer, Gary, got hit in the face with all dat shit an' look . . .' He showed Cory his sweater disdainfully. 'I got it all over me as well. Fuckin' sick innit?'

Cory nodded, looking over Sean's clothing and shaking his head.

'Blatant. Me an' Sonnie heard on the news he's in critical condition star. I don't think he'll last the day myself.' Cory's voice was a deathly baritone.

So that's how she knew so much, Sean thought to himself, at once feeling as though every eye in the street was on him. He turned to Cory, his mind replaying what he'd just heard.

'How come you was stayin' at Sonnie's den, you tryin' t'sting me?' he muttered, pretending to be sullen.

Cory went unusually quiet and refused to look his cousin in the face. Sean glanced at him, looked away, then snatched his head back, at once seeing the guilt-stricken look all over his face. A cold feeling went through him and he felt hollow inside, his stomach clenching nervously. He imagined his girl and his cousin, all alone for the night in her flat.

'Cory, what the *fuck's* goin' on?' he spat, hoping his cousin would completely disprove his suspicions. Fatigue tore at his judgement and he looked at Cory with an irrational rising anger. Cory's reply was completely unexpected.

'All right Sean, it was me,' Cory confessed, looking at the youth mournfully.

Sean screwed up his face, not understanding. 'Wha' you talkin' about man, I'm baffled . . .'

They were both silent. Cory quickly realised he'd put his foot in it. He continued, preferring things out in the open so he wouldn't have to lie to Sean. Tentatively, he explained.

'It was me dat tol' Sonnie you was doin' the move. She come to our drum dis mornin' all upset, an' I had to tell 'er man . . . The girl was in tears, makin' up a whole 'eap o' noise an' Shannon nearly came in on the whole thing. I'm sorry blood, but it had t'be done man—'

'You gee'd me up to Sonia?' Sean broke in, sounding angry. In fact, he was relieved that neither Sonia nor Cory had betrayed him. He was a little disturbed that Cory grassed him, but felt equally keen not to let on what he'd been thinking moments before. He decided anger was the best emotion to fake for now. Still, by the look on his cousin's face, he wouldn't be able to keep that up for very long.

'Fuckin' 'ell Sean, I dunno what come over me man . . . I tell you summick, it won't happen again, believe. I only done it for you y'know Sean – you don't know how worried I was yesti-day . . .'

That did it. Sean turned away from Cory, once again looking at the sky and the forest of blocks surrounding them. He couldn't pretend anger when deep down inside him he knew he was in the wrong. An image of the man in the jewellers, shotgun pellets peppering his body, flashed across his brain. Sickened, he strove for normality in his voice.

'So what, you up for coverin' me or what?' he asked, changing the subject as sullenly as he could.

Cory stopped dead, forcing his cousin to stop also, with a speculative half smile on his face. He tapped the rucksack with one crutch, not returning the smile, his expression serious.

'Yeah, I'll back you up man – on one condition. After dis move, you have to call it a day, serious t'ing. I don't even like dis side of you. It ain't right man, it ain't *you*, y'unnerstan'.'

Sean's grin broadened, but it was slightly self-conscious. His own confession spilled from his guts – words he'd been unable to say to Sonnie and words he'd probably never repeat to anyone besides his cousin.

'You better believe it ain't me star. I threw up when we got to Levi's house man, thinkin' about dat brer. I ain't even shocked he's critical to tell the truth, true he took a point-blank shot. I still feel queasy all now, believe me. I ain't goin' through dat shit again, especially the way Sonnie looked at me.' He jerked a thumb back at the rucksack. 'It ain't worth ten o' these man.'

'So wha' you sayin',' Cory pressured. 'You gonna stop movin' wi' dat fake Dredd now or what?'

They stared at each other, a tense silence filling the gap between the boys. Sean suddenly burst into an easy smile.

'Yeah man – dem t'ings are done wid f'real . . . I swear on my life, dis is the las' time Cory . . . I'm *out*.'

Cory nodded, unsmiling, and they resumed their walk, each feeling a little better now. Laughing at a sudden thought, Cory turned to Sean. 'Well, jus' as soon as we get you an' the bait bag off the road, you c'n give it to me, if you feel dat way!'

Sean cackled and threw his head back. 'Fuck you man. Furthermore, I got a dett sterlin' silver ring dat would suit you, if you want it. You could even give it to Rosie if you want.'

Cory joined in Sean's laughter, feeling better and more alive than he had in days. Sean had seen the light. He'd realised Levi was no good. It was tragic a man had to get blasted almost in half for this realisation to come, but such was life, and life was a bitch with PMT. He smiled at Sean through his good-natured haze.

'You always bin a stingy git man,' he spat, cracking up. 'I shoulda realised how you stay when you wouldn't share your *Star Wars* toys when we was yout's.'

They laughed as they walked underneath the tower block's awning, waving at the old African lady who was manning the reception desk as they passed her counter. They then waited for the lift impatiently, still chuckling and shaking their heads as they watched the floor numbers falling as the lift got closer. Just before it came, Cory had an idea, which he relayed to his cousin as soon as it hit him.

'Hear what now spee, I feel dis good news calls for a celebration y'get me? I'm gonna go shops an' hol' a bottle o' brandy, I won't be long.'

Sean smiled his agreement, but inwardly he was a bit dubious, as he didn't feel they had anything to celebrate yet. He was also tired enough to sleep for the whole day. Drink was the last thing on his mind, but Cory looked so pleased, he felt he owed it to the teen. He patted his pockets for money.

'Safe man, I got a little change, I'll cover it,' Cory said, backing away.

'Respec' blood,' Sean looked at Cory gratefully.

'Soon come,' the injured teen told Sean, swinging away.

The lift arrived almost at the same time, chiming gently, calling for people to step inside. Sean entered, thinking of Sonia and her reaction to him back at the flat.

She'll calm down, he told himself, not even sure if he believed she would. She'd been vex, more vex than he'd ever seen her. That was not a good sign at all. I'll phone her tomorrow, he decided, as he pushed his floor number and watched the dimpled metal door slide shut. He'd made a mistake acting the tough man in front of her; he should've just told her the truth – he was frightened by what he'd seen and was ready to throw the towel in for good. He wouldn't be able to stand losing Sonnie now. He had to get her back.

Full of good spirits (and hoping to fill himself up with more, soon enough), Cory hopped his way to the shops in the bright sunshine, already feeling some heat on his back. Even though it was early in the morning, the streets were busy and when he got to the off-licence, he was amazed to see just how many loafers were lazing outside. In deep thought, he completely ignored the figure that rushed out of the bakery past him and then stopped, recognising him.

'Cory?' A male voice was calling him from behind. 'Cory man, wha' you sayin'? Walk right past me will ya, ya cunt!'

Cory spun around to see his old school friend, Craig Price, staring at him with his familiar wry smile. The teen was surprised to see him, as he had thought Craig was long gone from the West London scene. He swung his way over to the boy, beaming.

'What's up man, long time star,' the teen said, sincerely. Craig smiled, reaching out to shake Cory's hand. After some fumbling with his crutches, the teen managed it with an embarrassed grin.

'I've bin hearin' about you!' the boy said, his Cockney accent even stronger now, helped along by a stint in the army. 'What the fuck's bin happenin' man?'

Cory sighed. 'Craig I tell you, it's too much to go into right about now believe me. I jus' had some trouble with some boys from dat little estate up the road man. I'll tell you more another time.'

He paused, glad to see his old friend and wanting to talk about something else for a change.

'So what, when d'you lan', where you comin' from star?'

Craig gave a blissful smile and stretched fully. 'Me? I tell you Cory, I jus' come back from Mecca boy, serious t'ing, it's heaven out dere.'

'*Mecca*?' Cory peered at the teenager, stunned. 'Don't tell me you turned Muslim?'

The boy cracked up, shaking his head. 'Nah man, I bin Amsterdam blood, the Mecca for drugs takers, y'get me! You should see it out dere, 'ave you bin?'

Cory shook his head sadly, laughing at the same time.

'Man it's the lick I'm tellin' you. Hundreds of different weeds man, you can smoke a ziggy right in front of the Rads, even though they got guns and the beautiful girls . . . aw man, you'd love it out dere, I know you would man.'

'So how long was you dere?'

'A week an' it was well worth it mate.'

Craig still looked like he was there; his eyes were clear, yet glazed and he seemed full of energy.

'So what's up with the army shit? You on leave or summick?' Cory questioned inquisitively.

Craig chuckled again. 'Yeah, I'm on leave man: permanent leave. They kicked me out, cause I got caught sellin' green with dis other brer I linked up with in the base.'

'Ah man!' Cory was incensed. 'What did your paps say?'

'He was all right y'know, gimme an' ear bashin' an' that was it boy. I might look a nex' job, I might not y'get me? Depends how I feel man. How's Sean anyway?'

'Ah he's safe, jus' coolin' man.'

'What about Garvey, he still jugglin' Es?'

'On an' off,' Cory replied, thinking that lately, it was more on than off.

Craig gave him a speculative look, as if balancing something in the scales of his mind, before beckoning him over to the road-side where cars were parked and there were fewer people passing by. Intrigued, Cory followed, wondering what was on the boy's mind.

'I'm gonna tell you summick spee an' dis is between me an' you, yeah?' he began, in a serious tone of voice.

Cory nodded, showing he understood.

'When I come out the army, they chucked me out straight-away, the same day they found the greens, y'get me? I'd had an idea for a scam for weeks an' me an' the brer that was sellin' the weed had bin smugglin' guns out of the base for months man an' stashin' 'em with dis girl that I was seein' out dere, don't even ask me how. Let's jus' say that the security were a little partial to a bit o' the white stuff, y'know? Anyway, I got about two bags of 'em before I got kicked out, chock filled with rifles, hand pistols, even a few grenades that we nicked, all fairly new an' virtually unused, y'get me?'

'So what, you lettin' 'em off?' the teen asked, getting to the point.

'Yeah man, any one you want, at ridiculous prices man, true I wanna get rid of them, quick as poss'. I heard about that grief you was havin' an' I was wonderin' if maybe you could use one man, true I know none o' them 'ave bin used in anythin' else, so they're as clean as Gary Lineker's reputation mate. Things are gettin' fucked up around here since I bin away, so you never know when you might need some protection.'

'Sure is,' Cory said truthfully. 'But I reckon the way t'ings are goin' nowadays, I'll hol' that bucky an' get shif', without even gettin' a chance to let it off star. Look at me as well man, I can jus' about stan' up, let alone hold a gun. I'll tell you what, I'll 'llow it for now, but gimme your number still, jus' in case.'

'Yeah yeah,' Craig replied, searching for a pen.

Cory produced an old Underground ticket and Craig wrote a mobile number and home number on the card. When he was done, he handed it to the teen, who scanned it, then placed it in his pocket.

'The mobile's me, but the other number's my partner, Petey. If I'm not around deal with him, he'll sort you out neatly. That goes for anythin', green, bone, Es, y'get me? If you see Garvey, give 'im my number too yeah? I gotta doss man, my dad wants to see me, so jus' ding me any time, all right?'

'Definitely,' Cory replied. 'I'll bell you star.'

'Later on,' Craig yelled, turning and walking away briskly.

Smiling, Cory turned and went into Kareem's store, looking at the mass of bottles behind the counter for a bit, eventually deciding to settle for a quarter bottle of Martell. He paid, fielding questions from the shop's assorted staff about when his cast would be coming off, then stuffed the bottle into his jacket pocket, before checking his change and leaving. He hadn't gone far when he bumped into Shannon coming out of the Sunshine Fruit 'n' Veg store, her hands full with bags.

'Hiya hopalong! What's up, lost your parrot?' she said, looking bright and cheery as usual. Cory 'ha ha'd' sarcastically and made as if he hadn't heard.

'You're up early innit, what's the occasion?'

'Breakfast,' Shannon replied, holding up her bags like a fisherman showing off a prized catch. 'You'd better be nice to me as well 'cos it's gonna be dett man!'

'I ain't the one who was takin' the piss outta you,' her cousin moaned, putting on a sullen look. She 'aahed' and put an arm around him, squeezing their cheeks together tightly and making him fight her off, laughing while he looked around cautiously to see who'd noticed her embrace. Shannon rolled her eyes, waving the bags around recklessly.

'Where you comin' from anyway, Rosie's?' she questioned, the bloodhound in her taking over.

'Nah man, you're jokin'. I was jus' gettin' some ciggies,' he lied, not wanting his cousin to think he was hitting the bottle and also not wanting to explain why he and Sean were celebrating. She frowned in reply.

'I got browns,' she told him, patting her pockets to reassure herself.

'Yeah well, I want my own star. I'm a independent kinda man, y'get me?'

Shannon snorted as if she had heard something both unbelievable and funny.

'Please yourself den. I'll walk up an' wait for you on the corner, OK?'

'Yeah yeah, I won't be long.'

The newsagent's was situated next door to the fruit 'n' veg store, though if he'd really wanted cigarettes, he could have bought them from Kareem's. He purchased ten Silk Cut instead of his usual Benson's, thinking distractedly about the low tar, then made his way back along the pavement towards his block, whistling cheerfully.

He vaguely noticed Levi's gleaming Frontera double parked not far from Sue's Cafe on the opposite side of the road. He only recognised the tall, bulky shape of the man when he realised he was talking loudly at Shannon, who was steadfastly attempting to ignore him. The men who stood around laughed in encouragement.

He closed in on Levi until he was only a few paces from him, before stopping and glancing around, as he still wasn't sure the Dredd was without his roughneck henchman.

Scanning the street behind him, he could only see one threat, a solitary policeman, just making his way past Eltham House, with the flatfooted tread that all Mets adopted. He was still more or less a block away and Cory mentally warned himself if he didn't shout too much at Levi, there was a good chance the lawman would walk right past. Pleased with his logical thinking, he covered the last few steps between himself and the older man, steeling himself in fear, but determined to have his say.

Levi was studying Shannon's body, eyeing her legs clad in black leggings and admiring her ankle boots loudly. The other men were also making signs of appreciation, chuckling and joining in with the Dredd occasionally.

'Mmm, *mmm*, dat t'ickness look ready star!' he was saying, still unaware of Cory's presence. 'What'm baby, come chat wi' de man dem nuh!'

Levi gestured at the men and, as one, they all smiled over at Shannon, with grunts of approval as they looked her over once more. Cory swung directly behind the man and spoke in a strong voice, as Shannon abruptly turned, her face angry, then alarmed.

'Levi?' he said.

Levi turned slowly and the men went quiet at the sight of the tall teenager on crutches, some of them recognising him from around the area. When the dealer was fully turned, he smiled at Cory with a grin about as endearing as a crocodile's.

'*What'm* my yout', yuh lan'?' he beamed.

'Yeah I'm out Levi an' it looks like it wasn't a minute too soon innit? I jus' wanted to tell you, real friendly y'know, to stay away from my family from now, right? Both of 'em.'

He gave a mental groan inside his head as he realised he'd given Shannon more reason to suspect something was going on. He looked at her to see if she'd noticed and saw her forehead wrinkling as she tried to figure out what he meant. Levi, not wanting a scene, waved his hands as if he was physically trying to smooth things over.

'How yuh mean star?' his smile was fighting to stay in place. 'Joke me ah mek wid yuh cousin, no need . . .'

'Jus' shut up will you!' Cory snapped. 'I'm warnin' you Levi, leave my fuckin' family alone star, I ain't rampin' wid you!'

Some of the men moved forward at that, anticipating trouble, while the others laughed quietly behind their hands, looking at the concrete.

'A wha' de . . .?' Levi looked as if he couldn't believe what he'd heard, before erupting. 'Ey yuh lickle pussyclaat, min' I don' brok yuh other leg f'you star!' he snarled, stepping forward, his eyes wild, his hand raised and his fist bunched, ready to swing at any moment.

There was an explosion of movement from the corner as some men stepped away and others rushed at Levi to hold him back. Shannon dropped her bags screaming, 'Leave him alone, leave him alone!' as she ran headlong into the cluster of men, jostling the ones on the outside of the crowd out of her way. The sound of scuffling feet filled Cory's ears and somewhere he heard a man shout, though he wasn't sure if it was at them. The dealer's bulk filled his vision and for a moment, Levi was the whole world.

Simon, Johnny's cousin, was one of the men in the gathering. He decided to step in, as he knew that Cory was a respected friend of his relative and thought it might even make him look good in front of the dark beauty they'd been teasing moments ago. He grabbed the Dredd's raised fist with his own, just before Shannon reached them, turning the dealer's wrath on himself. Cory flinched, stumbling on his crutches. Levi snatched his hand away, fixing Simon with a wide-eyed stare.

'Leggo me han' star, wha' do you?' he seethed crazily at the young man, who was slightly built and no match for the bulky Dredd. Simon put the offending hand down as Levi rounded on him, speaking quickly to prove he meant no harm.

'Cool nuh Levi, look a casian right dere star, checkin' over yuh car. Yuh lookin' to get shif' spee.'

Everybody turned their eyes to the road to see the policeman Cory had spied looking over Levi's double-parked car with great interest. As they watched, he tried the doors. He peeked through the windows. He checked the tyres.

When he took out his notepad and a pen to write the car's number down, Levi stepped to Cory and pushed his shoulder, causing him to start. For the first time in his life Cory'd been thanking God for a policeman's actions. He met Levi's hateful gaze and thanked his maker again.

'You better min' yourself yout' man,' the man breathed menacingly, not wanting the others to hear him. 'You won't even see me comin' star.'

His piece said, he turned around and strode away, staring at both Simon and Shannon as he passed them, before he walked past the tall fence of the primary school and was gone from their sight.

The policeman put away his pen and his pad and was walking towards the shops, looking in through the windows in an attempt to establish ownership of the vehicle. Cory thought now was as good a time to leave the scene as any and, nodding to Simon in silent thanks, he motioned to Shannon and lurched away, while his cousin pointedly ignored the lustful stares Simon was shooting her way. When they were on the Denver side of the road, Cory looked back and saw the policeman walking up and down the empty street corner, before eventually reaching for his radio. The teen supposed that now the jeep would get towed away. Good, the cunt, he thought uncharitably, half smiling. Shannon caught his expression and turned on him.

'Oh, I suppose you thought dat was funny did you?' she snapped as she rounded on him.

'No, I—'

'I should fuckin' well think not, 'cause you're an idiot, plain and simple. You was virtually offerin' my man out dere, what's wrong with you? You couldn't even fight a baby like you are now, let alone Levi.'

'Yeah, I know dat, but it's the principle cuz—'

'What, to almost get t'ump up in the street proves some fucked-up macho principle eh? You're lucky dat Rad come, or it would 'ave bin all over star.'

'Yeah you're right, I'm a speng, fuck it man. I can't help my feelin's, I was jus' worried for you Shan.'

The tremor he'd been holding back so long crept into his voice. He turned away from the girl bashfully in the clutch of emotional fatigue.

Shannon looked reproachfully at Cory as they entered their block, feeling bad for having a go at him. They were silent as they passed the reception desk, making the African woman look up. The Bradleys ignored her and waited by the lifts in silence, until suddenly Shannon impulsively hugged the teen, to his surprise, then kissed him on the cheek, her face carrying her apology much more than words could. Glad she seemed to have forgotten about his minor slip up for now, Cory hugged her back, his mind on the immense love he had for his family and the relief he felt of getting everything over with.

They stayed that way, arms wrapped around each other, grinning like teenage lovers until the lift arrived, both of them oblivious to the stares of the people who were waiting in the lobby with them.

PART THREE

The Frying Pan Syndrome

It doesn't matter who is punished, provided that somebody is punished.

George Bernard Shaw

Chapter Sixteen

Two months had passed. The weather that had been in the offing the month before finally arrived on the estate at the beginning of July and then hung around for the rest of the month, bathing the streets in sunshine. It had become one of those summers when you could wake up at nine o'clock and put on a T-shirt without even bothering with a jacket, as you knew that by one o'clock you'd be hot enough to feel like throwing it away.

The cats took to the street in large numbers. Crime in and around the area increased sharply, as pipers who'd normally confined their activities to the nocturnal hours began to feel the long, slow roast, due to rocks as much as the heat. The local constabulary were faced with a spate of muggings and burglaries, most taking place in broad daylight, often with many witnesses.

Sean and Cory heard all of these tales, but they both made a pact to stay out of trouble, at least until the end of term after their exams. Sean felt glad he had a second chance as gradually the fuss about his armed robbery with Levi died down, mostly because of the other news reports that took over almost immediately. The man who'd been shot was alive, although he was still very unwell. The cousins had heard rumours he'd left London for a while to convalesce in peace and quiet.

Sean felt a little better after hearing that and thus, relieving himself of some of his guilt, he turned his attentions to his family, taking a few much-needed driving lessons, and passing his end of terms.

Cory forced himself to do the same, believing his negative

influence on his cousin had at least partly led to the events that had occurred. Instead of loafing at his friends' houses, smoking and rowdily playing computer games, he headed for the library and revised until his head felt as though it would burst. Most of these sessions were with Sean, and they'd usually leave when the librarian shut the room at seven in the evening. It was hard work, and he managed to sustain it until the middle of June, when he ran out of money and, unbeknown to his cousin, he linked up with Art to begin robbing houses again.

Despite his attempts to rekindle their relationship, Sean was dismayed to find Sonia intransigent. In college, she was coolly polite and no more. When he pushed her she would say she 'needed time to think' and that he should 'give her some space'. So he did.

Those were the times when the urge to buy a rock was strong, stronger than he would have believed, not long ago. He confessed his craving to Cory, who understandably got very upset and responded by plying Sean with weed. It helped, as it soothed his anger rather than fuelling it, but sometimes that cool taste haunted his tongue, desperately.

He brooded and studied and when the exams eventually came around, he was pleased with how he'd fared. Amanda Brooks lent him her notes and jokingly said that if he passed, it was due to her. Sean had a good feeling he'd get through on his own merits. He had to.

On the first week in July, Sean received a call from Sonia. She'd promised to take her sister (who'd returned with her mother from Jamaica in mid-June) to Whiteley's shopping complex in Queensway to see a film called *Free Willie* and then on to Burger King for lunch. She'd just been paid and was wondering if he'd like to join them.

When they finally got to Whiteley's, Sean stood to one side while Sonia waited in the queue to buy their tickets. He watched her with a sense of pride, still seeing her as 'his' no matter what her attitude towards him was. Before he'd met up with her that day, he'd been worried she'd called him up to tell him it was over between them. Now he was fairly confident she still checked for him, as it'd been just like old times on the tube ride up to the complex.

Sean liked the UCI's cinemas. He'd been there many times before with Sonia. It was clean, it was cool and most of all, he liked the neat little hole at the side of your seat to slip your drink into when your hands were full. Tamika loved the film and she sat between the two teenagers, cheering and laughing, along with the hundreds of other kids. She insisted on staying until the very last credit rolled away, then they left the empty cinema and made a beeline for Burger King.

Sean insisted on paying for the meal, something that irked Sonia no end, but she eventually relented, not wanting to make a scene in front of her sister. They sat downstairs and, after they had stuffed their faces and Tamika had gone to the toilet, the couple finally found themselves alone. Sonia brushed the corner of her mouth with a napkin and smiled at Sean.

'So, how d'you reckon your exams went?' she probed.

'Ah, not too bad y'know. I had to cram a little, but Amanda gave me some of her notes so I jus' put my head down, y'get me? Cory helped me as well y'know.'

'Dat's good,' Sonia was still smiling. 'You know Amanda likes you innit?'

'*Nah* man, don't gimme dat!'

'It's true, she's bin tellin' people! I don't mind, I think it's quite funny to tell the truth.'

'Yeah, well *I* mind.'

Sean didn't know how to take Sonia telling him she didn't mind.

'I only wanted notes off her that's all. It's you I'm on star, not Amanda. I mean, she's cris' an' everythin' but—' He broke off as Tamika came back, her Kid's Club toy tightly clutched in her hand.

'Can we go to dat big park now?' she asked her sister, gazing at her with deep brown eyes. Sonia kissed her head lovingly.

'All right babes, we'll go and let you 'ave a swing about, then we're off home. I'm well tired star.'

'*Yaaaay*!' Tamika yelled happily.

They binned their rubbish and left for the streets, arm in arm again, with the little girl running and leaping at their side.

'So how d'you reckon you did den?' Sean asked as they walked towards the main road.

'I'm not sure,' Sonnie replied truthfully. 'I'm like you, I had a lot on my mind an' I really needed to study hard to catch up again. I answered most of the questions, but only the results'll tell if I got 'em right. It's horrible innit, waiting for 'em to come back?'

'Sure is. My stomach's in knots star.'

Sonia laughed. 'Tellin' me! I . . . Oi Tammy, come away from that dog!'

They'd crossed the road and were at the park gates where Tamika had found a friendly Staff, tightly held by its owner. It was a smooth beige colour, with muscles bulging everywhere and dopey-looking brown eyes. As Sonia disliked dogs, she only saw the sharp teeth and dripping tongue. Tamika, who was laughing with glee, looked up at Sonnie reproachfully.

'It's only a *Staff*,' she said simply, which made Sean and the owner laugh.

'She won't bite, she loves kids,' the middle-aged white man with the leash told them. It made no difference to Sonia.

'Come babes, let's go, come on,' she urged her sister, who reluctantly turned and walked through the park gates, looking back occasionally and leaving Sean to shrug at the owner, his expression saying it was a 'woman thing'.

They walked along a wide tarmac path, headed for a large playground packed full of kids of all colours and ages, climbing, swinging, see-sawing and digging, all of them loving the weather. Sean and Sonnie sat on a bench where they could keep a close eye on Tamika. The teen poked his girl, urging her to look at the kids.

'Looks like a Benetton advert innit?' he commented, smiling. Sonia agreed.

'Innit. It gives us a little hope though I reckon. I mean not everywhere's as fucked up as Greenside. It makes me happy to see dem playin' like dis, it really does. I shoulda brought my camera.'

They watched the kids some more, then Sonia turned to Sean and took his hand. Sean felt his anticipation rise. This was it.

'Sean, uhhh, you musta guessed that I wanted to talk to you about somethin' pretty important today . . .'

Sure did, Sean thought.

' . . . An' I also wanted to say sorry for the way I bin actin' these last few weeks, but it's jus' dat I've bin goin' over things in my mind turnin' 'em over and over, trying to come to some solution about us two, y'know? I . . . I suppose it did us some good bein' apart from one another . . .'

So what you tryin' to say? Sean wanted to ask, but didn't.

' . . . 'cause it . . . well, I don't know about you, but it strengthened *my* feelings, y'get me? Then the exams come an' I really wanted to pass, so I had to block you out for a while y'know, 'cause it was drivin' me crazy . . . I mean dis whole Levi thing was . . . Uhh . . . boy . . . I love you still, I can't get away from dat, but dere's one minor complication buggin' me, although it's pretty major when I check it . . .'

Sean tried to keep his mouth shut, but his brain took over, full of thoughts of Marcus, wondering if the teenager had anything to do with this.

'Who's bin buggin' you . . . *Marcus*?' he asked impatiently, forgetting himself.

Sonia was talking on automatic and, reflecting back later, Sean was sure she never heard him.

' . . . I . . . Uhh . . . Well, I think I might be pregnant. In fact, I'm almost positive I am.' *Pregnant*! His thoughts screamed at him.

Sean sat back on the bench with Sonia watching him carefully, taking in deep breaths, staring at the kids but not seeing them. Pregnant! He'd be eighteen in a few weeks and Sonnie thought she was pregnant. It didn't make sense. He hadn't touched her. He wanted to ask if she was sure it was his, but he knew they'd be finished if she even sensed what he was thinking. Besides, in his heart he knew it could be no one else's. He thought back and remembered the time when he'd gone over to her flat and had found Marcus there . . . Did they? Yes, they had, he remembered. It had to be then, that was the most recent time they had . . . had . . .

He couldn't think it for now. He realised he'd forgotten Sonnie and he turned to her, his mind reeling.

'It was dat time . . .'

' . . . When you come over an' Marcus was dere? Yeah, dat's

what I reckon anyway,' Sonia finished for him, her eyes slightly amused. Sean's mind flashed back to his earlier thoughts on how radiant she was looking and decided it all added up now.

'Are you sure?'

'It was that time? Fairly . . .'

'No, I mean, are you sure you're pregnant?'

It hurt him to say it. Sonia nodded.

'Kinda. I ain't had a period dis month or the las' either an' I bin sick nearly every mornin'. I was gonna go doctor's or get a test from the chemist's, but I thought I'd see you first an' let you know what might be happenin'.'

'You jus' ate *Burger King*! You should 'llow that junk food in your condition!' Sean spluttered, choked, still attempting to get his head around the idea. Sonnie was giggling at him.

'I ain't even sure if I am yet, so don't have me on lettuce an' celery jus' yet! Then I gotta think about whether I want it or not . . .'

Tamika ran up to their bench with a Mediterranean-looking girl in tow, asking for an ice cream and pointing at a small Wall's hut cleverly placed near the playground's iron gates. Sonia went and dealt with the girl's request, returning with a cherry brandy ice lolly for Sean and a cider one for herself. When she sat back down, the teen wasted no time in getting straight back into the conversation.

'What d'you mean if you wannit or not?'

Sonnie stretched out her legs and sucked on her ice lolly for a bit before answering.

'I dunno, I mean . . . of course I wannit for myself, dat goes without sayin' . . . But I look around me at what goes on in dese sides an' I'm like, do I really wanna bring a kid into dis world? There's even a flasher on Greenside y'know, showin' himself to little girls an' boys, the disgustin' bastard an' dat was in the *Gazette* jus' dis week. You know what I'm sayin' anyhow, we've talked about it enough times ain't we? We was gonna wait an' get a career for ourselves, a house an' all that—'

'Yeah, yeah, yeah, but we ain't got dem t'ings Sonnie,' Sean broke in. 'An' you gotta remember how I feel,' he continued. 'We talked about it, as you said. I would like to have a yout' when I got money an' a car an' a house an' all dat shit, but we ain't got it 'ave we? What we have got, is a yout' on the way—'

'Maybe . . . ' Sonia muttered.

'All right *maybe*. But if you are pregnant Sonia, don't come to me with dat abortion shit man, cause I ain't hearin' it, y'unnerstan'. Dat's my yout' star, it has to live.'

Sonia was quiet for a minute, then she poked her half lolly at the teen and narrowed her eyes at him.

'It's a good thing I want dis kid too an' not a career or summick, 'cause we'd be in trouble wouldn't we?'

Sean said nothing.

'I mean, it's a good thing that I want to give up nine months, an' realistically, the rest of my life, lookin' after our kid. I know I'll be dere. I won't have no choice, unless I kick the bucket, God forbid . . .'

'Sonia man—' Sean looked pained.

'No Sean, I'm dealin' in bere realities from now on, fuck not bein' prepared for things. The point I'm makin' is I'll be around when dis yout' shits its nappies, or when it starts school, or when it gets its first girlfrien' or boyfrien' an' it wants to have dem over to stay. Will *you*? Think about it, 'cos Sean, I ain't raisin' no kid on my jacks star, later to dat. I seen enough of it on Greenside to know it's fuckin' hard work y'get me an' I ain't able for all dat star. *Sooo*, if I am preggers, I need to know exactly how you feel about it an' whether you're ready to commit your life, not even to me . . .'

She paused dramatically.

' . . . But to the child. You have to promise me you'll do your best for it an' take your fair share of the load, 'cos it ain't gonna be easy, I'm tellin' you. An' if you have any doubts or any feelin' you might wanna doss out, tell me *now* Sean! I'll get it over an' done wid quick an' easy.'

Sean listened carefully, then he put a tentative arm around Sonia's shoulders. She slid over to him, resting against his chest, so he had to look down to speak to her.

'Hear what now Sonnie, I'll admit I ain't thrilled to bits about the prospect of bein' a father so soon. Shit, I ain't got nothin' to give a yout' 'cept love, y'get me, but you know what? I'm gonna work at it, f'real. I didn't wanna kid jus' yet, but if things go along the lines we're thinkin', I want you to have dat yout' Sonnie. I wanna see it grow up an' play an . . .' He broke off wistfully, searching for the right words, looking at the clear sky.

'Have the kid Sonnie man, believe me, I'll be behin' you a hundred per cent. Have the yout' star.'

'No more gangster business,' she warned him.

'If you are pregnant, I'm gonna get you to throw away dem fuckin' pills star,' he said, a little angrily.

'It's only ninety seven per cent sure anyway, or somethin' like that,' she told him. 'Knowin' me, I'm one of the unlucky three.'

'*Innit*,' he muttered vaguely. 'Does your mum know?' he asked, wincing slightly, as he was pretty sure of the reply.

'Uhhh, yeah she does y'know, well, I told her I suspected anyway. Don't worry, she knows we wasn't fuckin' around. Well we *was*, but I don't mean in dat way . . .'

Sean boomed laughter.

'Yeah man, she's as safe about it as she can be, she knows it couldn't be helped. We took precautions an' it didn't work. What more could we do?'

Sean nodded, remembering it was Sonia's mother who'd advised her to try the pill, rather than have her fall unexpectedly pregnant. What a fuck up, he mused.

'What about Tamika, does she know?'

'Nahh,' Sonia smiled up at him. 'I'll tell her when I'm sure. She'll be an auntie! She'll love it.'

'F'real,' Sean replied.

A week after Sean found out about his approaching fatherhood, Cory was enjoying the heat in Greenside's only park with an assortment of friends. The park had become a meeting point for almost everybody and usually by one o'clock, the grass would be alive with crews of teenagers, smoking, drinking, flirting and playing football. Today was no exception. Cory sat the game out, not because of his leg (his cast had been removed two weeks before) but because he was waiting for Rosie to appear. He didn't want to sweat himself up kicking a ball around. He was clad in a casual shirt and blue jeans, and was sporting a brand-new pair of Reeboks he'd bought with money from his jobs with Art. He had no intention of scuffing his trainers kicking a ball either, at least not when they were brand new.

Smoking a zook, he surveyed the crowd of teenagers, smiling as he listened to their conversations. Garvey was there, sitting with his head in Claire's lap, so was Jason Taylor and little Stacey, talking with some other kids his age. A little further away sat Raymond and a crew of boys: Nazra, his broken arm fully functional again, a tall skinny black boy called Maverick (who sold rocks) and a massive muscular guy with skin the colour of varnished pine, called Howie, nicknamed Mr Strong. Everyone simply called him Strong.

Amongst the girls was Tara, who was gazing at Garvey and Claire jealously, even though she had a man. Cory was sure some OPP had been going on between his friend and the girl and he intended to ask him about it later on in the day. There was also a bunch of Claire's friends whom Cory had yet to be introduced to. All of them were wearing shorts high on the thigh and thin tops. It was hard for him not to look.

While the others talked, he'd kept a close vigil on the girls sitting across the way from him. He swore that one girl, a light-skinned beauty who reminded him of Tanya, kept snatching glances at him and smiling as she looked away. Claire caught him staring at her friends and smiled, before nudging Garvey and pointing at him. Garvey rolled his eyes and tutted, which made Cory focus back on Maverick and Nazra again.

'So what, you still jugglin' bone?' he asked the dark boy.

'Yeah man.'

'How's t'ings runnin'?'

'Neatly boy, you see I got my ride innit? I'm jus' tryin' to save enough money to sen' my grandparents back to Trinidad y'know. They've bin wantin' to get outta dis shithole for summick like thirty years y'get me, so hopefully I can save enough before winter comes back, then I'll be out like a snout.'

Maverick lived in Devonshire House, and although he'd attended different primary and secondary schools Cory had a lot of respect for him. He'd seen him work up from a half ounce of weed, to selling ki's in nothing less than an ounce, letting his customers take care of minors like draws. Early this year he'd started on the rocks, yet Cory had never seen or heard of him ever smoking a bone. His mother knew what he was doing, but when her son put four hundred pounds in her hand for a month's rent, and earns in one night more than she did in a month, she learned to overlook those things.

'Yeah man, you got your head screwed on, dis country ain't no place for old people, especially old black people. They don't give a fuck about us man,' Cory responded sourly.

The others snorted morosely and shook their heads, their respective futures a hazy dot on the horizon that defied any attempts to zoom in on it. Cory relaxed for a bit more as Tara passed him his zook, then jumped as warm hands covered his eyes and the world around him went dark.

'Hiya!'

He turned his head and saw it was Rosie, dressed in grey tracksuit bottoms, trainers and a colourful T-shirt, her bag swinging from her shoulder. She bent over and kissed Cory on the lips, before sitting on the grass next to him, beckoning Tara to come over and waving at the other girls animatedly. Cory passed her his zook.

'So where you bin then?' he teased.

'You *know* where I've bin an' don't grin at me like dat Mister Bradley, 'cause nex' time you don't get out of it so easily.'

'I'm sorry, shoppin' with one woman is bad enough, but you an' your aunt too? Later *on*, I'm not involved.'

Cory was speaking with his hand on his heart, as if he was taking a pledge. Rosie batted the hand away and cut her eyes at him.

'Chicken,' she teased back. 'I had fun anyway, even if you couldn't be bothered to turn up. I bought loads of garms up Ken High Street and Maddy nearly even had a fight in Tesco's with some posh woman who couldn't steer her trolley straight. I thought she was gonna bash her with her brolly star. It was so funny.'

Tara shook her head and giggled with her friend. Cory tried to sneak a look at Claire's friends and almost got caught by Rosie, who'd turned to talk to Nazra. He pretended to wave to Garvey who realised what he was up to and threw over his bag of weed. Cory caught it deftly and whipped out the blue Rizla, trying to find a place where the thin breeze wouldn't blow it over.

'Hey.'

Rosie touched his arm, smiling gently.

'I gotta present for you.'

'Yeah? So where is it den?'

'Look, in my bag, I ain't gettin' it out in front o' these lot,' Rosie replied, letting one strap of her leather shoulder bag fall open. Cory peeked inside, frowning at the bits of tissue and paper that were inside.

'Can't you see it?' she muttered.

Cory squinted, then laughed out loud as he saw what she meant. In the corner of the bag was a twelve pack of Durex. Rosie joined in his laughter and closed the bag up quickly as she noticed other people looking over. Cory continued with his zook, giving her a sidelong, but happy look.

'So what, is dat how you're goin' on?'

'F'real!'

Rosie's eyes were sparkling like precious stones in her face. 'I was thinkin' we could jus' slip away a little later, true my aunt's got a meetin' at the church 'till late. I got some wine at home, a spliff of skunk weed . . .'

'Yeah man, dat's a date,' Cory replied. They smiled at each other in anticipation of things to come.

Suddenly from far away, the roaring sound of car engines came to them, making Cory and several others look up, even though it was barely audible over the ordinary street noises. Slowly but surely, the roaring came closer and closer until everyone was looking in the direction the sound was coming from, which most took to be the east of Greenside. People outside the park's fence could be seen looking around to see what was going on, while the footballers broke off their game and ran to the pitch's chain-linked barrier, some of them clambering up it like army cadets on an assault course. They climbed all the way to the top to get a bird's eye view.

In a blaze of sound, with tyres screeching like demented demons, came four police riot vans, two smaller dog handler's vans, a lone Metro and a Vauxhall Cavalier, with fluorescent stripes down its side. They accelerated down the straight that ran along Somerford, Brownswood and Goldsmith Houses, before taking a left at the corner of the Greenside adventure playground. Two of the riot vans almost touched taking the corner and the drivers had to fight to keep them from crashing. They careered past Belsize and Devonshire, until they could be seen no more.

At once, the watching crowd went crazy.

'Yuh see dat! Yuh *see* dat!'

'Dem casian's are out for someone today star, f'real Neil!'

'You see dem nearly crash on the corner!'

The footballers were coming over to discuss what they'd seen, swaggering towards them, glad it wasn't them the police were after.

'Boy, dem man ain't rampin' speego, I pity the man dat gets nabbed by 'em!'

'Hear what, if dat was me, I'd jus' get my bucky an' shoot my way out star.'

This was Maverick speaking. Nazra shook his head in despair.

'You wouldn't have a chance spee. First gun gets let off an' you ain't comin' outta dere alive star. It'd jus' be one less nigga to dem man.'

'Later, I'd fuck up a few on the way if I'm goin' out, I'm tellin' you,' Maverick argued, not giving up.

Cory looked over at Rosie, wondering if she was thinking what he was. The vans looked like they were heading towards Beechwood House to him and, in the light of everything that had happened, he wondered what the significance of that could be. Inclining his head at the girl, he got up, lit his zook and brushed the grass and dry mud from his jeans. When Rosie got up, Cassandra called out to her.

'Oi, where d'you two think you're goin'?' she yelled, aiming to bring attention to their movements.

'None of your business star,' Cory shot back, as he didn't really like the loudmouthed girl anyway.

They said their goodbyes and abruptly left. As they walked away, Cassie stuck her middle finger up in the direction of Cory's back, which made her friends crack up. The only other person to take notice of Cory's hasty departure was Garvey. He watched the boy's back move steadily away from him, a worried frown on his round face, until Rosie and Cory were out of his sight.

*

The couple headed out of the park gates at a modest speed, silent until they reached Caldervale House. There, Rosie took the teen's hand and swung his arm gently, watching his face, trying to shake him out of his reverie. A group of ten boys were surrounding a car parked across the road from them, listening to loud rolling Hip Hop beats, making the car rock in time with the slow tempo. The couple looked over and waved dutifully.

'I can't stand dat Cassie, gets on my fuckin' nerves,' Cory growled as they walked. Rosie frowned, sensing the girl wasn't the real reason for his displeasure.

'Ah, she's all right,' she muttered, then she almost whispered her next words. 'D'you reckon it was Levi's they was goin' for?' she said hoarsely. Cory shrugged.

'Who knows? We'll find out soon enough though innit? If it is I'll jump for joy star, I'm tellin' you. They should put him away and t'row the key in the Thames, f'real.'

'You're worried about Sean though ain't you?' she asked.

'Yeah,' he blew out smoke. 'If it is Levi's crackhouse gettin' it, Sean could be in danger man. I don't know what shit he was doin' while I was in hospital an' I don't know what evidence of it is parked off at Levi's drum, y'get me? He could be in trouble an' I can't do nothin' man.'

Rosie sighed and squeezed his hand. 'My poor baby. It jus' don't stop does it?'

'Nah, it don't fuckin' stop man,' Cory grumbled, kicking a stone across the road in anger, his face glum.

They walked the rest of the way to Beechwood House, in a tense, speculative silence.

The first Levi knew of the danger was when he heard the series of loud thumps on his door, floating down the corridor into his ears. He strained to hear better, his tense posture causing Spider and Kenny to eye him, then start, as they also heard thuds and muted voices from outside. Kenny was clutching at a browning a crackhead had brought in earlier that day. There was a moment of silence, then, instant action.

'*FUUUCK, IT'S DE BEASTBWOY DEM!*'

Levi was out of his chair in a second though he wasn't even sure what was going on. As he'd been paranoid all his life and was still alive so far, he let his instincts take over and guide him, hopefully, in the right way. Better to be safe than sorry he'd always thought. With that in mind, he ran to the pipe room to warn them of the danger.

'Get rid o' de fuckin' shit, they comin' star!' he yelled loudly.

Glassy-eyed people were piling into the corridor, asking what was going on, as the smoke flooded the flat in an instant. Losing his temper, Levi pushed them back inside the misty room angrily, often using his fists when someone didn't move quickly enough for him.

'Where the fuck you goin' star? Geddinside man what'm t'you to raas—'

'What's goin' on, I don't wanna get shif' man, what's goin on?'

Art and Johnny peeked over the milling bodies, only to see Levi glaring at them, teeth bared, his forehead wrinkled with rage.

'Geddin the *fuckin*' room!' he shouted, pushing the people back inside, then shutting the door with a bang. Kenny rushed up to him, his eyes alive with excitement.

'Everyt'ings done man, they won't find jack shit star.'

'Where'd you put the t'ings?'

'In their usual places y'get me? We should be all right, providin' they don't search the place too t'orough.'

'It'll 'ave t'do,' Levi muttered. If only he'd had time to think clearly about things – he was meant to be warned in advance about any raids on the flat by a detective sergeant from the drugs squad. Clearly the police were not into helping him any more. Either that, or he'd been informed on. .

The very real possibility of this grew in the Dredd's mind as they made their way to the back room, ignoring the frantic shouts from the pipers whom Spider had locked in.

Voices sounded outside the door, loud and full of authority.

'Lawrence?' There was a pause. 'Lawrence Patterson? This is Sergeant Bailey of the Shepherd's Bush drugs squad. We've a warrant to search your flat, so open up in there, or we'll have to force our way in. What's it to be mate?'

Inside the flat no one said a word. Kenny glanced at Levi, his forehead shiny with sweat, his eyes wide with apprehension, none of which he could wipe away. The Dredd raised an eyebrow at the unknown officer's mention of his given name. The bags of crack, hidden underneath the kitchen floorboards were very much in the centre of his mind. He'd only bought it from his safe house yesterday. The Dredd couldn't believe his bad luck.

Time dragged by. The second hand on his Rolex seemed to jerk itself around for an eternity before the sergeant's voice came back to them again, sounding drunk with the confidence of authority.

'All right Levi, you've had your chance. We're comin' in!' he shouted, his voice almost a whisper to the people in the back room. On the landing, one plain-clothes policeman had produced a compressor unit with which they opened up the door frame. Then, measuring the front of a short pole against the lock, he held it, legs spread wide apart, swinging it experimentally back and forth a few times, finding it hard to manoeuvre in the confined landing area. When he was satisfied he had a decent angle for the job, he smashed the end of the pole directly on the door's lock three times.

On the third strike, the lock gave and the door swung inwards, before hitting the short poles that barred their entrance behind the actual door. Although the scaffolding poles were strong, the door frame and the bed of metal that held them in place were not. After the police kicked the door a few times, the wooden frame gave and the poles clattered noisily to the ground.

The armed response officers were the first to enter, looking like soldiers in their regulation body armour, though the uniforms and plain clothes weren't far behind. They surged through the council flat like a human tidal wave, eager to feel some collars and seize some product. Having been briefed on the layout of the flat, the Sergeant knew exactly where to head for, his eyes set on the closed pipe room door at the back of the flat.

Art drew his knife as the door to the pipe room flew open slashing the first man to enter across his face, smiling at the sibilant whisper as it chopped the air. He watched in delight as the skin of the man's cheek split apart cleanly before his eyes, sending blood dripping onto the policeman's shoulder and onto the floor.

The rest of the pipers put up some fight, but most of them were too charged to even move. They were easily overwhelmed by the sheer number of officers that had laid siege to their Class A community. They were subdued and made to sit huddled in a corner of the room, while the dog handlers tried various means of calming their charges down, all to no avail. Even the men could smell the crack in the air, dominating others of sweat, sex and vomit, so for the dogs the odour must have been overpowering.

In the back room, Levi, Kenny, Spider and Alice had all given themselves up without a fight, their hands raised in the air. Sergeant Bailey showed the stunned dealer his badge, then patted the man down himself, unable to conceal his pleasure at having him in this very sticky situation. Levi eyed him, his jaws clenched in pent-up fury, as he hadn't met this young officer before. His enthusiasm for the job only meant he'd be harder to bribe.

'So where you got the crack hidden Levi? You might as well tell us and save everyone a great deal of time.'

The young Sergeant was cocky and full of self-assurance, speaking directly into the older man's face. Levi turned his head, causing his locks to swing around gently.

'So what about you Spider?' the officer said, moving down the line, sneering at the man's long tangle of hair and his rough unshaven face. Spider opened his mouth to reply, but before he could speak, another officer came in, with a collection of self-sealed bags in his gloved hands.

Levi closed his eyes as if experiencing a great inner pain, as Baily's sardonic smile widened.

'I think the decision's bin made for you lot already,' he threw at them, while he looked the bags over. Although it seemed impossible, his smile widened even more.

'Levi Patterson, Kenny Saunders, Dean Willow and Alice Cooper?' he said tentatively. They all looked up as one. 'I'm arresting you, under the Misuse of Drugs Act and formally charging you with suspected possession of a Class A substance, with intent to supply. *Also* . . .' Bailey motioned once and an AFO (authorised firearms officer) wearing plastic surgical gloves stepped forwards. Levi focused on keeping his head straight as he saw the Browning Kenny had been fiddling with, nestling in the officer's palm. Bailey was in his element.

'I am arresting you for suspected possession of an unlicensed firearm, plus suspected possession of live ammunition. You do not have to say anything, but it may harm your defence if you don't mention when questioned, something which you later rely on in court. Anything you *do* say, may be given in evidence. Understand? Good. Now cuff the fuckers an' let's go.'

'*Fuck you!*' Levi yelled, unable to hold his rage back. '*Fuck all you beas' bwoy!*'

In an instant he lunged at Bailey, his fist swinging as he fired himself at the man like a catapult, all of his anger behind the wide sweeping blow.

He missed Bailey by centimetres as the policeman moved back instinctively, but Kenny took his chance as soon as Levi jumped and drove his fist at full force into the face of the burly man who stood in front of him, hearing the bone in his nose crunch with a sound like dry cornflakes. As he doubled over, he brought a knee to the policeman's face, sending him crashing to the floor, out cold. To his left and to his right were Alice and Spider, grappling with the policemen guarding them and not having much luck. He moved to join in.

Levi's main objective had been to gain possession of the gun the AFO was holding. But before he could make his next move, the room was packed with police officers. He was attacked by at least five men, their truncheons bringing flashes of light to his head everytime one connected. He could hear Alice screaming in rage and pain and the muffled voices of Spider and Kenny, cursing loudly. He tried to cover his head, but to no avail.

More policemen surrounded him, still beating him savagely, until they held his limbs still. His writhing body was first cuffed, then lifted by six men, taken out of the flat and carried down the stairs, closely followed by the others.

Halfway down the stairs, Levi screamed he wanted to walk into the waiting TSG carrier on the ground floor. The men carrying him refused at once, but Bailey strangely enough agreed, though he refused to do the same with Kenny, or the crackhead couple. Hands held behind him by the metal cuffs, Levi was turned onto his feet and prodded down the hard steps until he emerged on the ground floor, shocked by the waiting crowd that stared as he stepped into the light. Some smart arses started cheering as he appeared, but the Dredd's hardman stare soon put a stop to that. As he looked over the crowd, a respectful silence fell. It was then he saw Cory.

Their gazes locked for a second, the teen's unafraid and flat and Levi's cold and threatening. He stepped towards the back doors of the van, turning his head as he passed Cory, so the youth knew it was him he was looking at. The Dredd saw the girl he was with clutch Cory's arm possessively as he passed by. He winked at her before entering the van, causing fury to flood the teen's face, which in turn made Levi smile.

I bet any money it was him who grassed me up, the dealer thought to himself as Spider, Alice, Bailey and two other officers, all squeezed into the back of the vehicle. Kenny was lifted into a van all to himself, which to Levi looked ominous, as he could see several policemen getting into the vehicle, their faces hard and flushed. He stared at Cory's figure as the van moved away, not taking his eyes away from the teen, sure that today's puzzle had been irrefutably solved.

Cory and Rosie stood apart from the others, saying nothing. They watched the van disappear from sight then eventually, they went inside her aunt's flat, their faces thoughtful and worried.

Chapter Seventeen

The Uxbridge Road in Shepherd's Bush was a lively place. Homeless kids sat in shop doorways with blankets on their knees. Teenage girls pushed prams and crews of boys roamed, searching for some rich-looking person to mug. Convertible cars cruised by slowly, beeping at girls as they cruised past them, trying not to knock over the cats as they recklessly weaved in and out of the afternoon traffic.

A few people looked up as the procession of seven police vehicles wound its way towards the station, but for the most part nobody took any notice. The procession pulled into the car park situated at the back of the station. The policemen from the first van carefully prodded their cuffed captives through a door in a large metal gate and through another door which led into the back of the station. Their charges complained and grumbled all the way.

Sergeant Alvin Bailey watched his captives like an army general scrutinising his prisoners of war with cold satisfaction.

He was more than pleased with what he'd achieved this afternoon and he was sure Detective Inspector Pollock, his superior officer, would be equally impressed. The raid (code-named Operation Tree, with reference to Beechwood House) had taken a lot of planning, manpower and taxpayer's money. Although he wouldn't have been directly blamed if anything went wrong, it wouldn't have done his flourishing career any good to have any fuck-ups on his unblemished record.

Bailey had been sixteen years in the Metropolitan Police

Force, first as a lowly constable at the tender age of nineteen, eventually making sergeant by the time he was thirty. His life-long ambition as a child had been to be a policeman and once he was installed into his coveted job, he soon became recognised and respected for the many 'collars' he felt in his days as a patrolman. He got on well with his colleagues and kept himself busy by working out in the gym, jogging, swimming and play-ing football with the lads in various 'friendlies' against other stations.

As the years went on, crack cocaine started to figure more and more in the crimes he and his fellow officers had to deal with. Slowly but surely the police found themselves on the losing end of a battle they'd had no forewarning about and next to no train-ing for.

The Greenside Estate became the focus of Detective Inspector Pollock's attentions as most of the crack trade seemed to centre around there. It wasn't long before Lawrence Patterson, a prolific 'juggler' otherwise known as 'Levi', was beginning to reckon very highly in their sights. They had decided to keep him under surveillance and see what developed.

Bailey watched as the last of the crackheads were thrown into their cells to roast for a few hours, then he went outside into the car park again to oversee the movements of the second, more important set of captives.

Levi, Alice and Spider emerged from the back of their carrier pretending indifference to all that was going on. Kenny, looking the worse for wear, was still struggling. He was pushed force-fully out of the vehicle and Bailey watched him through narrowed eyes. One of two custody officers sitting at a broad table looked at him, then snapped a curt order at the men.

'Search 'im an' put 'im straight in a cell till he cools down,' he instructed the men. Bailey smiled and turned away, his eyes scanning the sleek white lines of the Vauxhall Cavalier ARV that'd accompanied them on the journey to and from Greenside.

He went back inside the custody suite which housed a row of dreary grey filing cabinets along one wall and a broad table set in the middle of the room. Behind the table were the two cus-tody officers, who were now asking Levi and Alice to empty their pockets.

Alice produced forty pounds in crumpled notes, some keys and a self-sealing bag full of weed, which made the officers loitering in the large room laugh and make jokes about everyone getting high tonight.

Levi simply produced more keys, his Mercury phone and a large wad of cash, which he wordlessly placed on the wooden desk before the officer. The man spotted the dealer's gold Rolex Oyster and pointed at it, and at his rings and chains, then at the bag with a smile.

'Let's 'ave those as well Mr Patterson,' he said, jovially.

Levi unclipped the watch and pulled off his jewellery (he had to struggle with some of the older rings) then placed them with his keys. He appeared unruffled and relaxed as Bailey watched him, feeling his anticipation rise at the thought of the coming interview.

The custody officer put Alice's bag of weed into another larger plastic bag with numbers on it. He then instructed the arrested men to watch, as he went over to a small rectangular machine on the wall, pulled a handle, then heat-sealed the plastic, so that it was completely airtight and could not be re-opened without considerable force.

They were then taken, in turn, into a side room, where they were made to strip naked and turn their socks inside out. Levi was instructed to lift his genitals, while both prisoners were told to spread their legs and touch their toes.

The routine dealt with, Levi ambled nonchalantly to his cell, his composure not falling even for a second. Bailey called to him from where he was standing, leaning against the back wall, facing Spider's seated back.

'See you in a few hours Levi!' he yelled at the Dredd.

There was a murmur of mirth from the policemen still in the room.

Detective Inspector James Pollock was a large, robust-looking man, standing at six feet three inches, with a broad chest and wide shoulders. He'd been in the force for twenty-six years and, now approaching his fifties, he was well respected by the younger officers who were coming up in the ranks. Pollock had seen a lot of action in his time, first pounding the beat, and eventually behind a desk where things were less dangerous but no less hectic. He sat in his office looking over reports made by the officers involved in the crackhouse raid. He was waiting for the sergeants to finish their interview with Levi. A knock on the door made him look up with a smile on his face.

'Come in!' his voice rolled across the room.

Bailey entered the office, looking as pleased as his superior officer. He walked across to the cluttered desk and sat down, barely containing his excitement.

'How goes it?' Pollock asked.

'Lovely at the minute sir,' Bailey replied. 'We told Patterson we know about the armed robbery in Arnos Grove, and he's gettin' in a right old sweat over that warrant y'know. We've given him half an hour to think it through, see if he feels like giving up anyone on the shooting. I'm fairly confident he'll tell us what we want to hear.'

'As soon as we get those names off Patterson, phone Sergeant Hutchinson at Arnos Grove and let them know what's happening here. They might even be able to get a warrant to raid those addresses on the basis of the information we've obtained, so if things go well, we'll still be able to get a hold of those guns. Whatever happens, they've *got* to be taken out of circulation.'

Bailey nodded. In November of '94 PC Patrick Dunne was shot dead after a call for assistance by a gang of men who had just murdered a black man called William Danso. Although this happened in Clapham, South London, police all over the city (and no doubt the country) were calling for arms, while waging an unspoken war against people like Levi, who supplied arms to the man on the street making the average bobby's job twice as dangerous.

More important than putting Levi away, the cache of guns was the grand prize in this deadly game.

'What about the others guv? Shall we interview them or what?'

'Fuck 'em for now; Patterson's the main man at the moment. As for Spider, Kenny and those other crackheads, wait until you've got the statement from Patterson, then interview them, if only to see what little bits of gossip they might know. When you've done that, you can just charge 'em an' let 'em go.'

'Will do guv.'

Pollock looked at his watch.

'Half an hour did you say? I think his time's up isn't it?'

'I'll say,' Bailey replied, laughing as he got up to leave.

Pollock joined in, his booming guffaws following the sergeant out of the room and into the corridor.

Derek Chambers, Levi's solicitor, sat on the end of his client's hard metal bed regarding him calmly. On the other end sat the Dredd, drinking a can of Sunkist Chambers had brought in for him. A metal tray lay on the concrete floor with a plate of a half-eaten dinner of sausages and mash. A policeman stood by the door watching them.

'I really think you should give them what they want,' Chambers told Levi, yet again. Levi knocked back his drink, smacking his lips when he was done.

'Don' worry boss, me nah go jail. Me gaan gi' dem *everyt'ing* dem want . . .'

Levi snatched a look at the policeman guarding the door, wanting him to overhear his words. The look wasn't lost on Chambers, who understood completely what his client was doing.

'Be careful what you say,' he warned. 'When you get to the dock it won't be easy.'

The dealer shrugged, wanting to get away from the subject before Chambers said something incriminating.

He knew the police had only granted this meeting because they thought he knew more than he was letting on. He was very aware of the man at the door, his ears twitching, straining to hear everything they said. Well fuck him. He was getting out of this and he would lic his whole way through statements, trials and newspaper interviews if he had to. Going to jail was not in his plans and if the Rads thought he intended to just disappear without a fight, they had another think coming.

'The best thing you could do is push for bail in exchange for the shooter in that robbery. With a bit of luck we could have you out by the day after tomorrow, maybe even tomorrow night. Have they fingerprinted you yet?'

Levi shook his head tiredly.

'Well they'll have to soon, it's the law. When they do, tell 'em you can help them find the shooter, if they'll grant bail. They'll try to ignore you at first and act like they're not listening, but just tell 'em that. Ten to one they'll agree. They'd prefer it was you risking your life looking for an armed teenager than them.'

The policeman guarding the door gave a tight smile at that, but refused to look at them and said nothing.

'Dat soun' easy enough,' the Dredd rumbled. 'But who's gonna bail me out? Kenny in y'asso, Shawna cyaan get involve . . .'

Unseen by the guard, Chambers winked at him casually.

'Don't worry Levi, I'll take care of that. You just think about what you're gonna say to Sergeant Bailey later on. I'll deal with the rest.'

The two men looked at each other, locked in years of understanding. The guard ever watchful, saw nothing.

Chapter Eighteen

Sean picked up a carton of strawberry Ribena from Sonia's fridge and walked into the living room, where his girlfriend's mother Samantha was sitting, peeling potatoes with a speed that only came with years of practice. She was tall, with a kind of rugged beauty and a weathered bronze complexion, as well as the family's trademark brown eyes. Her hair was wrapped in a blue head scarf and she wore a T-shirt and a long skirt despite the heat. Gold teeth flashed at Sean as he sat down restlessly, his eyes on the television, but his mind elsewhere.

'Cheer up nuh. Yuh face look *sour* bwoy,' she informed him, putting down a potato to look at him.

Sean shrugged and tried to smile.

'I'm OK, I'm jus' thinkin' about Sonnie man. I really should've gone with her, she needs me.'

He sighed, his face serious once more. Sonia had left the flat alone earlier, against his wishes, to visit a chemist's in Shepherd's Bush for the results of her pregnancy test.

They'd followed the instructions on a box they'd purchased the day before and in those hours between then and now, things had taken on a surreal quality. He'd spent the day at Sonia's, talking with her and her mother after Tamika had gone to bed, discussing what they would do if the test read positive.

'Sonia's stubborn and independent,' Samantha said. 'Sometimes she jus' waan show everyone she's in control, y'know? I remember when she was a chil', she wouldn't even let me tek her to school. She had to go on her own, even when de teachers did start to complain she wasn't safe. I try tek her a couple o' times, but she'd sulk an' mek up noise an' I jus' let her go alone in the end. So don' you feel a way, jus' 'cause she feels she has to go fe de test results by herself. It her way, that's all.'

Sean nodded.

'Yeah I know dat . . . Still, I reckon I shoulda gone too. This involves both of us, y'get me?'

He ran his hands over his head agitatedly. 'Furthermore, if Sonnie wants me to wait, I'll wait man. I jus' hope if she is pregnant, she'll start bringin' me in a bit more man.'

'I'm sure she will,' Samantha replied, going back to her peeling. 'Yuh spoke to yuh mudda yet?'

'Nah man,' Sean shook his head. 'I'm gonna wait an' make sure it's a definite t'ing, before I let any of dem lot know.'

To tell the truth, Sean was a little afraid and unsure of the reaction he'd get from Bernice, given her present state of mind. His mother had had a lot to deal with over the past few months and she didn't even know the half of what was really going on.

The night before after he'd got back from Sonia's, he'd sat by his desk, watching his cousin sleeping in the bed across the room from him, his mind in a whirl. Cory would be proud of him, he'd thought – he knew he could count on him for support, no matter what happened. Strangely enough, over the last few weeks they hadn't seen a lot of each other, each of them busy with their own lives. Sean intended to try to resolve that, no matter what the results of the test were.

He finished his Ribena and was in the kitchen, throwing the carton in the bin, when the front door slammed and Sonia's voice called out a greeting. Sean took a deep breath then entered the living room, feeling the familiar pangs of nerves in his stomach. Sonnie had flopped on to the sofa and was stretching herself out.

'Boy, I'm *tired* yuh see!' she groaned, her arms spread out, smiling at Sean. The teen bent over to plant a kiss on her lips and was surprised when she held him tight, then pulled him so he sat next to her.

'I'm pleased to see you're in a good mood!' he told her, meaning it. Samantha was looking at them both in anticipation.

'Well don' keep me in suspense any longer, wha' 'appen Sonnie?'

Sonia gave a little smile and clutched Sean's hand.

'Well, the pharmacist says I'm a perfectly healthy specimen, full of energy an' vitality an' all dat . . .'

'*Sonnie* . . .' Sean warned, giving her a stern look that said it all. Sonia beamed again, looking beautiful.

'I'm sorry, I'll get on with it.' She shrugged and made a face, 'Prepare to be a father Sean. That woman at the chemist's says I'm nearly three months' pregnant.'

Sonia's mother squealed with delight and dropped the potato she'd been peeling to run over and give her daughter a hug, all the while crooning, 'My baby, my baby . . .' over and over again.

Sean sat smiling, scarcely believing his ears, but happy just the same, knowing that this changed everything.

He would go home and tell his mother and the others his good news as soon as possible. He smiled at Sonia, then gave her a hug, thinking he would stay here for half an hour more, then go home and work out how he'd tell them.

Whistling, Cory strolled out of his block, feeling good, the sun pleasantly warm on his face. He crossed the road and made his way to the football pitch, eyes hidden by black Ray Bans, all the while thinking of Rosie. It was plain to him that life was looking up and all he needed to cap things was a good result from his end-of-term exams. It was about time he and his family had a run of good luck; he felt that the previous day might be the beginning of a lovely winner's streak.

Yesterday, he and Rosie had left the crowd milling outside and had headed straight into her bedroom, climbed into bed, not wanting to waste any more time even talking. For the remainder of the afternoon, that was where they stayed, exploring each other's bodies and using almost all of their condoms.

He smiled again as he entered the pitch through tall gates and saw his friends gathered at the opposite end, clouds of smoke billowing around them.

As he got closer to the knot of people he groaned, recognising one of them as someone he really didn't like. Martin Pitt was a half Asian, half black Greenside boy and Cory had always seen him as an impostor, trying to be somebody he wasn't. He was a tall skinny youth who smoked rocks, always making out he was some kind of American gangster, and talking about 'bitches' and 'niggas' and 'muthafuckas'.

Martin had a large canvas holdall sitting open beside him and all of the boys in the group were holding packaged brand new cotton shirts, or studying the cuts on dazzlingly blue pairs of jeans. Cory knew the boy had been selling knocked-off clothes for a while, but he had never had any money when he was around. Martin always had the top of the range Ralph Lauren or Armani wear in his holdall, passed on to him by girls who either went into shops and stole them, or worked cheque books and cards.

'Yaow star, yuh finally lan'!' Garvey shouted at Cory, his hands wrapped around a neatly packaged sky blue shirt. The others nodded his way and a burning spliff was passed to him by an eager hand.

'I won't say no,' Cory told them, raising the zook to his mouth. He sniffed once, then sneered.

'Raa, dere's a makka seed in dis spee! Look 'ow it's burnin'!'

He lifted the spliff up to show the crew, smiling. One side was letting out thick smoke in a winding trail into the air. The comments from the boys were varied.

'Cha, if yuh don' waan smoke dat, pass it *here* star.'

'Dig it out man, what'm t'you?'

'Who built dat ziggy man?'

'Hey Cory, if you blas' dat you'll go mad spee, sen' it here nuh?'

'Fuck you lot man,' Cory replied to one and all, sitting down in the nearest available space.

He got out his switchblade and dug the offending seed out, watching as it burned into nothing on the grass. He took a few more quick tokes, before passing the ziggy to Garvey.

'Where's all the gullies man?' the teen asked. His friend rolled his eyes.

'I dunno star. Maybe it's too early f'dem. Maybe they ain't comin'. I saw Rabana an' she said Hyde Park's the lick today. Then again, they might all turn up later. Claire's comin' by at some stage, I know dat much.'

The half-caste boy lay back, obviously not bothered. 'Anyway,' he continued, 'Wha' you worryin' about girls for, I thought you had your hands well full yestiday.'

'They're *never* full enough star,' Cory cackled, flexing his fingers and screwing up his face like Benny Hill. The boys laughed.

'So what, did you wuk it?' Garvey wanted to know.

'Yeh man.'

''Bout fuckin' time star. What's it sayin'?'

Cory thought for a second.

'Put it dis way. Y'know when you've bin ravin' an' you drink nuff, then you wake up the nex' mornin' with a hangover sayin', "I musta had a good time star, true my head's killin' me"?'

'Yeah yeah.'

'Well, my dick needs some Nurofen boy, serious t'ing. It's poundin' man!'

Garvey cracked up.

'My man's bin bangin' 'is balls star!' he gasped, causing the ripple of laughter to turn into a roar.

'F'real!'

The teen cracked up, with the others joining in around him, slapping the grass. Of course, Martin Pitt had to get his two pence's worth in, once he saw everyone was enjoying the joke.

'So what Cory, you're seein' Rosie den?' he wheedled nosily, as he snatched up some Rizla. Cory turned a distasteful gaze on him and spoke in a sarcastic tone.

'Yeah man – whenever she's standin' in front o' me.'

'Ha ha mate. Are you or aren't you?'

'What's it t'you? I don't wanna know your business, so keep your nose outta mines,' Cory said easily, though he felt his good mood continue to leave him rapidly.

'Hear what now, the only reason I was askin' is 'cause I thought she might wanna earn some wong man. I got some cheque books dat need workin', but they're in bere ho's names, so I thought maybe you could chat to your bitch an' we'll split t'ings halfway, y'get me? Den afterwards, you can jus' give her however much you wanna, innit?'

'Outta my cut I suppose?'

Martin gave a large shit-eating grin. Cory got even more riled up.

'You're a proper jooks y'know dat,' the teen snapped. 'What makes you think I'd ask any gully to go out there f'*you*? An' wha' you talkin' about, "my bitch"? Where d'you think you are man, Harlem? Dis is *London* y'know, in case you forgotten. Furthermore, you bes' min' the police don't nick you mate, there's nuff about since dat raid yestiday.'

'Cory, Cory,' Martin chuckled, shaking his head, 'I was jus' tryin' to help you get some money together star. I see how you're always lookin' on the garms I'm yellin', that's all, don't feel a way. It's cool if you ain't got no money y'know, jus' say, no one'll laugh.'

Some of the boys sniggered and spluttered at this, no doubt Martin's intention from the outset. He had a sly sneer on his lean angular face and Cory could've easily strangled him at that point.

'Star, what makes you think I'm inna your shit garms? You're full o' doo doo spee.'

Martin gave another cheerful laugh and threw over a couple of shirts.

'Check, check, check, check it owwwt!' he drawled in his favourite American accent, as the spinning packets flew into Cory's lap. The teen wanted to throw them back as hard as he could, but he remembered his earlier promise to himself and got his anger under control.

'They the phattest Versace shirts you can buy star, eighty poun' in the Wes' End, gimme *t'irty* dollars an' they're yours. The Polo's the same t'ing an' the Hugo Boss as well, plus the Armani . . .'

Cory looked the garments over.

'All right, I tell you what,' he muttered. 'Gimme dem for a score each an' you got a sale.'

'A *score*!' Martin squealed. 'Later, you're rampin'! What'm I gonna do with a score Cory man?'

The teen grinned derisively.

'Same t'ing you'd do wid thirty boys star, buy a bone innit, you fuckin' cat. Hear what, you was makin' noise about wantin' to help me out, so help me out nuh?! Dis time now, I want t'ree items y'unnerstan' an' I'll buy dem now, if you come correc'. Wha' you sayin' Mart?'

The other boys joined in the bartering, Garvey the loudest, agreeing that the price should come down, with coarse and profane yells. Now Martin looked uncomfortable.

'I can't do it,' he whined. 'Everyone'll want it for that price if I do.'

'Don't sell it man,' Cory pressed, smelling victory. 'Put your garms where your mouth is.'

The noise from the circle was deafening, nearly drowning Cory's words out.

'All right, all right!' Martin said, giving up. 'But only f'you Cory sccin' as you're so brok.'

'Respec',' Cory replied, trying to hide his smile.

He went over to the bag and when he'd made his choices, he put them to one side and reached into his sock where he had a small velcro bag wrapped around his ankle. He pulled the velcro apart, then retrieved a fat roll of notes from inside the bag, making the boys gasp collectively. Art's houses had been proving most profitable these days and Cory was sure that Lionel, Greenside's resident pimp, paid almost twice the amount Levi previously had been paying them for their goods. He'd been looking to go shopping for clothes today anyway, but seeing as the shops seemed to have come to him, he was glad he had a decent amount of money for a change.

'I . . . I . . . I . . . I thought you said you was brok,' Martin stuttered, while the boys around him creased up, shouting the fact that the boy had been, 'played like a sixteen bit'. Cory smiled sweetly and winked at him.

'Nah man, you said I was brok. I jus' said I wanted dem shirts for a score each. Maybe you'll see now you can't judge me so easy, y'get me? Jus' 'cause I don't run off my mout', don't mean I can't flex, y'unnerstan'? Enjoy yuh bone will yuh?'

Straight faced, Cory picked up his garments and made his way over to Garvey, the only teenager there not shocked by his seemingly instant wealth. While the others resumed talking and Martin sat looking morose, Cory edged close to his best friend's ear.

'Hear what now, you see how much garms is in my man's

bag?' Cory inquired quietly. The boy smiled.

'Hundreds of pounds worth,' Garvey whispered, his hazel eyes sparkling like crystals.

'Wha' you sayin' den? I feel say it's time for pussy bwoy Pitt to get robbed innit?'

'*Blatant*,' his friend agreed. Cory lay back on the grass.

'When he dosses, we'll follow 'im,' he muttered out of the side of his mouth, his lips not moving, knowing his friend constantly walked with his knife. Garvey laughed and passed him another zook.

'Raa, raa, my man's due to get stung twice in one day,' he giggled darkly. Cory laughed too, admiring the way the silk Armani caught the sun's rays. He'd give that shirt to Sean, as a return present for the gold chain his cousin bought him months earlier.

Gavin Hall, an athletic youth from Devonshire House, pointed to the gates outside excitedly.

'Raa, see Art an' dem man dere star! They musta got let out boy. *Oiiii*! Oii! Wha' gwaan?!'

There was silence for a moment as everybody looked over, squinting at the gates. The figures gestured back and Gavin laughed and waved again, signalling them to come over.

'Come nuh!' he shouted as he waved.

'I wonder if they got charged?' Makuja, a boy with African parents asked the circle.

'Course they charged 'em man, they wouldn't let 'em out so quick if they weren't charged,' Garvey answered seriously. 'Dem man don' skin teet' y'know. Even if they can't fin' nuttin' on you, they'll hol' you for a lickle y'get me, so they can put you out of action for a while, innit Cee?'

'Yeah man, they'll lock you up for as long as they can,' Cory muttered, detachedly. He was watching Art's progress across the pitch.

Mak shook his head in disagreement.

'Well *booyy*, one time I was charged with muggin' dis rich gully from Kensington. She had bere tom on her star, 'lexes, diamonds, the lot! Anyway, I got nicked and I was charged an everythin', but the Rads left me in the cell for two days man!'

There was immediate uproar.

'Two days? You're gowin' man!' Martin proclaimed. Mak's face was spirit-level straight.

'Nah man, I ain't lyin', I was dere for two fuckin' days. They fed me an' dat, but they didn't chat to me or nothin', or tell my mum where I was either. I was only fourteen at the time and I feel say it's against the law for dem to keep you in a cell for dat long, but what could I do man? When they let me go I stank man, I was fuckin' brewin' believe.'

'Dat's grim,' Cory growled. 'You shoulda reported their raas man, f'real.'

'Yeah I would've, but my mum ain't too clued up about law an' all that stuff,' the boy replied.

The boys left the subject closed there and looked up as Art, Johnny and Teresa, a local crackbitch, approached them, all of them looking the worse for wear.

'What'm people?' Art croaked roughly, as he lurched up to the boys. Everyone nodded and touched fists with Johnny and Art, while giving tentative hellos to the white girl, who looked as though she was going through some serious cold turkey. None of the trio could keep still for a second and eventually Garvey offered Art the chance to build a spliff, just to make him sit in one place for a while.

'Yeah all right,' the boy replied. 'But I wanna talk to Cory for a second man, so hold tight. Furthermore, let Johnny buil' it innit an' I'll jus' blas' it when I come back.'

Cory looked up sharply as he heard his name mentioned and found himself looking straight into Art's watery eyes. He held the young man's gaze for a second before nodding, picking up both his knife and his shirts and following him a little way, until they were out of earshot. When Cory looked back, nearly everyone there turned their heads, as though no one had been watching him walk away. He laughed to himself, then touched Art's elbow so he stopped by the pitch's chain link fence. The hot sun even made speaking seem like a major task and Cory didn't waste time small talking.

'What's up man, wha' you gotta chat t'me about?' he queried, feeling perplexed and at a loss as to what the boy could want.

Art gave a thick cough, spat through the fence into the park next door and placed a friendly hand on the teen's shoulder.

'Boy Cory, I got some *dread* news f'you star, somethin' I don't think you're gonna like at all man. I feel say certain man was gee'ing up the place las' night an' lettin' off on bere names y'get me? I jus' felt I had to warn you, 'cause it don't look too healthy, y'unnerstan'?'

'Eh? Wha' you talkin' about star,' Cory grumbled. 'Who's bin grassin' me up?'

Art looked confused and he took his hand away from his friend's arm, not getting what he was saying.

'Nah man, I ain't talkin' about *you*, you're safe spee, no worries. But I feel say man's tryin' to get your cousin in some shit to cover himself, you get what I'm sayin'?'

'What, someone gee'd up Sean y'mean?'

Cory looked at Art, the full implications of his words finally crashing down on him.

'Boy, 'fraid so spee.'

'*Who*? Tell me man, whodunnit star.'

Cory was unconsciously grasping the handle of his switchblade tightly and his eyes were wide and hard in an instant. Art stared at him, wondering if it would be wise to pass on what the police had told him in his interview last night, and knowing Cory had a strong dislike for Levi already. He very much feared the boy's wild nature could lead him to doing something he would deeply regret later.

Art sighed inwardly – it was too late to say A and not say B. If he tried to keep the grass undercover now, he was risking Cory taking his frustrations out on him and that was out of the question, seeing as he was weaponless at the moment. Shrugging to himself, as well as Cory, he spoke hesitantly.

'Hear what now, it's like *dis*. I had an interview wiv a couple o' Rads las' night an' they was talkin' about me at first, but then they started askin' about Sean—'

'Askin' *what*?' Cory snapped.

'You know man, what does he get up to, who does he move wiv, dem talks dere y'unnerstan'? Two two's, they asked me if I ever seen my man wiv a gun an' I told 'em "No". I goes that Sean's a straight A student an' they laughed an' said "Yeah yeah, very likely", like they didn't believe me. Anyway, they goes one of the people that was taken in yestiday was tellin' 'em

Sean was involved in some robbery an' he shot some black brer not long ago.

'I was like; "*Raa* that don't soun' like the brudda I know", y'get me, but dem man was sayin' they had a very good source, tol' em Sean done it y'know?'

'So who's dis source den?'

Art shuffled a bit and said nothing.

'Art don' fuck me aroun' man,' he warned, on the edge of violence now.

'The Rads slipped up man,' Art said unwillingly. 'They tol' me they'd interviewed nuff people from the raid, but we was all on the same row and I know I was the firs' out y'get me, 'cos I could hear when they opened the doors. Then, when I was waitin' for my brief outside the interview room, I heard two minor Rads talkin' about how, "the long-haired coon had spilt his guts, no problem". One of dem see me lookin' an' they shut up quick, but I heard 'em blatant, y'get me an' I think they knew. Now, how many black man from Levi's 'ave got long hair, except for—'

'*Levi* . . . ' Cory breathed at the same time as Art, glad to hear the name and his suspicions out in the open.

Levi, the name that always came back to haunt him, wherever he went. Whenever he thought that he and Sean had shaken free of the Dredd, he popped back up, giving them more and more grief each time he appeared. The hate for the man that had been building in the teen had now reached epic proportions. He imagined making him bleed, hurting him, making him beg for mercy as revenge for all he'd put them through this summer.

Cory was incensed as his mind raced, thinking yet again of what he could do to alleviate a situation that was mostly his fault. His first reaction was a need to lash out and hurt the Dredd, make him see that the Bradleys were not some family he could fuck around with and use as scapegoats for his own intentions.

Maybe he could talk to someone from Grove or something; somebody who would throw acid in Levi's face for a price, just as a warning, or a deterrent, so he'd keep his mouth shut. There were plenty of people he knew who'd do it, but when he thought about it, that wasn't safe either, as it would involve him asking around, a sure-fire way of getting grassed up if the shit hit the fan. He had to do something to shut the Dredd up, but he couldn't think of anything quick and simple enough, besides . . .

Suddenly, Cory knew exactly what he could do to solve his problem.

'Yeah . . . uh thanks Art man, I appreciate you tellin' me that,' Cory said, his thoughts obviously elsewhere. Absently, the teen shoved Art a purple twenty-pound note, which he gaped at for a second, before taking it and putting it in his pocket quickly.

'Safe star, anytime,' he replied with a forced confidence, regretting that he'd told Cory anything. Everyone knew how protective the two cousins were of each other and he could see the rage in Cory's eyes every time he looked at him. The best thing would've been to find Sean and let him know what Levi was up to, but it was too late now. Cursing himself, he thought that in his ignorance he'd just made a bad situation much worse.

But hey, he had a score in his pocket and he might even be able to get a shiners out of Teresa in exchange for a blast of the pipe, so things weren't that bad. The two boys ambled back to the group easily, before Cory abruptly turned, tapping Art on the elbow.

'Listen Art, tell dem man I soon come all right, I jus' gotta sort out some t'ings yeah?'

'Yeah, yeah,' the crackhead replied, his mind now taken over with the thought of lighting that pipe, taking in the smoke, the blast as it hit his brain. Goosebumps formed on his skinny arms and he barely noticed the teen leaving his side and backtracking out of the park behind him.

'Hey! *Hey*, where's Cory goin' spee?'

Garvey was up on his feet, watching Cory's lithe figure leaving the park gates once again, in a military stride. He looked at Martin Pitt once, then back at his friend, feeling a flash of *déjà vu* as the teen walked.

Art shrugged at the boy's question. 'I dunno man, he said he'd soon come, got some t'ings to deal wiv man.'

'Wha' d'you say to 'im star?'

'I was jus' talkin' about a nex' move man, what'm t'you?'

He dismissed the boy and turned to the crowd.

'Hear what anyway, anyone up for some bone, 'cause I got a score an' if we put our money together . . . '

Art smiled at Teresa. The girl gave him her best 'come hither' smile, which in her current dishevelled state wasn't even very sexy.

Garvey looked on in disgust, before picking up his weed and, without a word to the others, headed in the same direction as Cory, wanting to find out once and for all what was really going on with him.

He'd had a feeling things were not right with his friend for some time now. Over the last few months, the happy-go-lucky Cory had turned into an anxious person, always looking over his shoulder when he walked the streets. His temper could be roused in seconds over the most trivial things. Garvey believed he knew the teen inside out, and right now, he had all the symptoms of a guy in a lot of trouble.

Jungle was blasting from Shannon's room, just above the high-spirited voices of Shannon and her friends. No doubt they were smoking, drinking and enjoying themselves to the full. Sean, who was in the kitchen, fixed himself a ham sandwich with coleslaw and a dash of Encona hot pepper sauce, then picked up his glass of Coca-Cola and slowly made his way to his bedroom, taking small steps so he didn't trip on anything.

As he passed Shannon's room he could feel the heavy bass shaking the door. Smiling, he kicked it lightly with his foot as both his hands were too full to knock. There was a chorus of voices telling him to enter, then the door opened and he walked in, unable to see who had let him in, as they were hidden behind the open door.

The girls were all wearing short dresses and jean shorts to combat the hot weather and the sight of their smooth, dark, firm bodies started a pang deep in the teen's stomach that ended somewhere near his groin. Since he was very young he'd always thought his sister didn't seem to have any ugly friends. He smiled at Shannon as she emerged from behind the door and gave him a hug, not wanting him to leave.

'Y' all right Sean, how's Sonnie?' Shannon asked, going back to her spot at the head of the bed.

'She's all right man, jus' relaxin' for today, y'get me?' he replied, taking a token sip of his drink.

'Where's Mum?'

'Gone Greg's for a bit, she said.'

'What about Cory?'

'I dunno, he jus' tol' me he was goin' out, then he left.'

His sister knocked back a mug that no doubt contained some alcoholic beverage, then lit a zook and pulled happily away on it.

'Yeah well, I ain't stoppin' anyway, I jus' popped in to say hello. If you got a spare moment later on though, I wouldn't mind a word Shan.'

Shannon squinted at him from across the room, then made as if to get up.

'So what, talk t'me now innit?' she insisted seriously.

'Nah man, it's a minor star, don' worry about it for now. When you're ready yeah?'

'OK then.'

'See ya!' the girls shouted as he left. Shaking his head, he went into his own room, switched on the TV, then hungrily devoured the ham sandwich, while the lunchtime news came on.

He reached into his jeans pocket and pulled out a half-smoked crack spliff he'd been puffing on this morning, on his way over to Sonnie's. It made him feel guilty to do it, but since she'd told him that she might be pregnant, he couldn't help the craving that came over him sometimes, more often when he was alone. He stopped telling Cory about it because he didn't want him to think he'd turned into some kind of junkie. He would go to the many dealers on Greenside, choosing a different one each time, so no one thought he was becoming a regular smoker.

He took slow, deep tokes on the crack zook, holding the smoke in his lungs until his chest ached. When he was virtually smoking cardboard, he put it out fiercely, blowing plumes through his nose and mouth as he lay back. He was buzzing – the spliff had hit the spot. He lay back on the bed enjoying the sensation. When the phone rang in the living room it sounded as if it was wrapped in cotton. Lazily, he waited until he heard Shannon go to answer it.

He was surprised when she called his name.

'Comin'!' he called, as he stumbled towards the door. His sister looked at him strangely as he took the receiver from her, and shrugged when he asked who it was. He waited until she was gone, then pressed the plastic to his ear.

'Yeah yeah?'

He could hear the sound of breathing, then, 'Yes my yout'.'

Levi? he thought, startled. What did he want?

'What's up man?'

'Cool star . . . me on vacation, y'unnerstan'?'

'Yeah, Cory tol' me you'd gone away.'

There was a silence, then the Dredd chuckled.

'Listen blood, me 'ave a propasition fe yuh . . . Me need a man fe come collec' me from y'asso tomorra, 'bout alf ninc, dem times dere. True Kenny an' dem man lock up me cyaan fin' nobody fe drive me y'get me. So me start wonder if you woulda min' earn some wong, yuh 'ear me?'

'Boy y'know,' Sean said slowly. He thought about what he'd promised Cory weeks ago. Up until now, the temptation to move with Levi again hadn't come his way, and he'd been safe, but now. He closed his eyes, his head hurting him. Why couldn't life be easy for once? Now that he knew his baby was on the way, he had an obligation towards his child as well as his cousin. He needed money badly, more than he'd ever needed it before, but he'd promised.

'Come nuh star, me nuh 'ave all day.'

Levi's voice brought him back to reality.

'Listen Levi man, I'd like t'help you out but—'

'So my yout' yuh waan t'row way a monkey?' the man broke in, cutting him off like a sharp pair of scissors.

'*Wha*'?'

Sean looked at the receiver in amazement.

'Yeah man, I'll gi yuh a monkey, jus' to pick me up an' tek me 'ome. Yuh cyaan loose star . . . Wha' yuh ah say, bring me in nuh?'

'Levi man,' Sean grumbled, giving in already. Half a grand . . . he was almost spending it already.

'All right den, I'm in,' he told the man, confidently. Somewhere inside him, a voice sounding very much like Cory screamed at him to stop. He closed his eyes again, as Levi drowned the voice out.

'Wicked my yout', yuh bona fide, y'get me? All right, me waan yuh go Shawna drum—'

'*Shawna's?*' the youth spat. The Dredd laughed.

'Yeh man, me never mention dat?'

Sean grumbled a reply. He laughed again.

'Yeh man, me 'ave a box o' tricks she's keepin' f'me y'unnerstan'?'

'Yeah yeah,' Sean said morosely. He knew exactly what the Dredd was talking about.

'Me waan yuh go to 'er yard an' collec' dem t'ings, den drop dem off, an' come look fe me. T'ink yuh can do dat supe?'

'I suppose so,' the teen mumbled. 'A monkey yeah?'

'Yeh man. Jus' come t'de station an' wait outside, 'bout nine, half nine, seen. Shawna should 'ave some money fe me too, so don't forget to ask fe dat, seen.'

'All right Levi, I'll be dere.'

'Later . . .'

Sean got up, went into his room, then opened his desk and pulled out his SIG-Sauer. He checked the safety catch, before pushing it into his waistband. A little more rooting around, produced a pair of dark glasses and his black gloves, which he shoved into his back pocket.

Time for some of that easy money, he thought, as he closed the door behind him. After a knock and a yell to Shannon, Sean left the flat for an appointment with Levi and fate.

Garvey strode, full of purpose, through Greenside's many blocks, searching for Cory. He headed for Denver at first and was pleased when he saw the other Bradley, Sean, come out of the foyer, heading his way. He raised a hand and touched fists with the lanky teen.

'Yes blood.'

'Nice one Garv's. Where you off to man?'

'I'm lookin' for your cousin as it goes. He ain't in your drum is he?'

'Nah man, it's jus' Shannon an' her bredrins dere at the moment. I ain't seen Cory since dis mornin' myself.'

'Shit.'

Garvey stood with a hand on his chin. Sean studied him from behind his sunglasses.

'Why, is somethin' up?' he said, his curiosity aroused.

Garvey looked up, considered telling him what he knew, then thought the better of it, as what he knew wasn't very much. The teen couldn't have gone far and Garvey was a cautious boy, not given to acting blindly. He decided to continue his search and not worry Sean over something that, more than likely, was nothing.

'Nah man, it's jus' dat Martin Pitt's got nuff Versacc garms an' I was thinkin' we could rob 'is claat an' make some wong, y'get me?'

Sean laughed, as a black man clutching a Bible walked past them in the middle of the road, shouting out psalms at the top of his voice. Cars beeped at him, but he paid thcm no mind, except to shake the Bible at them menacingly. The teenagers watched him walk away, silently, then Sean turned back to Garvey, his smile gone.

'Anyway, I gotta run man. If you see Cory, tell 'im I'll catch up with him dis evenin', I gotta talk to him seriously.'

'Yeah yeah.'

Garvey watched Sean head for the bus stop, then break into a run as a red single decker pulled up, its doors swinging open to admit him.

Turning away, Garvey walked back, past the football pitch towards Caldervale House. The heat was pounding on his head, making him feel irritable and tired, even though it was still quite early. At the rate things were going, it would still be hot at eleven or midnight, which meant another sleepless night for the youth. He shook his head and uncapped his bottle of Snapple, hating the warm taste of it, but necding something for his throat. He drank and walked, his feet slapping rhythmically on the street's hard paving slabs.

He turned left at Caldervale, cruising with no real destination, then he saw a familiar figure by the corner of Devonshire by an open-air phone box. As he watched, the figure put the receiver down, felt the coin slot for change and sat on a wall, obviously waiting for someone, his trio of new shirts lined up beside him. Garvey grinned and trotted over.

'Cory!'

The teen looked up, then smiled, distantly. 'Yes Garv's.'

Garvey walked closer, then joined his friend on the wall, all the while shooting concerned looks at him.

'What's up man, how come you jus' ducked out like dat spee?'

Cory shrugged.

'Boy . . . Garv's, to tell the truth, it's a long story man. I can't even go into it now y'get me, not in full anyway.'

'How you mean?'

'Man . . .' Cory pulled a face and rubbed his shaved head, 'I've bin meanin' to tell you for time, but there's bin too much goin' on spee, an' my head's confused man.'

'What, like mine is now?'

Cory chortled, but the laugh sounded hard and somewhat forced.

'Buil' a ziggy man,' he offered.

'What here?'

'Yeah man, I'll look out f'you.'

Garvey took out his king size, tore it once along one side, then broke in the cigarette. Cory passed him the weed, looking everywhere.

'I can't wait to get rich, so I can stop smokin' browns,' he complained. Garvey gave him a look as he rolled and licked.

'You don't smoke browns man.'

'Yes I do. Every time I smoke green.'

Garvey shrugged and lit up.

'Dat's a minor though, innit? The way I see it you don't even use a third of browns for a ziggy.'

Cory nodded.

'Yeah true, but we ain't using no filter are we? All dat tar an' nicotine an' shit's goin' in our lungs wid *no filter man*.'

He said this last in a sepulchral voice. Garvey chuckled deeply.

'What's wrong with you man,' he muttered. 'Dat's morbid star. I don't even think about dem t'ings man, you do an' you're more likely to worry yourself sick innit? Lung cancer an' all dat. Fuck it man. We're all gonna die sometime. I mean, check dat brer.' Garvey pointed at a white tramp staggering their way holding a blue can of Tennants Super. 'You think he's worried about lung cancer? Nah man, he's livin' for the moment y'get me?'

Cory stared at the man, before turning to his friend.

'Yeah well, I don't mean to sound rude, but dat example don't really do your argument any justice man. The only reason he's not worryin' about cancer is 'cos 'is kidneys are fucked instead. Dat's not much consolation, is it?'

They laughed a bit and sat in a friendly silence, watching the world go by. Garvey passed the zook, spitting tobacco.

'So wha' you waitin' here for?'

Cory shrugged.

'I jus' spoke to Craig Price an' I'm gonna go up his estate for a bit, to cool out.'

'Oh yeah, he's back on the manor again innit?'

'Yeah yeah.'

'My mum said she seen 'im, but I ain't.'

Garvey peered at Cory. 'Dat's a bit sudden innit?'

Cory looked at the boy, then laughed.

'Garvey man, 'llow me star. Listen, the only reason I ain't tellin' you what's happenin', is 'cos it's a long story an' Craig's comin to pick me up on his moped now, seen. But as soon as I'm back in Greenside I'll link you an' show you the ku, serious t'ing.'

'What, you can't even bring me in *slightly* spee?'

Garvey was holding his first finger and thumb together and squeezing up his face to show how 'slightly' he wanted to be confided in. The teen laughed again.

'*Naaah* man, I ain't worth it star. I swear on my pap's grave, I'll tell you everythin' when I get back.'

'All right den man, whatever.'

Cory passed the zook back for the last blast. Garvey looked up quickly.

'Ah shit, I knew dere was sumthin' I had to say! We forgot about Martin Pitt!'

Cory slapped his head.

'Damn—' He stopped. A moped's engine could be heard, coming from nearby.

'Sounds like Craig.'

Garvey kicked the roach away.

'It's comin' dis way,' he commented.

They waited for a few more seconds, before Craig's red Vespa chugged into view. The teenager was riding one handed, his left hand holding a spare helmet. He came to a neat stop in front of the two friends and swung a heavy head Garvey's way.

'All right mate, 'ow's it goin' den?'

'Safe spee,' Garvey walked to the kerb and shook hands with the boy, grinning.

'You're lookin' tense boy, the army musta treated you well!'

'S'all dem veggies innit?' Craig replied, his Cockney drawl a little muffled by the mask. He turned to Cory and lifted a fist in greeting.

'So what, you ready Cory, we gotta run man, Petey's waitin'.'

'Yeah man.'

He walked over to the moped and climbed on, talking to Garvey as he got comfortable.

'You gonna be in later den?'

'What time?'

'I dunno, about . . . six, or den again, *Eastenders* time.'

Garvey made a face. 'Who can say? Try me anyway. If I'm not dere, I'll be at Claire's man an' you're more than welcome to pass, you done know.'

'All right blood. Hey Garv's, c'n you look after dem shirts f'me, till I get back to these sides?'

'Yeah man safe, you can pick 'em up from my drum whenever man.'

'Cheers blood. Later on.'

Craig gunned the engine, sending black smoke from the exhaust in a murky carbon cloud. He nodded at Garvey, tooted his horn and then was off, with Cory holding a fist up as they powered away, the Vespa's gears sounding like a shrill throaty voice, before fading away.

Garvey watched the vehicle go, feeling apprehensive, wishing he had the words to make Cory stay in Greenside with him tonight. He didn't know why he felt so edgy, or then again he did. Cory was making him nervous. He'd said some strange things, not just today, but over the last few months too. So had Sean come to think of it.

'Fuck!'

He remembered he'd been meant to give Cory a message from Sean. He looked up at the road the teen had taken, picked up the packets of shirts, then walked on, his head down, thinking he should've used Sean as an excuse for Cory to stay around. A little annoyed, he walked towards Oakhill, premonitions rattling in his head like a pea in a whistle.

Garvey never saw Cory again.

Chapter Nineteen

Sean followed Shawna into her flat, feeling apprehensive now that the high of the rock had left him. The young woman had her child in one arm, a zook in the other and her face was calm, even after the bad tidings that Sean had passed on from the front door. They walked into the living room, where a white girl with long brown hair and a round chubby face sat spread out on the wide sofa, a zook between her short fingers. A top-of-the-range Akai video played back a muted recording of *The Real McCoy*, as two black stand-up comedians took to the stage, sending the on-screen audience into silent hysterics.

Shawna put the baby in a cot in the corner of the room and sat at the Ikea table, one hand on her head, looking doll-like in a bright patterned summer dress. When she looked up, her pretty grey eyes were tinged with red.

'So what, when did they shif' 'im?' she asked Sean.

Sean rubbed his face, trying not to look at the zook dangling between the girl's fingers.

'Uhh, yestiday I think. It was some kinda bigtime raid man. They probably bin surveying Beechwood for ages. Levi wants to get all the t'ings out of here an' back there, as quick as poss.'

'Is that smart?' Shawna queried. 'I mean, takin' everythin' back to the squat's a bit risky innit?'

'Yeah, but it's no riskier than leavin' everyt'ing here. If they bin surveyin' Levi, they must know about you Shawna.'

The girl sitting next to Sean passed him her zook. When Sean smiled his thanks, Shawna slapped her head.

'Oh I'm sorry, I'm *sooo* rude. Sean this is Patricia, Patricia this is Sean.'

'Hi,' Sean puffed.

'Hi,' the white girl replied. 'You don't have to call me Patricia, everyone calls me Patty.'

'OK den, but I like Patricia y'know,' Sean told her, babbling with the immediate rush he had got. He sat back in his seat while Patty started to natter to Shawna, looking pleased.

'That's what Mark says, but he usually calls me Patty anyway. Big Batty Patty that's what he calls me. Fuckin' piss taker! I can't help it if I got a big bum, it's the way I was designed. Mark don't business though, he likes my arse f'real man! Las' night we—'

'Patty please!' Shawna cut in. 'You said you weren't gonna talk about Mark no more an' here you are, off again . . .'

Patty covered her mouth with her hand, looking like a playful cherub caught in the act of some terrible naughtiness. She removed her hand and drank from a wine glass near her feet, her face flushed and slightly red.

Sean ground out the zook, blowing smoke out, before looking up at Shawna, impatient to get the job at hand done.

'So you ready den?' he asked.

The girl nodded, wiped her jet black hair from her face and got up, a little unsteadily.

'Cor, headrush,' she said, standing still for a couple of seconds. 'Back in a minute Patty.'

When her head cleared, she walked out of the living room, through the short corridor and down some dark stairs, with Sean following carefully behind her. When they got to the bottom of the stairs, she flicked on a light switch and Sean could see three doors, two at opposite ends of the passage they were now standing in and one directly in front of them. The young woman made for the room opposite them, then paused with her hand on the doorknob.

'Be extra quiet will you, Patty's yout's in dere sleepin'.'

'OK.'

Sean's voice sounded gruff and heavy to his own ears, loud in the thick silence. Shawna opened the door a crack, then closed it and turned back to him again. This time her face was puzzled and slightly suspicious.

'Wait a minute, how do I know you're tellin' the truth about all this? For all I know, you could be after the guns for yourself. Levi would go mad if I gave the box away without even knowin' who you were.'

Sean looked confused. He hadn't even thought of it that way.

'But you know me man, you see me dem times we did the robberies innit?' he argued.

Shawna stared at him, her grey eyes still visible, despite her dilated pupils. Her brow furrowed, as she thought hard.

'*Yeah*, but you an' me both know that don't mean nuttin'. I can't jus' let you take a box of weapons away jus' like that. It's not really sensible is it?'

Sean cursed himself, realising that she was right. He would have reacted the same way himself. He thought a bit more, then gave her a desperate look.

'C'mon Shawna man, Levi's known me since I was a yout'. I can't run away wid the t'ings or nuffin', we live on the same estate. How c'n I sting him if he knows where my mum lives?'

She pondered over this. To Sean, the silence was very long.

'All right go on den. But I don't afta tell you what'll happen if anythin' fucks up, do I?'

Sean nodded once, but stayed silent.

'Come we go in,' she muttered.

Pushing the door they entered the room which, Sean could immediately see, was a playroom.

As he stepped warily inside, he stepped on something soft, which squealed loudly, making both him and Shawna jump. He bent down to retrieve the toy and saw it was a bright blue dinosaur, with menacing teeth and claws.

Shawna laughed as he squeezed the toy again, then beckoned him to a dark corner of the room. The cache was sitting there, a heavily padlocked illegal alien in the room, a stark reality that didn't belong in this world of make believe and innocence that surrounded them. They bent down in front of the box and Sean could smell Shawna's perfume faintly next to him, sweet, but not overpowering. He gave the cache an experimental tug, then gasped at the pain in his fingers. The box didn't move a millimetre.

'Shit, that's heavy,' he stated, looking at Shawna. 'How'm I gonna get it to Greenside man? I doubt if I can even get it up the stairs.'

Shawna thought, then looked at him. 'You c'n drive innit?'

'Yeah, yeah. It'll be bait, but I can do it.'

'OK then, you c'n borrow my car yeah? Jus' min' how you drive it all right? You can hand it over to Levi when you bail him out.'

'Wha' you got?'

'A Tipo.'

'Ah man, dett! Cheers Shawna!'

The girl smiled, her face looking like a child's.

'S'OK. To get dis into the car we need some help though, cause I ain't liftin' it, I tell you that much.'

'Nah man,' Sean agreed.

Shawna got up, lowered herself slowly onto the bed, mindful of the sleeping child, then thought again.

'All right,' she pondered, 'I suppose I could ask the guy from upstairs to give me a hand. He's an ol' boy, but he's ever so nice, always helpin' me out when I need someone to watch over Kyle. He wouldn't screw at all.'

'Yeah, that makes sense,' Sean agreed again.

His mind was wandering, busily thinking of the name Kyle for his child, if it was a boy of course. Then again, having a child with the same name as Levi's wasn't something that appealed to Sean, besides he wanted a Christian name that meant something, whether the child was a boy or a girl. He shook his head to discard the thoughts almost as soon as they had come. It was the wrong time and definitely the wrong place.

'All right then, I'll jus' go upstairs an' see if my man's in, all right?' Shawna was saying, before she disappeared upstairs.

Sean nodded and sat on the large box. A little while later, the bedroom door swung open and a burly middle-aged white man with a face full of wrinkles came inside. Shawna was close behind.

'Wot, so that's it, is it?' he said, his loud Cockney accent, making Patty's child stir and turn over once, before breaking into snores again on his stomach.

'Sssh Georgie!' Shawna said, with a faint smile. 'Dis is my friend Sean, he'll grab the other end yeah?'

'You ready then mate?' Georgie asked Sean. He smelled old-people musty, like stale air that had been locked in a room for months, his crumpled face reminding Sean of a bloodhound's.

Sean moved down to the bottom end of the cache then waited as the older man grasped the edges at the top.

'Don't forget to bend your legs!' Shawna warned them both. 'I don't want anyone doin' their back in or anythin'!'

'Take the strain,' Georgie said, which made Sean want to laugh.

'*Lift*!'

They lifted at the same time, Sean's arms straining almost at once from the weight of the box. They dolly-stepped out of the corner, Georgie going backwards, then exited the room slowly, until they reached the foot of the stairs, where they put the box down. Shawna watched them from a couple of steps up, the keys for her car jangling in her hands. Georgie's face was slightly red, but Sean was impressed by the older man's strength. The box was heavy, but at least it was manageable now the Cockney had made an appearance.

'Ready?' Sean said. The man gave a grunt.

They lifted the box again and carried it one step at a time to the landing, with their arms aching. Shawna opened all the doors on their way out of the flat and, soon enough, they were outside on the street, panting. They dropped the cache somewhat heavily on the pavement, then watched as Shawna opened the boot and pushed the back seat forward, her summer dress lifting and showing a rounded butter-coloured thigh as she bent over.

They then gave the box one last lift and slid it into the back, before shutting the boot. Shawna rubbed her hands together and smiled.

'D'wanna beer you two?' she asked, when the boot was safely shut.

'That'll do nicely,' the older man said, as he let out an exhausted gasp. 'What d'you lot 'ave in there, a bazooka or summick?' he grumbled.

Shawna and the teen looked at each other and grinned. 'Close,' the girl muttered, under her breath.

Sean laughed.

*

Sean took a long, meandering route into Greenside to avoid being spotted most of all by his mother. He drove with a little more confidence now, thanks to the few lessons he had been taking and he was careful not to speed, though the only police cars that he did see dashed past him in a rush of gears and blue lights. He cruised sedately past Flaxman, Nelson and Lexham, then turned right into Beaumont Road, eased past Woodcroft and drove on, past the roundabout and into Beechwood, congratulating himself on his safe journey.

When he got to the block he parked, turned off the engine, then went stiff with realisation. Who was going to help him get the box upstairs to the squat? He had been so busy concentrating on other things, the thought hadn't crossed his mind and now here he was, in a car he didn't own, no insurance, no licence and a box of guns in the boot. He was practically screaming to go to jail.

He opened the door, feeling pissed off and stared up at the bulk of the building, debating his next move. He had the keys to the flat, but there was no reason to go inside if he didn't have the cache with him. He had some money Shawna had given him for Levi, so the best thing he could think of would be to get back inside the car, drive to the station and come back with the dealer, so that he could help him carry the weapons up to the flat.

He stood still for a while longer, paranoid about driving to the station with the guns in his possession until a voice called him, shaking him out of his reverie.

'Raa, this is a strange place to come sightseein' innit?'

Sean looked down. 'Hey, what's up Rosie? How long you bin watchin' me?'

'Since you pulled up. You was daydreamin' for time,' she informed him candidly. Tara was with her.

'Ain't seen Cory today 'ave you?' he asked the girl, thinking more on how his cousin's choice of women had taken a turn for the better. The girl frowned, then shook her head, her Puffs jiggling slightly.

'Nah I ain't, but I seen 'im yestiday.'

Tara giggled to herself and Rosie shot her a look, then turned back to Sean, shamefaced.

'Why, is anythin' the matter?' she asked, peering up at him.

'Nah . . . Well I suppose . . . *ahhhh* . . .'

Sonia had him like this sometimes, hitting the nail bang on the head, usually throwing him off balance for a second. He wondered if Cory had lasted long keeping the intelligent girl in the dark about their goings on.

'Rosie, c'n I chat t'you for a second in private?' he eventually managed, giving Tara a look of apology.

Rosie walked past her concrete front garden and followed him down the pavement. When they were far enough, Sean turned to the girl, his face earnest.

'Rosie, I want you to give Cory a message if you see him, yeah?'

'Okay,' she drawled, sounding a touch unsure. He ignored it and continued.

'Tell 'im that I'm busy helpin' Levi get bailed out, but in the meantime he should stay home an' wait for me to come back. Tell him that I'm safe an' everythin' an' that I'll be back later, but he must wait for me to come home. I'll drop Levi back here, then I'll be straight over, got that?'

'Yeah I got it, but how come you're helpin' my man out? I thought you'd wanna keep away from him.'

Sean gave a start, shot the girl an odd look, then dismissed what he had heard again.

'It's worth wong for my man to be on street, he's losin' nuff dollars sittin' in a cell. He's offered to pay me as well, so the way I see it, it's money for nothin' jus' to go an' get 'im an' bring 'im back.'

Frown lines creased Rosie's forehead. She put her small hands on her hips and narrowed her eyes, her gaze distant, her thoughts flashing across her face.

'*Yeah*, but I still don't understand why he wants you to come an' get him out, when there's nuff people closer to him that could do it, jus' as easily. I ain't tryin' to jinx up your programme or nuffin', but don't you reckon it's strange that all of a sudden Levi's pally wiv you again? I'm sorry, but I don't trus' that brer, he's a snake in the grass star.'

Sean shrugged, looking at the floor, then faced Rosie stubbornly. 'Boy, it's like what that brer on *Mastermind* says, "I've started so I'll finish" innit? I've already borrowed his girl's motor, so I might as well go an' get 'im now, don't you reckon? I can't afford to turn down wong, I'm not that rich yet, y'get me?'

Rosie squirmed a little, not looking at him, then she sighed and pouted sulkily. 'All right Sean, do what you're doin', but be careful will yuh? Cory'd be properly cut up if anythin' happened t'you, I can tell, he talks about you all the time. He really loves you man, so jus' watch yourself, if not for your sake, for his OK?'

'I'll try,' Sean replied, touched at her words. He gave the girl's hand a squeeze, then backed away and opened the Tipo's door, climbing inside the clean interior slowly, as though he was forcing every movement that he made. Rosie watched him start the engine, then reverse until he was facing the main road and accelerating flawlessly out of Beechwood, the car's engine purring gently as he disappeared from sight.

As usual, the streets had come alive with the sun and the whole area was buzzing with a vibe that was so strong, Sean felt he could almost touch it. He often slagged off London in the winter, but he had to admit when the sun was shining and the women were out in force, there was nowhere else like it for him. Bicycle riders flew past him as he pulled away from the lights, their mouths covered with painters' face masks to avoid car fumes. The teen smiled and thought that they had the right idea.

Soon, he arrived at the police station and he eased past, then decided to park a few streets away from the building, out from under the Met's watchful eyes. When he was done, he checked his gun was still firmly against his stomach, then sat back in the driver's seat, preparing to doze for a bit as he was early. Eyes closed, he thought of his cousin once more, then impatiently tapped the sides of the chair, feeling bored and wanting some action.

Chapter Twenty

When Cory finally got back to Greenside sometime later in the day, the sun was a huge orange ball, barely visible over his high-rise block and turning the sky into a mosaic of colours. The moon was a hazy spotlight in the heavens, faint, but becoming more apparent as its opposite number moved away. The teen thanked Craig for the lift and the pistol, promised to come and see him soon, then took off his shades and went into his building, holding a plain carrier bag, the expression on his face dead serious.

He heard voices coming from inside the flat as he turned his front door key, but thought nothing of it, his mind on future scenarios, his ears shut off for the moment. When he was inside though, he heard his aunt yelling hysterically and his cousin's lower tone, speaking in comfort through every pause. As best as he could, he ran down the stairs and into the living room where the voices were coming from, preparing himself for the worst.

Bernice was sitting on the sofa, her hands clenched and her face taut, the TV in front of her ignored in her abject despair. She wasn't crying (Cory felt a dull relief about that) but her eyes darted about the small room as if she was being hunted and she feared that her predator was in the room, waiting to pounce. Shannon was leaning over her, a cup of tea in her hand, her own eyes hard and angry, even though they were slightly glazed. As Cory rushed into the room, both women looked up at him expectantly, then their faces changed to show disappointment.

'*CORY*!' both of them chimed at the same time.

'What's up, what's up?' Cory cried, fumbling into the room.

Bernice looked at him, her eyes fluttering crazily. Cory felt like running out of the flat right that second, not even wanting to wait and hear what his aunt had to say, but he steeled himself and walked further into the room, his insides churning.

'We've just had the police here, bangin' our door down lookin' for Sean, sayin' they got a warrant out for his arrest!' Bernice told him. Cory tried to keep a moderately surprised look on his face.

'I asked them if they were sure that they had the right house an' they said, "Yes", then I said, "Are you sure you've got the right *person*" and they said "Yes" again. Then they barged in here an' searched the whole flat lookin' for him, walked in on Shannon an' her friends smokin' in her room . . .'

Shannon blushed and looked down.

' . . . Then they went into your room an' found some jewellery an' a whole 'eap of money in there, almost two thousand pounds the policeman said. What's two thousand pounds doin' in your room?'

Cory opened his mouth, but the only thing that came out, was a faint croak. We've blatantly bin bagged man, he thought sickly.

Bernice didn't even wait for an answer to her question. ' . . . Then they went on, askin' us where he was hidin' an' tellin' us that he may as well give himself up, askin' for his friends' names and addresses. They said that he was involved in that armed robbery in Arnos Grove an' that he shot someone! What's goin' on Cory, they're lyin' aren't they?'

There was a minuscule pause, as the women turned to look at Cory.

'Yeah . . . they're lyin' auntie. Sean wouldn't shoot no one, he ain't into dem t'ings man.'

Shannon was glaring at the teen, clearly disbelieving his words. Bernice nodded, hearing what she wanted to hear.

'I knew it, *I knew it*!' she hissed. Then she thought for a second. 'But where did all that money come from then?'

Cory sighed as he had anticipated that question and he had no real iron-clad answer.

'I dunno auntie, I didn't even know it was dere. Where did they fin' it?'

'Under Sean's bed,' his aunt replied, looking at him strangely. She had found stolen goods belonging to Cory hidden under Sean's bed many times before. The following silence was very, very loud.

'Cory, it wasn't you who was involved in that robbery was it?' The teen tensed under her gaze.

'No auntie, it wasn't me—'

'Cory—'

'It wasn't I swear! I'd have a hard time nickin' a football off a load o' kids with my leg, let alone doin' a robbery. I dunno what's goin' on man, but I wasn't holdin' up no jewellers, I promise you.'

Cory felt like a bastard yet again, as he dropped Sean further and further in the shit. He moved around a bit then looked at his cousin, who was glaring at him.

'So what, where is he den? 'ave you seen 'im?'

'Yeah,' Shannon looked grim. 'Las' time was this afternoon, but he left without sayin' nothin' about where he was goin'. He ain't bin back, cos I bin in all day.'

'You're lucky you didn't get arrested too,' her mother informed her.

'I know man, but dem Rads was so busy tryin' to look up our skirts, they hardly even noticed us bunnin'.'

Shannon put her head in her hands, looking dejected and fed up with life. Bernice sipped her tea, tutting every now and then, but looking a little calmer. Cory studied his hands, then, unable to take the atmosphere anymore, he got up and went into his room, swinging his bag and cursing under his breath as he did so. He opened the door then gasped as he stepped inside. Their bedroom was a tip.

Clothes were everywhere, the rubbish bin had been over-turned and searched and the police had obviously been through all of their drawers and cupboards, searching for clues to Sean's whereabouts, as well as evidence that would link him to Levi. A strange smell was in the air, one that the teen recognised and hoped that the police hadn't. Cory saw his digital scales lying on the floor and he was glad that all of his weed was in his pocket, otherwise he would have been up shit creek now. He picked it up, flicked it on and off to make sure it was still working, then looked about again, trying to remember what he had put where.

From his sock, he pulled out a small length of copper piping Craig had given him. He had asked the white boy whether they sold silencers too and Craig had laughed and given him a strange look.

'Fuckin' 'ell mate!' he chortled. 'Don't you know, if you're nicked wiv a silencer alone, you can get up to seven years inside star. That's like confessin' that you wanna murder someone spee, premeditated, y'get me? I tell you what, I got somethin' that's jus' as effective an' a hell of a lot cheaper too.'

The boy had disappeared into the back room again, then returned with the piping in his hand. It was about fourteen centimetres in length and fitted snugly over the barrel of the gun when Cory had tried it out.

He paced around his room, the copper piping in his hand, until he found the rucksack Sean had used to carry the jewellery from his raid. He slipped the piping in, as well as a baseball cap, then took out the shoulder holster from the plain carrier bag, put it on underneath his T-shirt and put the gun inside. He then peered into the mirror, finding that the gun was a visible lump beneath his armpit everytime he moved his arms; but with them by his side, it was unseen. He looked out of the window at the fading light, then decided to put the holster over his T-shirt. He could wear a jacket over that and the gun would be virtually unnoticeable.

He made adjustments quickly, then looked in a drawer on his side of their desk and pulled out a small blue Helix safe and opened it with a tiny key attached to his keyring. The money he'd been saving over an eight-week period, some two hundred pounds, was still lying neatly inside under the coin tray. He put it in his back pocket happily, in case the police came back, then laughed out loud to himself, pleased that he had salvaged something. There was a knock on the bedroom door and he stopped abruptly.

'Come in!' he yelled, hands by his sides, hoping it wasn't Bernice.

It wasn't. It was worse.

'What the fuck's goin' on Cory?' Shannon growled, looking wild as she stomped into the room. She sniffed the air then, wanting to say her piece, dismissed the odour and let rip.

'I dunno who you're tryin' to kid, but it ain't workin' one bit, I'm tellin' you now star. Mum can see summick ain't gellin' she ain't stoopid y'nuh an' I bin watchin' this get bigger an' bigger for ages, but like a fool I said, "Wait, let dem lot take care of it, they're capable people now". Capable *what*? Hear what, you bes' jus' show me the ku now man, cos if you don't, I'm liable to knock you out right now, y'hear me?'

'Damn Shannon.' Cory sat on Sean's bed, taken aback. 'It ain't as simple as that man—'

'It's exactly that simple!' Shannon almost yelled. Cory was thankful that, although she was vex, she was keeping her voice at a reasonable level, aware of Bernice and the flat's thin walls.

'Cory I wanna know right now!' she warned him, her foot tapping as if it wanted to fly over and boot the teen in his chin.

Cory got up, put on his jacket and slid the rucksack onto his shoulders.

'Listen Shannon, I don't even want to mask t'ings from you no more, there ain't much point now,' he said truthfully. 'But I gotta go find Sean man, before dem Rads get to him an' I ain't got time to talk. Now tell me dis: did the Rads mention Levi at all?'

'*Fuck you*!' Shannon half whispered, half screamed. 'I hate you sometimes Cory. Why d'you always have to have your own way man? Furthermore, I ain't tellin' you nuthin' till you answer *my* question firs' y'unnerstan' so you better hurry up an' get on wiv it, before I get *really* vex star.'

'Ah, suit your fuckin' self man. I'm gonna find Sean,' Cory spat and slid past Shannon, out of the slightly open door. She was following him in an instant and she reached out and stopped him by her own bedroom door, her face screwed up in earnest as he faced her.

'All right then, let me come with you,' she suggested.

Cory considered it for a second, then shook his head. 'Nah man. I'll be quicker by myself.'

'*CORY*!' his cousin growled through clenched teeth, almost trembling in anger and frustration. Cory rolled his eyes and turned around again.

'Later man—'

'All right Cory wait!' Shannon whispered again. Cory sighed, his breathing harsh, sounding like a man at the end of his tether.

'Hey Shannon you gonna let me go look for my man or what? I ain't got all day—'

'Well shut up an' listen!' Shannon cut in, her own temper reaching its frayed ends too. The teen could have snapped back and a fight might have started right there, if it wasn't for the girl rushing on with an explanation for her harsh words straight afterwards.

'Jus' *listen* Cory OK? When the police was here and Mum was with 'em in your room, they made all dem lot, y'know Pamela an' dem, they made 'em leave y'get me? Raa, we was in the sittin' room an' I said to one, "Hey does this have anythin' t'do with that Levi?", 'cos I kinda guessed the ku an' at first they wouldn't answer me, but when I got persistent they eventually said "yeah".

'So now, they start takin' the piss, sayin' that Sean's in deep shit, true they want 'im for attempted murder or manslaughter, or one o' dem t'ings dere. So one goes to me that it's such a shame, true Sean's done a runner while Levi's sittin' pretty, got his bail, probably won't even do long inside. Y'know, tryin' to see how much I know an how much I'm willin' to let off. So I said "When was that?" talkin' about the bail an' he goes to me that it should have bin done about an hour ago y'get me?'

'An hour?' Cory muttered, his brow scrunched up.

'Yeah, but that was ages ago,' Shannon admitted.

Cory was quiet, thinking, then he nodded grimly at the distraught girl. 'All right Shannon cheers, yeah? I'll tell you the whole story top to bottom later man, I gotta run star.'

She wordlessly followed him into the living room, where Bernice still sat, staring without interest at the television. Cory went over to her, kissed and hugged her, then told her he was going to look for Sean and that he 'Wasn't coming back without him'. His aunt nodded blankly and clasped his hand in hers before letting him go, then he walked briskly to the front door, Shannon on his tail and the rucksack thumping on his back.

'You stay away from Levi if you see 'im,' she warned the teen when he was by the door, then, as if by some weird sixth sense, she touched the bag on his back.

'What's in here?'

She fingered the bag lightly. Cory turned and flashed his grim smile again.

'A little helpin' hand,' he told her enigmatically, turning his back on her once more.

Cory hit the darkening streets like a vengeful spirit, his mind fully focused on the task that lay ahead of him. He knew that Levi might have been bailed out hours ago – but he was prepared to take the risk to find out, if it could aid his cousin in any way. His plan was to force Levi not to testify in court against Sean by putting the Dredd in hospital. He wholeheartedly believed Sean that it had been the dealer who shot the courageous yet foolish black man in the jewellers, and he didn't see any reason why his cousin should take the blame for something he didn't do.

Cory knew that he was taking a big risk and he also knew if any of his friends had any inkling of what he had in store for Levi, they'd think he'd lost his mind. Maybe he had. At the end of the day it didn't matter, because Cory was prepared to go to almost any lengths to make amends for the way that things had turned out. He thought of all the people who had been upset, indirectly perhaps, through him. Even Bernice had instantly known he had *something* to do with all the ruckus; didn't that prove it was always that way?

He took shortcuts and back streets to the police station, his jacket undone as the evening was crisp and warm. A black girl crossed the road in front of him, heading his way and he almost called out Rosie's name, but as she got closer he realised that it wasn't her. It was wishful thinking. Suddenly he missed the calm, thoughtful presence of the girl and he knew that if it had been her he'd seen, he would have told her everything in a second and she more than likely would have been able to talk him out of his plan. He vaguely wondered if that was love.

Fuck dis up an' you'll never know, he told himself wryly.

He wouldn't mind having the type of relationship that Sean had with Sonia, if it meant him concentrating his attentions solely on Rosie. With Tanya things had been good, but he had always suspected their pairing would end the way it had.

Sometimes he'd envied the closeness Sean and Sonnie shared.

He rubbed his stomach and forced his mind to concentrate on what lay ahead of him, thinking Levi, Levi, Levi. He slowed down, not wanting to look like he was hurrying anywhere, and without appearing too obvious, he started scanning the street to see if he was being watched.

The road was quiet, the cars on either side still silhouettes, parked motionless by the kerb. Up ahead, he could see figures walking, but there was nothing behind him save a small tabby cat that came out from underneath a hedge, its eyes shining as it watched him walk past. He looked over the cars. Some of them were quite expensive and Cory judged from the look of the houses he passed that this was a well-off street. It made him all the more glad for the rucksack on his back. He smiled and started to cross the road.

Halfway across he stopped to survey a line of cars parked in front of him. He squinted, his eyes wide and his mouth open. He stared harder, then realised that he must look very out of place, standing in the centre of the street peering at the vehicles, so he made his way to the other side, his eyes locked on what he had seen. Part of his mind told him that he was wrong, he was just being optimistic, but his other more instinctive side said that for once in his life, luck was on his side.

The car that he was so interested in was a blue Tipo, fairly new, with a cool grey interior and three-spoke alloys. The words 'sixteen valve' were written on the side by the petrol cap, but to Cory none of that really mattered. What mattered to him was that he was sure he had seen Levi driving this car, many times before.

There was one way to be sure.

He moved around to the back of the car and seeing what he wanted he let out a pent-up 'Yes!' through his clenched teeth and gave a little jump of joy on the spot.

On the back window, there was a black plastic car sticker, bearing the legend, '*NUBIANS DO IT BETTER IN THE DARK*', with a picture of a black man looking up at a half moon and a cluster of five pointed stars.

Cory could remember when Levi had first bought the Tipo on a hot summer's day, much like the one that had died down not three hours ago. He had been cooling with Art and some other Greensiders on the Dredd's block, waiting to pick up some weed, when Levi had cruised along, pulling in, then revving the engine a couple of times so that everyone could hear sixteen valves in action. They'd gone over and Cory noticed the car sticker, asking where the dealer had got it from.

He looked the sticker over once more, then hurriedly continued his walk to the station, almost positive the man he was looking for would be inside.

When he eventually stood across the road from the building – a tall sturdy three-storey construction – he stopped and gazed at it, very aware of the beeping car horns, the soft whisper of passing cars and weight of the rucksack, comforting against his spine. He stood there for two minutes psyching himself up, as if he was preparing for a testing game of football, then he walked past the building, crossed the main road and headed for a church wall, where he could sit and watch the entrance to the station, unnoticed by anyone who left or entered. There were some lights on in the rooms upstairs, but as far as Cory could see, nobody had their eyes on him.

He settled himself, his eyes keen on the bright entrance, his face cast with a thousand worries.

Levi was also waiting.

His wait was perhaps the most agonising, as he had no idea what was going on in the very building he was in, let alone the world outside. He forced himself to relax and be patient. He had faith in his solicitor and he knew if Sean did what he had asked of him, he would do it well. More fool him. Levi had a nasty little surprise up his sleeve, a sting in his tail that he would unleash with no regrets and even less sympathy. He pondered on Sean's warrant, wondering if the police had found the teenager yet. He had a strong feeling they wouldn't.

This way, Sean would come to bail him out, Levi could make some excuse to go back into the station then he could inform whoever was at the desk that the person they were looking for was standing right outside. Levi planned to make a quick break for it as soon as he'd achieved what he wanted. He would be free and the young man would be behind a cell door.

He felt the urge for a crack spliff, though weed, or even Ecstasy crushed into a powder would have done him right then. He lay on his bunk and tried to ignore the dry roasting in his mouth, his mind, if not his body, very busy and alive.

Forty-five minutes later, there was a click and the jangle of keys. Levi stayed motionless, eyes on the ceiling, hands behind his head as his cell door swung open. A white-shirted policeman with keys stared at him, then strolled inside, his manner saying that he meant business.

'Come on Patterson, time to go,' he said.

'So soon?' the Dredd replied, a broad grin on his face. He walked to the booking room and seated himself down in front of the main desk, looking smug.

Bailey came through a side door and stood to one side watching the Dredd. The whole area was quiet and solemn.

'Sign here for your things please Mr Patterson,' the officer at the desk ordered curtly.

'What about Kenny an' de others? When they comin' out?' Levi yawned loudly, being melodramatic about the simplest bodily function.

'When somebody comes to pay their bail Mr Patterson. Now if you could sign here . . .'

Levi signed and pushed the sheet over to the officer, watching as he unlocked one of the many steel grey cabinets behind him.

'There you are,' he muttered, as the officer handed over the plastic bags containing his keys and his phone. Levi took them, looked them over, then looked back up expectantly.

'So wha', where de res'?' he seethed.

'The money and the jewellery we're keeping and *under the circumstances* . . .' The Duty Officer behind the wide desk raised a hand and spoke louder as Levi tried to interrupt, drowning the Dredd's arguments with a trained 'taking charge' boom. The officers who stood around were smirking now, pleased to see Levi brought down a peg or two.

'I'm sure you'll understand why,' the policeman continued, glad to have the last word. 'Now if you've collected everything, you're free to go Mr Patterson . . . for now. This form will tell you when you need to come back and you'll get a letter in the post about your court appearance. Make sure you don't get too busy and forget will you? Goodbye.'

Levi stared at the officer, fuming.

'C'mon Patterson,' Bailey ordered, tugging the Dredd's arm as he stared coldly at the Duty Officer, his mask of good humour slipping for a second, revealing the real Levi. Bailey took his arm to steer him away, but the Dredd snatched it away, then walked out, with the younger man close on his heels.

'You know the way then,' Bailey kidded as he strode to a door leading to the front desk. Levi grasped the handle, turned back to the policeman and snarled at him under his breath. 'See you soon, *mate*.'

He opened the door and stepped into the reception area, steaming like a bowl of rice on a hot cooker. When he saw Sean, sitting on some plastic chairs in the waiting area, he immediately felt better.

'Yes yout'!' he cried, as he pushed through the middle doors. 'Wha' gwaan?'

'Yes blood,' Sean grinned, standing up and shaking a dead leg, his fist raised and ready to be touched. Levi noticed the boy easily matched his height and he smiled wryly at nothing as he knocked fists with the teen, knowing he'd made the right choice.

'I bin waitin' here *ages* man!' Sean complained, scowling yet looking pleased.

They left the building and emerged into the night air.

You'll be here a hell of a lot longer soon, the dealer thought evilly. Out loud, he said, 'Yeah man f'real, dis place is depressin' star. Come we go Greenside yout' man, we got t'ings to talk abou'. You fin' yourself a ride yet?'

'Nah, I borrowed Shawna's.'

'*Hmmmp.*'

Levi smiled. 'So you're movin' in on me gyal ee? Two day me inside an' de man sting me properly boy.'

Sean laughed and shook his head, hearing the jokey tone in the dealer's voice.

'Nah star, you know I ain't on dat man.'

'Betah know,' the dealer warned.

They walked a little way further, Levi ready to enter the car park behind the police station. Sean continued walking past the entrance and further on down the street. Perplexed, the Dredd stood in one place.

''Ey where yuh ah go? Where yuh park star?'

'Two streets away.'

Sean gestured with one hand, taking quick looks behind him, but not stopping, wanting to get back to his estate on the double. Levi caught him up, his face annoyed.

'So wha', wha' you do dat for?'

''cos your box o' tricks is still in the boot,' the teen informed him, not slowing down.

'*What*?!'

Levi looked stunned.

'Dere wasn't anyone to help me get it up the stairs, so I had to bring it with me innit? It's no big t'ing, it's jus' the sooner we get it out of here, the sooner we can get it somewhere safe, don't you reckon?'

'Yeah,' Levi said softly, thinking he might've been a bit too clever this time. Now, with the cache in the picture, he would have to handle things a little differently as the Tipo could be traced back to him, quicker than a dog's hind leg could scratch fleas. Quickly he mused on how he could angle things his way.

'So y' all right supe'?' he drawled, his bounce returning.

'Yeah man, I'm safe star,' the teen assured him.

'Still studyin'?'

'Nah, I'm on summer holiday. My end-of-term results come soon though, so hopefully I'll be up for my second year an' after dat . . .' he smiled wistfully. 'The world's my oyster man.'

'Yeh?'

'Yeh man.'

Levi looked at the teen, his gaze a little wistful too. It was a strange look, a mixture of pride and liking, with a touch of envy thrown in. For the first time, a paternal feeling for Sean overtook him – for a moment it flowed as deep and as strong as the blood in his veins. He thought of his brother again; supposing someone had tempted *him* into crime, would he be a bank manager now? Not a chance in hell.

Confusion swept over him as he stared at Sean again, suddenly unsure if he could go through with his plan. They both edged out from behind a large van, then crossed the road carefully.

'Star, I was t'inkin', maybe we should get back togedda, run a few t'ings y'nuh? There's plenty t'ing need tekin' care of, what wid Roger bein' out o' action an' all that. I need someone like you, wid some brain inna yuh 'ead, to look after runnin's an' mek sure everyt'ing gwaan nice, y'unnerstan'? You could mek some real money, 'stead a all dis pocket money you bin earnin' up to now.'

Sean screwed up his face and made a distasteful expression.

'Man . . . I don' think so Levi, I'm tryin' to run t'ings proper star. I shouldn't even tell you dis, but boy . . . star, I got a baby on the way, Sonnie's pregnant innit? I gotta think about responsibility a lot more man, gotta keep my nose clean too an' gettin' involved in any illegal runnin's ain't on f'me. I shouldn't even be here now, only I figured it won't do me no harm, helpin' you out an' that. But it stops dere man. I wanna be around for my kid, not like my dad, who couldn't even be bothered to be there for me.'

The teen's litany flowed of its own accord, his mind on how hard it was to say the word 'No'. Sometimes, you had to say it – you had to detach yourself from the life of your peers around you and go for what *you* wanted. Sometimes you had to dig in your heels and do what *you* believed was right, what *your* heart told you was the best course of action. The teen decided to follow his own heart and leave the Dredd to his old devices when this was over. Then he could bring his child up the right way, his conscience could be free of guilt.

He turned to Levi, not able to express the full extent of his feelings. 'Nah Levi, I think I'm out for good man. Not that I was ever really *in*, y'get me . . .?'

'It's cool, it's cool,' the Dredd murmured easily, knowing it made no difference really. He mused on Sean's most interesting confession, feeling a bit bad, but burying it neatly with thoughts of his own immediate needs where it wouldn't worry him.

'So Sonia's pregnant?' he breathed, surprised that the sensible girl had taken the age-old route. 'How Samant'a tekin' it?'

'Ah, not too bad,' the teen replied. 'I think she's kinda pleased actually.'

They were now standing in front of the Tipo and Levi looked it over to see if there were any noticeable dents or scratches,

Sean watching by his side. Everything looked ship shape and he felt pleased with the teen yet again, hearing a quiet voice in his ear that told him maybe he had got the wrong boy after all.

Trying to ignore it, he gestured for the keys to the Fiat and unlocked the door. The teen marched over to the passenger side and waited for him to open his side too.

Cory sat on the church wall for twenty minutes, before he spotted Levi coming out of the front entrance of the police station, instantly recognisable by his flowing locks, along with a man who could have been any one of a thousand different people he knew.

He pushed away from the wall, his eyes on their progress up the dark street, keeping a decent distance between himself and the two men. He crossed the Uxbridge Road and followed them on to the opposite side of the street, fifty or sixty yards behind the pair. They seemed to be talking animatedly and at one point, just by the police car park, the Dredd stopped and looked around, perhaps sensing that he was being hunted, while the other man walked on.

Cory ducked down behind a car, reached inside the shoulder holster and slipped the Walther into his jacket pocket for easy access. When he looked up again, Levi had walked up some more and he half crouched, half ran between the shadows of the parked vehicles, hoping that no law-abiding citizen would come out to see what he was doing hiding there. When the men crossed the road into the street that ran parallel to this one, Cory waited until they had disappeared around the corner, then dashed across, making sure that he was still opposite them and keeping a safe distance between them all the time.

He tried to get a decent look at the other guy to see if he knew him, but he was walking faster than Levi and Cory wondered if his senses were running overtime too. He couldn't be a solicitor, the youth mused. The man was wearing straight-cut jeans, Reebok trainers and a dark sweatshirt, with a baseball cap. Cory knew that that was the standard streetwear for black youths all over London. He cursed the man's presence, still sure that he knew him, and narrowed his eyes as they reached the Tipo.

'Shit,' he whispered underneath his breath, as he saw them study the car then both climb inside.

He removed the gun from his pocket and put it back in his shoulder holster, his eyes locked firmly on the small Fiat.

'Ah shit!' Levi cried, his hands against his head.

'What's up man?' Sean inquired, wanting to be on his way as quickly as possible.

'Dem fuckin' Rads man, they didn't gi' me back my wong!' Levi complained bitterly, looking at the teen.

Sean stared back dubiously. 'What, d'you reckon they would, seein' as they know it's crack money? More than likely, they'll hol' onto that until the trial innit?'

'Yeah,' Levi said, thinking quickly, 'but they might jus' gimme it back now, an' if they do, I can pay you off intermead, y'get me? Oh yeah, speakin' o' wong you got some money f'me?'

'Oh yeah,' Sean replied, easing the wad out of his pocket and slapping it in the Dredd's palm. He counted it, nodded, then glanced at the youth once more.

'Besides,' he suggested, 'I waan see if I c'n sort out Kenny's bail too. I might as well see if I c'n kill two bird wid one stone, nuh true?'

The teen thought about it.

'Yeah man. Won't Kenny's bail be the same as yours?'

'Who knows? You might as well come wid me yout' man an' we'll fin' out togedda innit?'

Sean screwed up his face and pushed himself deeper into the seat, his expression displaying exactly what he thought of *that* idea.

'Can't I jus' wait in the veic's man? You won't be long innit an' at least I can listen the radio star.'

The Dredd decided not to push his luck any further. He had already made a mistake by implying that he could bail Kenny out and, if he insisted, Sean would get suspicious. He wasn't stupid, and getting the teen locked up outweighed retrieving the cache, at least for now. Levi checked himself over then spoke.

'All right yout' man, I'm gonna go an check t'ings out. I'll jus' have a lickle slash over dere firs', go an' see the Rads an' den I soon come, yeah?' The Dredd pointed towards an alleyway across the road from them, the perfect place to have a private piss.

'Safe man,' Sean muttered, his head against the seat's headrest, tired beyond words.

The Dredd glanced at him once more, confident he was going nowhere, even if he wasn't sure what to do with the youth. He nodded, then got out, shutting the door behind him and crossing the street into the alleyway.

It was a shortcut between streets he had often used as a youth and he followed it through to the middle where he was completely hidden from the roads at both ends by the alley's twists and turns. High wooden fences surrounded him, protecting the back gardens of houses that loomed over his head. Levi wasn't bothered by the lights. He unzipped and let out a stream of steaming fluid, sighing a little as the ache in his bladder receded, his left hand against the fence, propping him up.

The night around him was very still. He pondered a moment on the silence, then shook his penis, wanting to leave the dark and the shadows and get back to business.

Cory watched in amazement as Levi got out of the car, slammed the door, then made his way into the alleyway. He fumbled the gun back out of the leather holster and withdrew the copper pipe from the rucksack. He checked the motionless silhouette in the Tipo, then, as quietly as he could, followed Levi into the alley, breathing lightly through his mouth. He could hear his heart thumping in his chest like a kettle drum in an orchestra and his mouth was dry, though his hands were not shaking and his face was set and firm. He took small steps, hiding behind the cars until he reached the alley's entrance, then he darted inside, the Walther now in his hand. From deep in the alley, echoing off the walls, Cory could hear the trickle of water and he smiled, realising what had driven the Dredd to this place. He rounded the corner and saw his prey, leaning and urinating against a wooden fence and his smile widened.

It was strange, Cory thought, levelling the pistol at the dealer's back and placing the piping over it with his left hand, how a small item in someone's possession could create such a shift in the balance of life's status quo. Right about now, although nobody knew it but him, Levi, one of the most feared men in Greenside, had his life hanging in the balance. Fuck that, he thought, in reality he, Cory Bradley, had the man's life in his own hands. It was up to him what happened to the Dredd from now on. The feeling was a sobering one and, although he would deny it, it was a feeling that he also liked a lot.

Power.

He lined the man up in his sights, his mind thinking; *What time you 'ave deh Dredd?*

He shook his head, relined, then spoke in a confident whisper. 'Yo! Levi!'

The Dredd turned around, pure reflex action working now. He faced Cory, his mouth open wide in recognition of three things: the boy, the instrument of destruction in his hand and the dire situation he was in. In that second, he knew that Cory knew exactly what he'd planned for Sean.

'Wait nuh—' he started, fumbling. He never got to finish.

Cory pulled the trigger and the gun bucked in his hand, the bullet making a hollow scraping sound as it raced the length of the pipe, exited and smashed into the Dredd's outstretched hand.

Levi stared open-mouthed at the stump of where his finger had been, the bone between his first and second knuckle glistening whitely. When he looked back up, the colour had drained from his face, yet his expression was barbaric in its menace.

Cory was already aiming again, the fingers in both hands tingling, his stomach churning, as the Dredd rushed at him like a speeding Underground train.

'*YAAAAAH!*' Levi bellowed, running at the teen.

Cory fired reflexively, twice.

The first shot hit Levi in the stomach. He let out an 'ooof' sound and fell to his knees, his injured hand clutching his reddening belly, his head thrown backwards.

The second shot hit him in the side of his face.

Cory stood in one place, hypnotised, before taking a step closer, his eyes popping out of his head. This had not been part of his plan.

He wanted to cry out he'd never meant this to happen – he

wanted to scream things had gone too far – but it was too late now, the damage was already done. He found himself willing the Dredd to get up, even though it meant scaring himself half to death if he did. He took a tiny step closer, smelled the excrement coming from the man's still body in waves and knew Levi was gone.

'Ah man, *no*!' he whispered, his body starting to tremble. It wasn't fair. Everything that he did went wrong, every move he made resulted in a checkmate against himself. What could he do now? He was looking at murder, and if he didn't leave now somebody was going to come strolling down the alley and find him in this terrible scene from a gangster movie. He remembered Levi's friend in the Tipo and he wondered if he was carrying too.

Hating himself, Cory put his gun in his pocket and the copper piping down next to Levi's head. He forced himself to search the Dredd's pockets, his teeth clenched in disgust, averting his eyes from the grisly half face. He kept expecting the corpse to jump up and start throttling him in revenge, but the only time it moved was when he dug deep into the pockets. He found a thick wad of cash, as well as Levi's Mercury and his keys. He left the phone, but took the money and the keys, then, without looking back, he followed the alleyway into the next street.

Chapter Twenty-One

Sean was listening to some old-time Raregrooves on the Tipo's radio, his fingers keeping time impatiently, his eyes closed tightly. Sometimes he opened them a crack to look at the car's digital clock and, not long after the Dredd first left, he thought he heard the older man's voice yelling something unintelligible. When he listened further he heard nothing, so he closed his tired eyes again and got into the relaxing music, wanting his girl very much.

After the clock told him twelve minutes had passed, the teen kissed his teeth and looked towards the alleyway.

'Don't tell me he's still pissin',' he muttered to himself stroppily.

When he thought about it, he hadn't noticed the dealer walk by him, though he easily could have done while his eyes were closed. Fed up with all the stalling, Sean decided to speed things up a little. He switched off the ignition and slipped the keys out, then opened his door and got out of the car, making sure that he locked up everywhere. Satisfied that he had done well, he then walked across the road to check if Levi was still watering the flowers, while fighting an inexplicable urge to leave this place.

As he crossed, he thought of Rosie's earlier words. He liked the girl and thought that she would be good for his cousin, maybe even to the point of calming him down a bit. She had brains, looks and a personality to go with it, so he considered her thoughts on Levi carefully, still hearing the sincere ring in her voice.

Maybe the dealer *was* up to something. He had been acting strange enough tonight, talking about getting back money that both of them knew was long gone. The way that he was looking at him as well . . . That was even stranger and now there was his untimely disappearance. Things were starting to add up in Sean's mind and he didn't like the answers he was arriving at one tiny bit. Still, he advanced boldly into the alley, thinking that if the Dredd didn't make a move soon he would walk his short way home alone.

The first thing he noticed was the atmosphere.

The hairs on the back of his neck stood up and there was a tingle in his fingers. The moon was like a giant eye staring at him through the darkness, and the clouds passing by it made him feel as if the ground underneath him was moving too, causing him to stumble and lurch like a drunk.

When he saw the corpse, he knew what his body had been trying to tell him.

He covered his face but rapidly looked up again, sure it would have moved. It was in the same place. He could now see the thick splash of blood streaked along the wooden fence, the dark pool underneath the corpse and even what seemed to be particles of flesh scattered in amongst all the mess on the wood. He retched and got up, trying to go closer so he could take the man's pulse, but unable to bear the deathly wide-eyed stare. Eventually, he looked as far the other way as he could and walked over, bent down and felt his wrist.

Nothing. He had thought as much.

Scared, looking around himself, Sean wondered how long ago this had happened. The killer could still be in the area. He looked at the body once more, then saw the copper piping lying next to the corpse. Without even thinking, and certainly not recognising it for what it was, he bent down and picked up the pipe.

Confused, he studied the object in his hand for a moment, wondering what it was doing there, knowing it had to mean something. His fear of the body waned, and he fought the fatigue and shock, attempting to force his mind to think hard, harder than it ever had. He would've stood there indefinitely, if it wasn't for the sound of hushed voices and furtive footsteps, echoing down the alley towards him.

That did it for Sean. He dropped the pipe, his ears deaf to its clatter, hearing only the footsteps, coming closer and closer. He ran out of the alleyway as fast as he could and headed full pelt back down the road he'd come from. His only thoughts were that a rival dealer had shot the man and that if he'd killed Levi he could be looking for him now. Sean was also very aware he was the last person seen with the dealer and was keen to detach himself from any police inquiry. Cory didn't pass his mind for a second. As far as he was concerned, his cousin was at home, waiting for him to come back.

Sweating and shivering, he burst through the police station's doors and made his way to the reception, where a sullen man was standing at the desk, talking to a Chinese kid in baggy black trousers and an even baggier T-shirt. The policeman eyed Sean coolly as he pushed into the reception area, one eyebrow raised in a bored expression.

'Can't you read mate? One at a time, moron,' he said, as the Chinese boy grinned apologetically at Sean. He heard nothing through the loud roar in his ears. He stood completely still for two seconds, causing both the boy and the man to stare at him. To Sean, it was an eternity before he found his voice.

'*Levi's dead! Someone fuckin' shot 'im man!*' he spat and the Chinese boy shrank away from him at once. The burly Met man looked at him quizzically.

'Who's Levi!'

'Uhh, uhh, Lawrence Peterson . . . I think.'

'Y'mean Patterson!'

Sean nodded then lurched forward, his gorge rising at a sudden memory. He struggled to keep his food down and managed, but only just. The policeman jumped over the desk (Sean had time to think that he must've always wanted to do that) then helped him up and unlocked and steered him back through the side door, into a plain room with some easy chairs and a broad, bare office desk.

'Where is he?' the burly man ordered as soon as he'd sat down.

'Two streets west. In an alleyway,' Sean muttered, his head between his knees, his voice thick.

'All right, I think I know the one. Now wait here, don't move a muscle OK? What's your name again?'

'Sean Bradley,' the teen told him, without thinking.

He looked up to see the policeman staring at him. Sean held his eye, knowing he was in deep shit now, his heart going a mile a minute in his chest. The man gave him another inscrutable stare, then turned and went through another door.

As soon as he was gone, the teen went for the side door and tugged on it. Locked. He sat back down, wondering if there were cameras in here.

Then he remembered the SIG-Sauer at his waist.

Then he remembered the cache of guns in the Tipo.

He placed his elbows on the office desk and held his head in his hands, the full weight of what was happening hitting him. From the car park, sirens wound themselves up, making the teen jump at the sound of their manic wailing. The door through which the sullen policeman had departed opened again to reveal two Met men in civilian clothes.

The casually clothed one came forward, a predatory smile on his young face.

'Sean Bradley?' he asked.

Sean nodded, for once in his life wishing he wasn't.

'I'm Sergeant Leonard, this is Sergeant Bailey. If you could follow us please,' the older one requested, stepping back from the door.

Sean got up, detached completely from his situation and thought about his mother, sister, cousin, girl and child to be. He wondered if he'd see any of them as a free man again, or whether his child would ever know him outside a prison visiting room.

When the four solid knocks sounded on Rosie's door, she was in her bedroom busying herself varnishing her nails, the radio playing low tunes and her night light casting a mysterious glow over everything that it touched. Her window was opened slightly, as the tiny room was an oven in the summer. As she made to get up she heard her aunt letting their visitor in, the breeze from the half-opened door making her curtains billow and lift gently.

She strained her ears and heard a deep male voice answering Madeleine's higher pitch. The girl smiled as she recognised it and waited expectantly for the bedroom door to swing open, wanting some company on this hot, beautiful night. Yet, when Cory walked inside, closing the door firmly behind him, her smile faded and her hand went to her mouth in shock. The breath in her lungs caught for a second, as the bag that he was carrying slipped off his shoulder and onto the floor with a thump. She then watched him ignore it, turning his face to the door, his head pushed into the crooked V of his elbow.

'Cory?'

He stepped towards the bed, his teeth chattering as though it was the middle of winter, sending a ripple of goosebumps across Rosie's arms, though whether it was in fear or from the chill he had brought in with him she couldn't tell. Had she just been thinking that it was warm? She reached for her window and slammed it shut noisily as Cory sat down, hearing her aunt's wail of complaint from the other room. Ignoring that, she slid down beside the shivering boy and wrapped her arms around him, pulling his head to her breast, cradling him in her arms.

'What's up, huh? Are you sick babes?' she murmured, becoming even more frightened as she realised that Cory was trying to stop his trembling to no avail. She ran a finger down his clammy temple, smelling the strong varnish on her nail with the motion: he was ice cold. Cory's teeth chattered loudly over the music. She could feel him clenching his jaws together to stop it.

'I'm . . . cold . . .' he chattered, holding on to her for dear life. Rosie sniffed around her boyfriend, trying to smell alcohol, but there was none on him. She then felt underneath his chin, the nape of his neck and his forehead, clinically.

'Well, you ain't got a *temperature*,' she stated, looking a little puzzled now, but still holding him, and rocking him. Cory said nothing, merely moaning a little as if in pain, and with each moan Rosie would kiss his forehead and rock him some more, not knowing what else to do and thinking that he would tell her what was wrong soon enough, otherwise why had he come to her?

Madeleine knocked on the door and told her she was going to bed half an hour later. The couple sat on the bed in a silence broken only by Cory's moans, the radio's chatter and the bed springs' squeaks.

'Ssssh, shush babes,' Rosie muttered, feeling silly talking to him like a baby, but letting the words flow anyway. Soon he looked up, his eyes still out of focus, like he was staring *through* her, but she forced herself to lock her eyes with his.

'What's up?' she probed again, softly. Cory snatched his eyes away, shuddered, then spoke to his hands.

'Rosie . . . Rosie, tonight I did somethin' really fucked up man. I don't even know how to tell you—'

'Cory wait . . .' the girl breathed, wanting to take back her question right away. She knew that he had stabbed someone before, after all, she had seen him directly after the incident, but he hadn't looked anything then like he did now. She reflected that if he could plunge a blade into someone badly enough to put them in intensive care, what chance was there that this thing here and now wouldn't be worse? Over all the time she'd known Cory, she'd never seen him this distraught about anything. Rosie knew he was a person that handled trouble casually, as if it was an occupation. All of the signs spelt danger, but she made a vow to stand by him, whatever he'd done.

'What happened to your hands?'

She changed subjects, releasing her hold and taking both hands in hers gently.

The right palm was a stinging red, while the left had blotches in small flushed patches across his fingers. On closer inspection the girl thought that she could see a line going across all four digits. Cory stared at them, then pulled them away, seeming to draw somewhere deep for his old self. When he next looked at her, his eyes were still glazed, but a lot more composed than they'd been.

'Rosie listen man . . .'

Deja vu, the girl thought.

'I got somethin' important to tell yuh. Uhh . . . Damn . . .' He sighed. 'I'm leavin' London OK?'

She glanced up quickly, confused.

'Tonight. I come to tell yuh that it ain't 'cos of you or any-thin'—'

'Den what *for*? she cried.

Cory looked at his hands again, speaking slowly so she caught every word. His voice was as slow and steady as a large steam-roller, crushing any chance of her speaking until he'd moved on, having said his piece.

'Rosie . . . I killed someone tonight man. I murdered some-one star.'

The girl looked at him blankly, frowned, then laughed ner-vously, pushing his shoulder like someone who knew they were being teased and had just got wise to the joke.

'Yeah, get out o' here man!' she giggled, her eyes still serious.

Cory pushed a hand under his T-shirt, then pulled it out, holding the Walther, its sharp angles looking quietly deadly by the lamp's sparse light.

'I killed someone tonight,' he stated again, his lips accepting the words more easily, the second time around.

She heard herself from far away, mumble, 'Who was it?' hoping if it had to be anyone, it was Roger, or even that brer Insane Shane. She found herself very aware she hadn't passed on Sean's earlier message. It seemed as if Cory would never answer.

'Levi.'

Rosie covered her eyes, unable to look at him, feeling the sureness, the instinctive belief, that things were worse than she could have ever imagined. She moaned now and Cory stared at her until she took her hand away from her head, her eyes shin-ing with tears.

'I didn't know the brer meant so much to you,' Cory growled, sounding both cold and babyish at the same time. His girl looked up in surprise, then scowled, her voice taking on a dupli-cate tone, her anger directed at herself as well as Cory.

'Oh, don't be so stupid!' she snapped and was sorry at once, mainly due to the stung look on his face. Gently, she took his hands again, her face reproachful, not wanting to say a single word, but knowing she had to.

'Cory, I seen Sean earlier today . . .'

The teen's eyes lit up.

' . . . And he gave me some message to give to you, if I saw you. I phoned your house, but there was no answer an' I see Garvey an' he said you was up Kiplin' an' he didn't know when you'd be back. So you see? I couldn't find you at all—'

'So what, wha' d'he say?' Cory asked roughly, only half listening.

Rosie closed her eyes painfully. 'Ah *shit* man . . . I dunno how to say dis . . . Baby, Sean told me that he was goin' over to bail Levi out earlier, that was this evenin' sometime man. Did you see him dere or—?'

She stopped dead, as a look of plain simple comprehension grew on his face, like a hard and ugly-looking dandelion, in the midst of a rosebush.

'Ohh no . . . Ah man . . . I seen 'im man, I don't *fuckin'* believe it,' Cory moaned, his last three words a hoarse cry in the back of his throat, his hand lashing the bed in muffled thumps.

'Art tol' me Levi gee'd Sean up. So I went to the station wiv dis bucky to warn 'im off y'get me? Show 'im to stay away from us, y'unnerstan'? So I wen' up there an' . . . an' . . . I seen the guy y'know. An' I swore that I knew him . . . but he was too far away to see . . . too fuckin' far man. Levi went down some alleyway an' I crept up on him . . . I didn't mean to kill 'im! It was meant to be a warnin'.'

Cory gulped this last. He couldn't tell the girl Levi had been urinating when he'd shot him, or that he'd taken his money either. That last, he would keep to himself forever.

'He fell down . . . I shot him in the *face* man. Then I run all the way here . . . left Sean in the car . . .'

He swung around to her, making her flinch slightly. '*I left Sean in the car*,' he said again, in a clear voice.

He paused, then got up quickly, heading for the door in an abrupt burst of motion.

Rosie had sensed such a move and she rapidly got up with him, grabbing his arms and wedging her body in front of him, blocking his exit.

'Woah, hold on sec' where d'you think *you're* goin'?'

'I'm goin' back to get Sean,' he told her bluntly. Rosie let go and gave him a withering look.

'Are you crazy or summick? It takes at least fifteen minutes to go from Bush t'here an' you bin here nearly a hour now. You go back dere now, it'll be jam packed wiv Rads man. How long d'you think a dead body can lie unnoticed in an alley for?'

He shrugged, stone-faced, not answering her question.

'So wha' you gonna do?' she whispered, thinking she knew exactly what he was planning.

'I'm *missin*',' he muttered flatly. He looked up just in time to see the surprised look on her face. Reading her wrong, he spoke quickly.

'I'm sorry about all dis shit I put you through Rosie, I know you deserve better than dis, blatant. I dunno . . . maybe they'll catch me or summick, or maybe I'll come back an' check you when it's blown over a bit. But I gotta flash, now, before they realise it was me. Kenny'll definitely know – an' all Levi's other bredrins'll be brewin' when they hear what's happened. Nuff people must know man, Art musta tol' all the footballin' crew . . .'

He stopped, seeing the truth of the statement, while Rosie looked around lost, not knowing what he was talking about.

He bent over and pulled the rucksack back from where it had fallen as Rosie sat beside him on the bed, her dark face lined with worry. When he retrieved the bag and sat back up, the girl was studying her clear nails, as if they held the key to the world.

'What about Sean?'

Her voice was husky. Cory wriggled uncomfortably, wrinkling the duvet.

'Boy Rosie . . . What can I say man? I love 'im, but I don' wanna go jail man, I couldn't face it. Y'know what I'm lookin' at wiv the gun, the bullets an' a premeditated murder? I'd be all thirty before I come out, I'm tellin' you—'

'But Cory, Sean's *innocent* . . .'

The unfairness of it all brought fresh tears, burning her eyes again.

'I can't do it Rosie.' Cory was staring at his red palms. 'I jus' can't. I know what you're sayin', but I can't. Hopefully he got out of dere before the Rads come, but it's like you said, what's done is done now. I can't do nuffin' to help him, all I can do is get myself nicked too, which don't help either of us one bit, y'get me?'

The girl made no reply, amazed by his selfishness, while understanding his reasoning, even though she believed that in his position she would have given herself up for her cousin. But then, how she could really tell? Maybe she would have run too, for hadn't she stopped the teen from going out after Sean moments before?

'Can't I come with you?' she asked, knowing that it wasn't possible, wondering why she had even bothered saying such a thing.

Cory shook his head, his eyes closed tight.

'Rosie, you don't know how bad I want you to come man. All the way to that alley I was thinkin' of you man. I . . .' he stumbled. 'We . . . we could've had summick dett together, you hear what I'm sayin'? I fucked up everythin' man, everyone's lives, from when I was a kid.'

The tears clogged his tongue. He cleared his throat harshly, swiped at his eyes and coughed into the silence.

'Well . . .' he muttered and left it hanging.

Rosie fidgeted in her place.

'You better go then. Before they come lookin' f'you,' she told him, hoarsely. His eyes glazed over again and he made for the door slowly, his head bowed and his whole manner deeply subdued.

'Hey,' she said, weakly.

'Huh?' He turned around once more.

'Don't I get a kiss den?'

She got up, on legs that felt as weak as a newborn foal's and stumbled a few steps, throwing her arms around him, wanting the feel of him to stay locked in her memory.

'I don't want you to go. Ain't dere any way you can hang around?' she complained tearfully.

Cory gritted his teeth and she knew she was making it harder for him.

'I know, I know, I wanna stay too, but I can't man, simple. Do me a favour and give dis to Bernice on the sly will you?'

He reached into his pocket and pulled out something, splitting it into two piles, then giving her one and pushing the other back into his jeans. It was a wad of money; hundreds of pounds in crumpled, used notes. Rosie grasped it, opened her mouth to ask where he'd got it from, then guessed herself and threw it on the bed without a backward glance, her fingers crawling as if a thousand microscopic insects were wriggling all over them. She rubbed them together quickly, not even aware of what she was doing.

'Call me,' she breathed, trying to forget the feel of the notes.

'I'll try,' he promised, holding her eye. 'Go to bed Rosie. I'll see myself out, yeah?'

'Be careful . . .'

'Yeah yeah. Take care, all right?'

Then he was gone, the bedroom door shaking slightly from the draught before the front door clicked shut. Rosie looked on the bed at the money, wondering how she'd be able to touch the notes, never mind hand them over to Cory's aunt.

But she knew her pain was nothing compared to what the Bradleys would soon be feeling, starting tomorrow morning – sentences for armed robberies ranged from anything between seven and fourteen years – and there was little or no chance of Sean getting off now, not with the way the courts viewed gun crime these days.

As for Cory – Cory would either live life on the run hounded by Levi's vengeful gang; or he'd be caught for the murder and made to serve at least as long inside as his cousin. Deep in her heart Rosie thought – or rather hoped – he'd get away. There were plenty of cities in England where a black youth could disappear – Birmingham, Manchester or Liverpool – and Rosie imagined Cory would do just that.

She wandered blindly over to her bed and lay on the duvet, staring at the ceiling, wanting to cry for her loss. Dry eyed and motionless in the half light she listened to the radio play, wondering how it all could have gone so wrong.

In the long confines of the now brightly lit alleyway there was a bustle of Met men around the prone body of the late Lawrence Patterson. Police tape barred both street entrances.

The ambulance men and coroner waited for the relevant murder squad detectives to arrive. Forensics picked up three shells, the copper piping and two bullets from the back fence. The items were all placed into transparent bags, to be analysed back at their labs. After that, the paramedics took over, stepping in with their usual quiet confidence.

Rolling a red blanketed stretcher underneath the tape, they lifted the stiffening body, and buckled it in, making sure the torn face was securely covered before they left the alley. Wheeling Levi back out, the crowd parted *en masse* for them, trying but failing to get a look at the body, some even straining on their tip-toes for a peek. The paramedics pushed the stretcher into the back of the ambulance, then one climbed in behind it, while the other took the driver's seat, eager to get back to Hammersmith Hospital, where a nice cup of coffee and a chat with a pretty nurse were both waiting.

In the back of the ambulance, the second man eyed the covered body, pulled back the blanket hiding Levi's face and let out a low whistle between his teeth, shaking his head in disbelief. He was an old hand and had been riding in an ambulance since the early eighties, the decade of the riots, yet still it never ceased to amaze him how violent the city of London was becoming these days, though he couldn't fathom why. It wasn't ten years ago that he would get three, maybe four jobs like this a year, but now he got them almost all the time, as if suddenly everyone had gone gun crazy, with no regard for the law whatsoever.

He reflected on this in disgust as the ambulance started up, moved forward, then lurched to a stop, throwing him onto the corpse. His face fell onto the dealer's stomach. He got up quickly, his mouth open in shock and then clambered up to the frontseat, talking loudly.

'What the fuck happened *then*?' he cried in surprise. His partner growled back at him from over his shoulder, equally shocked.

'Some idiot walked right in front of me, I had to swerve like a mad bastard. Almost hit that fuckin' Tipo.'

The second man peered over his friend's shoulder while holding his nose as the gases from Levi's stomach filled the back of the vehicle like a rank mist.

'Nice car,' he honked.

'Yeah, good thing I missed it too,' the first one replied, sounding relieved.

The ambulance drove slowly down the street and turned the

corner without any particular hurry, its occupants the only ones to notice the blue Fiat which sat on the dark side of the street, its alloys sometimes catching reflections from the Met men's torch beams as they paced the alleyway's entrance. Sometimes the beams played on the rectangular sticker whose message had sealed Levi's fate, *Nubians do it better in the dark*. Now Sean and Cory were lost to the darkness too.